THE
ALCAZAR

SEQUEL TO *THE CERULEAN*

AMY EWING

HARPER TEEN
An Imprint of HarperCollinsPublishers

HarperTeen is an imprint of HarperCollins Publishers.

The Alcazar
Copyright © 2020 by Amy Ewing
Map art copyright © 2020 by Tim Paul
All rights reserved. Printed in the United States of America.
No part of this book may be used or reproduced in any manner whatsoever
without written permission except in
the case of brief quotations embodied in critical articles
and reviews. For information address HarperCollins
Children's Books, a division of HarperCollins Publishers,
195 Broadway, New York, NY 10007.
www.epicreads.com

ISBN 978-0-06-249002-5 — ISBN 978-0-06-299871-2 (intl. ed.)

Typography by Anna Christian
20 21 22 23 24   PC/LSCH   10 9 8 7 6 5 4 3 2 1
❖
First Edition

For Matt,
spring to my summer, winter to my fall

THE

ALCAZAR

PART ONE

Arbaz, island of Thaetus, Pelago

1

SERA

SERA WAS PERCHED IN THE CROW'S NEST OF THE *MAIDEN'S Wail* when the Pelagan coastline came into view.

She liked it here best, where she was high up and could see for miles. They had been at sea for fifteen days since fleeing Kaolin and Xavier McLellan. Sera still shivered remembering that night—the theater with all those people staring at her, the way the sprites had burst forth from beneath her dear Arboreal friend Boris, Errol the mertag clinging to her back as he shattered the glass ceiling, running across the rooftops of Old Port City until they reached the Seaport. She could still see Boris's beautiful silvery bark charring as the sprites lit her leaves and branches aflame, still feel the twist of anguish that the gentle tree had sacrificed herself to give Sera and Errol the chance to escape.

But the only thing Sera could do to honor that sacrifice was to be free, as Boris had wanted. To find the tether that connected this planet to the City Above the Sky and return home.

"Land, Sera Lighthaven!" Errol cried out as he erupted from the water, his filaments flashing in shades of pearl pink and lilac. Then he vanished beneath the waves.

Sera swung over the rail and climbed down the rigging to join Leo McLellan where he stood alone on the deck. His sister, Agnes, had been welcomed warmly by the sailors, but not Leo. Violetta had made it clear at the very start that if he gave her crew any of that "patriarchal Kaolin horseshit," he would promptly be thrown overboard. They tolerated his presence because he was a guest of hers—the Pelagans thought Sera was Saifa, the goddess of life. Sera did not know how to explain to them how wrong they were.

"Pelago," she said eagerly, jumping the last few feet and landing lightly on the deck. "We're almost there, Leo."

"I never thought I'd see it," Leo confessed as he tied back his thick black curls with a leather thong. His hair had grown long and unruly over the course of the voyage. He'd complained about it for days until Sera told him she thought it suited him quite nicely. It made him look freer, somehow, and different from the person she had met back in Kaolin. He never mentioned cutting it again after that.

"I wonder what it's like," Sera said. She hadn't realized how uncertain she'd been that they would ever reach the country at all. But even now that they had, the island of Braxos where the tether was planted was still miles away, far to the north. There was a lot more journey left to go.

"Did you see?" Agnes came running up to them, her eyes bright, her cheeks flushed. "It's Pelago! We made it!"

"You will love the city of Arbaz, I am thinking," Vada said, sauntering up behind Agnes. "It has the largest market in all of Pelago. Even the one in Ithilia cannot compare. Though don't tell the Ithilians I said that."

Vada was the only sailor who treated Sera like a normal person, the only one who actually called her Sera and not Saifa. Sera had a suspicion that Agnes had much to do with that—the two girls were very close and had grown closer over the voyage.

"I can't wait to see it," Agnes gushed. "And Leo, Eneas said his sister works in the market; perhaps we'll be able to meet her."

"Sure," Leo said, tugging at his shirt, "we can meet whoever you want, as long as I can get some new clothes."

Vada grinned. "You are not enjoying Jacoba's leftover things?"

Agnes choked on her laugh. Leo had been wearing one of the tallest sailor's hand-me-downs, since his fancy clothes from the theater were entirely inappropriate for life on a ship.

"Surprisingly, no," Leo said dryly. "At least, not after two weeks in them."

"You know, I think you will be looking very fine in Pelagan clothes," Vada said. "You have the figure for them."

"Fashion is the least of our concern," Agnes said, tucking a loose strand of hair up into her bun. "And it's Ithilia we need to get to, not Arbaz."

Ithilia was the capital city of Pelago, on a different island called Cairan. Pelago was nothing *but* islands, and even though Sera had been looking at maps of it for two weeks, she still felt disoriented by them all. When she had gazed down at this planet from the City Above the Sky, Pelago had seemed so small, a collection of misshapen brown-and-green dots. But now she was realizing just how big this world was.

"Actually, it's *Braxos* we need to get to," Leo reminded her.

"But our grandmother is in Ithilia," Agnes said. "She's expecting me. And I know she can help us."

"If there is anyone in Pelago who can be helping you besides the Triumvirate itself," Vada said, "it is Ambrosine Byrne."

Sera hoped Ambrosine was a kinder person than Agnes and Leo's father. She did not have an ounce of pity for the man who had imprisoned her, but however cruel and callous, he was still the twins' only living parent. They knew almost nothing of their mother, Alethea Byrne, or her family, except that the Byrnes were very powerful and influential in Pelago. Agnes clung to the idea of Ambrosine the way Sera clung to her star pendant at night, the one her best friend, Leela, had given her.

She pulled the moonstone necklace out from beneath her shirt and rubbed it with her thumb, grateful that she had this one tangible reminder of her City. The stone was cold today—it seemed to have a mind of its own when it came to temperature, rarely reflecting the air around it or even the warmth of Sera's body. She wondered if it had always been like that when it had sat hidden in Leela's bedroom in the City Above the Sky. And the other night, Agnes said she had woken abruptly in the room they shared and swore she heard it humming from around Sera's neck.

"I'm coming, Leela," she murmured. "I'm coming, mothers."

Leo squeezed her shoulder. "We'll get you back to them."

But he didn't know that for sure, not really.

"What did she say?" Vada asked.

Sera felt a familiar surge of frustration. She was convinced there must be a way for her to communicate—not just understand, but speak and be understood—with the humans on this planet, whether they spoke Pelagan or Kaolish. She could not believe that the Cerulean of old would have gone down to a planet and blood bonded with perfect strangers, or given their blood away, willingly or not. So far those were the only two ways Sera had managed to make first Agnes and then Leo understand her. There had to be a way of communicating without her having to sacrifice quite so much. Especially now that she knew blood bonding with humans meant sharing memories.

She kept thinking back to that night when she had accidentally blood bonded with Leo while she was trapped in the crate. She hadn't been touching him, yet she had seen into his mind and he into hers. He had had her magic inside him already, of course, but Sera was certain there was some way for her to speak to everyone on this planet as naturally as she had spoken to Errol that first night when she woke up in the theater.

Leo translated for her now and Vada gave her a sympathetic look.

"I am still not quite understanding where it is you are coming from," she said. "But I am hoping you can return there safely."

Sera smiled at her in thanks.

Suddenly, Errol appeared again, and this time the filaments that hung over his bulging eyes flashed in dire grays and reds, his webbed hands flapping as his fishtail wriggled wildly.

"*Ships,*" he called. "*Ships are coming, with dark sails and cruel faces.*"

"What did he say?" Agnes asked, worried.

But before Sera had a chance to translate, a horn sounded. Vada jumped as sailors began pouring onto the decks.

"Triumvirate ships!" Vada's mother, Violetta, cried as she raced up to them. "Vada, hide Saifa. Now!"

The Triumvirate was the ruling body of Pelago, composed of three queens. Vada had told them that these queens didn't always get along or agree, and so depending on which one you were loyal to, things could get dicey if there was a conflict within Pelago.

Violetta snapped orders at other sailors to make sure the cargo they were carrying was safely hidden as well, and to bring out the diversions, whatever that meant. Sera didn't know what sort of ship the *Maiden's Wail* was, but could only guess it was carrying something illicit—besides herself, of course.

"What in the name of Bas are Triumvirate ships doing

out in these waters?" Vada said as she grabbed Sera by the arm. She led her over to a low wooden bench along the railing and lifted it up to reveal a small rectangular hiding space. Sera needed no urging to climb inside.

"Get the boy in too," a wizened old sailor named Breese said. "We do not need the Triumvirate thinking we have kidnapped a Byrne."

Apparently Leo looked so very much like his mother that he was actually recognizable in a country he'd never stepped foot in. It was quite tight with the two of them, but with a little bit of shifting, they made do. Sera's heart was in her throat as Vada closed the bench. Thankfully there was a narrow crack running between two planks of wood, and if they positioned themselves just right, they could see a fair amount of the deck. Leo's head was level with her waist and her feet were jammed against his stomach. Sera felt a strange lurch in her chest. She'd never been this close to him before.

There were several thumps as Vada put things on top of the bench to cover it, and Sera heard her mutter to Agnes, "Keep your head down and your mouth shut. Your Pelagan is very good, but no need to risk it if we don't have to."

Vada had been teaching both Agnes and Leo Pelagan and had been shocked at how quickly they picked up the language. Soon both twins could easily converse, though Leo seemed to have a slightly better ear and grasp for it than Agnes did. Vada commented that perhaps it was their Pelagan heritage that had given them some unknown advantage, but Sera suspected it was her own magic, living inside both twins, that was responsible for their startling aptitude.

She was grateful Agnes had that ability now, to appear as Pelagan—if there was one thing she knew about Kaolin and Pelago, it was that the two countries hated each other. And the discovery of Braxos had only made things worse.

"We've been at sea for so long," Leo muttered. "We have no idea what's been going on with the rest of the world."

He did not sound optimistic and Sera's heart sank—they were not the only ones headed for Braxos. The humans believed the island was filled with treasure or possessed some magical properties. Could they damage the tether if they reached the island before Sera did? She bit her lip and tried to swallow her fear. Right now, the important thing was to stay quiet and escape detection.

It seemed forever before she heard shouts and cries of, "Hold there!" Agnes and Vada were lined up on the deck alongside the other sailors, hands clasped, heads bowed. There was the sound of wood creaking and then the thudding of footsteps. Sera barely held back her gasp as the most frightening woman she had ever seen stalked into view.

She was very tall and wore a high-necked sleeveless leather tunic of mottled black and purple that covered her thighs, split in front and back to allow for freedom of movement. Heavy boots laced up to her knees over dark, rough-spun pants, and her forearms were enclosed from knuckle to elbow in leather cuffs woven with overlapping circles of copper. Her high collar was adorned with matching disks and her hair was cropped short, sticking up in spikes to frame a face cold and devoid of emotion as she stared down at Vada.

"Who is the captain of this ship?" she demanded.

Violetta stepped forward. "I am. Violetta Murchadha, at your service. The *Maiden's Wail* is a simple merchant vessel, returning from a journey to Kaolin."

The woman snorted. "Merchant vessel." Then she turned to others Sera could not see. "Search it." Other women dressed in similar garb passed by the bench—Sera heard some of them going down into the hold. She felt Leo tense beside her.

The woman turned back to Violetta. Her tunic was belted with an assortment of short, curved knives that glinted cruelly in the sunlight. A silver moon was emblazoned on her chest. "I am Rowen Drakos, head of the Aerin's guard," she said.

The Aerin was one of the queens, Sera recalled. Another one was called the Renalt, and she couldn't remember the name of the third. When they ascended the throne, Vada had explained, they gave up their first names and assumed only the family name. Sera thought that rather strange and sad—she could not imagine having to suddenly call Agnes the McLellan.

Violetta gave a curt bow. "An honor to meet you," she said. "My family has paid its respects to the Aerin since the days of my grandmother's grandmother."

"I am not interested in your respects, I am interested in the truth. Do you carry any Kaolin passengers, perhaps ones seeking the sacred shores of Braxos?"

"I carry nothing but a few platters, some rugs, several spools of copper wire, and a cracked urn that I paid far too much for in Old Port City," Violetta replied smoothly. "My crew and I were grateful to leave that filthy country behind and return home. By the grace of the goddesses we have made the journey safely. But I must say, never in all my years has a Triumvirate ship stopped me before entering Arbaz."

"Times are changing," Rowen said. "All the eastern ports have been closed and no one is to dock without permission—the Triumvirate voted not four days ago. Three to zero in favor."

Violetta looked surprised. "A unanimous vote?"

"Desperate times," Rowen said. "Kaolins are pouring into this country, all seeking to pillage what is rightly Pelagan. Even the Lekke could see that drastic measures must be taken. Anyone harboring or aiding a Kaolin will be arrested and imprisoned. The dungeons of Banrissa are quickly filling up with Kaolins and traitorous Pelagans alike."

"A bold move," Violetta said, "and a wise one. Was it the Aerin's idea? She has never been one to shirk from a call to action."

That seemed to please Rowen—her mouth quirked into an imitation of a smile. "It was," she said. Her gaze traveled down the line of sailors. "This is your whole crew?"

"It is," Violetta replied.

"And you trust them?"

"With my life. We have no interest in Braxos—we only wish to return to our homes."

Rowen smirked. "That would make you the only crew in the entire country that has no interest in Braxos."

Violetta hesitated, then said, "Has anyone found it yet? As you can see, we have been woefully ignorant of the happenings of the world."

"No," Rowen said. "It has not been sighted since those damned Kaolins first stumbled upon it. Six vessels have vanished looking for it so far—at least, six that we know of. The Aerin is putting together an elite team with specially designed ships to begin her own search."

"May Farayage bless their journey," Violetta said, touching her forehead.

Rowen snorted. "They would not need the sea goddess's blessing if Ambrosine Byrne weren't such an uncompromising bitch."

Agnes shifted, and Rowen glanced at her, but then one of her comrades was calling out, "Nothing belowdecks!" and Rowen's attention was diverted.

"Very well," she said. "Violetta Murchadha, I grant you leave to dock in Arbaz, by the power vested in me by our blessed queen, the Aerin." She handed the captain a slip of paper. "Present this to the dockmaster when you arrive. May the goddesses go with you."

"And with you," Violetta said, bowing again.

Sera held her breath as the soldiers returned to their ship. There was another creaking of wood and then a splash. For a long while, no one on the *Maiden's Wail* moved. Sera's back ached and her legs cramped, but she stayed as still as stone, waiting. . . .

"Do you think they've gone?" Leo whispered just as the top of the bench was flung open.

"They're gone," Agnes said breathlessly, reaching down to help Sera out. She blinked in the sunlight and saw the ship off in the distance, a black outline against the horizon.

"This is not good," Vada said as Leo climbed out after Sera, stretching his arms over his head. "Misarros stopping Pelagan ships?"

"Misarros?" Leo asked.

"The elite fighting force of Pelago," Vada explained. "They guard the Triumvirate and some of the wealthier families who can afford their protection."

Violetta strode up to them. "Never in my whole life have I needed permission to dock at Arbaz," she said, waving the paper as if it personally offended her. "I fear what awaits us when we arrive. Things are changing." She looked out across the water to where the Misarro ship was sailing away. "And not for the better."

2

LEO

LEO HADN'T BEEN ABLE TO FULLY SHAKE OFF THE JITTERS left behind by the Misarros, but then the port of Arbaz had come into sight and he found himself momentarily struck dumb. He'd spent all his life hating Pelago so much, he'd never really thought about what it might actually look like. He was shocked to find it . . . beautiful.

Structures like terra-cotta fingers pointed up toward the sky, glittering in the light of the setting sun as if their surfaces were encrusted with diamonds. There were clock towers and spires and domed buildings made of yellow or orange stone, wisps of smoke curling upward from rose-colored chimneys, and somewhere far off Leo heard a bell tolling. The city was ringed in hills, houses painted in cheery colors clustering around the central market, which Leo imagined was just inside the enormous white stucco structure with a red tile roof that loomed over the docks. The water was crystalline blue, a color that almost hurt to look at. It was all so idyllic, especially compared with the smog and steel and murky waters of Old Port. For a moment he wondered why their chauffeur, Eneas, had ever left this place.

He shuddered to think about what would have happened if he himself had never left, if the escape plan had failed— he'd be on a train somewhere in Kaolin right now, getting his palm sliced open daily by the actor James Roth. He'd be selling Sera's blood along with Boris's and Errol's replenishing powers—well, not Boris's, not since the poor tree burned. But the very thought made bile rise in his throat.

"What are you thinking of my heretical country, *moulil*?" Vada asked, slapping him on the back. *Moulil* was the Pelagan word for mule. She was always calling him things that weren't his name. Mule, jackass, Face of Byrne, patriarchal idiot . . . it had bothered him at first but he didn't mind anymore. It was just how Vada was.

"I think it's beautiful," he said, and his compliment seemed to both startle and please her.

"It's gorgeous," Agnes agreed. "But I don't like the look of those ships."

Off to their left was a sleek black schooner flying a flag with five red stars on it.

"Another Triumvirate patrol," Vada said, her face darkening. "From the Lekke. You see the stars? Five red stars are the symbol of the Lekke. The Renalt crest is a golden sun and the Aerin, as you were seeing by her Misarros, uses a silver moon. I am not liking that all three queens voted to close the ports."

"Is that unusual?" Leo asked.

"Most votes are two to one. And the Lekke is the most levelheaded of our queens and slow to take such a drastic action. If she has joined the other two in this decision, then I fear . . ."

Her voice trailed off.

"Fear what?" Leo asked, wondering if he really wanted to hear the answer.

"War," she said.

It would be foolish of Kaolin to declare war on Pelago—their naval fleet was not nearly as skilled as Pelago's armada. But then, if it was known that Kaolins were being arrested left and right and thrown in jail, how could the president of Kaolin do nothing? At some point, his hand would be forced. Leo just hoped they'd be well on their way to Braxos before that happened.

The schooner cruised up slowly to the port, only allowed to dock and lower the gangplank once Violetta had produced Rowen's letter.

"Right," Vada said. "Face of a Byrne and I will be going to the market. You all need new clothes, disguises." She glanced at Sera. "Especially you. I will have to be asking my mother if the *Maiden's Wail* can carry you to Ithilia—she may not be wanting to risk it after what happened today. Maybe I wait until she has had a few whiskeys."

"I'd like to go to the market too," Agnes protested.

"No," Vada said firmly. "If something were to happen, Sera would be on her own. Besides, I would very much like to walk the markets of Arbaz with a Byrne." She cackled. "Diana Oleary will not be charging me twelve aurums for that honeyed piss she calls mead today!"

They waited until the other sailors had unloaded the ship's cargo before disembarking. The last piece was a crate with a heavy padlock on it.

"What's in there?" Leo asked.

"None of your damned business," Vada replied. "And remember, no more Kaolish. From now on, you speak only Pelagan."

Leo huffed and made a face, but Vada's back was to him, already striding down the gangplank, leaving him no choice but to follow.

The docks were swarming with people, mostly sailors and other rough types with weathered faces and tough, tanned skin. But there were Misarros too, striding through the crowds with imposing looks, various metals glinting at their necks and on their arms. Leo thought they would easily give the Old Port City police force a run for their money.

"I am not liking this one bit," Vada muttered as a Misarro with a moon on her tunic grabbed an urchin boy by the collar and dragged him off. Leo kept close as they headed toward the entrance to the market, a huge archway in the center of the red-roofed structure with the words *MARGORA DE ARBAZ* carved above it. A woman in dark pants and a green vest eyed him as she twisted a sapphire ring the size of a walnut on her finger. There was a young man behind her about Leo's age, with long brown curls and a slim figure. He wore a silk shirt open to his navel, and pants so tight Leo thought they must have been painted on. The woman whispered to the boy and he sashayed up to Leo.

"Looking for a date?" he asked coyly in Pelagan.

Leo had never been propositioned by a man before. "No," he replied in Pelagan without even really thinking about it. Vada grabbed his hand and pulled him away.

"Stop that," she hissed.

"Stop what?" he said. "I didn't do anything."

Suddenly, he was caught up in the crowds pushing and shoving to get through the arch, and he had to struggle to keep sight of Vada and her auburn braid. The white building was a massive portico that stretched out as far as Leo could see in either direction, its stone halls reverberating with the sounds of so many people. Then he emerged into the market itself and Vada was dragging him toward a golden building about the size of a small house, with a striped awning. Leo didn't need to use his Pelagan to understand the sign posted on its face.

KROGERS—AURUMS

Vada turned to him, her voice low. "Okay, jackass, let's see how precious this face of yours truly is. And act like everyone here is beneath you. Shouldn't be too hard, no?" He resisted the urge to roll his eyes as she started shouting, "Out of the way! Mr. Byrne coming through! Make way for the Byrne!"

Leo watched in awe as the crowds parted and people in line stepped aside to usher him and Vada to the front. Many of them looked at him wide-eyed or bowed their heads when he passed.

"Give me your money and let me do the talking," Vada

muttered as they approached the window. Leo quickly shoved a thick wad of krogers into her hand.

"Dorinda, you lazy bastard," she said, slamming the money down onto the sill, "look sharp and change these bills at once!"

Dorinda was a rail-thin woman with a mass of bright red hair pulled back from her face by a band of mussel shells. A set of bifocals was perched on her nose and her nails were long, sharpened to points, and painted jet black.

"Vada," she said, drawing out the last *a* with apparent relish, a sickly sweet smile spreading across her face then suddenly vanishing. "Get to the back of the line, you little shit. I told you last time, no special favors. I don't care who your mama is. You want me to call the Misarros?"

Leo hid his shudder at the thought—he might look like a Byrne but there was no way he would be able to pass himself off as one once someone started asking questions.

"If you are wanting to call the Misarros on Mr. Byrne here, then by all means, go ahead," Vada said. "I'm sure Ambrosine would be delighted to hear how her family is treated in this market."

Dorinda started as she looked at Leo, then immediately adopted an obsequious expression. "In the name of the goddesses, I did not see you, sir. I will change these for you right away."

Once she was gone, Vada grinned at him. "This is working even better than I had been thinking."

Dorinda reappeared a few minutes later with a heavy leather purse that clinked as she set it down. "Would you like me to count them out for you, sir?"

Leo shook his head, then rested a hand on one hip and stared out into the distance, as if looking for something far more interesting. His father always did that when he was speaking to someone he felt was lesser than he.

Vada snatched the purse and tied it to her belt. "May the goddesses bless you," she said to Dorinda.

But Dorinda was eyeing Leo with interest and he saw a disconcerting flash of recognition. "I was wondering, sir, if you could tell . . . it is being said that Ambrosine has cut off the passages around Culinnon, ones that lead to the Lost Islands. Does this mean she has found Braxos?"

The name Culinnon sparked something in his memory, but Leo couldn't quite place it.

"I'm sure if Ambrosine wanted you to know what she was doing, she would have hurried right here to tell you herself," he said before remembering he wasn't supposed to speak. But Vada looked quietly pleased as Dorinda's cheeks flushed. Leo felt the best course of action was to leave as quickly as possible.

"Vada, come," he said sharply. He turned without waiting and strode off through the crowds with no idea where he was going. Tents in bright colors dotted the landscape alongside pens of animals, little brick houses with thatched roofs, and grocer stalls boasting baskets filled with all sorts of fruits and vegetables—ripe peaches, dark purple plums, and some sort of orange fruit with spiky blue leaves were nestled among shiny cucumbers, red tomatoes, and thick bunches of carrots. He finally stopped between a fruit seller and a butcher shop and Vada clapped him on the shoulder.

"Well done," she said. "That was getting dicey, no?"

"Yeah," Leo said.

"Well, now we know you can pass yourself off as a Byrne."

Leo didn't find any comfort in that. "What if she tells the Misarros about us?"

"The Misarros would not wish to be messing about with a Byrne," Vada reassured him. "Unless the world has gone truly mad. Come, we need to get you clothes. And something to eat; I'm starving."

She bought them each a pear and Leo felt his anxiety ease slightly as he sank his teeth into its sweet flesh, letting the juice dribble down his chin. It had been fifteen days of salted pork, stale bread, and hard cheese. He was fairly certain this pear was the best thing he had ever tasted.

"We should bring one back for Sera," he said through another mouthful.

Vada raised an eyebrow.

Leo's face went hot. "I only meant . . . just because she doesn't eat meat," he stammered.

"Yes. I am sure that is what you were meaning," she said with a sly smile.

They made their way past a silversmith, urns and platters and spoons reflecting the late afternoon sun, then ducked down an alley that led to a little square ringed with stalls in various shades of umber and maroon whose vendors only seemed to sell rugs. They skirted a woman on stilts dressed in flowing robes of brilliant green juggling four striped balls, then pushed through a band of musicians playing a cheery tune on fiddles and pipes and drums. Misarros seemed to be around every corner, but Vada always found some path to avoid them. Leo kept his head down until they had turned a corner and he was nearly blinded by a stunning array of jewelry.

"How big *is* this market?" he wondered.

"Very big," Vada said. "There is a famous story that a wealthy woman from one of the northern islands came to see its splendors and was lost for twelve days. When they found her, she was skin and bones and nibbling on a dead rat."

"Ugh," Leo said, and Vada laughed as she ducked underneath a thin sheet of colored silk hung between two apothecaries, pungent herbal smells emanating from their open doors. Leo followed and found himself in a row of tents dyed in shades of lilac and lavender and violet. Pants were folded neatly on tables inside one, shirts hanging in another, and a third had the most stunning collection of dresses Leo had ever seen. There were tents selling seashell headdresses and ones displaying all types of shoes and still others with a wide selection of scarves.

"This," Vada said, spreading out her arms wide, "is the best place to buy clothes in all the market. The question is where to start. . . ."

"Agnes will want pants," he said. "Something comfortable and functional."

Vada nodded. "We can dress her to have the look of the daughter of a merchant or a wealthy sea captain or a high-placed servant." She glanced at him. "Perhaps servant is working best for our scheme."

His sister wouldn't like the servant part, but she'd be happy about the pants. "What about Sera?" he asked.

Vada's brow furrowed. "If anyone sees her skin or her

hair it will cause a fuss and we are not needing fusses right now. . . ."

They passed down the line of tents and stopped abruptly at a pair of Misarros with golden suns on their chests patrolling the outside of the fanciest tent in the whole row. *Ofairn's Fine Gowns*, Leo translated as he read the sign above it, right before Vada pulled him back. But there were Misarros behind the tent as well. Vada cursed under her breath and, in a movement so fluid Leo barely registered it, sank to grab a knife hidden in her boot and cut a long, delicate slit in the tent. She slipped inside and pulled him in after her.

The dresses that hung on the walls were shimmering things of lace and silk, all expertly tailored, some with long sleeves, some strapless, some adorned with shells or beads, others with what Leo realized were river stones, pebbles in shades of periwinkle and slate and olive. The tent itself was empty except for a lone girl, maybe fifteen, with brown skin, copper-colored hair, and big doe eyes. She was clearly in for a fitting, wearing a dress that covered her completely in head-to-toe lace.

To Leo's surprise, Vada made a sort of choking sound and then fell to one knee, nudging him with her elbow to do the same.

"Princess Rahel," she said. "We did not . . . I am sorry . . . we were just . . ."

Leo had never seen the sailor so out of sorts; at the same moment his mind was registering her words. Princess?

"You may rise," the girl said, then she giggled. "That's not the door to the tent. Did you get lost? Don't you know what doors look like?" They stood, and she wrinkled her nose. "You smell. Are you sailors? Have you ever been to Kaolin? My mother said it's full of heretics. And their clothes are all rather drab. Don't you like this gown? Mistress Phebe designed it herself. I'm getting married in a month, isn't that exciting?" Her eyes turned to Leo and he saw a flash of recognition and also something he used to get all the time from the girls in Old Port—desire.

"You look like a Byrne," the girl said.

"I am one," Leo replied because Vada was just kneeling there, dumbstruck. "My sincerest congratulations on your upcoming nuptials."

Rahel grinned. "I thank you, sir," she said, making a low, elegant curtsy. Then she leaned forward and whispered, "My family hates your family."

If there was one thing Leo was good at, it was flirting with rich girls. "My family hates *your* family," he said with a wink, and was rewarded with another giggle. "But since our families are not here at the moment, can we remain friends?"

Rahel looked delighted. "As long as we keep it a secret," she said.

"Of course," Leo said, bowing. It occurred to him that the Misarros guarding this tent were actually guarding the princess. The golden sun on their tunics meant she was the daughter of the Renalt. "I'm surprised you traveled to Arbaz in such dire times."

Rahel clapped her hands together. "I know, it's so exciting isn't it? Though I don't understand why Mother had to vote to close the ports. Ithilia is so much more thrilling with all the new people. She didn't want to let me come here but of course I had to have a dress by Mistress Phebe, didn't I? She's the best in the whole country! And who cares about silly old Kaolin ships? I hear they barely sail at all in Kaolin and ride around in big honking machines. Are you here for new clothes as well? Those ones aren't very fitting on you. Why is a Byrne dressed like a common sailor? Is she your girlfriend?"

Vada snorted at the suggestion and Leo shook his head.

"No, she's my servant," he said. Rahel looked very pleased to hear that.

Just then the tent flap opened, and a woman entered carrying a very elaborate headdress. "I have found just the one, princess," she was saying, then stopped short at the sight of Leo and Vada. She was probably in her late forties, with wavy black hair and brown skin, her curvy figure hugged by a gown of iridescent blue-green scales, and while Leo was absolutely positive he had never seen her before, there was something familiar about her face.

"Look, Mistress Phebe, a Byrne has come to see you!" Rahel declared. "But he didn't use the door. He certainly needs new clothes, doesn't he?"

Leo's knees locked together, wondering what this woman would do as she stared at him, but then she turned to the princess with a wide smile. "Yes, he does," she said. "And we have finished our fitting. You may change next door and I will be with you shortly."

Princess Rahel did not seem eager to leave Leo's company, but she acquiesced. Once they were alone, Leo felt his heart pounding in his ears. Vada struggled to her feet as the woman folded her arms across her chest.

"Leo McLellan," she said, and Leo felt a shock run through him.

"No," Vada protested weakly. "He's a Byrne, he—"

"Oh, he's a Byrne all right," the woman said. "Those eyes, the nose, the chin . . . my god, he even has her hair, if not the same color." She cocked her head. "But this Byrne was not raised on the estates of Culinnon or in the majestic streets of Ithilia."

"I . . ." Leo didn't know what to say and from the looks of it, neither did Vada.

The woman smiled and extended a hand to him. "My name is Phebe Ofairn. I believe you know my brother, Eneas."

3

AGNES

THE SUN WAS SETTING, AND LEO AND VADA STILL WEREN'T back.

Agnes paced the length of the captain's cabin as Sera stared out the porthole window over the bed, fascinated by the sights and sounds of Arbaz.

What was taking the two of them so long? Agnes fingered the letter in her pocket, the one her grandmother had sent her. She kept it on her at all times, right next to the photograph of her mother. They were touchstones reminding her of who she was and of her purpose. She took the letter out now and read it for the millionth time.

My dearest Agnes,
I hope this letter reaches you. I have friends at
the University of Ithilia and received surprising (and
welcome) news. Come find me when you arrive. I will
say no more here except that I have longed to meet you.
Your loving grandmother,
Ambrosine Byrne

The date for Agnes's interview with the Academy of Sciences was already set and mere days away. Agnes didn't want to miss it—she *couldn't* miss it; she had been waiting her whole life for this opportunity. But Sera needed to get home. Agnes felt terrible asking her friend if they could delay the journey even for just a day.

"I know what you're thinking." Sera's voice made her jump. Agnes quickly put the letter back in her pocket.

"I was just worrying about Leo," she lied.

"No you weren't. You are thinking about that school, the one you are hoping to attend. You have an interview there soon, don't you?"

Agnes was confused and surprised—she had barely spoken about the university, as if that would make real the possibility of failure.

Sera smiled. "Leo is more impressed by you than he lets on."

Agnes felt her cheeks grow hot. "It's not important," she said. "The main thing is to get you to Braxos."

"Agnes." Sera stood and took both of Agnes's hands in her soft silver ones. "This journey was never only about me.

We are all changing, making new paths in our lives, me and you and Leo. You are my friend. I would never want you to miss an opportunity because of me. We will go to Ithilia and you will interview at this school and then we will continue on to Braxos. I would never forgive myself if you lost this chance. I would never want you to resent me after . . . after I'm gone."

Agnes felt like a thorn was stuck in her throat. She wanted Sera to return to her people, but she was going to miss her desperately. She'd never really had a true friend before. She had Vada now, but Vada was something else—Vada was need and want, Vada was in her dreams at night and on the tip of her tongue in the morning. Vada was all sorts of things that Agnes had never felt before.

"You are the best friend I've ever had," Agnes said. "I'm so glad I met you. Well, I'm not glad that my brother caught you with a net launcher and my father locked you up in a crate, but . . ."

Sera laughed. "How strange the way this all began. But you were always kind to me, right from the start. You made me believe that not every human was evil."

"Chalk one up for humanity—we aren't all bad."

"Those Misarros were awfully frightening," Sera said with a shudder. "I fear it may be even more difficult to get to Braxos now than we had thought."

"But you said Errol knows the way," Agnes pointed out. "So we have an advantage over everyone else."

Sera nodded. "I wish he could tell us how far it is, how long it will take to get there. But he speaks in terms of swims and shoals. I don't think he understands distance like we do."

Agnes collapsed onto the bed and stared at the ceiling. Sera sat down beside her.

"I felt so confident back in Kaolin," Agnes said. "Focused. Like I knew what I was doing. Now we've made it to Pelago and I feel like I never understood just how big the world is."

"Me neither," Sera said. "I had only ever seen the City Above the Sky until I fell. But there is so much more in the universe." She sighed. "I always wanted to see this planet. And then I got my wish, but not in the way I thought."

"Do you really think the tether will help you get home?" Agnes asked.

"Yes," Sera said, and Agnes looked up to see stark determination on her face. "It is the link between my City and this planet. It *must* be the way home. In days of old, Cerulean would always travel to the planets they were tethered to. They had to have a way to get back somehow." She turned to look out the porthole. "The closer we came to this country, the more I could feel my magic getting stronger, multiplying and bursting in my veins." Suddenly, she gasped. "They're back!"

She and Agnes scrambled off the bunk and opened the door, running to the hatch as footsteps echoed overhead. Then it was thrown upward, revealing a square patch of sunset-colored sky and Vada's face.

"Well," she said. "That was an interesting shopping trip, to say the least. Here, catch."

She dropped several parcels, wrapped in soft, colorful paper and tied with twine. Agnes caught one wrapped in blue that felt sturdier than the green one that followed. Leo had to pass his packages down carefully—he had quite a stack of them, boxes tied with green ribbons in addition to paper-wrapped clothes. The fanciest one by far was for Sera, wrapped in gold foil with a stamp on it featuring a swan with three stars over its head.

"I will be helping you into this," Vada said to Sera as she and Leo climbed down into the hold. "There are many buttons." She turned to Agnes. "You and your brother go change, quickly. We don't want to be late for dinner, and I am not liking the thought of walking the market after dark."

She gave Leo a push and shuffled Sera down to the captain's cabin.

"Dinner?" Agnes asked. "Where are we going for dinner? What happened in the market?" She followed Leo to his room, which wasn't a cabin so much as an unused storage room. There was a dusty bench with a blanket and pillow, and a couple of empty shelves built into the walls.

"I'll explain once we're changed," Leo said as they turned away from each other.

Agnes unwrapped the sturdy package and gave a cry of delight. "Vada got me pants!" she exclaimed.

Leo snorted. "*I* got you pants. I figured you'd want them."

"Oh. Thanks."

"They should fit better than your old lab attire."

She bit back a retort and began to undress. She was still unused to being grateful to her brother.

The pants were navy-blue wool and fit as if they had been tailored just for her. Her new shirt was linen with long cuffed sleeves, and a third package held a vest of dark red suede, similar in cut to the black one Vada wore but much finer. There were boots of supple leather and a small headband with an arrangement of scallop shells on one side. By the time Agnes was fully dressed, she wanted to cry.

She had never felt so comfortable or so much like herself—at least, the self she had always wanted to be. In these clothes, it was as if she had peeled off a layer of Kaolin and left it behind.

"Oh, Leo," she said, unable to find one snarky thing to say in this moment. "It's perfect."

"I had to guess your size," he said. "I've only ever picked out dresses for you."

"Are you done yet?" she asked.

"Yes, I'm ready," he said, and he sounded nervous. "Just . . . promise me you won't laugh, okay?"

"Why would I laugh?" She turned at the same time he did, and her mouth fell open.

"*Leo*," was all she could bring herself to say.

Her brother had always cut a dashing figure in his suits and tuxedos, but to see him in Pelagan clothes, it was like looking at a different person. She wondered if that was how he was feeling as he stared at her.

Leo wore a pair of sleek black pants that tapered at the ankles, scarlet shoes with large gold buckles and chunky two-inch heels, and a champagne-colored shirt of the finest silk made in the traditional style favored by elite Pelagan men: large, billowing sleeves that cinched at the wrists with the front open in a wide V, its point plunging to his breast-bone, exposing quite a bit of his chest. A turquoise sash that matched his eyes was tied around his waist.

"They made me buy this," he said morosely, but before Agnes could ask who *they* were, he sighed and looked down at himself. "Never in my life would I have thought I'd be wearing the stupid Pelagan clothes Robert and I used to make fun of."

"Robert was a small-minded idiot," Agnes said. "And I don't think you look stupid at all." He gave her a withering look and she held up her hands. "I'm serious! I mean, it's different from your usual style, but . . . it honestly sort of works on you."

"I'm practically naked," Leo said, tugging at the open V of silk. "Why don't they button their shirts? Why don't their shirts even *have* buttons? These pants are so tight I doubt I'll be able to sit down. And why do I have to wear heels?"

Agnes couldn't suppress her laugh. "At least yours aren't dumb pointy things designed to make you teeter and fall. Those are very sturdy. Very practical." Before he could protest further, she opened the door. "Now tell me what happened at the market and where we're going for dinner."

"Well, everyone was right about my face," he said, taking a few cautious steps in his new footwear. "The woman who changed money for us didn't doubt for a second that I was a Byrne. She asked me if Ambrosine had cut off all the passages to the Lost Islands. Our grandmother might be even more powerful than we realized."

That made Agnes thrilled and queasy all at once. "But

even if she's cut off the passages, surely she would let *us* through," she said.

"That's not all," Leo said as they started down the narrow corridor back toward the captain's cabin. "We sort of ran into a princess. The Renalt's daughter."

"You *ran into* a princess? How?"

"Trying to avoid Misarros," Leo said like it was obvious. "Anyway, she was buying a dress from a woman who turned out to be Eneas's sister. She's a big-deal dressmaker in Pelago. She recognized me immediately and helped us pick out all these clothes. She invited us back to her house tonight. So that's where dinner is."

"What?" Agnes yelped. "You found Eneas's sister? What's she like? Where is her house? Why didn't you tell me all this right away?"

"Because I knew you would ask a million questions and it would take ages for you to get dressed and then we'd be late. You didn't see the market, Agnes; it's heavily patrolled by Misarros. We need to blend in or we'll end up in jail or worse."

Agnes's heart skipped a beat. "But they wouldn't arrest a Byrne, would they?"

"If Ambrosine has cut off the passages to the Lost Islands, I'm not sure being a Byrne is such a great thing at the moment. Besides, we're half Kaolin. They're arresting anyone who they suspect of having anything to do with Kaolins."

He was right, Agnes knew, and she didn't like it. They needed to find her grandmother. Once they were under Ambrosine's protection, they would be safe. She was about to pepper him with a few more queries when the door to the captain's cabin opened and Leo stopped so abruptly that Agnes crashed into him.

Sera stood in the doorway, her hair tied back in a bun, a smugly grinning Vada behind her, wearing an outfit similar to Agnes's own but with a dark yellow vest.

"She is looking perfect, just like Phebe said," Vada declared.

Sera's lace dress clung to her slender figure, rich purple and patterned with flowers, tulips and violets and marigolds. The sleeves were so long they crept over her hands to encase each finger in lace up to her knuckles. The neck climbed to brush the base of her chin, and around her waist hung a belt of bone white clamshells limned in gold filigree. The dress fell to cover her feet, a long train spreading out behind her. The overall effect was one of wealth and loveliness.

"She looks beautiful," Agnes said.

"This is the traditional dress worn by an upper-class Pelagan woman who is about to be married," Vada said. "Princess Rahel was being fitted for one just like it. It's a brilliant disguise. Sera will be playing the part of a blushing bride for your brother."

Leo's cheeks turned pink.

"But what about her hair?" Agnes asked. "And her face?"

Vada snapped her fingers. "I have not yet added the best part." She vanished, reappearing a moment later with a large headdress in her hands. Carefully, she placed it on Sera's head. It was crafted out of myriad small shells—slipper snails and shark eyes and pointed venuses grew to form two distinct points, like delicate horns. In between them nestled a gorgeous pale pink conch. Strands of purple and turquoise beads dangled to her collarbone, covering her face and hair completely.

"See? Perfect." Vada beamed. "Agnes, you and I will be pretending to be their servants."

"What?" Agnes cried.

"You wanted to leave the ship, did you not?" Vada said. Agnes grumbled, but there were far more important matters at stake than one night of pretending to serve her brother.

Sera turned her head side to side and the beads made tiny clacking sounds. "It's a bit difficult to see," she said.

"Don't worry, we won't let you trip on anything," Agnes said.

Vada frowned at her brother. "Where is your *kommheart*, Kaolin fool?"

"His what?"

"She made me get a headdress too," Leo grumbled before turning on Vada. "I told you, this outfit should be enough."

"Oh, I am sorry, were you born and raised in Pelago? Are you knowing all our ways and customs as if they were your own? No? Then close your mouth and put your *kommheart* on," Vada snapped.

Leo muttered something under his breath and stalked off back to his room. Sera smiled at Agnes beatifically.

"It's a very pretty dress, isn't it?"

"It is," Agnes agreed.

She examined her arms, encased in purple lace. "I like

this color. We only have robes of white or blue in the City Above the Sky."

Agnes was always happy when Sera found something to love about this planet. Even though she knew it wasn't for her, she knew the girl had to return to her people, it made Agnes happy to think her own home wasn't all bad.

"Your clothes are very nice as well," Sera said. "You look much more comfortable."

"What is she saying?" Vada asked.

"She likes my outfit," Agnes said. "She thinks I look comfortable."

Vada winked at her. "You do, little lion. You look as if you were born to wear it."

Agnes flushed. Leo appeared then, a circlet of speckled junonia shells crowning his curls. For all his moaning about it, the headdress was subtle and suited him perfectly.

Vada clapped her hands together. "Well, my friends," she said. "Let us go to dinner."

4

SERA

As soon as Sera stepped foot on the shores of Pelago, she felt her magic surge within her, a thrilling force that made her feel at once powerful and out of sorts. She had an overwhelming sense of certainty that her City was still tethered here, that this country was welcoming her like an old friend.

Then they entered the market and she became overwhelmed by all the people. There was an undercurrent of tension in the air. Misarros prowled everywhere, occasionally stopping to question a patron or a vendor. But Vada's disguise had worked—no one bowed or knelt or treated her like a freak or a goddess.

When people did notice them at all, it was Leo they

focused on. She saw an old man touch his forehead when they passed and a young girl do a double take. She was glad that Leo, at least, could pass himself off as Pelagan. And no one seemed to take any notice of Agnes.

Sera's legs didn't stop trembling until they were fully past the enormous market. They came out upon a wide boulevard bustling with horses pulling carriages decorated with shells or stones or jewels. People on foot wove in between them, alongside the occasional palanquin carried by broad-shouldered servants, curtains open to let in the cool evening breeze and revealing the man or woman reclined within.

Leo stopped and looked up and down the boulevard in confusion.

"Which way?" he hissed to Vada, but before she could answer, a man wearing a uniform of dark pants under a white tunic and low-heeled sandals rushed up to them. The same seal on the package her dress had been wrapped in—a swan crowned with three stars—was printed on the right side of his chest in red.

"Mr. Byrne," he said, making an elaborate bow. "What a true honor to meet you. Mistress Ofairn has sent me to escort you, your bride, and your servants to dinner. Please come this way."

Leo responded with a curt nod. They crossed the boulevard, deftly maneuvering between carriages, before entering a smaller street lined with dwellings made of light-colored stone, ivory and rose and pale gold. It was quieter here and Sera felt her heart rate slowly return to normal.

The servant made a sharp right, onto a street paved with

blue-gray stone. It rose up in a steep incline, the dwellings on either side colored in teal and cobalt and jade. Leo was breathing heavily by the time they reached the top, and even Sera was a little winded. She liked the air in this country better than the sticky heat of Kaolin. The faint taste of brine and the fresh breeze off the water made her feel stronger, more alive. Though she was ready to take her headdress off—it was growing heavy and the beads that hung in front of her face were beginning to bother her.

The dwelling that sat at the crest of the hill was a blue as brilliant as Sera's hair, and she liked it immediately. A low stone wall surrounded the neatly kept yard and the door was painted a welcoming yellow. A thin finger of smoke rose from the chimney and curtains patterned with flowers fluttered in the open windows. From inside, Sera heard the faint sounds of children laughing.

The man hurried up a walkway lined with forsythia, its sun-colored flowers matching the door. He ushered them inside and called out, "Mistress Phebe, I have brought Mr. Byrne and his company!"

The room was large and airy, its walls painted white and adorned with shells and flowers. On one side was a long table made of driftwood with two benches and an assortment of candles in its center, all burned down to varying heights. On the other, closest to the door, was a large bay window with a curved couch in front of it, a rocking chair, a small pouf, and a low table covered in books and newspapers. A wooden horse sat in one corner surrounded by other toys—a duck with wheels on a string, a spinning top, a miniature watering can.

A woman came hurrying into the room. She had brown skin like Agnes, but with black hair that was swept up and pinned with seashells. She wore a simple gown of pink silk, and her face broke into a smile when she saw them.

"Thank you, Aeden," she said to the servant. "That will be all for this evening."

The man seemed reluctant to leave. "Are you certain, mistress? I could—"

"That will be all," the woman said again, a lick of iron in her tone, and the man bowed low and left the dwelling. She took a step toward them, her eyes fixed on Agnes. "So," she said. "You must be Agnes."

"I—I am," Agnes stammered.

"I am Phebe Ofairn. My brother has told me so much about you. It is an honor to have you in my home."

Agnes shifted, uncomfortable with the praise. "Well, um, thank you for having me. Us. Eneas was always . . ." Her voice trailed off. "Is he all right? Have you had any word from him?"

Phebe gave her a gentle look. "Don't fear, child. He is fine. I received a letter from him—he left Old Port not a day after you did to return to Pelago. He felt it altogether too dangerous to stay in the city. Now that he had helped you escape, he could not risk working for your father anymore."

Agnes exhaled. "Oh, that's wonderful news."

Phebe's dark eyes turned to Sera. "And you must be Sera. Leo told me all about you."

Sera felt the time for hiding her face was over. She carefully lifted off the headdress and Phebe gasped, one hand flying to her chest.

"In the name of the goddesses," she murmured. "You *do* look just like Saifa."

"I am no goddess," Sera said. "I am a Cerulean."

Phebe's eyes grew wide at what must have sounded to her like musical gibberish—that was how Agnes had described Sera's voice before they blood bonded and were able to understand each other. Leo translated for her now. Sera clenched her teeth in frustration. There *had* to be a way to communicate without the help of translators or the dangerous intimacy of blood bonding.

"You said that before, in the market. Cerulean." She sounded it out as if unsure. "I still don't know what that means, but you are welcome in my home, Cerulean or Saifa or whoever you may be. Come, you must be starv—"

But she was cut off by a young boy scampering into the room.

"Mama, Mama!" he said, tears in his eyes. "Parisa took my—" He stopped and frowned. "Why you speaking Kaolish, Mama?"

Sera could never tell who was speaking what language since they all sounded the same to her. She thought it very kind of Phebe to speak to Leo and Agnes in their native tongue. But now she realized it was also dangerous—and even more dangerous for this little boy to see a goddess in his house. Quickly she put the headdress back on.

"Carrick, go back to the kitchen to your father," Phebe said sharply. "Mama has visitors, I told you that before."

A wiry man with pale skin and long hair the color of honey came hurrying in, an infant squealing and stretching in his arms.

"I'm sorry, love," he said, taking the boy's arm. "He got away from me. I'll—"

But he stopped short at the sight of Leo and gasped. "He looks *exactly* like her."

"I told you," Phebe replied.

"Princess Rahel?" Carrick asked, looking up at Sera. "Mama, you bring princess home?"

"No, darling, these are Mama's friends," Phebe said. "Princesses don't come to dressmakers' houses; she came to my shop like I was telling you, remember?"

Carrick smiled at Sera smugly. "My mama is *famous*," he said.

Phebe shot her husband a pleading look. "Get him to bed, Davin."

"Did you see the evening papers?" the man asked.

She gave him a curt nod that effectively ended the conversation.

"Come now, Carrick," Davin said as the baby in his arms let out a wide yawn. He kissed Phebe on the cheek. "Dinner's all ready. I sent Tabitha away, as you asked." He glanced at Leo. "I see why now."

Once they were gone, Sera removed the headdress again and shook out her bright blue hair.

"My apologies," Phebe said. "The children weren't meant to be up now but, well, with a seven-year-old, a five-year-old, and an infant, Davin and I have very little say over how things go in this house. Though I wish Carrick hadn't heard me speaking Kaolish." She sighed and rubbed her forehead.

"We didn't mean to put you in any danger," Agnes said.

Phebe gave her a weary smile. "You are the closest thing to children Eneas ever had. It's no trouble, we'll just have to have a talk with him tomorrow. Please sit," she said, gesturing to the driftwood table. "I'll be right back."

"I'm so glad Eneas is okay," Agnes said as they took seats on the benches. "I was worried."

"Phebe seemed quite accepting of Sera," Leo said. "That's a good sign, isn't it?"

"She is one person and was prepared for her," Vada said. "I do not think we would be getting the same reaction in the market."

Sera agreed.

"What did her husband mean about the newspapers?" Agnes asked. Sera had noticed that too.

"We should have been buying one when we first arrived," Vada said. "But with the Misarros and Dorinda and Princess Rahel, I forgot."

Sera wanted to know more about this princess they'd seen, but Phebe returned then and a most familiar and delicious scent filled the air.

"Fried squash blossoms," she said, placing a platter on the table. "An old Ofairn recipe. And here are some dates dipped in honey and stuffed with blue cheese. We would have made lamb but Leo tells me you are vegetarian. I'll be right back with the main course."

The squash blossoms were not quite the same as the ones she was used to—the flowers were orange, not yellow, and they did not seem as crispy. But hot tears filled Sera's eyes at the sight of them.

"Are you all right?" Leo asked.

"They remind me of the ones my green mother used to make for me," she said. "They were my favorite."

Agnes squeezed her hand under the table.

"Right," Phebe said, returning with a large dish of steaming butternut squash, sliced in half with its insides scooped out, filled with farro and onions, feta cheese and dried cherries. It all looked agonizingly good. "Let's eat, shall we?"

Sera piled her plate with as much food as it could hold, and for many long minutes there was no sound but chewing and swallowing and the occasional gulp of water. When at last their bellies were full, Phebe pushed her plate back and let out a contented sigh.

"Well," she said. "I'm told you are all trying to get to Braxos, but the details were a bit vague back in the market. Not that I blame you. It's dangerous to speak of such things in public now. Especially with a princess so close by." She gave Leo a wry look. "Rahel was quite taken with you."

This rankled Sera, though she wasn't quite sure why, but then Agnes launched into an explanation of everything—how they had found Sera in the plains of Kaolin, how her father had put her into his final play, the escape to the Seaport, and the journey to Pelago. She did not mention the power of Sera's blood or the tether, only that they believed that the way to return Sera to her home was to get her to the ruins of Braxos.

"And we need to stop in Ithilia first," Agnes said breathlessly. "I've got an interview at the university. My grandmother is expecting me there."

"That will be difficult," Phebe said. "I've heard it's even

worse in Ithilia than it is here—you will be hard-pressed to find docking there. I would be shocked if Ambrosine was in the city, with the way she's been aggravating the Triumvirate." She glanced at Leo again. "You're *lucky* Rahel was taken with you."

"We heard something in the market," Leo said. "About closed passages?"

Phebe got up and walked over to the coffee table, returning with a newspaper.

AMBROSINE BYRNE CLOSES PASSAGES TO LOST ISLANDS, the headline screamed. And beneath it read,

> In violation of Triumvirate orders, the matriarch of the infamous Byrne family has closed the passages around the elusive island of Culinnon, the most direct routes to the Lost Islands. Rumor has it she is pressing her northern allies to do the same. Does this mean Ambrosine Byrne has found Braxos herself? Are the bodies washing up on the shores of Brilsin and Adereen the result of failed attempts to find this mysterious island—or is there a more sinister reason behind these deaths? Could Ambrosine be protecting her newest treasure? This reporter thinks it's high time the Byrnes were reminded that they do not control the northern islands—that all of Pelago is under the rule of the Triumvirate. Just how the Aerin, the Lekke, and the Renalt decide to deal with this affront to their power remains to be seen, but one thing is certain: The island of Braxos is stretching this country to a breaking point. And the Kaolins flooding our ports are only making matters worse. President Vance of Kaolin has sent a furious letter

to the Triumvirate demanding release of all Kaolin pris-
oners being held in Pelagan jails. It would be impossible
to imagine the Triumvirate giving in to these demands,
so the question then is—what will Kaolin's response be?
Could this mean war?

Sera read the last word with a lump in her throat. War.

"This is bad," Leo said.

"It is worse than I was thinking," Vada agreed.

"What's Culinnon?" Agnes asked.

"Yeah, I've heard the name before," Leo said. "I mean, I
get that it's an island, but what's so special about it?"

"When did *you* hear about it?" Agnes demanded.

"Back in Old Port, after that dinner with Elizabeth
Conway and her friend," Leo said, rubbing his temple like
the memory was fuzzy. "And the woman who changed our
money said something about it in the market."

Phebe looked from Agnes to Leo as if trying to decide
whether the twins were pulling her leg.

"You . . . neither of you know about Culinnon?" she
asked. "He never *told* you?"

"Who? Told us what?" Agnes said.

"I always thought Eneas was exaggerating," she said,
leaning forward to rest her head in her hands. "That complete and utter *bastard*." Then she sat up, adjusted a seashell
pin in her hair, and said, "Culinnon is an island owned by the
Byrne family. It is their home and the seat of their power, the
most mysterious island in all of Pelago, at least until Braxos
was discovered. Besides the fact that here, people do not own
entire islands—not even the Triumvirate families—no one is

allowed to set foot on Culinnon without Ambrosine Byrne's express permission. It is said to contain wealth beyond anything known in this world, and those who are fortunate enough to have walked its shores leave never being able to speak of it again, or reveal what they saw there, beyond a few hazy descriptions. Eneas could never even tell *me* about its wonders and he lived and worked there from when he was a young boy until the day Alethea moved to Ithilia. It is guarded by Ambrosine's own personal force of Misarros, but stories say there are other, more powerful methods of protection put in place. Culinnon is a living legend, as ancient and formidable as the goddesses of Talmanism."

It all sounded fascinating and frightening at the same time, Sera thought. Then Phebe turned and fixed Agnes with penetrating look.

"And it will be yours, Agnes," she said. "By birthright. When Ambrosine Byrne dies, Culinnon will pass to *you*."

5

AGNES

AGNES COULD FEEL EVERYONE'S EYES ON HER, FEEL THE blankness on her own face as her heart pounded out a frantic rhythm against her ribs.

She could acknowledge the words Phebe was saying, but when put together in that order, they made no sense. Inherit an *island*? And not just any island but a secret, powerful one that she hadn't even known existed until this very moment?

All the years she'd yearned for her mother, she'd never considered that Alethea might have left her something. Sera was gazing at her wide-eyed, Leo's jaw appeared to have become permanently unhinged, and even Vada seemed dumbstruck.

"I am being furious with myself for not making this connection," Vada said, shaking her head slowly, as if in a daze. "I thought Culinnon would be going to what's-his-name, the oldest son . . . Hektor. I am forgetting Alethea left a daughter."

"Why . . . me?" Agnes managed to croak out. "My grandmother doesn't even know me."

"In Pelago, names and titles and property pass through the mother," Phebe explained. "Alethea was Ambrosine's only daughter, and her eldest child. When Alethea died, Ambrosine was left with sons, two of them." Phebe grimaced. "Vada is right, Hektor likely assumed that he would be inheriting Culinnon, since Alethea's heir is half Kaolin and was living in Old Port City. He will not be pleased to hear you are in Pelago."

Agnes felt as if a cube of ice had just slipped down her spine. She was still getting accustomed to the idea of an inheritance, and now she had two uncles she'd never known who would be angry at her for it? Agnes had always been aware that she didn't know very much about her mother's family, but she was beginning to understand the sheer breadth of information her father had kept from her.

Leo gripped the table, his knuckles white. "This is . . . wow, Agnes. Do you think Father knows?"

It was the first time either of them had mentioned their father out loud, and Agnes flinched. But Xavier McLellan was miles away, across the Adronic Ocean—she did not have to live under his roof, or abide by his rules, and Agnes would not let herself be frightened by him anymore. Her mother had left her an *island*. In Pelago. Suddenly, Agnes's heart lifted. She would never have to leave this country. She belonged here.

"Oh, he knows," Phebe said, and Agnes was surprised to see Vada nodding. "Marriage contracts in Pelago are not taken lightly. I do not know the details of your mother's, of course, but regardless of her choice of husband, there is no way either she or Ambrosine would allow Culinnon to pass to anyone but Alethea's firstborn daughter. If it wasn't made clear enough to Xavier when they married, it certainly would have been once Alethea became pregnant."

"This is true," Vada said. "My mama had no marriage contract, but it is written that I will inherit the *Maiden's Wail* upon her death."

"There is something else," Phebe said. "Something you both must see." She turned to Leo with a faintly pleased expression. "You aren't quite as arrogant as Eneas used to describe in his letters. He pitied you, pitied the hold your father had over you. But he loved you too. Both of you." A tear shone in her eye. "He loved you like you were his own."

She stood and left the room, leaving the four of them looking at each other, confused.

Vada let out a low whistle. "Culinnon," she said.

"It certainly tops inheriting the brownstone on Creekwater Row," Leo said. Agnes couldn't tell if he was being sincere or hiding jealousy with sarcasm. She hoped it was the former.

"It doesn't get us any closer to Braxos," Agnes said.

"It might," Vada said. "The passages are closed, but maybe not for you. Why would Ambrosine Byrne deny her own granddaughter?"

"Do you think she's found Braxos already, like the papers say?" Agnes asked.

"No," Vada said. "I think if she had found it, the world would be knowing. Whatever is on that island, I do not think any person, Kaolin or Pelagan, would be able to be keeping it secret."

Phebe returned clutching a paper yellowed with age. "Here," she said, handing it to Agnes.

> *My darling Phebe,*
> *By the time you read this, you may have heard the news already. Alethea is dead. I do not know if I will ever be able to return to Pelago. I promised her I would take care of her children, that I would watch over them. A deal was made and a deal was broken and there may be repercussions that I cannot yet fathom. But I fear that's all I can put into writing. I'm doing everything I can to keep the twins safe, even if it means my home is lost to me. My dearest sister, know that I miss you and you are in my thoughts every day. And please, listen to your little brother this one time and heed my warning—stay away from the Byrne family. I hate to think of what Ambrosine might do to retaliate against me, if she has deduced my role in this. Stay safe, Phebe. May the goddesses go with you.*

Agnes had to read the letter three times before she fully understood it. "A deal?" she said. "What deal?"

"I don't know," Phebe said. "But not a week after I

received this letter, I had a visit from a pair of Byrne Misarros. They questioned me about my brother, when the last time I'd seen him was, when I had last heard from him. I lied, of course, about this letter. I told them I had not seen him since Alethea married Xavier and he left to live in Kaolin—that at least was true. I showed them a previous letter, one filled with stories of Alethea's nervousness at having children, of her excitement, with little bits of news about Old Port City and questions about his home country. A letter that was fully benign. They confiscated it and I have not seen a Byrne or their Misarros in Arbaz since. Not until now." She glanced at Leo.

"He never said anything." Agnes felt dazed. "Eneas never told us . . . I don't understand. Why didn't he tell me about this?"

"I think maybe he tried to," Leo said. "When he drove us to the Seaport, remember? He said to be careful around Ambrosine. He said to see things as they are and not as you wish them to be."

Her father's words came back to her then, from a day so many weeks ago in Xavier's study when Agnes had insisted that her mother would have wanted her to know Ambrosine.

The Byrnes are not who you think they are, Xavier had said. *They are selfish and greedy. They are arrogant.*

"But your grandmother knows you are coming," Phebe said. "And after Leo's meeting with Rahel, there will be no doubt she will hear of your arrival. You must get to Ithilia as quickly as you can. Her protection may be the only thing that can save you. If the Triumvirate finds out who you are, I don't know what they'll do. Holding the heir of Culinnon hostage certainly seems like an excellent bargaining chip."

Agnes felt her throat go dry. The *heir*. She'd never imagined the word applying to her. Nor could she have conceived of the danger that accompanied it. Would these three queens really use her as leverage against her grandmother?

"I wish I had known all this before," she said. "I wish my mother had been alive to tell me."

Sera gave her a sympathetic look as Phebe said, "Oh, child, I'm sure your mother would have wanted to be there for you more than anything. Life does not always turn out the way we expect."

Agnes reached into her pocket, ignoring the letter from Ambrosine and instead drawing out the photograph of Alethea.

"This is the only picture I have of her," she said quietly. "The only one."

Phebe took it as if it were more delicate than a moth's wing. "I had forgotten," she whispered. "How radiant her spirit was." She turned it over and read Alethea's inscription on the back.

Taken by X, March 12. Runcible Cottage, the Edge of the World.

"Do you know what that means?" Agnes asked without much hope.

"I do not," Phebe said.

"What was she like?" Sera asked, leaning over Agnes's shoulder to study the photograph. "She looks very brave."

Agnes translated and Phebe smiled.

"Brave, indeed. She had a wild spirit. And the parties she threw in Ithilia were legendary. She was creative but short tempered, gracious yet stubborn. Very stubborn. Eneas used to say there were mules with more sense than her." Phebe chuckled softly. "But he loved her all the more for it. And she knew how to cause a commotion. The day it was announced in the *Ithilia Star* that Alethea Byrne had married a man from Kaolin, you'd have thought the oceans had risen up and swallowed Whitehall. The whole country was in a frenzy."

Agnes felt tears well in her eyes and blinked them back. Her mother had never seemed quite so real to her as she did in this moment.

"What's Whitehall?" Leo asked.

"The sacred shrine of Talmanism," Phebe explained. "An outcrop of land just off the coast of Ithilia, connected by a narrow bridge to the great Palace of Banrissa, from where the Triumvirate rules."

"And not a place we are wishing to be visiting," Vada said. "Not if the Triumvirate is seeking to retaliate against Byrnes."

"No," Phebe agreed. "I wish Rahel had not seen you, Leo. It would be best to avoid Ithilia altogether."

"We can't do that," Agnes said.

Suddenly, there was a pounding on the door. Everyone at the table froze.

"Open up, in the name of the Triumvirate!" a deep but distinctly female voice called.

"Put your headdress on," Phebe hissed at Sera, who hurried to cover herself. From upstairs, the baby began to wail. Phebe took a deep breath and walked calmly to answer the door.

"Good evening," she said. "How may I be of service to the Triumvirate?"

"Good evening, mistress," another female voice, as smooth as velvet, replied. "We are inquiring after the Byrne who was in your shop earlier today."

"The one with a raggedy sailor companion and Alethea Byrne's face," the first voice growled. Agnes recognized it with a jolt—Rowen, the head of the Aerin's guard.

"Dorinda." Vada muttered the name under her breath like a curse.

"What do you want with him?" Phebe asked, but Rowen pushed past her and into the house. When she caught sight of Leo, satisfaction spread across her face.

"The moneylender was right," Rowen said. "You do look just like her. But Alethea's children are in Kaolin."

For a second Agnes thought Leo would try to deny it. "Not this one," he finally admitted.

Rowen seemed amused. "The prodigal son," she said. There was a cold pause. "Where is your sister?"

Agnes had never been so grateful to have her father's face.

"Still in Kaolin," Leo lied smoothly. "I came here myself, to be married." He gestured to Sera. "Like mother like son, I suppose."

"Please excuse my companion," the second Misarro said, coming up to stand beside Rowen. She was heavier set, with auburn spikes and a golden sun emblazoned across her chest declaring her to serve the Renalt. "The Aerin's Misarros aren't known for their manners. I am Eireen Connor, head of Princess Rahel's guard. The princess has requested your presence on her great ship the *Gilded Lily*." Eireen's eyes roved over the table and the remnants of dinner. "She wishes for you to join her for dessert." As an afterthought, she added, "You may bring your fiancée if you wish."

Something in the way she said it made Agnes think this princess would rather Sera not attend.

"That's very kind of her," Leo said. "But I'm quite comfortable here, thanks."

Eireen smiled at him pleasantly. "This is not a request."

Agnes could see two more Misarros looming just outside the door and wondered how many might have come to carry out Rahel's wishes.

"Very well," Leo said. "But my fiancée will remain here."

Eireen looked relieved by this, but Rowen frowned.

"Take off your headdress," she commanded Sera. "Let us see what sort of Pelagan would attach herself to such a . . ." She looked Leo up and down. "Half-breed."

"No," Leo said, stepping in front of Sera. He seemed to realize his mistake immediately. Rowen pulled a knife from the assortment that were strapped around her waist.

"She will remove the headdress or it will be removed for her," she said.

"Come now, Rowen, there is no need for threats," Eireen said. "I'm sure the girl does not mind. All one has to do is ask nicely." She turned to Sera. "You don't mind taking that off so we may see what I am certain is a beautiful face, do you, my dear?"

Sera seemed to have sensed that this, too, was not a

request, because she stood and placed a hand on Leo's arm. With careful, deliberate movements, Sera lifted the head-dress, her blue hair spilling down her back, her silver skin glowing richly in the light of the candles. Eireen let out a cry of shock but Rowen froze, regarding Sera with a mixture of surprise and disgust.

"What devilry is this?" she hissed. "Have you thought to craft some . . . some replica of Saifa to seize power? What sort of heresy are you Kaolins capable of?"

"She's not Saifa and she's not a replica," Leo said. "She has nothing to do with Pelago *or* Kaolin."

"Then would you be so kind as to explain exactly . . . *what* . . . she is?" Eireen asked, clearly struggling to main-tain her composure.

He pressed his lips together. "I can't tell you that."

Rowen's nostrils flared. "You will both come with us."

"Rowen," Eireen snapped, but Sera stepped forward, her face oddly serene.

"Tell them we will go with them willingly," she said to Leo. "Tell them there is no need for knives or violence. We can't let them have Agnes, Leo. And we don't want to put Phebe or Vada in danger either."

"What is she saying?" Rowen demanded. "What lan-guage is that?"

Agnes felt her throat tighten, her stomach lurch. Was she just going to stay here and let the Misarros take them? But if she declared who she was, they'd only take her too.

"We'll go with you," Leo said. "No one needs to get hurt."

"Excellent!" Eireen exclaimed. "The princess will be delighted. And with such an unusual guest as well." Something raw and hungry flickered in her eyes. "I simply cannot wait to hear her story."

There was an undercurrent of threat in her words that sent icy shivers up Agnes's neck. But she felt glued to the bench. Eireen gestured them to the door—neither looked back at Agnes or Vada as they left, though Agnes saw Sera reach out and take Leo's arm as if to steady herself. Rowen stalked after them and Eireen turned to Phebe.

"A thousand apologies for the interruption, mistress," she said. "Do enjoy the rest of your evening."

She left, and Agnes slumped, her heart pounding, her breath coming in gasps. She'd lost them. Her brother and her best friend in one fell swoop.

"They'll let them go, though, won't they?" she said. One look at Vada's and Phebe's faces told her the answer. She knew it anyway. Once they knew who Leo was, and especially once they'd seen Sera . . .

"No," Phebe said gently. "I don't think they will. I don't think they will harm your brother, but I fear for what will become of your silver friend. If they believe her some Byrne or Kaolin trick . . ." She trailed off. "I should have seen this coming. I should not have had you come here. Rahel is a silly girl prone to infatuation. And used to getting what she wants, when she wants it."

"So what do we do?" Agnes asked again. But she knew the answer: Ithilia. They must get to Ithilia. It had been calling to her all her life. She pressed the heels of her palms into her eyes.

"I know what you are thinking," Vada said. "But you must be patient. They will be leaving tonight and we will not be able to find a boat to Ithilia until morning."

"We?" Agnes blinked up at her.

"You think I would be leaving you to make your way alone? I promised I would get you to Ithilia. I swore on my *endexen*." She touched the fang hanging at her throat, from the shark her grandmother's grandmother had hunted and killed, the most precious thing she owned. "Vada Murchadha does not break a promise."

Agnes flashed her a watery smile. "Tomorrow, then," she said.

"Tomorrow." Vada squeezed her shoulder.

"You may not need to wait at all," Phebe said. Fear and exhaustion were etched across her face, but there was a determination there as well. "When it was four of you, that was too many, but with only two . . . you can sail, can you not?" she asked Vada.

Vada snorted. "I have been sailing since before I could walk."

Phebe's mouth set in a thin line. "Good. Because I have a boat."

6

LEO

Leo wondered if Sera was as terrified as he was.

"Tell her to put that headdress back on," Rowen commanded once they were out of the house. "She'll cause a riot in the market, whatever she is."

"She can understand you," Leo snapped, then cursed himself for letting his fear and irritation get the better of him.

"Really?" Eireen said. "How fascinating."

Sera quickly hid beneath the strands of beads, her fingers digging into his arm as they walked down the hill back toward the market of Arbaz. He wished he'd just agreed to go with them right away—maybe they wouldn't have taken Sera. He was certain that Rowen would hand him over to the Triumvirate the moment they landed in Ithilia. At least they hadn't taken Agnes too. He wondered if he would be as valuable as a hostage, not being the heir to anything.

The main boulevard was bathed in the warm glow of gas lamps; carriages and people alike stopped short to let the Misarros cross. Leo heard small gasps turn to excited mutterings.

"Is that a Byrne?"

"A Byrne in the custody of the Triumvirate!"

"Ambrosine won't take this lying down."

The voices seemed to follow them as they entered the portico. Leo's jaw was clenched so tight he thought his teeth might crack. He'd imagined his face would be a positive attribute once they arrived in Pelago, but it was bringing nothing but trouble.

They arrived at the docks and Eireen led them to a ship that Leo knew at once was the *Gilded Lily*. Made of smooth white wood, its every detail seemed to have been dipped in gold, right down to the glittering figurehead. A row of Renalt Misarros stood waiting by the gangplank, a line of golden suns. Eireen led them onto the ship, where tiny white lights had been strung over the deck. There was a table set for two with white linen and a candle flickering in the wind. Rahel was seated at it, fixing her hair, but she jumped up at the sight of Leo, then frowned when she noticed Sera.

"My lady, I have brought you—"

"Leo," he said, interrupting Eireen.

Rahel seemed enchanted. "Leo," she breathed, her doe-brown eyes growing even wider. Sera gripped his arm tighter.

"We must leave now," Rowen was growling. "The Aerin will not want to be kept waiting."

"You are on a Renalt ship, Rowen. You do not give orders here," Eireen said tartly, but turned away from her and shouted, "We sail at once!"

There was a flurry of activity as the Misarros readied the ship. Rahel looked around, confused. "But I thought we weren't leaving until tomorrow."

"Alas, my princess, things have changed. Your new friends are coming with us to Banrissa, isn't that exciting?" Eireen said.

Rahel's face lit up with delight. "I get to keep him?"

"Keep him?" Sera said, disgusted.

Rahel gasped. "What was that?" she asked, trying to peer through the beads covering Sera's face.

"Why don't you show your guests belowdecks," Eireen suggested. "I'm sure they would love to see all of your beautiful rooms. And they are most interested to try dessert."

The princess nodded, eager as a puppy. "Dessert!" she exclaimed, shooting a sulky glance at Sera before leading them to a set of stairs. "I didn't know you were engaged," she said to Leo as the ship began to move out into the water. But her petulance faded quickly as she began chattering to Sera. "Did Mistress Phebe make that dress for you? She's the best there is in Pelago, isn't she? She's making one very much like it for me. What was that language you were speaking earlier? Are you from the northern islands? My mother says they speak funny up there. I like your headdress too, it's awfully ornate. Isn't it hurting your head, though? They're heavy. You can take it off now if you'd like."

Though he couldn't see her face, Leo could tell Sera was bemused by all the questions. He certainly was. They had entered a hall with golden carpets and gold sconces on the walls and every door had a golden knob. It was all making Leo's temples throb. Sera pulled off the headdress and Rahel let out a shriek.

"Saifa!" she cried.

Leo was getting very good at explaining that Sera wasn't Saifa. But it was even easier with Rahel because she seemed to decide after a moment that she did not care who Sera was. Especially not after Leo told her they weren't actually engaged.

"What did you dye her hair with?" Rahel asked. "She would have caused a *scene* in the market. Is that why she's dressed like your bride? That's a brilliant idea, you are so smart. I heard the Byrnes are smart but also cruel, that's what Mother says. She says they're out for power. Ambrosine wanted to marry Hektor to a Triumvirate princess but they all said no, even the Lekke. I was too young, though, when she asked. Wouldn't it have been grand, a Byrne marrying a Renalt? But Mother didn't like that much. Which Byrne are you?"

"Alethea's son," Leo said. He could hardly keep up with Rahel's questions and found he was too tired to lie.

"So you're Kaolin!" Rahel exclaimed. "How exciting." She opened a door to a parlor with golden chairs upholstered in pale pink, gleaming mirrors encrusted with pearls, and a gilded table set with a stunning array of desserts.

"What a beautiful room," Leo said, because he felt that was what was expected of him.

Rahel beamed. "I designed it myself. Wait until you see where I sleep! I've got a pink comforter and pink pillows and a golden dresser. Do you like pink?" she said to Sera, then just as quickly turned back to Leo. "Can you make her talk again? Her voice is so pretty."

"I'm not a windup toy," Sera said, and Rahel applauded.

"My mother is going to love you!" she said. Leo's stomach sank. He didn't want any of the Triumvirate getting their hands on Sera—or worse, finding out that her blood contained magic.

"These desserts look magnificent," he said, changing the subject. Rahel needed no further encouragement.

"Aren't they? These are wine-poached apricots, and that's a chocolate lava cake that's so gooey it makes you want to scream. What's your favorite dessert?"

She was looking at Leo like he was the treat. He made himself give a long, slow smile, the kind that always worked best on the tavern girls back home.

"Well," he said. "I do love a good cobbler. Peach if I can find it. With whipped cream."

Rahel licked her lips. "I can get you that! My chef makes anything I tell her to. I'll be right back!"

She slipped out and left Sera and Leo alone.

"What . . ." Sera sank down onto a plush pink chair.

"Yeah," Leo said. "She's a lot to take in."

"What do you think she'll do with us?"

"It's not her I'm worried about. It's her mother, and the other two queens."

Sera nodded. "She doesn't seem to care about who I am. But she likes you quite a lot."

Was Leo imagining the hint of resentment in her voice? He was pretty sure Sera liked girls, given that she had three mothers and came from a city of only women. Why would she care if Rahel thought him handsome?

He moved to look out the window, a large circle covered in gauzy gold curtains. The lights of the market were already tiny as stars in the distance. "We're moving pretty fast. Wonder how long till we reach Ithilia."

"What do you think Agnes and Vada are doing?" Sera asked.

"They'll make a plan," Leo said, and he hoped he sounded surer than he felt. "They'll figure something out. Agnes wasn't born with all those brains for nothing."

"At least we kept her out of the Triumvirate's hands," Sera said. "Being the heir to Culinnon and all."

Leo was relieved that he felt no jealousy about that whatsoever. His sister could have all the islands she wanted. He felt like he didn't know who to trust in this country—as much as Agnes had been longing to meet their grandmother, Eneas's parting words plus the letter he'd sent Phebe had left Leo with a cold sense of foreboding. Whatever the deal was that had been made and then broken, it seemed Ambrosine wasn't happy about it. But she was also their best chance at surviving the Triumvirate and getting to Braxos—especially if she was controlling the flow of ships to the Lost Islands.

Silence wrapped around them and Leo dreaded the moment when Rahel would return. The girl was exhausting. There was a clock on the mantel that ticked loudly and his heart picked up speed with each passing second. There was nothing he could do in this moment, no way to escape and no idea of what would happen when they reached Ithilia. Finally the quiet grew too much to bear.

"What would you be doing right now?" he asked Sera, the words rushed to cover his increasing panic. "If you had never come here."

She seemed relieved by the question, as if she had been fighting against the silence as well. "I would likely be working in the stargem mines," she said. "That was my next apprenticeship. Though I do not think I would have been any better at that than I was at cloudspinning, or tending the seresheep, or working in the orchards." She poked at a gelatin mold and watched its thick green body undulate. "There was meant to be a wedding season coming, that's what Koreen said. I'd never seen a wedding season before. I was so excited."

"You have a season for weddings?" Leo asked, leaving the window to take a seat on the couch beside her chair.

She nodded. "And a birthing season follows after. I was born at the end of the last birthing season, so there has not been a wedding season in my lifetime yet."

"Did you . . ." Leo cleared his throat. "Was there someone—well, two someones—who you wanted to marry?"

"Oh, no," Sera said, and Leo felt a selfish pang of relief. "No, I . . . Leela had been kissed, but not me." She twined her fingers together and glanced at the door Rahel had gone through. "I did not think that sort of love was meant for me."

"But you do now?" he asked, tensing in anticipation of her response.

"I know it," she replied. Leo was certain she could hear

his heart pounding through bone and skin and muscle.

"What happened to change your mind?"

She turned to him and her eyes were a burst of refreshing blue in the golden room. "I came to this planet," she said. "And discovered I am attracted to males."

She confessed it as if it were the easiest thing in the world, as if she could not hear the bells ringing out inside Leo's chest. This was not where he'd expected the conversation to go and he wasn't sure if he'd truly allowed himself to acknowledge his feelings for Sera until this moment.

"Are you all right?" she asked. "Your face looks . . . strange."

"Does it?" His voice sounded unnaturally high. "No, I'm fine, I'm . . ." He searched for a change of subject, but Sera found one for him.

"Oh," she said, and her hand flew to her necklace.

"The moonstone?" Leo asked.

She nodded. "It just went cold."

She took it out from beneath her dress and Leo found his eyes drawn to it. The stone was a white purer than a swan's wing, shot through with delicate ribbons of color.

"Is it as smooth as it looks?" he asked. He'd never touched it before, never even dared to ask.

Sera smiled and held it out in her palm. "Would you like to feel it?"

Their hands touched as he ran his fingers over it, Sera's skin igniting a greater thrill in him than any magic stone ever could. The moonstone was like an ice cube that wouldn't melt—Leo found himself compelled to stroke it over and over again, its smoothness almost compulsive. Sera laughed, a richer, kinder sound than Rahel's giggles.

"It's pretty, isn't it?" she said. "My friend Leela found it on the banks of—"

All of a sudden, the moonstone flared up in their hands, so hot Leo wanted to pull away but found that he couldn't. Sera's palm began to glow and Leo had the same sensation he'd had when he and Sera had blood bonded and shared memories—a disorienting weightlessness, a feeling of heat zipping through his veins until it finally reached his heart. Sera gasped, and he knew she felt it too but he couldn't unstick his jaw to ask her what was going on.

There was a crackling sound, like static through a radio, and Leo's vision blurred—for a second he saw a different place, almost like an overlay across the opulent room, shadows of another location with columns and paths and clear pools of water.

"Did you see—" Sera began, and then there was a hard jerk behind his navel and he felt like he was being pulled upward very quickly through a narrow tunnel. He found himself rising through one of the pools, except that it wasn't filled with water and he no longer had any sense of his body at all. Glowing blue columns loomed all around him and a chain of silver-gold-blue was shooting up through the pool he was in, or maybe down from the cone of moonstone that was protruding from a circle of pure white vines covering the ceiling.

At the edge of the pool stood a girl with silver skin and blue hair, a few inches shorter than Sera and with a rounder face.

"Sera?" she whispered, staring at him. And he knew he

was seeing through Sera's eyes, her magic linking them, or maybe it was the moonstone they had been holding—this had to be the City Above the Sky.

"Leela?" Sera said.

Tears were tumbling down the girl's cheeks, even as her face broke into a wide smile.

"It's me," Leela said, and her voice cracked, but there was a clear ring of triumph in it. "It's me, Sera. I found you."

PART TWO

The City Above the Sky

7

SERA WAS *ALIVE*.

Leela emerged out into the Moon Gardens, still stunned by the vision she'd had below of Sera on a ship, crossing an ocean and gazing up at the stars, such tiny things, mere pinpricks in a blanket of ink black. And not only that, but there were Cerulean trapped in stalactites beneath the City. Leela's head was so full of questions she wondered how it didn't simply burst and spill her thoughts all over the moonstone statue of Faesa, who was staring at Leela with her wise, sad eyes. Who were these Cerulean? What had the High Priestess done?

Without even realizing it, she called on the statue to slide back over the hidden staircase that led down to that mysterious underground garden beneath the City. It was as if the moonstone was reacting to her very instincts and desires.

Leela looked up at the temple of Mother Sun, wondering where the High Priestess was now. She could still hear the faint *swish plop* in her ears, the sound of the High Priestess feeding the trapped Cerulean with that odd golden fruit. It was bad enough when Leela had first discovered that it was the High Priestess and not Mother Sun who had chosen Sera to be sacrificed—but after tonight she had no idea how deep her treachery ran. What was she doing with those Cerulean? Why keep them in stalactites?

The Moon Gardens seemed so alive now after all that stillness below—the snuffling of rodents and the buzz of insects sounded louder than usual. Leela realized she needed to move, she needed to get home before anyone saw her. It was not expressly forbidden for her to be here, but it wouldn't do to have anyone asking questions.

The temple was on an island in the middle of the Great Estuary, in the center of the City, with three bridges connecting it to the mainland. Leela crossed Dendra's Bridge in a fog, her mind pulled in a hundred different directions. But there was one thought that overpowered all.

Sera is alive. She repeated it over and over, numb shock giving way to joy as she passed the Aviary, the birds silent in their nests at this late hour. She wove her way through the domed sunglass dwellings until she reached her own home, nestled near the Apiary, and climbed through her bedroom window so as not to wake her mothers. She lay down and gazed at the ceiling, clutching her hands to her chest as tears seeped from her eyes and dripped into her hair.

"I'm going to find you, Sera," she whispered to the ceiling. "I'm going to bring you home."

How to actually accomplish this, she had no idea. But for now it was enough to know that her friend was alive, that she had not lost her forever.

It was all connected to moonstone, Leela was sure of it. The moonstone obelisk by the birthing houses had revealed markings and moved aside for her like Faesa's statue did. It had shown her first a vision of a dark room with glowing flowers and a pretty tree with turquoise leaves, then another vision, a smaller room with a person with pale skin, turquoise eyes, and curly black hair. Perhaps it was even the moonstone itself that had saved Sera's life. Leela exhaled in a gust. Could her gift have been responsible for keeping Sera alive?

Kandra, she thought with determination. She had to tell Sera's purple mother. Not only had Leela found Kandra's long-lost friend Estelle among the Cerulean imprisoned beneath the City, but Kandra needed to know that her daughter had not died. Except Kandra was living in the birthing houses now, far away in the Forest of Dawn, along with all the other purple mothers who had been chosen to bear daughters during the newly announced birthing season. How was Leela supposed to speak to her in secret there?

She bit her lip, regretting that she could not seek help from Sera's other two mothers. But that would require far too much explanation of things Leela did not know or think it safe to reveal. She had no idea for what purpose the High Priestess was using the trapped Cerulean, nor could she actually prove to anyone that Sera was still living, since she seemed to be the only one struck by the visions, the only one with this connection to the moonstone.

She tossed and turned all night, but when dawn's pale fingers crept in through her window, she was no closer to figuring out what to do next. She needed help. She needed Kandra. Leela fretted over the impossibility of the task before her as she made her way to the kitchen. But of one thing she was certain—she had to go back to the City's underbelly as soon as she could. It was the only place she'd seen Sera and she felt certain it held the answers to seeing her again—and hopefully the solution to bringing her home.

"Why, you look even more tired today than you did after the Night of Song!" her green mother exclaimed as Leela took her seat at the kitchen table. Her purple mother was stirring a large pot on the stove, the smell of oregano, carrot, and onion filling the room.

"I'm afraid I did not sleep well," Leela said with a yawn. "Is that all for us, Purple Mother? I do not think I have much of an appetite this morning."

Her purple mother laughed. "No, I am bringing food to the birthing houses today. The purple mothers there must keep up their strength."

Leela's heart somersaulted in her chest. "But I thought the birthing houses were sacred and forbidden by anyone save the High Priestess to enter now that the birthing season has begun."

"They are sacred indeed, but it is the duty of other purple mothers who have borne daughters before to provide those blessed to bear a child with nourishment and support," her purple mother said.

Leela saw what might be her best opportunity.

"Might I accompany you there?" she asked in what she hoped was an innocent tone.

Her green mother's face lit up, and Leela knew it was because she had not shown interest in much of anything recently.

"That is not allowed," her purple mother said. "I'm sorry, darling."

"I know," Leela said, and made a show of looking crestfallen. "I was just hoping to see how Plenna is doing. Now that I have lost Sera"—her tongue tripped over the name—"I was hoping to find solace in my other friends. It would be such a blessing to see Plenna happy." She sighed, hating the lie but knowing it was her best chance to see Kandra.

"Come now, Ilianne," her green mother said, "let her walk with you to the forest at least. Leela would not disturb anyone, nor would she ever threaten the sanctity of the birthing houses."

Her purple mother hesitated and a moment passed between her two mothers where Leela felt like they were having a silent conversation.

"All right," her purple mother said at last. "I cannot argue with you both. We will not stay long, though. And you will have to wait outside the sacred circle. I shall ask after Plenna for you."

Leela's spirits soared—she could not believe her luck. "I swear I will do as you ask. Oh, thank you, Purple Mother!"

Her mothers exchanged a pleased glance and Leela knew they were happy to see her returning to her old self, not the raw angry girl she'd been in the days after Sera's sacrifice. And she was happy they were happy, even as she hated being untruthful to them.

Though she was not hungry at all, she forced herself to eat some toast with pine nuts and blackberry jam, then changed into a fresh dress and waited while her purple mother poured the stew she'd made into a ceramic bowl, covering it with a length of cheesecloth.

"Are you ready?" she asked. Leela nodded and kissed her green mother on the cheek.

"It is so good to see you becoming yourself again," her green mother said, smoothing back her hair. Leela hid her guilt beneath a smile.

She and her purple mother took the path that wound its way past the Aviary, birds chirping cheerfully, then followed the line of the Great Estuary, dipping through the orchards and the seresheep meadows before they came to the Western Bridge. It was the same path Leela had taken to meet Kandra for so many nights, when they would sit by the obelisk at the birthing houses in the moonlight and talk of Sera and Estelle or muse over the High Priestess's motivations.

Kandra had also known of the High Priestess's falsity— she had just been tricked into forgetting it. Years ago, she had thought her friend Estelle was dead until she saw her one evening by the obelisk. Frightened, she had run away and confided to the High Priestess, who had placed her hands on Kandra's head and told her not to worry. After that, the memory of Estelle had faded from Kandra's mind—until Sera had fallen. The loss of her daughter had broken whatever spell the High Priestess had cast. And so Kandra and Leela would meet in the Forest of Dawn and puzzle over what to do. The High Priestess needed to be stopped, but how?

The Forest of Dawn was so different in daylight with her purple mother beside her. It made all those other nights feel like something out of a dream. Or perhaps *this* was the dream. With so many new mysteries, her world felt as upside down as the dying gardens beneath the City that grew from the ceiling.

They met Olfa, another purple mother, as they entered the forest, an empty basket in her hands.

"Good morning, Ilianne," she said to Leela's purple mother. "My goodness, that smells wonderful."

"It is my famous carrot stew," she replied, beaming.

"I'm sure the purple mothers will appreciate it," Olfa said. "I was just bringing another batch of fruit from the orchards, but I must return the basket to Freeda." She eyed Leela with an expression of polite confusion. "Good morning, Leela."

"Good morning, Purple Mother," Leela said.

"Leela is hoping to hear news of Plenna," her purple mother explained. "I told her she may accompany me to the forest but she must wait outside the sacred circle."

Olfa looked relieved. "Well, I'm sure Plenna will be happy to hear she has a friend who cares so much. I can report that she is most impatient to become pregnant."

Leela's purple mother and Olfa traded knowing smiles.

"I won't keep you," Olfa said, and she waved goodbye

and left Leela and her mother to make their way through the forest. The familiar smell of magnolia and crabapple filled Leela's nose as they walked, bees humming pleasantly in the background. Morning sunlight dappled the ground through leaves of brilliant green.

They were about thirty feet away from the birthing houses when her purple mother stopped. Leela could not see their small domes through the trees but she could faintly hear voices and occasional laughter. "This is as far as you can go, my love," her purple mother said, gesturing to the ground. White and blue pebbles were scattered to form a line that stretched out in both directions. Leela had not seen this yesterday when she had come to see Kandra and tell her about the moonstone necklace she had given to Sera and how she had heard Sera's voice coming from Aila's statue. Kandra had not wanted her to go beneath the City, thinking it too dangerous. And she had warned Leela to stay away from the birthing houses and not do anything foolish. And now Leela was back again to see her. But she had to. Kandra needed to know.

"The birthing houses are all filled now," her purple mother said. "Lyron Sunbringer arrived this morning, and she is the last one. There will not be another Cerulean blessed to have a child until one of the waiting mothers becomes pregnant. Then she will leave the houses to make room for a new purple mother, returning to her own dwelling until her time draws close. She will only come back to these houses to give birth."

Leela felt a tug of selfish joy that Kandra would be allowed to leave at some point, followed by a pang of sadness that it would come at the cost of bearing another child so soon after losing Sera.

But she has not lost Sera, Leela thought fiercely. *And I will find a way to tell her that.*

"You will wait here for me," her purple mother said, and Leela nodded. But as soon as her mother was out of sight through the trees, Leela began to follow the line of stones. Even if she had not been so familiar with this part of the forest already, the voices that grew louder were a beacon calling to her. Finally she stopped. She could not see the houses but she knew where she needed to go. And she would not be afraid of breaking the rules anymore. If the High Priestess could lie, and sacrifice Sera, and trap Cerulean in stalactites, then surely Mother Sun would forgive Leela for this infraction.

She took a breath and stepped over the line. When nothing happened except a sparrow singing loudly in a nearby birch, Leela let out a light-headed giggle. She was not sure what she had expected—a lightning bolt, perhaps, or a sun flare? She marched forward, feeling braver than she ever had, or maybe simply accepting her bravery in a way she hadn't before.

But being brave did not mean being rash, and she slowed her pace when the first domed house came into view, flitting from tree to tree to stay hidden.

The birthing houses looked the same as they had yesterday, rounded one-room dwellings made of sunglass, but the clearing with the moonstone obelisk was changed. Garlands of flowers had been strung from its tip to the doors of each house, daisy chains and ropes of fire lilies and strings of silvery moonflowers. Bouquets of forget-me-nots and tulips and chrysanthemum were piled high around its base. Tables had been set up on the grass and Leela saw Treena and a few of the older midwives stitching together a canopy to prop over them. There were a handful of purple mothers bringing food, and Leela caught sight of her own mother talking with Plenna. Of Kandra, however, she saw no sign.

Quick as a sunlizard, she darted to hide behind another tree, then another, letting her intuition guide her. She found Kandra sitting at the foot of an old spruce between two houses, her head leaning against its trunk, a length of blue seresheep wool in her hands. It looked as though she had been trying to sew something and given up halfway through.

"Kandra," Leela hissed. Kandra did not seem to hear her; her eyes were as dark and vacant as they had been in the days after Sera's sacrifice. "Kandra," Leela tried again, as loud as she dared.

Kandra started and looked around. When she caught sight of Leela she gasped and hurried to join her.

"Leela, I told you—" she began, but Leela had no time to spare for a scolding.

"I know, I know, I came with my purple mother and I must get back to the spot where I was told to wait for her. But I went to the Moon Gardens last night. I found a set of stairs beneath the statue of Faesa. Stairs that were not blocked by sunglass as the ones beneath the obelisk were." She gripped Kandra's hands in her own. "I went below the City and found what the High Priestess has been hiding."

Kandra's eyes widened. "Tell me everything," she said. "And quickly."

The story poured out of Leela and when she got to the part about discovering Estelle, Kandra made a sound that was half cry, half gasp.

"Estelle?" she choked. "She's still alive?"

Leela nodded. "I don't know what the High Priestess is doing with her, though. And there were so many others trapped just like her. The High Priestess was feeding them golden fruit that grows among the vines surrounding the tether. And then she held her hands out and all the stalactites began to glow and the ground shook and the tether . . . the tether . . ."

Leela could not find the words to describe its brilliance or the way the High Priestess's face had contorted in silent agony.

"I wish I could *see* it," Kandra said.

"So do I," Leela said. "But that is not all." She took a breath. "I saw *Sera*."

Kandra blinked. "In a stalactite?"

"No. I saw her in a vision, like the other ones I've had, only this was the clearest one yet. She is on the planet, Kandra. She is *alive*."

Kandra jerked her hands away. Leela was surprised to see her mouth set in a hard line.

"That is not a funny jest."

Leela frowned. "It is no jest at all. I saw her. It was real."

"You don't know that," Kandra said. "You don't know what these visions are. You said so yourself. They could be lies or tricks. They could be some dark magic of the High Priestess. She was able to take my memories of Estelle away; who is to say she cannot implant memories as well?

You don't *know*, Leela."

"But I do." This was not at all the reaction Leela had been expecting. "I mean, I didn't before, but I do now. It was no trick or spell. I *felt* Sera's heart beating in my chest as if we were blood bonding. It is a heartbeat I would know anywhere. Besides, the High Priestess did not even know I was there. Sera has my moonstone and I think it saved her. I've been seeing her through it, or . . . or it's connected us in some way. But those other visions were from the planet too, I'm sure of it. She's down there, Kandra. And I'm going to find a way to bring her home."

"Stop." Kandra's voice was sharp as ice breaking and she stepped back as if frightened of Leela. "Please," she whispered. "Don't . . . she is gone. She is *gone* and I must bear a new daughter and you cannot come here and tell me otherwise. You cannot give me false hope."

Leela felt a sharp twinge of anger. "There is nothing false about it," she said. Why did Kandra not believe her?

"Kandra!" one of the midwives called, and the two of them jumped.

"I must go," Kandra said, turning away. "Do not come back."

Leela felt empty as she watched her only confidant hurry toward the flower-strewn field to join the other purple mothers. This was not how she had imagined the conversation would go. She'd thought Kandra would be overjoyed. She'd thought she was bringing good news, not sadness and heartbreak.

"I'll find a way to show her," Leela muttered aloud to herself. "I'll prove that Sera is still alive."

She would return to the City's underbelly and learn all she could about that underground garden and the clear pools and the stalactites and what it all meant. If Kandra could not help her now, Leela would do this on her own. The weight of it threatened to crush her but she was determined to shoulder it.

She turned to make her way back across the stones to the path and abruptly found herself face-to-face with the last person she wished to see.

"Leela," the High Priestess said, gazing down from her impressive height with a mixture of confusion and horror. "What in the name of Mother Sun do you think you are doing here?"

8

LEELA'S HEART POUNDED IN HER EARS, HER FEET GROWN into the ground like roots.

"It is forbidden to cross the sacred circle once the birthing season has begun," the High Priestess said, and Leela nodded mutely. Had the High Priestess overheard any of her conversation with Kandra?

She folded her hands together and fixed Leela with a hard stare. "Please explain yourself."

"I wished to see how Plenna was doing," Leela said quickly. "My purple mother brought me along with her to deliver food and made me promise to wait at the path. But I . . . I did not listen. I thought if I could see Plenna happy, it would help heal some of the pain of Sera's loss." She looked down in case the High Priestess could read the lie in her eyes. "My heart still grieves for her."

"Of course it does, my child. But grief is no excuse for breaking such an important rule." The High Priestess placed a hand on Leela's shoulder, her skin hot through Leela's cloudspun dress. She'd never been touched by the High Priestess before, and Leela felt her magic jerk inside her, as if she had just touched a burning stove with bare fingers. "I am afraid a conclave must be called. And a penance must be decided."

Leela could only vaguely remember the last conclave, when she was just a little girl, called to deal with a Cerulean who had refused to aid in preparations for the Festival of Light, one of the three major Cerulean holidays. The woman had been old, Leela recalled, and lonely. She had lost both her wives and had retreated from Cerulean life. Leela remembered feeling both sad for her and frightened of her, as her penance was announced in front of the entire temple. She was tasked with preparing for the festival all on her own. And she had done it, to the City's great surprise.

She had died a month later. Leela felt ashamed that she could no longer remember the woman's name.

"Come," the High Priestess said. "We must tell your purple mother what has happened."

The look on her mother's face when she was told that Leela had disobeyed her made Leela want to slink under a rock. The other purple mothers and midwives had gathered in shock, listening to the High Priestess recount Leela's breach of faith and announce the conclave. Leela felt she could see her own purple mother's heart breaking at the thought of her daughter receiving the harshest Cerulean reprimand possible.

There was only one face missing among the crowd—Kandra's.

Leela was not allowed to accompany her purple mother home. She was not allowed to go home at all. She was marched by the High Priestess straight to the temple. The walk was long and peppered with gardens and dwellings so that Leela had to watch the news of her shame spread throughout the City. All the bravery she'd felt earlier evaporated, leaving her flat and lifeless. She did not know what her penance would be, but she was certain it would not leave her free to roam about the City any longer, even in the dead of night. How was she to get back to the stairs beneath the Moon Gardens? How was she supposed to see Sera again?

She cursed herself for being so reckless. But as they made their way across Faesa's Bridge, Leela felt her resolve harden. Whatever this penance was, it couldn't last forever. She would pay the price and she would return to finding a way to get Sera home.

They skirted the hedge that surrounded the Moon Gardens, novices inclining their heads as the High Priestess passed, then shooting Leela curious looks.

The High Priestess had not spoken a single word to Leela throughout the entire walk, and while Leela was beginning to feel the weight of the silence, the High Priestess herself did not seem to notice. She moved so gracefully she appeared to glide, her face set in an expressionless mask, and Leela could feel the heat of her body radiating through her long robe. The moonstone in the High Priestess's circlet gleamed in the sunlight and Leela was possessed with the sudden urge to pull the circlet from her head and pry the stone from its setting. She wondered if maybe there were more answers in that stone than in any of the statues in the Moon Gardens.

Leela felt weary as they approached the doors to the temple, her feet dragging, her head bowed. This morning, the world had seemed full of possibilities, but now everything had changed again. The freedom she had taken for granted was gone. She would be watched. Wherever she went, she would be seen as the young Cerulean who'd broken the rules.

But even worse—she had lied to her mothers and she had been caught. She had disappointed them, and Leela's stomach pinched with the shame of it.

Just then the sun lit on the temple's golden spire, a blinding flash of brilliant yellow that vanished as quickly as it had come. The High Priestess was still climbing the temple steps, but Leela's own legs had turned to stone.

She stared at the copper doors, where the markings of Mother Sun were etched in ever-changing, indecipherable symbols. Only they weren't indecipherable any longer.

Heal them.

Two simple words written over and over and over.

"Leela?" The High Priestess stood at the top of the stairs, staring down at her. "I know you are frightened, but this must be done. There are consequences to every action."

"What do the doors say?" Leela blurted without thinking.

The High Priestess froze for only half a second, but in

that brief moment Leela sensed uncertainty and a hint of what might have been fear.

"That is no concern of yours," she replied tartly. "The symbols of Mother Sun are meant for the High Priestess alone to decipher and share with the City as she will."

She can't read them. The thought came wild and unbidden to Leela's mind, and once there, she knew she was right. Another lie uncovered—for it was true, everyone in the City thought the symbols were meant only for the High Priestess to read. But who had told them that? The High Priestess herself. Leela did not know why or how she could understand the symbols all of a sudden, but she knew they were no hallucination. It took a great amount of effort to lower her head and trudge up the stairs. She could not afford to look upon the doors again, could not give any indication to the High Priestess that she'd been able to read them.

What is happening to me? They entered the sanctum, its ceiling painted with the sun and three moons and countless stars. There was a large smattering of orange mothers present and Leela was surprised to see Sera's among them. Though she shouldn't have been—of course her orange mother would be praying now that Kandra had been sent to the birthing houses. Orange mothers were teachers of devotion in the Cerulean family unit, and prayer was an important part of their lives, especially prayer for a new daughter. Most of the orange mothers were praying together but Sera's sat apart from the others, on a cushion alone in front of the Altar of the Lost: a giant sun crafted out of sungold and moonsilver and studded with dark blue stargems, one for each Cerulean lost in the Great Sadness.

The Great Sadness was the worst tragedy in all of Cerulean history, when two hundred Cerulean had been massacred on the last planet they had been tethered to, nearly nine hundred years ago. That was when the High Priestess had ascended to her role—the previous High Priestess, Luille, had died on the planet. The Great Sadness was why Cerulean were not allowed to go down onto planets at all anymore. It was too dangerous, the High Priestess said. But Sera was on the planet now, and while she had seemed anxious and sad, Leela did not have the sense she was in danger. The lies were piling up and making her head hurt.

Leela had the strongest urge to run to Sera's orange mother, to tell her everything and see if maybe she would believe her daughter was alive when Kandra would not. But she could only follow the High Priestess as she crossed the room in sweeping strides, novices and orange mothers scattering in her wake. Acolyte Endaria was hurrying across the chancel, the look on her face leaving Leela in no doubt that the news had already reached her.

"Her purple mother has been informed," the High Priestess said without preamble. "Send Novices Belladon and Loonir to her dwelling to tell her other mothers."

Acolyte Endaria pressed a hand to her chest and looked at Leela with confusion and pity. "Why would you break such a sacred rule, my child?" she asked.

Leela tried to appear contrite. "I . . ."

"She is young, Endaria," the High Priestess said, sweet sympathy in her voice, but it was too honeyed for Leela's liking. "And still grieving the loss of her friend. You remember how it was to be young and curious and sad."

Leela could not picture Acolyte Endaria as ever being any of those things, but the acolyte nodded fervently.

"Imima has prepared the chamber of penitence," she said.

"Excellent. The conclave will convene tomorrow at the hour of the serpent."

"Yes, High Priestess," Acolyte Endaria said, bowing her head.

The High Priestess turned to Leela and fixed her with a gaze so penetrating, Leela felt as if her skin was being peeled off. She forced herself to remain still, to take courage in the memory of Sera's heartbeat and the knowledge that her friend was out there and needed her, refusing in this moment to show either true fear or fake humility. The High Priestess had lies on her side—Leela had love and truth. She could feel her love for Sera shimmering in every facet of her blood. For one thrilling, weightless moment, Leela had the sense that the High Priestess was afraid of her.

Then the High Priestess's lips twitched as if she wanted to smile and Leela felt her heart crumble into a pile of hot ashes.

"We all make mistakes, Leela," she said. "We all challenge authority in some way when we are young. Do not despair. You will grow from this lesson and become an even better Cerulean than you were before. I am certain of it."

"You will," Acolyte Endaria echoed. "Now come with me. I will take you to the chamber of penitence, where you shall stay the night."

The High Priestess gestured for Leela to walk the stairs

that led to the chancel. Leela had never seen the room from this vantage point before—it spread out before her, endless yet also close, as if she could reach her arms out and wrap them around the entire space. The pulpit was made of nebula tree wood, silver as the moon and studded with crystal-clear stargems. Leela had never seen behind it; a single shelf lined its insides, empty now, but Leela guessed it would hold the sacred bowls the High Priestess would use for various ceremonies.

Acolyte Endaria led her to a space at the very back of the chancel that Leela had always thought was just wall but slid aside to reveal a narrow hallway curving along the outer edge of the temple. The walls glowed, lighting their way, and Leela followed the acolyte to a small room with yet another door. The only doors Leela had ever seen were the ones on the temple and those on the birthing houses, both made of copper. The door Acolyte Endaria opened was made of soft gray wood and inlaid with lacquered golden polaris leaves.

The room was round, simply furnished with a bed and gossamer blanket, and a dresser with a basin and pitcher. A lone, circular window was set in the wall too high above the bed for Leela to see out of.

"Novices will be stationed outside, to bring your meals and see to your needs," Acolyte Endaria said, but Leela knew that what she really meant was, "You are not allowed to leave this room."

"Yes, Acolyte," she said. It was only for one night, though Leela hated any amount of time that took her away from the world beneath the City, from the cone of moonstone that had shown her Sera's face.

And she had never once slept anywhere but in her own bed in her own dwelling.

Acolyte Endaria left, closing the door behind her. Leela curled up on the bed and rested her chin on her knees. The room felt even smaller with the door closed; she was not used to being so confined.

She wondered how her mothers were doing, and felt shame creep up the back of her throat. She would tell them everything one day, she vowed. She would make them understand why she was changing and breaking rules and sneaking around. She hoped they would not be disappointed in her. It had never been her intent to cause them pain. But she had come too far down this path to turn back now. She must find out what the High Priestess was doing with all those trapped Cerulean and right the wrongs her lies had caused. She must bring Sera home.

The day passed slowly. Novices brought meals for her, but Leela had no appetite and only picked at the food. A few times she would press her ear against the door, to see if there really was a novice keeping watch over her at all times. And she always heard the shuffling sound of feet or a soft hum or a whispered recitation of prayer.

The light coming in through the window grew dimmer as night fell. There were no candles or lanterns in the chamber of penitence and Leela let the darkness surround her. She would alternately pace the room or throw herself on the bed, unable to stay still for long, but with no place to truly go. It must have been past the hour of the owl but not yet the hour of the dark when there came a gentle knock on the door.

Leela was lying on her back, staring up at the window, and she sat up so quickly her head spun. No one should be visiting her and it was far past the time for any more meals. She was beginning to wonder if she had imagined it when the knock came again.

"Leela?" a quavering voice whispered.

Leela gasped and rushed to fling open the door. Standing in the hall, with a look of sheepish pride on her face, was Elorin.

9

"Elorin! What are you doing here?" Leela asked, pulling her inside and closing the door.

Elorin was a young novice, one of Leela's circle of friends who had found her calling in a life of devotion to Mother Sun. Leela had never been very close to the girl until after Sera fell, when she began to spend more time at the temple in hopes of learning about the High Priestess's treachery. Elorin had been an unexpected comfort, a friend when Leela wondered if she would ever be able to trust anyone again. It was Elorin who had told Leela about the secret place the High Priestess would retreat to when she wished to refresh her mind and recommit to her faith. But Leela knew the truth now. She had seen the secret place with her own eyes.

"I wanted to see you," Elorin said. "So I asked Novice Cresha if I could watch over you tonight instead of her. Oh, Leela, is it true what they're saying? Did you really breach the sacred circle of the birthing houses?"

"It's true," Leela said, and Elorin gave a tiny cry.

"But why? I hope you do not mind my saying so but . . . that sounds more like something Sera would have done."

Leela let out a breathy laugh. "Yes," she agreed. "It does."

Elorin's face was a mere outline in the pale circle of moonlight streaming through the window. "There has been a change in you since she died," she said. Leela nodded. That, at least, was no secret. "It seems to me as if you carry a heavy burden. Yet I do not know what it is or what I can do to help. And I would very much like to help you."

"I . . ." Leela's heart stuttered out a painful beat. She so badly needed a friend but she was unsure if she could truly trust Elorin. Besides, if she *did* believe, then was Leela putting Elorin in danger too?

"They said you wanted to visit Plenna, to see her happy because you miss Sera," Elorin said. "But I do not believe that. You were never close with Plenna. I asked myself, why would Leela break a sacred rule for a Cerulean she has no strong attachment to? And then I realized that there *is* a Cerulean at the birthing houses who you might break the rules to see." Elorin leaned forward and whispered, "Sera's purple mother."

Leela inhaled sharply, her eyebrows shooting up her forehead. Elorin's satisfied smile was a glint in the moonlight.

"I knew it," she said. "But I still do not understand why. Was it merely to comfort her? There are some novices who whisper that it feels too soon for her to bear another child. Others think she must be overjoyed by the chance to have a new daughter. It is not for me to question the will of Mother Sun, but . . . I think Sera's purple mother must be very sad. Yet I still cannot believe that you would go against such a firm rule without good reason, and comfort does not seem to be enough."

Leela listened to her work all this out and realized that Elorin was far more perceptive than she had ever given her credit for. Sera had never liked her much because she was so pious, but Leela was beginning to see that her piety was only one facet, that the girl as a whole was someone entirely more layered—that maybe she kept things about herself secret too.

"What if," she began hesitantly, "I told you that I did not believe it was Mother Sun who chose Kandra to be blessed to bear another child?"

Elorin blinked. "But who else could possibly do that?"

"Who indeed?" Leela held her tongue and waited; it felt like she could hear the wheels turning in Elorin's mind. Leela knew she could not suggest the High Priestess's name herself—it would not be as it was with Kandra, who already had a reason to distrust her. Elorin was a *novice*. She had chosen a life of devotion to Mother Sun and, by extension, the High Priestess herself. If she could not or would not make this connection, Leela thought, then she would know where the girl stood.

But she found herself gritting her teeth and hoping against hope that Elorin would see and believe. Because she did not want to continue down this path alone.

Elorin gasped suddenly, her hands flying to cover her mouth. "No," she whispered. "It cannot be." She peered at Leela over trembling fingers. "The High Priestess?"

"Yes," Leela replied, her shoulders melting with relief.

"But . . ." Elorin moved as if in a dream to sit on the edge of the bed. "But why?"

Leela sat beside her. "That is what I am trying to discover."

"How did you come to this conclusion? What proof do you have?"

Leela told Elorin of the conversation she had overheard between the High Priestess and Acolyte Klymthe through the hedge of the Moon Gardens, when it had become clear to Leela that the High Priestess herself had chosen Sera to be sacrificed. "I was as shocked as you are," Leela said. "I had always trusted in the High Priestess and her wisdom and courage. But *she* is making decisions that Mother Sun should make. And that is not right. That is not how our City is meant to work."

Elorin was shaking her head slowly, and for a heart-stopping moment Leela feared that the girl would reject this knowledge—that she would refuse to believe that the leader of their City was anything less than pure, that she would run to the High Priestess and reveal what Leela had told her.

"We trust in her so implicitly," Elorin said. "But I

wondered . . . first when the City did not move after Sera's sacrifice, and then again when I became a novice. Do you remember when I told you about the secret place in the temple where the High Priestess goes to sequester herself? And that she had been going there more and more recently?"

"Yes," Leela said. "I remember."

"I only knew because I overheard two of the oldest novices talking about it and they seemed . . . I would not say suspicious, necessarily, but there was an edge to the discussion that made me curious. And then you began coming to the temple more often, which wasn't something you ever used to do. It seems like since Sera fell, strange things have been happening in this City."

Leela could not suppress her smile. "You are very perceptive, Elorin," she said. "More than I ever realized."

Elorin shrugged and looked down shyly. "I do not think anyone thinks much of me, or takes me very seriously. It is only because I have trouble opening up to people. It is easier to be devoted to Mother Sun—she listens to me with a welcoming heart and a patient mind." Her face fell. "At least, I thought she did. Perhaps she has never heard me at all."

Leela took Elorin's hand in both of her own. "No matter what the High Priestess may be up to, I am certain Mother Sun hears you and loves you. You need not lose faith in that."

Elorin looked up, her eyes sparkling with her magic. "I want to help you."

A lump swelled in Leela's throat. "I would like that very much."

"Tell me everything," Elorin said. "Does Sera's purple

mother know? Was she helping you discover the High Priestess's secrets? Is that why you stole into the birthing houses?"

"She was," Leela said. "And I will tell you what I can, though there are some things I must show you, because even if I did tell, you would not believe me until you saw them with your own eyes."

Elorin's mouth formed a perfectly round O.

"But first," Leela said, "I must explain the reason why I went to the birthing houses, because even Kandra did not believe me." Leela didn't have the patience to tell her all about the moonstone and the other visions. There were more important words that she needed to say out loud—and be *believed*.

Elorin sat up straight and her face grew solemn and serious.

Leela took a deep breath. "Sera is alive," she said. "I have seen her. She did not die in the sacrifice. She is on the *planet*."

For a long moment, Elorin said nothing. Leela's heart was frantic in her ears. Then Elorin nodded slowly. "I believe you," she said.

Acolyte Klymthe came for Leela the next morning as the bells rang through the City, calling all Cerulean to the temple for the conclave.

"It is time," she said.

Leela felt a strange buzzing sensation all over her body as she followed the acolyte out of the chamber of penitence.

Sera is alive, she reminded herself as Acolyte Klymthe slid aside the door at the back of the sanctum. *No matter*

what penance they give me . . . if I can bring her back, it
will prove the High Priestess is a liar.

They emerged onto the chancel where the High Priestess
and Acolytes Imima and Endaria were already standing at
the pulpit. Leela's heart jolted at the sight of the City gathered, so many eyes fixed on her beneath blue hooded robes.
She saw her mothers sitting in their usual spot and her chest
twinged with shame.

By the Altar of the Lost, she caught sight of Sera's green
and orange mothers, looking so small and sad without Sera
or Kandra in their midst. They were holding hands, Leela
saw, and there was some strong emotion pulsing in the
depths of their eyes as they watched her. Leela did not think
it was disgust or consternation; it looked to her like love.

"My children," the High Priestess said, spreading her
arms wide as she addressed the congregation. "We are
gathered here today in the light and love of Mother Sun
to determine the penance of Leela Starcatcher. For she has
broken one of the most precious rules of the City and must
bear responsibility for what she has done."

On the pulpit were four blue candles of varying heights.
The High Priestess turned to her acolytes, the moonstone in
her circlet pale as bone.

"It is always grievous when a Cerulean defies the rules
of our City, never more so when it is one who has always
been so true and trustworthy. What shall her penance be,
my acolytes? How can we ensure that she does not commit
this transgression again?"

Leela's spine was as straight as the trunk of a polaris
tree, and she met the High Priestess's gaze unflinching. But

it was Acolyte Endaria who spoke first.

"She must fast for three days and three nights," the acolyte said. "To purify her body for Mother Sun."

She touched the smallest candle with one finger and a purple flame burst from its wick. Then Acolyte Imima stepped forward.

"She must beg forgiveness in front of the City and vow to never commit such an act again." She touched the second smallest candle and a bright green flame began to burn. "So that she may take full responsibility for her actions."

Acolyte Klymthe fixed her wide-set eyes on Leela. "She must clean the temple until the floors shine and the doors gleam and every last inch is spotless," she said. "To prove the value of hard work and her commitment to this City."

She touched the second tallest candle and a red flame appeared.

At last, the High Priestess moved forward. She towered over her acolytes and Leela felt a strange chill emanating from her, and her own heart went silent in her chest. She knew this was the penance that would mean the most, and be the most difficult to bear. The entire sanctum seemed to be holding its breath.

"She will relinquish her right to find her purpose in this City," the High Priestess said, "and join the novices to live a life in service of Mother Sun. For only in devotion will she truly be able to atone for her wrongs."

The gasps and shocked mutterings from the congregation filled the sanctum as Leela felt all the air seep out of her lungs. The room seemed to spin—she dimly noticed Acolyte Endaria's eyes flicker to the High Priestess as if she too was surprised by this pronouncement. The High Priestess touched the tallest candle and the flame burned black.

"And so the conclave has ended," she said. Just like that, the High Priestess had taken away her right to find her purpose, to ever become part of a triad, to choose her own fate as a Cerulean. She had taken away her home and her room, her mothers and her freedom, all in one fell swoop.

She caught sight of Koreen in the crowd, the prettiest Cerulean of Leela's age, sitting beside Atana, another of Leela's old friends. The two of them were whispering together, and Leela felt certain Koreen was enjoying this. She was the sort of girl who loved gossip.

She could not bear to look at her mothers. If she did, she would burst into tears. She would not give the High Priestess the satisfaction.

"It may seem as though we are requiring too much of her," the High Priestess was saying. "But this was no small violation, my children. Imagine if there are no pregnancies because of what she has done? The sacred circle exists to protect our beloved purple mothers and ensure fertility. How will we feel as a community if that has been threatened by one Cerulean's rash decision?"

Leela felt a shocking clarity flood her veins like ice—of course this was why the High Priestess was punishing her so. If Mother Sun was no longer deciding the chosen one, or the wedding season, or the birthing season, then things could go wrong, as they had with Sera's sacrifice. And so if no purple mother were to become pregnant, the High Priestess would have a ready-made scapegoat right at her fingertips.

Leela cursed herself for her stupidity. She was not seeing clearly enough, only looking at what was right in front of her. The High Priestess had been lying to the City for who knew how long—she must have prepared for a time such as this. How many Cerulean were being kept beneath the City? Leela guessed at least a hundred. Her eyes flickered to the Altar of the Lost as a new thought occurred to her.

The Great Sadness. The High Priestess was the sole remaining survivor of that tragedy left. Her account was the only one that existed. What if she had lied about that too?

Leela realized with a start that the temple had gone quiet. Acolyte Endaria gave her a tiny nudge and Leela stepped forward. It was time for her to apologize for her actions.

She wasn't sorry, not one bit, but she had learned to lie over the past weeks since Sera had fallen, and now she was grateful for that horrible skill. She caught sight of Elorin, standing with the other novices along the walls, her eyes wide, her hands clutching the front of her robe. Leela gave her the faintest hint of a smile. At least the High Priestess did not know how close they had become, or what Leela had confided in her. At least she had assigned Leela to the one place where she had a friend.

"I ask forgiveness," Leela began, "for the wrong I have done this City . . ."

10

SHE WAS COMMANDED TO STAY IN THE CHAMBER OF PEN-
itence until the end of her fast.

She hadn't even been allowed a moment alone with her
mothers to say goodbye. Once she concluded her apology,
she was swept off the chancel by Acolyte Klymthe, through
the sliding door at the back of the temple.

"Your fast begins at dusk," she said. "A final meal will
be brought for you and novices will provide a bucket in the
morning and evening for you to relieve yourself. You are not
to leave this room for three nights and three days." Leela's
breath quickened but she tried not to let it show. One night
had been awful enough, trapped in this small room—Leela
did not like the closed door, or the window too high to see

out of. Acolyte Klymthe's eyes were unyielding, like blue iron. "I should have suspected you might do something like this," she said. "Ever since that day you came to the temple seeking answers from the High Priestess for Sera Lighthaven's unworthiness."

That was the day Leela had realized Kandra was the only one in the City who might believe her about the High Priestess, the day she had dismissed the possibility of confiding in any of her other friends, including Elorin.

Leela wondered if Acolyte Klymthe knew about the stalactites below the City.

But she had a part to play now—she had already made one grave mistake that had led her right into the High Priestess's hands; she could not afford to do it again. So she bowed her head and murmured, "I am sorry, Acolyte Klymthe."

The acolyte sniffed. "Yes. Well. Your life is Mother Sun's now. Let us hope you will live it in her light and love."

But when she said Mother Sun, Leela felt with a shiver that she really meant someone else. She kept her head down, sure that if she looked up, Acolyte Klymthe would see her defiance. When she heard the door close, she collapsed onto the bed and stared up at the window.

I will be patient, she vowed. *It is only three days. And then I will return to the gardens beneath the City and I will see Sera's face again.*

How long could three days possibly be?

Long, Leela discovered.

Each hour felt like a day within itself. The room seemed

to grow smaller with every passing minute. Leela's stomach shrank and twisted and ached. She was allowed water, and those moments when a novice would deliver her a pitcher or bring the bucket for her to relieve herself became the highlight of her days. It was always one of the older novices, Belladon or Cresha or Baalin. She did not see Elorin again.

She thought of Sera, of where she was now and where she might be headed. If she was on a ship, she was likely on the sea between Pelago and Kaolin, but which country she was coming from and which she was going to Leela could not say. She tried to remember all she knew of the planet, but that had been Sera's fascination, not hers. She guiltily admitted to herself that she had never paid much attention when Sera spoke of the planet. She sifted through her recollections of the lessons her green mother had given her about it—she knew that family units were different there, with males and fathers and all that. And she knew that they worshipped different gods, not Mother Sun, though what sort she could not say. But she was hopeful that Mother Sun was watching over Sera, that she could see her even on the planet, so far away from the City.

She mulled over what Elorin had said, when she had wondered if Mother Sun even heard her prayers at all now that she knew of the High Priestess's deceptions. But Leela remembered the way the symbols on the doors to the temple had suddenly made sense—it was Mother Sun speaking to her, she was sure of it. Though if *she* could read them, then why not all other Cerulean? Perhaps it was a matter of awareness—Leela was seeing through the lies now, and so it was as if a veil had been lifted. Perhaps the High Priestess had cast some sort of spell over the entire City, the way she had taken Kandra's memory of Estelle away. And because the City believed only the High Priestess could read the symbols, then that was all they saw, a jumble of markings.

But it seemed to Leela as if Mother Sun was far away, farther than she ought to be. It was like trying to shout to someone who was in the Day Gardens from the top of the temple; there might be the faintest trace of a voice on the wind, but not enough to hear exact words. Else why had she not already righted this wrong and exposed the High Priestess herself? Leela felt as if perhaps Mother Sun had been lost somehow, as if she had been searching for the City Above the Sky and was only just now beginning to find it.

At long last, dusk of the third day of her fast arrived, and Acolyte Endaria came for her with a tray of broth and an onion roll sprinkled with poppy seeds. Leela's stomach roared at the scent of it.

"Eat slowly," Acolyte Endaria said as Leela gripped the bowl in trembling hands and slurped the broth. "It will be hard on your stomach after so many days."

Leela was so famished she thought she could eat an entire wedding feast, but she found she could only nibble on the bread once she'd finished the broth.

"Come," Acolyte Endaria said, standing. "I will show you to your bed."

Leela followed obediently, and had to shield her eyes at the light of the setting sun when they emerged from the temple—she had become too accustomed to the dimness of the chamber of penitence. The Moon Gardens were so radiant that Leela felt tears prick the corners of her eyes.

They passed Aila's statue, her laughing face turned upward toward the stars, and Leela wanted to throw her arms around the moonstone and cry with joy that she was finally outside again. The rich smells of grass and earth and flowers filled her nose. She felt so light she could fly.

Acolyte Endaria led her to where the novices' dormitory was, taking her down the steps to the large circular room beneath the temple. She had come here once before with Elorin, and she saw the novice's bed now, her nightstand laid with a golden comb and stargem ring. The vase, which had previously contained a moonflower, now held a pale blue rose. But Acolyte Endaria directed her to the opposite side of the room.

"This is where you will sleep," she said. A novice robe was folded neatly at the end of her new bed. "You may bathe in the Estuary this evening if you wish. Tomorrow you must begin your work cleaning the temple."

Leela picked up the robe with hesitant fingers. "M-may I see my mothers?" she stammered. "I did not get to say goodbye to them."

Acolyte Endaria hesitated. "I do not think that is allowed."

A solitary tear spilled down her cheek and Leela brushed it away. "All right," she said. She had to be strong now. She was no longer a child and her mothers could not help her.

But she missed them terribly anyway.

Acolyte Endaria's face was creased with pity. She was the youngest of the three acolytes, with a heart-shaped face and very long eyelashes. "But of course, this was all so sudden. I am sure it would be all right for you to see them this evening once you've bathed. But *very* briefly. You must return to the temple by the hour of the owl and no later."

Leela nodded, her heart lifting. "I will, Acolyte," she promised. "Thank you."

There were many novices returning from the Estuary as Leela crossed Dendra's Bridge. Some waved at her or smiled, but most gave her suspicious looks. Leela could not blame them; she had not chosen this life the way they had. She was not truly one of them.

Leela saw Koreen with Atana again and also their friend Daina, but the pretty Cerulean girl did not appear to see her—or if she did, she pretended she hadn't. Leela waited for a sting that did not come. The time when Koreen's opinions had mattered to her was long gone. She had new friends now, truer ones than Koreen or Atana or Daina had ever been.

The cool waters of the Estuary were a balm against her skin, washing away three days of dirt and sweat and exhaustion. Leela floated on her back and stared up at the stars, her blue hair spilling out around her face, gentle waves lapping over her stomach and her breasts. She remembered the last time she had bathed here with Sera, the day she had given her the moonstone necklace. How much had changed since then.

At last, she emerged from the water, clean and slippery as a sun trout, and dried herself with her old dress before pulling on her new novice robe. The walk to her mothers' dwelling felt the same and different all at once. It was a path she knew so well, but the dwelling was not her home any longer.

Lanterns were lit in the kitchen, golden light spilling out of the windows. Leela hesitated in the doorway, fearful all of a sudden that her mothers would not wish to see her. But then her purple mother came into the hall with a bolt of seresheep wool in her hands.

"Leela?" she gasped, and the wool thudded to the floor.

"Hello, Purple Mother," Leela said. She should call her Ilianne now, she thought, and her other mothers Rooni and Lastra. She did not live at home any longer, and so must address her mothers by their given names. But she found she could not bring herself to do that quite yet. She could not bear to part with that last piece of her old self.

Her purple mother flew toward her and flung her arms around her. And then her other mothers were there hugging her and crying, and Leela had never felt so loved yet so alone.

"We miss you so much," her green mother whispered.

"I miss you too," Leela whispered back.

Her mothers pulled away, her orange mother fussing over her robe while her purple mother tucked a lock of hair behind her ear.

"Are you all right? Have you eaten? You must be starved. We have some cauliflower cooking, and your green mother is making her famous purple barley salad, with arugula and lemon, just how you like it."

Her purple mother could not seem to stop the torrent of words, as if they might be the last she would ever say to her daughter.

"I have had some broth and bread," Leela said. "That

is all I feel I can eat. And I must return to the temple by the hour of the owl."

Her purple mother's eyes filled with tears. "Of course," she said.

"I am so sorry." Leela found she could not look at her. "Purple Mother, you did me such a kindness taking me to the forest and I repaid you with lies and deceit." This apology, at least, was sincere. "I did not mean to dishonor you, mothers. I only . . ."

But there were no words to explain why she had done what she did.

Her green mother lifted Leela's chin with a gentle finger. "You think we have not seen the change in you, my darling?" She smiled, and tiny lines crinkled around the corners of her eyes. "You think I did not hear you sneaking out of your bedroom at night?"

Leela felt her stomach swoop, as if she had jumped out of a tree that was taller than expected. "You . . . knew?"

"I knew when Sera would coax you out as well," her green mother said. "I thought you missed the adventures she used to take you on."

"I do," Leela admitted.

"We imagined you would confide in us," her orange mother said. "When you were ready."

Her purple mother fixed her with a look of bracing sympathy. "You did not sneak into the birthing houses to see Plenna, did you."

Leela shook her head. "But please don't ask me to explain, mothers. Only know that I am so sorry to have shamed you. I never meant to be such a disappointment."

Her mothers looked at each other, and then they were all hugging Leela again.

"My sweet child," her green mother murmured. "You could never be a disappointment to us. *Never*."

Leela felt some of her guilt ease, the tightness in her chest soften, and she held her mothers close and breathed in their scents, lavender and rosewater and citrus.

"We will still see you," her orange mother reminded her, "at the temple, and around the City. And you are always welcome here. This will always be your home."

A tear slid down Leela's cheek. "Thank you, Orange Mother. Or must I call you Lastra now?"

Her orange mother let out a choked laugh. "You may call me whatever you wish. If the High Priestess can issue four penances at once, if Sera's sacrifice was not enough to break the tether, then . . . well, it seems as if many things in this City are changing. What you call your mothers is the least of them."

"Perhaps it is time for change," her green mother said. "This City has been sedentary for too long."

Leela wanted to scream, she wanted to hold her mothers in her arms and never let them go, she wanted to cry and confess all. But it was not time, not yet.

She was grateful to know that her mothers were not wholly unaware. Perhaps there were other Cerulean noticing a change in the City.

She gave her mothers one final squeeze, then stepped back. "I must return to the temple."

Her orange mother nodded. "We are glad you came."

Leela smiled through her tears. "So am I. And as you said, I am not going far."

Her green mother pressed a hand to Leela's cheek. "We have been so proud of you. But there is a strength inside you that, I admit, I did not always see. It shines through your eyes now. I have never been more honored to be your mother."

"Nor I," her purple mother said.

"Nor I," echoed her orange mother.

Leela's throat was too swollen to speak. She kissed them each on the cheek, then turned and fled back to the temple, more determined than ever to return to the underground gardens, to bring Sera home and heal her City.

11

THE NEXT DAY, AFTER THE NOVICES HAD THEIR MORNING prayers, Leela was given a mop and bucket of soapy water by Acolyte Klymthe and set to cleaning the floors of the temple.

Leela found she did not mind the work—it allowed her mind to wander, to plan. She felt there was nothing to be done other than wait for the novices to fall asleep and sneak out of the dormitory, back to Faesa's statue. But she wanted to take Elorin with her. The young novice needed to see that place with her own eyes.

Leela's arms ached from mopping by the time evening prayers arrived. She had intended to stay awake until the hour of the dark to see which novices slept soundly and which might be woken by the slightest noise, but suddenly it was morning and time for more prayers and more cleaning, and Leela had not even remembered falling asleep.

The next day was the same, and the next, and the next. Leela's arms grew lean and strong, the mop feeling like an extension of her, the swish it made on the floors comforting, the splash of the water in the bucket its own music.

Swish swish plop swish. Swish swish plop swish.

It reminded her of the sound of the High Priestess feeding the trapped Cerulean with the golden fruit. She was just thinking that perhaps tonight would be the night to try to sneak to the Moon Gardens when a group of novices passed her, whispering, and Elorin trailed behind them. She paused for a brief moment, pretending to encourage Leela in her efforts, but then dropped her voice to a low whisper.

"The High Priestess has not been seen since the last evening of your fast," she said. "I tried to keep a watch on her as much as I could and I saw her enter the Moon Gardens, but she has not yet returned."

Leela's heart sank. She did not dare go beneath the City if the High Priestess was there—and if she had not been seen, Leela was certain she was down with her stalactites.

"There's something in the Moon Gardens, isn't there," Elorin whispered.

"Yes," Leela whispered back. "And I'll show you. But we must be careful."

Elorin glanced toward the gaggle of novices leaving the temple. "They do not think you belong here," she said. "They are angry about the penance."

"I know," Leela said with a sigh.

"I think it is a good thing," Elorin said. "I think this City might be waking up."

Leela thought so too, but Elorin scampered off before she had a chance to say so.

The next day, Acolyte Imima gave her a bristly brush and set her to scrubbing the walls of the temple. That lasted for another four days—Leela had to get a ladder to reach the higher parts and the work was less forgiving than mopping had been. She watched every day for a sign of the High Priestess but she never appeared.

The morning after she finished the walls, Acolyte Endaria gave her a cloth and a jar of polish and instructed her to clean the pulpit and the temple doors. Leela decided to start with the doors—she was quite sick of the inside of the temple. She took the ladder with her so she could start at the top and work her way down. The symbols seemed to shift under her fingers as she ran the cloth over them, though they did not spell *Heal them* or anything else today.

"Good morning, Leela." Koreen was standing at the top of the temple steps.

"Good morning," Leela replied politely, wondering what Koreen wanted with her.

"I am in a triad now," she said. "With Daina and Atana."

"What joyful news," Leela forced herself to say.

Koreen shrugged. "It is a shame we missed the wedding season. I would so love to be married."

Leela kept her mouth shut. She had no pity to spare for Koreen.

"I was hoping to speak to the High Priestess," Koreen

continued. "But Acolyte Klymthe says she is sequestered."

"She is," Leela said. "And has been for many days."

Koreen sighed. "It is such a trying time for her. First, Sera is deemed unworthy by Mother Sun, then you go and break one of the most sacred rules of the City. Her spirits must be very low."

It took all of Leela's strength not to make a sharp retort. "Indeed. Well, unless there is something you need, I'm afraid I must get back to my polishing."

Koreen pursed her lips as if this conversation was not going at all the way she wanted. "Very well," she said. "Atana and Daina and I are going to get our own dwelling near the Aviary. You may come visit us whenever you wish."

"What a kind offer," Leela said through gritted teeth. "If I can find the time, I surely will."

Koreen raised an eyebrow, then flicked her hair back over her shoulder in a way that Leela seemed to recall used to be attractive but now looked vain and silly. She turned and headed off toward Aila's Bridge.

Leela returned to her polishing when suddenly, the symbols beneath her cloth changed, and a waterfall of a single word tumbled down the copper door.

Tonight, it read.

Leela nearly dropped the jar of polish.

"Mother Sun," she whispered. "Is that you?"

Tonight. The word sparkled, the symbols growing larger, and Leela felt sure Mother Sun could hear her.

Then she heard a familiar voice.

". . . more food, and prayer." The High Priestess came around the bend of the temple, speaking with Acolyte

Klymthe. "I will go myself early tomorrow. Make sure they know they need not be concerned. They will all be pregnant soon enough. Mother Sun wills it so."

"Yes, High Priestess," the acolyte said, bowing her head.

"Ah, Leela," the High Priestess said. "Your penance is coming along nicely, I am told."

Leela forced herself to sound meek. "I hope so, High Priestess. I am working very hard."

"Carry on," the High Priestess said, and she and Acolyte Klymthe disappeared into the temple, walking past the doors without a second glance, making Leela certain that the symbols were speaking only to her.

"Tonight," she whispered to them, and the markings rippled and grew illegible once more, and Leela finished polishing with her heart in her throat.

She managed to get word to Elorin at supper that evening.

The novices ate in the Moon Gardens, on gossamer blankets with large bowls of food spread out among them. Leela was helping herself to rice seasoned with saffron and olives when Elorin appeared at her elbow.

"Good evening, Leela," she said politely. "May I have the spoon when you are finished?"

"Certainly," Leela replied, just as distant. Then she lowered her voice and said, "We must go to the Moon Gardens tonight at the hour of the dark."

Elorin inclined her head without looking at her, and Leela handed her the spoon and left to sit on a blanket near the statue of Faesa.

I'm coming back, she thought.

Faesa's eyes seemed to see right into Leela's soul. She felt as if the moonstone heard her, and was glad, though the statue remained as cold and impassive as ever.

She ate her rice without tasting it, and climbed into bed before any of the other novices, making her breath come slow and even to give the illusion of sleep. The waiting was torture as she listened to the conversations fade out one by one, replaced by light snores and the shifting of blankets. Leela did not know how, exactly, but she sensed when the hour of the dark approached and sat up quietly. From across the room she saw Elorin rise. The two girls ever so cautiously crept out of the dormitory.

Elorin followed Leela to Faesa's statue, where Leela stopped and touched the Moon Daughter's stone hands. They were bitterly cold, and she was reminded of the ice pops she and Sera used to suck on when they were girls.

Open for me as you did before, Leela thought, and her heart spoke the words with confidence. She was not afraid.

Markings appeared down the length of Faesa's robes, and the statue slid aside silently; the only sound in the quiet dark was Elorin's hushed gasp. Leela put her finger to her lips. Elorin's eyes were big as saucers as she gazed down at the sunglass steps. The cold was fierce and Leela began to descend, keeping her hands on the walls to prevent herself from falling. Elorin's footsteps were a faint patter behind her, and Leela drew courage from her presence.

Colored lights began to shine as they neared the end of the stairs, and Elorin made a little whimper when she saw them but said nothing. When they reached the bottom, Leela waited patiently as the girl drank it all in.

Glowing blue columns surrounded them, towering in icy splendor. Eerily lit green paths snaked around the crystal pools that dotted the floor, revealing clear glimpses of the planet below. It was utterly silent except for the faint hitching of Elorin's breath.

I see you, Sera, Leela thought, staring down at the outlines of Kaolin and Pelago. *I know you're down there.*

She met Elorin's gaze and pointed toward the ceiling. Elorin looked up and let out a cry of shock that vanished in the cavernous space. The upside-down gardens or forest or whatever it was stretched out above them. Trees and bushes, wildflowers and ancient shrubs all grew toward them, as if Elorin and Leela were standing in the sky and looking down upon the earth.

"The gardens wither and die the further out you walk," Leela said. "Come. I want to show you the tether."

"What are those pools for?" Elorin asked.

"I don't know," Leela said. "But I don't think we want to step through one."

They crept forward, keeping to the paths and avoiding the pools. At last they came to the vast circular space right beneath the temple, where the tether shot up through the largest of the pools. It planted itself firmly in an enormous cone of moonstone with a glowing red heart in its center— ice-white vines surrounded the cone, golden fruit hanging among the brittle leaves. Leela was unsure how the High Priestess had managed to reach them—the ceiling was very high. Elorin looked as though she were going to faint as she stared in wonder at the finely wrought chain of magic that connected their City to the planet below.

"The tether," she whispered. "It's so . . ."

She could not find the word to describe it.

"I know," Leela said.

"What *is* this place?" Elorin asked, gazing up at the vines surrounding the moonstone. "What are those golden fruits?"

It was time to show her—no amount of explanation would do, and Leela herself did not have all the answers anyway. She beckoned Elorin closer and knelt by one of the ice-covered circles on the floor.

Estelle, the symbols proclaimed. Leela brushed her hand over the ice so that it became clear.

"That's a Cerulean!" Elorin exclaimed, staring down in horror at Estelle's hunched naked body trapped in the stalactite.

Leela nodded solemnly.

"Is she . . ." Elorin swallowed the word.

"She lives," Leela said. "See, she breathes. Her name is Estelle. She was a friend to Kandra—Sera's purple mother—years ago. The City believed her dead from the sleeping sickness. But she has been here all this time."

"What does the High Priestess want with her?"

Leela pursed her lips. "Not just her," she said. She pointed to another circle, then another. Elorin clapped her hands over her mouth.

"There is a Cerulean beneath every one of these?" she whispered. "But why? What for?"

"I do not know," Leela replied. "But I saw the High Priestess feed them the fruit from those vines." She pressed a hand to the ice. "I don't know how she uncovered these circles, though. I can only make them clear."

"That is more than I can do," Elorin said, sweeping a hand over a circle with the name *Vaana* written on it. The ice remained opaque.

"Hmm." Leela did not know what that meant.

"This is not *right*," Elorin muttered. "This is unnatural. These Cerulean should not be trapped down here! This is not the City I know and love."

"I agree," Leela said. "But until we know what she is doing with them and find some way to get them out of these icy prisons . . ."

Elorin gripped her shoulder. "I cannot imagine," she said, "how frightful and lonely it must have been for you. To know of all this and carry it entirely on your own."

Leela's smile was tight but full of gratitude. "Thank you," she whispered.

Elorin turned to the moonstone's fiery red heart. "Is that where you saw Sera?"

"Sort of. It is hard to explain. The moonstone gives me visions of her, of where she is and who she is with." Leela quickly explained about the necklace she had given Sera. "I think it is connecting us—as if that stone is linked to all other moonstone in this City. But I cannot control it. The visions come as they please."

Elorin tiptoed forward and then curled up by the side of the pool. "Another vision will come," she said. "Even if we must wait here all night. I believe in you, Leela. The power of this place . . . it recognizes you. Can you feel it?"

Leela had not quite thought about it like that before. She sat beside Elorin and the two of them stared into the pool, watching the tether glint and twinkle as it stretched to the planet below.

"Do you remember the story the High Priestess told us during the wedding season?" Elorin asked. "The story of Wyllin Moonseer and the forming of this tether."

"I do," Leela said. "Though I am not sure how much of it I believe."

"Perhaps the High Priestess and Wyllin were not truly friends at all," Elorin mused. "Maybe the High Priestess chose her the way she chose Sera."

"But Wyllin died to form this tether," Leela pointed out. "And Sera was unable to break it. I always assumed it was because Mother Sun had not truly chosen her. That the sacrifice could not work because the choosing had been manipulated."

"Perhaps," Elorin said. "I am only wondering what life was like in this City nine hundred years ago. How much has been lost or changed. How much has been forgotten."

Leela had been wondering that too. She wished there were someone else to ask, but only the High Priestess was left from that time.

She did not know how long they sat for, but she was just about to suggest that they leave, her thighs growing numb with cold, when she felt another heart beating in her chest.

"Sera?" she gasped. Elorin turned, pushing herself up onto her knees.

"Do you see her?"

Leela shook her head. "I can feel her heart."

"Does it speak to you? Like a blood bond?"

"No. It is . . . calm. Slow and steady. Almost as if . . ."

She looked at the cone of moonstone and the vision came and she welcomed it with joy. The room was small and dark, with a square bed and a single round window, like the one in the chamber of penitence but not so high up. The floor beneath her tilted and swayed gently. Leela saw the shapes of two figures beneath the covers, both sleeping. Suddenly, a girl sat up—it was not the same girl she had seen before, the tall one with curly hair and turquoise eyes. This girl had brown skin and brown hair, disheveled from sleep, and though her face was half in shadow, Leela sensed a keenness in her gaze.

"Sera?" she whispered, but Sera slept on peacefully. Leela saw the glint of gold around her friend's neck, the pendant clutched tight in one silver hand. The girl was looking at the necklace too, and Leela wondered if she knew about the moonstone, what it was and where it had come from. They were sharing a bed together, so Leela imagined they must be friends at the very least, if not perhaps something more. Leela found herself glad that Sera had found someone who cared for her on the planet. She wanted to get a better look at the girl, she wanted to *move*, but she did not know how, when suddenly, Elorin was shaking her arm and the vision dissolved and Leela's heart ached at the loss of Sera's steady beat.

"What?" she asked.

"Someone's coming," Elorin whispered.

12

"HIDE!" LEELA HISSED AS THE UNMISTAKABLE SOUND OF footsteps came closer.

She and Elorin hurried as quickly and quietly as they could, pressing themselves against the cold surface of a column only moments before the High Priestess emerged into the clearing. They crouched low and peered out to watch her as she circled the main pool, muttering to herself, to the tether, to the moonstone. . . . Leela could not be certain which and she could not make out what she was saying.

At last, the High Priestess stopped and Leela saw her mask fall away, the ancientness showing on her face in hard, deep lines around her mouth and eyes, her irises darkening, her shoulders hunching as if she carried the weight of the entire City on her back.

"I have resisted for so long," she said, and it sounded like a confession. "But I must give in again. They need me. It is not enough. Not enough."

She held out a hand and a golden fruit fell into her open palm as if she had called it down from the vines. Her whole body seemed to tremble as she brought it to her mouth and took the first bite. The moonstone heart contracted, then pounded even more frantically, turning a furious crimson. The High Priestess moaned and Leela could not tell if it was ecstasy or agony or both. She took another bite and then another, until the fruit was gone and only a shimmering blue pit left. That she let fall through the pool and it flashed bright as a newborn star before burning out into nothing. The pool rippled, strange shapes and shadows passing over its once-clear surface, but Leela could not make them out from her vantage point.

The High Priestess watched them with an unreadable expression, her eyes darting this way and that. Then she clutched her head as if in pain and her skin began to glow, silver at first, then blue, then as red as the heart of the moonstone. Elorin's fingers were painfully tight around Leela's arm and Leela herself clutched at the novice's hand in terror.

Leela could feel the heat emanating from the High Priestess's tall frame, hotter than anything she'd ever felt before, a heat that writhed, that commanded, that consumed. One by one, the ice-covered circles containing Cerulean began to shine, a light so vividly white both girls had to shield their eyes, as the underground gardens were filled with their brilliance.

Then the light and the heat were gone, snuffed out as quickly as a candle flame; when Leela looked, the High Priestess was herself again, her face young and smooth and beautiful, her skin silver as the moon. She gave a great gasp, pulling in air as if surfacing after a long time underwater, and lifted her eyes to the vines.

"Thank you," she murmured. She knelt by the pool and spoke to the tether like an old friend. "This was not how I meant it to be," she said, her voice full of regret. "Perhaps it should have been me. Perhaps I would have been the better choice."

Then she stood and shuddered, and her gown rippled; she seemed to grow even taller. Without another word, she strode off down one of the luminous green paths and disappeared. Leela and Elorin waited, not daring to move or speak or breathe. When at last they felt it safe, they crept forward from behind the column and approached the pool. It looked the same as it had, crystal clear and still as glass.

"Did you see those shapes that rose on its surface?" Elorin whispered.

Leela nodded. "I couldn't make them out, though."

"Nor I." Elorin shivered. "And then all those lights and that . . . that *heat* . . ."

"Who do you think she was talking about?" Leela asked. "When she said she would have been the better choice?"

"Sera, maybe?" Elorin bit her lip.

That didn't make any sense, though. Something nagged at Leela, something she could not quite put her finger on. "We must go," she said. "We cannot be caught out of bed."

"Yes," Elorin agreed solemnly. Then she threw her arms

around Leela. "Thank you for trusting me with this," she whispered, her breath tickling Leela's ear. "It is scary and sad and worrying and so many other things, but . . . I would rather know the truth and be frightened than remain ignorant and live a life wrapped up in a lie."

Elorin's arms were hot in this cold place, her skin soft where it touched Leela's, and she smelled of nutmeg and cedar. Leela felt a faint stirring inside her. It was so nice to be held.

They hurried back up the stairs, and Leela found herself once again startled by the normalcy of her world. Elorin stood beside her, steadying her, giving her courage.

And more important, giving her hope.

The next day, as the sun set and Leela continued her work polishing the temple doors, the bells began to ring out, calling the City to gather.

Leela climbed down from her ladder, putting it away before joining the other novices in laying out the cushions for the Cerulean to kneel on.

"What is happening?" she asked Novice Cresha as they worked near the Altar of the Lost.

"You will hear along with everyone else," Cresha said. She was one of the novices who most resented Leela's presence among them.

"The High Priestess visited the birthing houses this morning at dawn," Novice Loonir whispered when Cresha left to gather more cushions. "I think one of the purple mothers is pregnant at last."

Leela's knees locked. Was it Kandra? She did not know

why, but she was certain that if Kandra became pregnant, it would kill her. Maybe not today, or tomorrow, but slowly, the grief would eat away until she was nothing but a husk of bone and forgotten magic.

"My children," the High Priestess said when the City had gathered. Her eyes were more vibrant today, her skin aglow like moonlight. Leela thought she could feel the heat of her from where she stood against the wall between Loonir and Cresha, but she may have only been imagining it. One thing was certain—she was stronger and more confident than she had been last night beneath the City.

"I bring you glad tidings from the birthing houses," the High Priestess continued. "Plenna Skychaser is with child."

The temple erupted in cheers. Leela saw Heena and Jaycin, Plenna's wives, embracing each other tearfully as other Cerulean offered them their congratulations.

"Isn't it wonderful, Leela?" Loonir said, grinning at her.

Leela forced herself to smile back. "Wonderful," she echoed.

She caught sight of Sera's other mothers, who had not risen to their feet or cheered with joy at this announcement, but only clung to each other. Leela wondered if they were sad because Kandra had not been chosen, or relieved.

"Such blessed news calls for a celebration," the High Priestess commanded. "Let us go to the Day Gardens. A new generation of Cerulean is about to begin! Praise Mother Sun and her everlasting light!"

"Praise her!" the Cerulean cried.

"Come, Leela," Loonir said. "We must go at once to the fermentation house in the orchards and gather as much sweetnectar as we can carry. What a joyous day! I confess I was beginning to worry myself."

"Worry?" Leela asked as she followed the throng of Cerulean streaming out of the temple.

"It does not usually take so long for a purple mother to become pregnant," Loonir said, frowning. "Not all of them, of course, but . . . at least one should have been with child by now. Perhaps it is only because the seasons are so close together." Then her face brightened. "But no matter! Plenna is pregnant. Heena and Jaycin must be so happy. I cannot wait to offer them my blessings!"

Leela could not bear the thought of going to the Day Gardens and celebrating. Her stomach was in knots as she descended the temple steps. This felt wrong, another lie of the High Priestess's, something unnatural. She reached the last stair and turned to look back at the doors just as the symbols began to swirl and shift. It took all her strength of will not to cry out, though she should have been used to reading them by now.

Eat the fruit, they said.

"Forgive me," Leela stammered to Loonir. "I have a gift for Heena and Jaycin on my nightstand; I will meet you at the fermentation house."

"I can wait for—"

"No, no," Leela said. "You go on. I will join you in just a moment. What a blessed day!"

Loonir acquiesced as a green mother swept her up in conversation. Leela scurried around the curve of the temple and paused in the doorway to the novice chambers, waiting for the crowds to pass over Aila's Bridge in the direction of the Day Gardens. The shouts and cheers and cries faded away, but still she waited just to be sure. She hoped Loonir would have forgotten about her by the time she reached the fermentation house.

The Moon Gardens were drenched in a honeyed light as the hour of the owl approached. The tips of the hydrangeas glowed jade-gold and Faesa's statue was waiting for her with knowing eyes. This time, Leela did not even have to touch the statue. Markings appeared as she approached, as if they had been waiting for her, as if they knew Mother Sun had told her to come. With one gentle beat of Leela's heart, the statue slid aside.

The cold did not seem so biting as it had on her previous visits; perhaps she was growing accustomed to it. The winding stair felt familiar, the blue and green lights a welcome sight as she emerged into the cavernous space with gardens growing from above like a plant-filled sky.

Sky Gardens, she thought. *That is what I shall call this place.*

Her feet carried her without thinking to the main pool, weaving her way through the circles where Cerulean rested beneath. The tether seemed dim today, fragile, as if some of the pure light had gone out of it. Leela turned her eyes to the heart of the moonstone. It pulsed weakly in its cone, more orange than red, and she knew this was the High Priestess's doing. She looked up at the vines crawling around it, heavy with fruit, and wondered how she was ever going to reach one. They were far too high and there was nothing for her to climb.

Plop.

She whirled around. A fruit lay on the ground, only a few feet away, on top of the circle with Estelle's name. Leela approached it cautiously. She was afraid to consume anything the High Priestess had touched, especially after she had seen the effect it had had on her. But Mother Sun had told her to—and while she didn't trust the High Priestess one bit, she knew the symbols were not leading her astray. She crouched down to examine it, like a peach but smaller and without a hint of pink. When she picked it up, it was hot to the touch.

"Mother Sun," she prayed. "Do not fail me now."

And before she could think about it another second, she plunged her teeth into the fruit's flesh.

The taste was everything Leela loved most in the world—toasted pine nuts and lavender tea and dates stuffed with cheese . . . it was her green mother's smile and her purple mother's laugh and her orange mother's embrace . . . it was the singing of minstrel flowers and the pale light of dawn and the crook of the old willow tree in the Day Gardens.

And it was Sera's heartbeat, most of all.

She did not realize she had eaten the entire thing until she held its small glowing pit in her hand. She stood and walked to the pool, dropping the pit through the water as she had seen the High Priestess do. And when it flashed in a light so bright and warm and strange and scary and perfect, the water began to churn around the tether, frothing in a foam of sea green and blushing pink and heliotrope. Leela felt her magic sing inside her, a song of heartbreak and joy, a song like the blazing colors of sunset and a night without stars, and her blood crackled and snapped, and her skin felt as if it was searing itself to her bones.

She threw her head back and laughed though she did not know why, only that it felt good, it felt right—hot tears streamed down her cheeks as she thought of Sera, racing with her along the banks of the Estuary or watching her climb the temple spire or chasing each other through the moonflower fields. Sera filled her mind and her heart, Sera expanded inside her, Sera Sera Sera . . . and when Leela looked at the pond again, the water had become thick and pliable, like newly crafted sunglass, and a shape was emerging from it, a shape that she knew, oh so very well.

When Sera's slender frame had finished forming out of the water, the pond rippled and she became more than sunglass. She became *Sera*, the Sera Leela had known and loved, the Sera she had shared her heart with and would share it with until the end of her days.

Leela let out a wild cry, like a trapped animal finally freed.

"Sera?" The name was no more than a fragile whisper on her lips, though she had meant to shout it.

Sera blinked and said, "Leela?"

Through her tears, Leela smiled a smile so wide and full, she thought she might split in two.

"It's me," Leela said, and the triumph rang through her louder than the bells of the temple. "It's me, Sera. I found you."

PART THREE

Ithilia, the island of Cairan, Pelago

13

SERA

SERA DID NOT KNOW WHAT TO SAY OR WHERE TO BEGIN.

She couldn't believe her eyes. Leela was here, *talking* to her. Real, true, perfect, sweet Leela. Sera's heart swelled up so big she feared she would choke on it.

She hadn't understood what was happening when the moonstone had flamed in her hand, like a miniature sunflare, a heat stronger than anything she had ever felt—one second, she and Leo were in Rahel's golden room of desserts and the next she was being pulled upward, flying so fast her vision blurred. She'd emerged through a pool of clear water, except it wasn't water—it was something in her magic that was shifting and shimmering, making her form mutable. The moonstone felt heavy around her neck, almost like an anchor keeping her from dissolving. She had an awareness of being in the pool and also of being on the ship below in Pelago. She was a vision here, albeit a solid one. She could not move her feet or turn her head or run to Leela and throw her arms around her. She existed only within this pool.

Leo was nowhere to be seen but Sera could feel his presence, could sense his heart beating alongside hers. It must be her magic in him that connected them, that held his consciousness here with her but unable to take form. She hoped he was not too frightened—this was all strange and new for her; she couldn't imagine what it must be like for him.

As she took in her surroundings, she realized she was *below* the City. She thought back to her sacrifice, when she had fallen wheeling through space and seen the underbelly of the City Above the Sky with its long stalactites protruding out like icicles. She had never considered there was a whole world contained within, one that glowed ice-blue and ghostly green.

"How am I here?" Sera asked, the words tumbling out clumsily.

"I think . . ." Leela turned her gaze up to where heavy golden fruit hung from white vines. "I ate the fruit and then I called to you and you came."

"The moonstone," Sera said, wishing she could touch it, hold it out, show it to her friend. "It went hot in my hand." She frowned. "What fruit? What is this place?"

"The moonstone," Leela muttered, as if answering a question Sera had not asked. Then she brightened. "I call it the Sky Gardens. This is a secret place beneath the City that until now, only the High Priestess has been to."

"Is she here?" Sera asked, hopeful that someone might be able to explain what was happening. She was surprised to see Leela's face cloud over.

"No," she said. "She is not who she pretends to be. This City is in turmoil, Sera. So much has changed since you fell."

Sera listened, thunderstruck, as Leela told her tale. When she got to the part about Cerulean trapped *inside* the stalactites, Sera let out cry of shock and disgust, and by the time she learned of Leela's penance, Sera wished she could sit down, but the pool held her still and steady.

When Leela had finished, Sera was quiet for a while, her head spinning with all these revelations. She did not know what to say or how to feel. Leela seemed to understand.

"It was hard for me too," she said. "To accept it. We have trusted in the High Priestess for so long."

"But why pick me?" Sera wondered aloud. "I was no threat to her. I was a nuisance."

"Kandra thought perhaps you had been chosen by Mother Sun to be the next High Priestess," Leela said. It was so odd to hear Leela call Sera's purple mother by her given name.

"That cannot be true," Sera said. "I would make a terrible High Priestess. No one in the City would accept me."

But she remembered the words she had seen on the bowl, the day of the choosing ceremony. *Heal them*, the symbols had said.

She had never told Leela about the symbols, but she did now. Leela gasped.

"So Mother Sun has spoken to you as well?" she said.

"I . . . I never thought of it like that," Sera said.

"I have begun to be able to read the symbols on the temple doors," Leela confessed. "They speak to me, they change for me so that I can understand them, but no one else sees."

"But Leela," Sera yelped. "If you can read the symbols, does that not mean *you* are chosen as the next High Priestess?"

Leela shook her head. "I would be just as wrong a choice as you," she said. "I think this has been another of the High Priestess's lies. I do not think she herself has been able to read the symbols for quite some time. And I fear she has done something, made it so that no one else can either. But you were always so different, Sera. Maybe that's why you could read the symbols. Or maybe Mother Sun somehow sensed that the choosing ceremony was wrong or being manipulated. Perhaps she was trying to send you a message, though you could not understand it at the time."

Sera did not know what to think of that. She felt a twinge of confusion that was not her own and wondered what Leo must be making of all this.

"We do not have much time," Leela said. "I am meant to be bringing sweetnectar to the Day Gardens, to celebrate Plenna's pregnancy. I have seen visions of you in the moonstone, Sera, but I do not understand them. Tell me what happened after you fell. I have seen you with two different girls, one with brown skin and hair, and another with curls and turquoise eyes. Who are they? Are they helping you?"

"Yes," Sera said, and had to suppress a laugh. Of course

Leela thought Leo a girl. Hadn't Sera thought the same thing that first night she had met him? Knowing that males existed and seeing one in person were two entirely different things. "There are two humans who are trying to help me get to the tether so that I can return home. But the one with the turquoise eyes is a male. His name is Leo and his sister, Agnes, is the girl you saw. They are my friends, along with a mertag, a sort of half-male half-fish, named Errol. He says he knows the location of the island where the tether is planted."

She took a breath and began to tell the whole story from the beginning. Leela's face grew round and bright with awe.

"They stole your blood?" she cried. "It is just like the humans from the planet of the Great Sadness!"

"That is how I felt," Sera said. "But Leo and Agnes are not like that. Not all humans are the same."

"It still sounds like a horrible place," Leela said.

Sera was surprised to feel a stab of defensiveness. Of course she had hated Xavier McLellan and his evil schemes, but the planet was not *all* bad. She had loved the days on the open sea learning how to sail. She loved not quite knowing what was going to happen when she woke up every morning. She had made friends who were just as different as she was and struggling to find where they belonged, all sorts of unusual friends.

She would not see a male again once she returned to the City, she realized with a start. She hadn't quite considered that. It made her sad to think she would never have the sort of romantic love she desired in her City—she would have to give that up completely. For a fraction of a second she wondered if there were others like her in the City Above the Sky, with longings and desires that didn't fit with what was considered the traditional Cerulean mold. But she dismissed the thought before it had a chance to blossom. No one else in the City had ever seemed as different as her, and wouldn't she have noticed if someone had?

Besides, she would have her mothers and Leela back. Surely that would be enough.

"How are we able to speak, though?" Sera asked.

"The moonstone," Leela replied. "I'm sure of it. It contains so much power that has been forgotten over the centuries. But Cerulean had to get down to the planet somehow, didn't they? Before the Great Sadness, I mean. I think perhaps the pendant I gave you saved your life."

"But then, why can it not return me? Why not take me back now?"

Leela frowned. "Well, I think it sort of has. You are here, but also not here. Perhaps this cone of moonstone is connected to all moonstone. Maybe this is the place where Cerulean would talk to those who were visiting the planets in the days of old." She rubbed her temples. "I don't know, Sera. I don't have all the answers."

"No," Sera said grimly. "But the High Priestess does."

"I do not think she will relinquish her secrets easily."

Sera agreed. How strange that her world had turned upside down and yet she accepted it without hesitation. But then, it was almost a relief, to think that there had been some reason that the ceremony had failed, some purpose to this no matter how dark.

"How are you to prove her lies to the City?" Sera asked. "What is your plan to . . . to . . . overthrow her?"

Leela's eyebrows knit together. "I had not thought of it like that. I do not—I am not doing this to rule. My only goal is to set this City right. It is up to someone older and wiser than me to lead it."

But Sera was seeing the change in her friend, the girl she used to tease as a scaredy-cat, who she had to cajole into sneaking out at night. The way she carried herself now, the ferocity in her voice, the passion . . . Leela was growing up just as much as Sera was.

"I must go," Leela said suddenly. "I have stayed too long. The other novices will notice my absence. I will see you again. We are connected, you and I."

Sera's throat grew too tight to speak. She drank in Leela's face, memorizing every line, every strand of hair. Leela gave her one last smile before she turned and fled down the paths and through the columns until Sera could not see her any longer. She felt herself dissolving, the tether and the cone of moonstone and the vines swirling and melting in her vision, and for one panicked second, it was like she was falling again. But then she was back in the cabin on the ship with Leo beside her, and no place had ever felt smaller or stranger or less real.

For a long moment, Leo and Sera just stared at each other. The expression on his face left Sera in no doubt that he had witnessed that entire exchange.

"What . . . was . . ." Leo couldn't bring himself to finish the sentence, his chest heaving.

"I can talk to her," Sera said, because she didn't quite

have an answer to his almost-asked question. "I can *see* her. Oh, Leo!"

She threw her arms around his neck and let out a wild cry of joy. Leo's arms wrapped around her waist. He was all biceps and forearms, a hard flat chest and broad hands with strong fingers. Sera felt an unexpected shiver run over her skin and a pinch in a place just below her stomach. He held her tight as if fearing she might dissolve.

"That . . . was . . . insane," Leo gasped, releasing her and stepping back, taking a quick physical inventory of himself, patting his thighs and his chest and running a hand through his curls.

"Were you there?" Sera asked. "I thought I could feel your emotions sometimes but once I was in the City, you vanished."

"Yeah," he said. "It was like I was a part of you, connected to you, seeing through your eyes. But I didn't have a body. And I was somehow aware of myself here on the ship too. It was all . . . incredibly confusing."

"It was confusing to me too," Sera said. "I have never experienced anything like that before. I didn't know it was a thing to experience at all." She looked down at the moonstone in awe. "I wonder what else this stone can do."

The door burst open then, Rahel entering triumphantly, carrying a platter that brought the scent of peaches and cream.

"Peach cobbler!" she declared, her eyes fixed on Leo as if seeking some kind of reward. Rahel seemed mostly harmless, but something about how she looked at Leo irritated

Sera in a way she could not quite explain. Her magic was bubbling, prickling and sharp, as if her talk with Leela had opened some sort of secret door inside her that had long been locked, the key only just discovered.

"I'm afraid I'm feeling awfully tired, Rahel," Leo said, and Sera was impressed at how normal he sounded after such an otherworldly experience. "Perhaps my friend and I could retire for the night?"

Rahel frowned and her gaze flickered unwillingly to Sera. "Well, you can't sleep in the same room together," she said. "That's not allowed. It's my ship so I make the rules."

Tears of frustration pricked Sera's eyes—she had not just visited with her best friend and discovered the woman she had trusted all her life was a liar only to be separated from her one companion by a silly girl who was used to getting everything she wanted.

The moonstone was a bright sun against her chest, a connection between her City and this planet, like a tendon with synapses on either end, and Rahel gave a little squeak of shock as Sera stepped toward her. Leo gasped too.

Sera's magic began to sing inside her, a song she felt she finally understood, though she could not explain how or why. Something had shifted within her, something that said *this is how it is supposed to be*, and a fire was lit in her heart, its heat spreading through her body. It felt like a blood bond except there was no one she was bonding with but herself. The heat began to climb, crawling up her chest, twining around her collarbone, curling into her throat, until it reached her eyes and a sudden clarity came upon her, a brilliant flash like a star being born, and she embraced the force of power coursing through her from the tips of her toes to the ends of her hair. The strength that had been building within her since they left Old Port was finally released and found it had purpose.

"I am a Cerulean," she said. Her voice rang and shimmered in the air and she felt as if the whole world stopped for a moment to listen and obey her. "My blood is magic. And you will not take my friend away from me."

Rahel's mouth fell open. "You can speak Pelagan," she said, but Sera had no time to acknowledge that she had finally cracked the secret to communicating on the planet because she could *see* Rahel, see her whole life laid out in a veil that draped over her body, shimmering threads of gold and pink intertwined with a dark meaty red. Her eyes burned in her skull as she turned to Leo—his veil was different, a patchwork of greens and blues laced with sad stormy grays. But she had seen Leo's memories before and would not think to intrude upon them again without permission.

It was Rahel she wanted to see. Without quite understanding how she was doing it, Sera plucked a thread from Rahel's veil with her mind, one of the red ones, her fiery eyes locking the princess in place as the memory unfolded before her.

Rahel was a little girl, playing with a jumping rope in a large opulent room. Another girl her age, a servant, stood watching her.

"Be careful, Princess," the girl said. "You'll break something."

"Who cares?" Rahel replied, skipping closer to a crystal vase filled with tulips. "This is my house, I can do what
I want."

The rope snagged on the vase and it fell, shattering on
the floor. A matronly woman with iron-colored hair and
small glasses bustled into the room. "What's this?" she
demanded, gazing in shock at the vase. "Rahel, what have
you done? Your mama will hear about this!"

Rahel began to cry then, big heaving sobs. "It wasn't
meeeee," she whined. "It was Hadley, she did it, she
smashed it on the floor, I told her not to."

"Hadley," the woman snapped, turning on the servant, who could only quiver, unable to speak. Rahel's tears
stopped as soon as the woman's back was turned. "This is
not how a companion to a princess behaves!"

The woman made a gesture and Hadley held out her
hand. The woman drew a ruler from her belt and slapped
it against Hadley's palm, so many times that it began to
bleed, the skin turning raw and red. Rahel watched with
greedy eyes. Hadley didn't make a sound.

"Now clean this mess up," the woman said. Then she
wrapped an arm around Rahel, who instantly began crying
again. "Come, Princess, let's get you in a nice warm bath."

Rahel felt a sense of satisfaction as she was led out of
the room. And just before the door closed behind them, she
heard Hadley let out an agonized sob.

They returned to the present with a jolt, the gilded room
too bright against the darkness of the memory. Rahel's
mouth was opening and closing like a fish's, but no sound

came out. Sera felt herself growing taller.

"You are a bad person," she said with no emotion, a statement of fact.

At that, Rahel's sweet, innocent eyes narrowed, her whole face turning feral. "Eireen!" she screamed.

And Sera knew something awful was going to happen.

14

AGNES

Phebe's boat was docked on an inlet north of the market, away from the bustling seaport of Arbaz; it was no more than a sloop with a single tiny cabin.

She led Agnes and Vada down narrow streets lit with simple gas lamps that wound up hills and through small squares. To get to the inlet they had to descend a set of steep stone stairs carved into the hillside. Phebe had brought a lantern and the light swung and swayed in the sharp breeze, casting strange shadows that made Agnes jumpy. She took each step with deliberate care, the stone unnervingly smooth beneath her feet.

Agnes couldn't stop her pulse from racing, her palms sweating, feeling like too much time had passed since the

Misarros had taken her brother and Sera. Vada put a hand on her shoulder and Agnes's heart somersaulted despite her fear.

"Ambrosine is waiting for you, remember," she said. "And now Phebe is lending us a boat. Once we get to Ithilia, we will find her. If anyone can stand up to the Triumvirate, it is Ambrosine Byrne."

Agnes fingered the letter in her pocket, nestled beside the photograph of her mother. Vada was right—her grandmother knew she was coming.

When they reached the sloop, Vada got straight to work readying it to sail. Phebe had packed them food and extra clothes in leather satchels, and Agnes stored them in the cabin. A cloud passed over the moon, the only light from Phebe's lantern, the only sound the waves lapping against the sides of the sloop.

"She doesn't look like much," Phebe said, holding up the light. "But she's a good ship. She was my mother's—she was the true sailor of the family."

"She'll be fast," Vada said. "And that's just what we need. What is her name?"

"The *Palma*," Phebe said. "After my grandmother."

"Thank you for helping us," Agnes said. "I don't know what we would have done without you."

Phebe touched her cheek, a surprisingly maternal gesture. "Good luck, Agnes Byrne. You are as brave as your mother was, and I can give no higher praise than that."

Agnes felt a tingle run up her spine at the sound of her mother's last name and hers together. Vada helped her into the sloop—it rocked unsteadily under her feet and she gripped the side to keep her balance.

"Best if you stay seated, little lion," Vada said as she pushed off the boat and hopped in, letting out the mainsail and angling the tiller so that the sloop cut through the waves, swift and sure. Soon Phebe's lantern was no more than a speck of light in the distance.

"We've got to go back to the docks," Agnes said suddenly.

"What?" Vada frowned. "Why?"

"Errol," Agnes said. "We can't leave him."

Vada's only answer was a pursing of her lips and an adjustment of the tiller. In almost no time at all, the lights from the port of Arbaz began to spread out over the water, tipping the waves in yellow and orange. Other ships had lights shining through their portholes but it appeared as though the crew of the *Maiden's Wail* had not yet returned from the market. The sloop slid silently through the water and Agnes peered over its side.

"Errol?" she called softly, feeling a bit silly. How was he to hear her? She didn't speak the flashing lights the way Sera did, though she could understand him to a degree—she had discovered that to her delight during the voyage. It must have been Sera's magic inside her. She was able to sense the intention behind the lights if not the exact words.

"Errol," she called again, and dipped her fingers into the water, wishing they could light up the way Sera's did. She tried to get her face as close to the waves as possible. "Errol, please, we've got to go, they've taken Sera, we've got to get her back. If you're there, if you can hear me or see me or . . ." She let out a growl of frustration. "What do we do, Vada?"

Vada plunged her hand into the water and wriggled it around, making small splashes. "Errol, you beautiful stubborn slippery little creature, you come with us right now, do you hear me? We need to be off, so no hiding or playing tricks or—"

Agnes let out a shriek as Errol's head popped out of the water, his lights flashing in shades of blue, which Agnes knew meant Sera. He looked from Agnes to Vada and back again, cocking his head.

"She's not here," Agnes said, gesturing wildly and hoping the mertag understood. His bulging eyes turned toward the *Maiden's Wail*. "Sera isn't there. We must go get her now. We must get Sera." She pointed. "In Ithilia. We must all go together, Agnes and Vada and Errol."

Errol stared at her blankly, then snapped his teeth together and jerked his head in what Agnes took to be a nod. Vada steered the boat back out into the sea, and to Agnes's profound relief, the mertag swam along beside them. His torso and scales glowed faintly green, filling the water around them with a murky light.

"Won't your mother be worried?" Agnes asked, realizing they hadn't had a chance to say goodbye to the crew of the *Maiden's Wail*.

"She will know where I am once she hears a Byrne has been taken by the Triumvirate," Vada said. "Besides, I do not think she was expecting me to be staying on the schooner much longer. A daughter must spread her wings at some point."

"But aren't you meant to inherit the ship?"

"Let's hope my mother will not be dying quite so soon," Vada said with a sardonic look. "It is time for me to set out on my own for a while. On the *Maiden's Wail*, I am Vada the Captain's Daughter. I wish to be only Vada. I am not entirely sure who I am without the shadow of my mother over me."

"I'm not sure who I am anymore either," Agnes said, resting her chin on her knees. "In Old Port I knew what was expected of me and I hated it. Perhaps it was easier that way. Now I'm in Pelago at last and I've managed to lose my brother and my best friend and anger two uncles I never knew I had without even trying."

"You are not giving yourself enough credit," Vada said. "You have pissed your father off as well."

Agnes laughed, and Vada looked pleased. Then her face grew serious.

"I would not judge myself so harshly if I were you, Agnes. I have been making the trip between Pelago and Kaolin since I was a little girl, and I have known many Kaolin women, of all ages and classes. Never have I met one like you. I am remembering the first time I saw you." She gazed up at the stars as if she could see the past in them. "You were looking at me as furtive as a mouse, in all your fancy things and that stupid little hat perched on your head."

Agnes pressed her hand to her mouth to cover her grin. "I had been meeting with my fiancé that afternoon," she confessed. "My maid thought the hat would make a good impression."

"Fiancé?" Vada cocked her head. "A very lucky gentleman. Is his heart being broken now that you have fled to Pelago?"

"No," Agnes said, flustered. "No, it wasn't like . . . my father arranged it, as a punishment, I think. I never—Ebenezer was a very nice young man, but not for me."

"And what sort of man is for you?"

Agnes's heart lodged in her throat and pounded there furiously. She'd come so far—she had crossed an ocean and made it all the way to Pelago, the country of her dreams. It was time to truly be herself. It was time to say the secret she'd been forced to keep for so long out loud.

"None," she said. "I don't like men that way."

Tears of relief mingled with pride stung her eyes and she blinked them back. Her shoulders felt suddenly weightless, her legs and arms puffs of air. The waves lapping against the hull were like the sound of Pelago cheering for her, welcoming her home. She saw a flash of white that was Vada's smile, but then it was gone, and the girl said nothing. After a moment, though, she began to whistle, a sweet, solemn tune that Agnes didn't know.

The wind started to pick up, and the sloop skimmed across the water. The night was growing darker, thick clouds eating up the stars and swallowing the moonlight. Errol's scales shone brighter, so the boat was haloed in luminous emerald.

Agnes shivered and settled back against the hull of the boat, feeling another layer of the girl she'd been in Kaolin slip away and wondering where her brother and Sera were now.

It took them three days to reach Ithilia.

Agnes was anxious to be back on land. The tiny ship was a great help, to be sure, but it felt like a prison. The only upside was so much uninterrupted alone time with Vada. They spent their days on the lookout for any Triumvirate patrol ships and the nights talking about their families and their hopes and fears for the future. Agnes was shocked to discover that Vada often felt insecure around her mother's crew, and the thirst to prove herself on her own terms with her own ship had been growing since before the two of them had met. Vada found the stories of Agnes attending premiers and fancy gatherings in Old Port hilarious.

"What I would not be paying to see you at a ball in all frills and ruffles," she'd said, cackling.

Agnes had rolled her eyes but her stomach fluttered at the thought of attending a dance or party with Vada. "I promise, you aren't missing anything. Leo's the one who cleans up the best in our family."

Vada had glanced at her slyly. "I am doubting that," she'd said. "I saw you in that red dress the night you came aboard the *Maiden's Wail*, remember?"

Agnes had flushed and the subject had dropped.

Vada taught her Pelagan dice games and in return Agnes taught Vada about photosynthesis and the properties of matter. Agnes felt herself equal parts relaxed and anxious in Vada's presence, especially since confessing she was attracted to girls. Always the desire to kiss Vada was there, growing more insistent with each passing day.

The closer they came to Ithilia, the more crowded the waters grew. Errol guided them expertly, avoiding the larger ships that could threaten their tiny sloop. Agnes saw that many were flying the Kaolin flag, red and white stripes and a golden sun. She wished the *Palma* had a flag to declare them Pelagan. She caught sight of armed Kaolins stalking the decks of a ship with rifles in their hands. But it wasn't until the afternoon of their arrival in Pelago's capital city that they truly saw what Phebe had been talking about back in Arbaz.

Two ships were locked in battle—they had heard the cannon fire and smelled something burning, then seen a ship with a mast missing and smoke pouring from its deck alongside an enormous galleon. They had been too far away to see the flags they were flying, but the sight made Agnes jittery and anxious. If Pelagans were openly attacking Kaolin ships, then things were only going to get worse.

They reached Ithilia just as the sun was beginning its descent toward the horizon.

Agnes could not help the way her breath caught in her throat. *Ithilia*. She had dreamed of it, but no dream could prepare her for its magnificence. The city was built into the side of a cliff, three massive rings of white marble stacked slightly above each other like a terrace, each one smaller than the last. And at the very top was Banrissa, looking like a toy castle perched at the cliff's tip.

Farther out from the shore, she saw what must be Whitehall, the sacred shrine of Talmanism that Phebe had told them about. A narrow stone bridge sprouted from the base of the palace and hung, delicate as a cloud, over the whitecapped waves below. All Agnes could make out of Whitehall itself was a glint of blue-green.

Misarro ships patrolled the waters, as they had around the docks of Arbaz. Agnes was grateful for their little sloop—it was too small to be of any interest, and with only two passengers and a little cabin, there wasn't much chance of them hiding anything. A schooner flying a flag with the five red stars of the Lekke pulled up alongside them and Vada deftly negotiated permission to dock in Ithilia with a surly Misarro with tin disks at her neck. Agnes held her breath until the ship passed, headed toward a Kaolin frigate making a run for the port.

A young girl with sunburned skin and a blue kerchief around her neck helped them tie up at the docks, then stuck out her hand.

"Twenty aurums," she said.

"Twen—you've got to be kidding me!" Vada cried. "It was four last time I was here."

The girl shrugged. "There wasn't so much Kaolin trash last time you were here, then. Price's gone up. Pay or we sink your boat."

Vada grumbled but forked over the money anyway. Agnes waited until the girl had gone and then crouched by the water.

"Errol," she called. His head popped up instantly, his filaments flashing blue.

"We're going to get Sera," Agnes said. "You stay here. We'll be back."

Errol snapped his teeth at her and Vada took some dried

meat from her satchel. "Think fast, you greedy monster," she said, tossing it under her arm and up into the air. He caught it expertly and let out his strange croaking laugh, and Vada grinned. Errol flashed mauve-lilac-gold before vanishing beneath the water—those were happy colors. Errol was always happiest when he was eating.

Vada took Agnes's hand and there was a sudden lurch in Agnes's chest, like she'd lost her balance. It was the first time Vada had touched her since they'd left Arbaz. As if she had sensed that Agnes needed the sea voyage to truly come to grips with her new life and all that it entailed. But now was the time to stand up and claim that life; Agnes felt a shivery lightheadedness at the feel of Vada's skin against her own.

"Come," Vada said. "We must get inside the city before they close the gates." Then she grinned and squeezed Agnes's fingers. "What soft paws you have, little lion."

Agnes's laugh sounded more like a hiccup. She was holding hands. With a girl she liked. In public. She undid her bun and shook out her hair, feeling a strange sort of wildness, a power filling her up unlike anything she'd ever known. Lion indeed, but there was nothing little about the way Agnes felt in this moment. Vada's smile was a dazzling thing, but she said nothing, only squeezed Agnes's hand once more.

The docks were full of stalls selling ropes and maps and compasses as well as charcoal braziers where chunks of cod and tuna cooked alongside strips of bell pepper and zucchini and onion. Misarros were everywhere. The air was heavy with the scent of salt and fish and sweat, and underneath it all, the stench of tension.

There was a boy selling copies of the *Ithilia Star* and Vada was quick to purchase one. BYRNE TAKEN FROM ARBAZ, it declared. And beneath, it read:

> The Triumvirate has taken a young Byrne into custody and he is currently being transported from Arbaz to Banrissa. No word on his name or which branch of the family he belongs to, but sources say Ambrosine is furious. Will she finally relent and open the passages around Culinnon?

The paper was dated today. "So they haven't arrived in Ithilia yet," Agnes said as she and Vada joined the swarming crowds bumping and jostling to enter the lowest, largest circle of the city. The walls loomed up over them, beautiful and impenetrable. They passed beneath the gate and Agnes marveled at the carved figurines of people and animals that decorated each side, oxen pulling carts, men pouring water from pitchers, doves in flight, women on horseback. The underside of the huge arch was detailed in squares of stone bearing the different symbols of the Triumvirate so that they formed a mosaic of silver moons, golden suns, and red stars.

Vada was skimming the rest of the paper. "Still no sign of Braxos, but there are more bodies washing up on the northern islands. A Kaolin ship was sunk trying to reach Ithilia two days ago, when it failed to heed the Misarros' warning to turn around. The president of Kaolin is threatening to send his navy if the Triumvirate doesn't stop attacking

Kaolins." She shook her head. "We must be leaving Ithilia as quickly as possible."

"We need to find my grandmother," Agnes said determinedly.

"We can hire a *metapar*," Vada said. Agnes frowned at the unfamiliar Pelagan word. "It is a horse-drawn cart with a driver," Vada explained. "Like your hansom cabs back in Old Port. But Agnes, I am not knowing where we will be finding Ambrosine Byrne. And I'm not sure it's safe to simply be asking around."

Agnes fingered the letter in her pocket. *I have friends at the University of Ithilia*, her grandmother had written.

"Don't worry, Vada," she said. "I know how to find her."

15

LEO

It had been three days since they'd left Arbaz and Leo hadn't seen a glimpse of Sera.

Not since that first night, after Sera had spoken to Leela.

He'd been so relieved to be able to feel his body again after the disorienting experience of seeing through Sera's eyes in that strange underground place. His brain had still been processing what had happened, and then Rahel was back with the peach cobbler, which he'd forgotten about entirely, but it didn't matter because Sera had begun to *glow*. Her eyes were fiery blue suns as she stared down the princess, and spoke to her in *Pelagan*. But even that surprise had had to wait because then Leo was *seeing* things.

It was like when he and Sera blood bonded, except this

time there was only one memory and it was Rahel's. He'd watched, half fascinated, half disgusted, as Rahel blamed a servant girl for breaking a vase she herself had smashed and then delighted in the girl's punishment. Then the memory had vanished and Rahel screamed for her Misarro.

Eireen had come running, taken one look at Rahel's blubbering face, her shaking finger pointing at Sera, and before Leo could move or think, the Misarro had grabbed Sera, pinning her arms down and dragging her out of the room, Rahel still shrieking, "She hurt me, she's cursed, she hurt me!"

But that was days ago. Leo paced his cabin, everything floral patterned and crusted in diamonds. They'd locked him up, Rahel no longer trusting him though she visited him daily. It had taken all of his considerable skill at flirting to get her to promise that Sera was not being mistreated but just held prisoner like him until they reached Ithilia and the Renalt could sort out what to do with her.

Leo's nerves had been gnawing a hole in his stomach. Just then there was the click of a lock and Rahel swooped into the room.

"Ithilia! Leo, do you see? We're almost home," she sang, like the two of them were on an adventure together.

He peered out his window and was shocked when he saw land in the distance. At least he would finally get to see Sera again and know for certain that she was all right. But he shuddered at the thought of facing the Triumvirate. "I'm eager to see it," Leo lied.

Rahel beamed. "There are so many ships coming to it now. Mother didn't even want me to go to Arbaz at all, she said it was too dangerous, but won't she be pleased when I bring her a Byrne! And that . . . thing." She shivered.

Leo's jaw clenched. "I do hope Sera is feeling all right," he said, choosing his words carefully. "You wouldn't want her to be unwell in front of your mother."

Rahel pouted. "She's fine. I promised you, didn't I? I'm a princess; princesses keep promises."

Leo was wholly unreassured by that statement.

Suddenly, there was a massive bang and the whole ship shook. Rahel shrieked and rushed to cling to him as Leo grabbed on to a golden chaise to steady himself.

"What's happening?" she cried as the ship shook again. The smell of gunpowder filled the air and then there was a great groaning creak followed by a thunderous crash. Leo ignored Rahel's nails digging into his arm, ignored the pounding of footsteps and shouts from above, because Sera was somewhere on this ship and he didn't know where and he couldn't do a damn thing to help her. Whoever had attacked the *Gilded Lily* was not likely to be a friend to a half Kaolin man and a girl who looked like a goddess.

Footsteps came closer and Rahel shrank into his side. There was another crash and the door was kicked in, the painted wood splintering by the lock. A Misarro stood in the doorway, her spiked hair like flames about her face, golden disks covering her throat, no crest on her tunic. She took one look at Leo, then quickly stepped aside to let a woman enter the cabin. She was in her sixties and very tall, thick black curls streaked with gray piled up on her head, studded with an enormous crown conch. She wore navy pants and a pinstripe blazer, a silver-topped cane in one hand.

And she had Leo's eyes, exactly.

When she caught sight of him, her expression seemed to fracture, revealing pain, raw and jagged. Then she blinked and it was gone.

"You must be Leo," she said, stepping forward. "By the goddesses . . . she has indeed been born again in you."

"W-who are you?" Leo stammered, but the answer was as plain as his face.

"I'm your grandmother," the woman said. "Ambrosine Byrne."

Rahel let out a whimper. "You can't be here," she said. "This is my ship, mine! You aren't sup—"

Leo's grandmother turned to Rahel with an expression reserved for unwanted vermin. "Rahel, do us all a favor and shut your mouth," she said. "Your ship has no cannons, a skeleton crew, and my Misarros are better than yours. And before you even think to say it, yes, of course I know who your mother is, you pitiful little fool, and as you can see, I do not *care*. I'm taking my grandson and that's all there is to it. Your guard has been subdued and your ship crippled. Now do be a good girl and *sit down*."

To Leo's shock, Rahel plopped herself down on the chaise, eyes filled with tears, lips pressed together, cheeks red.

"Come, Leo," Ambrosine said, and Leo followed, half dazed, until he came to his senses.

"Where's Sera?" he demanded, turning on the princess. Rahel raised a hand and dumbly pointed to the left. Leo turned to his grandmother. "I'm not leaving without my friend."

Irritation flashed in Ambrosine's eyes, but she gave an elegant shrug. "Very well." With a snap of her fingers, the Misarro was sent off down the hall, kicking in door after door until Leo heard Sera's shocked cry. His bones melted with relief.

"It's all right, Sera, it's me, we're safe!" he called, and the next thing he knew Sera was flying out of the room and down the hall. She was unharmed, as Rahel had promised.

"You're all right," she said, throwing her arms around him. Her warm softness and flowery-starlight scent engulfed him and he felt a stirring in the pit of his stomach. "I was so worried about you."

Leo realized then that Ambrosine and her Misarro were staring at Sera, the way everyone stared at Sera.

"She's not Saifa," Leo began, almost wearily, but then he remembered Sera could speak Pelagan now. Probably Kaolish too.

Ambrosine held up a hand. "Explanations can wait," she said. "We must be off at once."

Wherever Rahel's guard was, Leo didn't know—the decks were streaked with blood and smoke poured out of the hole where the mast had once stood. Destruction lay in the wake of where it fell across the ship, splintered wood and crushed golden rails. There were more Misarros, all with gold disks sewn into their collars, which Leo took to mean they were in the service of Ambrosine.

They crossed the deck to a large plank-like footbridge, that extended from a huge galleon, two cannons on its deck still pointing at the ruined mast.

Once aboard, Ambrosine shouted orders, her voice like

the crack of a whip, and the footbridge was raised as the ship was readied to set sail. She turned to Leo and Sera as a servant in a blue tunic hurried up with a tray of ice-cold cucumber water. Ambrosine waved her off.

"I heard my grandson had been taken along with a companion," she said, looking Sera up and down. "Aren't you magnificent."

"Thanks for saving us," Leo said, but the words felt clumsy, inept. Ambrosine wasn't at all like he'd pictured her. He'd imagined someone matronly, with a hunched back and horrific taste in footwear. Not this sleek woman in an expertly tailored suit with her own contingent of fierce warriors.

He hoped he wouldn't be expected to call her "Grandmother." That would be altogether too strange.

She looked at him and he was once again seized by the bizarre sensation of seeing his eyes in someone else's head. Ambrosine had his curls too, black like his except for the bits of gray. But her chin was squarer, her cheekbones more pronounced, and her nose was slightly beaked.

"You are my blood," she said. "Of course I would come for you. I wish the circumstances of our meeting were different. But once I read in the papers that the Triumvirate had taken a young Byrne in Arbaz . . . I knew."

"Knew what?" Leo asked.

"I knew that my daughter's children had returned to Pelago at last," Ambrosine said. "But where is your sister?"

"I don't know," Leo said honestly. "She could still be in Arbaz. We made friends with a sailor, though, so she might be coming to Ithilia. She was there when Sera and I were taken. This is Sera, by the way."

Something about his grandmother made him feel like everything he said was just a little bit stupid, as if her presence scrambled his thoughts.

"I am a Cerulean," Sera said, pushing her shoulders back bravely, and Leo felt his chest melt a little. "Leo has been helping me get to Braxos so I can get back home to my people. We heard you have cut off the ways to the island but we hoped you might allow us to get through."

Leo thought that was rather valiant of her to declare all at once. Ambrosine raised an eyebrow.

"Braxos," she said, then smiled. It was a startling change, like the sun coming suddenly out from behind a cloud. Her whole face softened into a kinder version of the woman who had shut Rahel up earlier.

Ambrosine snapped her fingers and two sailors appeared as quickly as if she had conjured them out of the air. "Gather a crew, take one of the stowed boats, and make for Ithilia. Half will search the city, the other half make for Arbaz. I must find my granddaughter before the Triumvirate does."

"We're not going to Ithilia?" Leo asked.

"Ithilia is far too dangerous right now," Ambrosine said. "But don't you fear; my people will find your sister. Now, look at the two of you," she said, clucking her tongue. Another snap and two young servant girls in blue tunics rushed to her side. Leo could not help but be impressed— even his father did not command such immediacy. Though he could tell the girls were fascinated by Sera, they were doing a decent job of hiding it. "Take my grandson and his friend below. I want hot water prepared for them to wash, and find some fresh clothes."

"Yes, mistress," one of the girls said, and gestured to Sera as the other motioned for Leo to follow her. Ambrosine took his hand as he passed, and there was surprising strength in her grip.

"We will speak once you have had a chance to bathe and change," she said. He nodded and watched her take in his face once more, but this time her eyes revealed nothing.

The servant he was following opened a hatch and Leo descended a steep flight of stairs after her. She led him down halls carpeted in crimson and gold, miniature chandeliers hanging from the ceiling, and then into a small room with a claw-foot tub already filled with hot water.

"Your stateroom is right next door," the girl said shyly. "I will lay clothes out for you."

Leo started to thank her but she was already gone. The bath felt like heaven after being locked up for three days, no matter how opulent his prison. Once he had scrubbed the travel and sweat and dirt from his skin, he padded next door to his room. A four-poster bed was hung with pale blue curtains and laid with a navy comforter and pillows; there was a thick carpet that swallowed up his bare feet and a leather armchair with a small table beside it next to a large porthole. Simple garb was laid out on the bed, pants and a shirt and vest much like what the sailors on the deck had been wearing. The pants were an inch too short, the vest a hair tight, but the clothes were clean and Leo was grateful for them.

He opened the door to the stateroom, unsure of what he was supposed to do now.

"Sera?" he called, but then the same servant girl was rushing down the hall toward him.

"Mistress Byrne is waiting for you in her private parlor, sir," she said breathlessly. "If you will follow me."

She led him to a small cabin with two armchairs around a table set for tea. His grandmother was already seated in one and smiled at him when he entered. This smile wasn't quite the same as the one on the deck—there were teeth behind it. A large window let in the golden rays of the sun, which fell on oak-paneled walls and illuminated a huge portrait of a woman standing at the prow of a ship, stormy waves crashing against its hull, one hand clutching the rail like talons. The woman had Leo's eyes and Ambrosine's beaked nose and she gazed out imperiously over the room.

His grandmother stood. "Thank you, Mckenna, that will be all," she said, and the girl vanished. "You look much refreshed, Leo."

"I am," he said, then added, "Thank you." He still felt out of sorts around this woman, a bit like he was just a boy again. "Where's Sera?"

"You seem quite fond of her."

Leo tried not to blush and failed. "She's my friend."

Ambrosine's smile widened like the answer both pleased and amused her. Leo wished he hadn't mentioned Sera at all.

"Please, sit," she said. "Have some tea with me."

She filled the two cups as Leo took a seat in the other armchair. She added honey to hers and stirred it slowly. Leo wasn't much of a tea drinker, so he just clasped the cup in both hands and waited for her to say something. While he was certainly grateful to be away from Rahel and the Triumvirate, and he had very much appreciated the bath, he wasn't entirely sure about his new situation. Eneas's warning to Agnes when he dropped them off at the Seaport still rang in his ears.

Be careful around your grandmother. Try to see things as they are, not how you wish them to be.

Leo shifted in his seat and took a sip of tea. It tasted of chamomile and lemongrass. When he looked up, his grandmother was watching him with the same expression as when she'd first seen him.

"I'm sorry," she said, leaning back into her chair. "You just . . ."

"I know," Leo said. He didn't need to be told again how much he looked like his mother. Though it did feel different, coming from Ambrosine.

"It's almost like she's alive again," she said, turning away to hide her face in a sip of tea. "Almost." Leo didn't know what to say to that. When she turned back, she was composed.

"How do you think your father is handling the news of his children gone, his empire shattered, his most prized possession fled?"

"You knew?" Leo asked. "About the play? You knew about Sera already?"

She let out a biting, humorless laugh. "Don't look so surprised; I make it my business to know the happenings in Kaolin, especially anything that concerns my grandchildren and that *man*." She spat out the word like it was vulgar. "I saw her picture in the *Old Port Telegraph*, an advertisement for Xavier's final production. Though I admit I did not think much of her, assuming she was some marketing prank of your father's. Thankfully no one in Pelago cares about the goings-on in Kaolin. I am one of the few who reads the Old Port papers." She cocked her head. "Your Pelagan is very good. I'm shocked your father allowed you to learn it."

Leo shook his head. "He didn't. The sailor Agnes befriended, the one who brought us to Arbaz. Vada. She taught us on the way."

"Did she teach Sera as well?"

"No," he said. "That's just . . . a part of who she is." He decided not to mention how recent a development it was.

"And she is linked to Braxos."

Leo had never thought of it like the two were linked. "That's one way to put it." He tried then to explain who Sera was without giving away too much information. He had to admit, it was impressive that his grandmother didn't flinch at the mention of a city in space.

"I've heard a great many strange tales in my life," she said. "But never one about a Cerulean." She sat back and crossed one leg over the other.

"Will you help us get her to Braxos?" Leo asked.

For a moment, Ambrosine was lost in thought. She added more honey to her tea and stared at the portrait on the wall as she stirred. "Yes," she murmured. "I will help you."

Leo's head swam with relief. "Thank you."

"The Triumvirate needs a good reminder of who they're

dealing with," Ambrosine said. "Braxos is of the north and belongs to the north. They've sat too long on their western thrones. They cannot claim what is not rightfully theirs."

Leo didn't see how Braxos was rightfully Ambrosine's either, regardless of geography, but felt it best not to say that out loud. For now, she was promising to help them, and that was all he could have hoped for.

"The Renalt won't like that you attacked her daughter's ship," Leo said.

Ambrosine finally tore her eyes from the painting. "Did I give the impression that I care what the Renalt likes or dislikes?"

Leo's face went hot. Talking to his grandmother felt like walking in a murky stream barefoot—he never knew when he might step on a jagged rock.

"Where are we going?" he asked, changing the subject.

She raised an eyebrow. "Why, to Culinnon, of course. Aren't you excited to see your true home?"

Leo wasn't sure he'd phrase it that way. As far as he could tell, at the moment he had no home. Not the brownstone on Creekwater Row or the mysterious island in the north of Pelago. He didn't seem to belong anywhere.

"I didn't know Culinnon existed until we came here," he said. "My father never told us anything about you, or my mother, or Pelago. We weren't even allowed to mention your name in our house."

Ambrosine slammed her cup down onto its saucer. "That *beastly* man," she muttered. "I should not be surprised that Xavier kept her from you. He kept her from me as well. He wasn't fit to shine her shoes, much less father the next heir to Culinnon." She pursed her lips and examined his face again. Leo wished she wouldn't. It made him feel like she was giving him a test and he was coming up short.

"You know," she said, "Alethea was my greatest love. I loved her more than my husband or my sons or any of the lovers I have taken over the years. And she was ripped from me, violently and completely. The unfairness of it has been difficult to bear at times, I admit. The pain of her loss. I can still remember the night she was born, on the estates of Culinnon where all Byrnes are brought into this world." She gave him a look he didn't quite understand and continued. "It was one of the worst blizzards in recent memory and the doctor was delayed. My husband couldn't stand the screaming and the blood, but then, he was always a weak man." She sighed and adjusted the conch in her hair. "Excellent family stock but spineless."

As little as Leo had thought over the years about his mother and grandmother, he'd never once thought at all about his Pelagan grandfather.

"Is he on Culinnon too?" Leo asked. "My grandfather?"

"He died years ago." She said it as casually as if she were commenting on the weather. "Anyway, the wet nurse used to say that the storm stayed inside my Alethea, the blizzard she was born into shaping the woman she became. It was nonsense but also true—Alethea was restless, she was rash, she was impetuous and could be brutally fierce when she set her mind to something."

Leo found he rather liked that idea, of his mother inheriting a storm.

"I kept her on Culinnon for as long as I could, but she wanted Ithilia and nothing else. She wanted the lights and energy of the city, the bustle of the markets and the glory of Banrissa. It was not enough that Culinnon holds magic and beauty and mystery. It was not enough for her to wander beneath trees that sing and swim in ponds that sparkled like twilight. It was not even enough that I let her keep Eneas." She fiddled with a button on her blazer. "I thought with time and patience and structure, she could be tamed. And the tighter I held her, the harder she tried to slip through my fingers. So what could I do? I let her go."

For a moment, Ambrosine looked older, weary. Her shoulders hunched and she rubbed her temple. "And I lost her. I lost her there forever, though I did not know it at the time."

Suddenly, a bell chimed out and she straightened, her expression once again cool and commanding. "It is time to dress for dinner."

She stood and Leo followed suit.

"What—what should I call you?" he asked.

Her mouth twitched like she wanted to smile, or maybe snarl, Leo couldn't tell. "Why don't you just call me Ambrosine."

He felt a pinch of relief. "All right."

Ambrosine opened the door. "Mckenna will bring you to the dining room when you're ready. I'm sure she's found some more decent clothes for you by now."

"Thank you," Leo said, then stopped. "Oh, there's

something you should know about Sera."

The flash of greed in his grandmother's eyes was as unmistakable as it was unnerving. "And what is that?"

"She doesn't eat meat," Leo said, then strode off down the hall, his head spinning at the day's turn of events.

16

AGNES

Agnes and Vada jolted along the streets of Ithilia in the *metapar*, which was just a cart with one horse and driver and seats that faced backward. The streets were crafted out of all sorts of material, mainly marble, like the walls surrounding the city, but others were cobbled and a few even had jewels studded along their curbs. Most of the buildings were painted white with blue doors and shutters, and all the roofs were lined with tiles that sparkled whenever light caught them.

They drove through bustling squares with fountains featuring various goddesses—Agnes recognized Saifa, and Vada pointed out red-skinned, black-haired Bas, the goddess of death, and Farayage, the goddess of the sea, with rich brown skin and hair as green and tangled as seaweed.

Cafés spilled out onto the sidewalks, with people in all manner of dress. Agnes saw one couple, both men, arm in arm—one wore a fine linen suit that might not look out of place on the streets of Old Port, the other a shimmering silk skirt paired with a lace top. Both had simple crowns of seashells in their hair and their eyes were lined with kohl.

She was once again stunned by the sense that she could be whoever she wanted here, that she could become the Agnes she never fully believed would ever exist. Her hair, free from its bun, tickled the back of her neck in agreement.

They turned up a street that rose steadily higher and when they reached the top, Vada tugged Agnes's arm and gestured for her to turn around.

The University of Ithilia sprawled out before her and Agnes could not contain her gasp of delight. A long gravel drive lined with cherry trees, their blossoms giving off a sweet fragrance, led up to an imposing, multistoried brick building with wings spreading out on either side and an impressive row of white columns on its front. A few students lounged on the large swaths of lush manicured grass or walked the smaller gravel paths between the main building and various outbuildings scattered throughout the grounds. Agnes's fingers began to tingle with anticipation—she could already picture the lab, so much bigger than her little closet at home, and all the equipment she would have access to. Professors to teach her instead of outdated musty old books. Her skin prickled at the thought of so much learning, so much potential. Most of the students she saw were women, but there were men among them as well. She could fit in here.

She wondered who her grandmother's friends were—maybe the dean, or some high-ranking professor. She hoped they would be able to connect her with Ambrosine.

The *metapar* pulled up to the front doors. Vada hopped down but Agnes climbed out slowly. Her heart was pounding so fast it was like a blur in her chest.

Low marble steps led up to a set of doors emblazoned with the university crest—a falcon with an olive branch clutched in its talons.

If only Eneas could see me now, Agnes thought as she followed Vada into the main foyer. It was a huge echoing space with high ceilings in a jigsaw of teak and maplewood. There was no sign of faculty or students—the foyer was completely empty. It ended at a pair of mahogany doors and just when Agnes was wondering if perhaps they should try another building, the doors opened and three students, two girls and one boy, walked out, chatting excitedly in Pelagan, their arms loaded with books.

". . . not at all like the rest of the family," one of the girls was saying. All three stopped short when they caught sight of Agnes and Vada. The other girl and boy wrinkled their noses and Agnes suddenly realized she had not bathed in three days.

"Hello," Agnes said, the Pelagan flowing off her tongue as if she had been born speaking it. "I'm—" She was about to introduce herself and then thought better of it. "I'm looking for the dean of admissions. I'm meant to have an interview this week."

The dean seemed like the most likely friend of

Ambrosine's, given that she had sent Agnes her initial acceptance.

The first girl frowned. "The dean has left for the day."

Agnes's heart sank. "Oh."

"Is there anyone else we can speak to?" Vada asked.

"The librarian," the second girl suggested. "He's always
here."

She jerked her head to the doors behind them.

Agnes wasn't sure how a librarian could help, but she'd
take somebody over nobody at this point.

"All right," she said. "Thank you."

The students left quickly, their whispers fluttering
around the cavernous space. Agnes waited until they'd gone
and then pulled the heavy door open.

The smell of books enveloped her the moment she
stepped inside, parchment and leather and oil, dust and
wood and sunlight. The library was enormous and Agnes
found herself momentarily stunned. She walked in a daze
down a green-carpeted aisle, shelves stretching out before
her, until she came to a large central area where tables with
little reading lamps and finely upholstered chairs were set
at neat intervals. Agnes lifted her gaze and felt dizzy at the
sight of three more levels of books, balconies open to the
central space with railings of polished bronze.

"Can I help you?"

She jumped as a man with thinning red hair and bifocals appeared from between two shelves. He wore a simple
linen shirt that was slightly rumpled, tweed pants, and
yellow suspenders. He held two slender books with gilded
spines in his hand. Behind the glasses was a pair of clever

blue eyes, so pale they were almost clear.

"I'm meant to have an interview this week," Agnes said. "For the Academy of Sciences. But . . . they told me the dean left for the day."

"She did," the man said. "I can leave your name for her, if you wish. Or you can come back tomorrow morning."

Agnes hesitated, then said, "Actually, I'm looking for someone else."

"Oh?" the man asked, raising one eyebrow. "How many interviews do you have?"

"It's not an interview, it's . . . my grandmother. I'm trying to find her and she told me she has friends here, at the university. I was hoping someone might be able to tell me where she is."

The pale eyes narrowed. "And who might your grandmother be?"

Agnes swallowed hard. "Ambrosine Byrne."

The books fell to the floor with a thud. "You are Agnes," he gasped.

Agnes blinked. "Um, yes."

He shook his head. "I'm sorry I didn't . . . you have the look of your father."

"How do you know who I am? Do you know my grandmother?"

The man smiled like the question was amusing in some way. "Yes," he said. "I know her."

Relief stabbed through her chest. "Can you help me find her?"

"She has just left Ithilia," he said. "Only hours ago."

"Left?" Agnes said, her head spinning. "No. She can't

be gone. She said she would be here."

"How are you knowing this?" Vada asked.

"Because she told me," the man said. "Please, allow me to introduce myself. I am Matthias Byrne. Ambrosine is my mother."

Agnes heard Vada mutter, "Holy shit," but didn't think herself capable of speech, though she agreed with the sentiment. She stared at the man who was her uncle and felt he was nothing like she'd been imagining the Byrnes. He seemed so mild mannered, so innocuous. Now that she knew, though, she could just make out Leo's features in his long nose and the shape of his eyes. Their color, of course, was nowhere near as vibrant, and his chin was rounder, his lips thinner, his cheeks plumper.

He seemed to understand what she was doing. "Alethea got the looks in the family," he said wryly. "Hektor too. I take after our father."

This was her mother's brother, Agnes realized with a start. She felt as if her brain should be keeping up better. Then she remembered Culinnon and took a step backward.

"I don't want any trouble," she said.

Matthias frowned. "I'm not sure what you mean."

Vada stepped up. "We are hearing that you might not be so happy that Agnes has come to Pelago. Word is the Byrne brothers may not want Agnes inheriting Culinnon."

Matthias's eyebrows shot up his forehead. Then he began to laugh. "Oh, by the goddesses, did you find the right brother," he said. "I haven't been to Culinnon since Alethea died. If I never set foot on its shores again, it will be too soon. This is my home now." He swept his hand out at the books around them. "And I would never judge someone based on their parentage. Believe me on that." He turned his keen, clear gaze to Agnes. "Culinnon is all yours if you want it. Though I can't say Hektor will be happy. But that isn't for him to decide. He knows how things work."

"I didn't even know about Culinnon until I arrived in Arbaz a few days ago," Agnes confessed. "I didn't know I had uncles at all."

Matthias's kind face crumpled with sadness. "Xavier never told you," he said, and Agnes shook her head.

"He never told me anything about my mother either," she said. "I've only ever seen one picture of her. I don't know anything about her family. I don't . . ." Tears sprang to her eyes, surprising her. She felt helpless and stupid and lost.

"Come with me," Matthias said, stooping to pick up the books he'd dropped, then leading Agnes and Vada through the maze of shelves until they reached a small office. A leather chair sat behind a desk covered in books and papers, a fountain pen tilted clumsily beneath a lamp with a green shade. There was a small sofa covered in papers against a wall filled with bookshelves and a hard-backed chair by a window with soft muslin curtains that looked out onto the university grounds.

"Please, sit," Matthias said, gathering up an armful of clutter to make room on the sofa. Vada plopped herself down and Agnes perched on the edge of the chair. Matthias walked around behind his desk, moved a stack of books aside, and picked up a silver-framed photograph.

"This is your mother," he said softly. "One year before she married your father."

He held out the photograph and Agnes took it with trembling hands. Her mother was sitting at an outdoor table at a restaurant, a glass of wine in one hand and a cigarette in the other. She wore loose-fitting striped pants and a fur vest, her curls done up on one side and pinned with various seashells. She was laughing at something Agnes couldn't see, as if someone just behind the camera had made a joke before taking the picture. A much younger Matthias with significantly more hair sat beside her, a shy smile on his face as he watched his sister. Beside him was a sterner man, with many of Alethea's striking features, but his eyes were dark and held none of her mirth.

Agnes ran her finger over the glass, tracing her mother's form. She looked so alive, so vibrant. She commanded the attention of everyone at the table. There was even an older woman at a neighboring table who was staring at her.

"She's laughing in the photograph I have of her too," Agnes said.

"She loved to laugh," Matthias said. "She loved to sing and be loud and break the rules. She reveled in being different. Hektor resented her for it. Father indulged her because of it. Mother . . ." He shook his head. "Well, Mother wanted her to be exactly like Mother. And she wasn't. Not even a little."

"What did *you* think about her?" Agnes asked.

Matthias cleared his throat. "She was my best friend," he said tightly. "She understood that I did not want the things a Byrne was meant to want."

"Things like what?" Agnes asked.

Matthias moved some more books and sat on his desk.

"I'm surprised your Pelagan friend here did not tell you of my family's reputation."

"I told her they were rich and powerful," Vada said with a shrug. "I don't concern myself with the affairs of the Byrnes very much. As long as I have a ship to sail and cargo to sell, the Byrnes and the Triumvirate can have as many pissing contests as they like."

Matthias chuckled. "Yes, that's a very apt way to describe it." He turned on the lamp as the light began to fade from the sky. "The Byrne family is one of the oldest in Pelago, and certainly the wealthiest. The northern islands are devoted to us, but the Triumvirate has always resented my family's power. Byrnes have been known to be ruthless. There is a story my mother loves to tell of my great-grandmother, Aileen Byrne, who was tricked by a healing woman into buying a tonic that would supposedly give her everlasting life. The tonic was just lemon juice and spices, and when Aileen discovered this treachery, she had the woman's tongue and eyes cut out."

Agnes gasped. "Is that true?"

Matthias shrugged. "It's a good story. And it is certainly effective. My family has held on to our power through a mix of money, mystique, and intimidation. And Culinnon lies at its heart. I wish I could . . ." He made a sort of strangled choking sound and sighed. "No, I cannot explain it to you. You will have to see it for yourself. The island possesses a sort of . . . well, I hesitate to use the word *magic*; it sounds so implausible."

Agnes and Vada exchanged a look.

"No," Agnes said. "It doesn't. Not to us."

Matthias scratched the bald spot on his head. "Very well—there's something about it that once you leave, you cannot form the words to describe it accurately. I suppose it is one of the island's ways of protecting itself."

"You make it sound like it's a living thing," Agnes said.

"Like I said, you must see it for yourself. Culinnon possesses greatness, but it is not enough for my mother. There is an even older story, from the earliest days of Pelago, one that my family does not like to tell. One that the Triumvirate would like to forget too." He glanced at Vada, as if uncertain that he should continue.

"You can trust us," Agnes said quickly.

Vada touched the fang that hung at her throat. "On my honor as a smuggler, I will not say a word."

Matthias inclined his head, and Agnes saw that Vada had given him a secret in exchange. A clever move, Agnes thought as her uncle turned back to her.

"Do you know the three ruling families?"

"The Aerins, the Renalts, and the Lekkes," Agnes said.

"Correct. But the Renalts weren't an original Triumvirate family. There was another, called the Shawnens."

"Shawnens?" Vada said. "I have never heard of them."

"No, you wouldn't have," Matthias said. "This was centuries ago. It has been forgotten why the Byrnes hated the Shawnens so much—a failed marriage contract or a broken deal or some other betrayal of trust. But whatever it was, the Byrnes and Shawnens fought until one side was completely decimated. There are no Shawnens left in Pelago." A shiver ran down Agnes's spine. "The Byrnes had hoped to be inducted as the third ruling family, but the Aerin and the Lekke were not wild about the precedent that would set. So they told the Byrne matriarch that if she wanted to be a part of the Triumvirate, she must give up Culinnon." Matthias took off his glasses and cleaned them on his sleeve. "Needless to say, she declined. And the Lekke and the Aerin had joined their forces together—the Byrnes could not fight two families at once. They retreated back to the north and the Renalts were inducted into the Triumvirate, and the matriarchs of my family have brooded over this slight for generations. It is often said there is a streak of insanity in the Byrne family. But that is not the word I would use."

"What would you call it?" Agnes asked.

"And insatiable lust for power," Matthias said. "My mother was furious when Alethea left. She'd had a plan, my sister told me. She wouldn't give me details but she swore she was never going back to Culinnon again. I was excommunicated soon after, so to speak. I wasn't Byrne quality, even for a boy. Too soft, Mother said. Too weak. Always with my nose in a book." Matthias rubbed the back of his neck. "It was drilled into us since we were children how important family was, how necessary our traditions were. But Alethea wanted to live her own life on her own terms. Mother could never forgive her for that."

He set his pale eyes on Agnes and she felt her stomach swoop. "She wants you, Agnes. She has a plan that was left unfinished with Alethea's death. So my advice to you would be: run. Go to another island, go back to Kaolin, go anywhere but where she wants you to be."

"But . . ." Agnes blinked. "I can't leave. And I won't go back to Kaolin, not ever. My brother, Leo, he's been taken by the Triumvirate along with a friend who needs my help. She has to get to Braxos, and not for the reason everyone else is trying to find it. She's . . . she's different, she's special, and I promised that I'd get her there and I can't abandon her or my brother, not now, not ever."

Matthias was quiet. "There is so much of her in your words," he said at last. "You say you need to get to Braxos to help a friend? Not for riches or glory?"

Agnes nodded. "I don't care about any of that."

Matthias stood.

"Then there is something you need to see."

17

SERA

SERA BATHED IN A LARGE COPPER TUB SIMILAR TO THE one she had used in Agnes's dwelling.

She was so grateful to be off Rahel's ship, to be free of her cabin prison. The three days without Leo had been full of anxiety and fear and exhaustion. She'd hoped perhaps that Leela might speak to her again, but the moonstone had remained frustratingly quiet. Whatever Rahel had told her Misarros about Sera seeing her memories, it had definitely frightened them—the only time she had human contact was when a Misarro would bring food for her, and even then they never fully came into the cabin, just slid a plate through the door, like *she* might hurt *them*.

So much had happened so quickly and she was only just

beginning to appreciate it all now that she was no longer headed to the Triumvirate. She could speak Pelagan! And see memories without sharing her own. Sera itched to try this newfound self blood bond again, but a deep part of her knew that this power should not be taken lightly.

The moonstone was cool in her hand now, at odds with the warm bathwater. She wished she could have seen her mothers as well as Leela, or some part of her City that wasn't strange and glowing and new, the City that she had known all her life. She remembered what her purple mother had said to her, the day after she was chosen to be sacrificed.

As long as the stars burn in the sky, I will love you.

Suddenly, her skin crackled and the moonstone flared up again like it had with Leela, but this time Sera was not pulled to that strange underground sky garden—she did not move at all, could still feel the freesia-scented water lapping against her body. And yet she could see twelve very familiar dwellings, except they weren't vacant like they usually were. The round birthing houses were covered in chains of flowers, the field with the obelisk full of people. She caught sight of her old friend Treena, now a midwife, with an armful of blankets. Then she gasped. Her purple mother was crossing the field, a bucket of water in one hand.

"Mother," she wanted to call, but her lips wouldn't move.

Sera was shocked to see how vacant and dark her eyes were. She had never seen her mother look so empty or so sad. Her purple mother paused and turned, staring at the obelisk with a furrowed brow, but then someone called out, "Kandra!" and she roused herself and kept walking, leaving Sera with an aching heart. There was another crackle and the image faded until only the walls of the washroom remained. Sera blinked and found tears in her eyes.

She looked down at the moonstone lying innocently in her palm. It was all connected, she thought. Leela was right. If she had visions of Sera on the planet and now Sera was having visions of the City . . . perhaps whatever moonstone was left in the City was finally coming alive again. It just took a Cerulean coming to the planet to waken its power.

The High Priestess would be able to explain all of this, Sera was sure of it. The one person who could not be asked. Sera could not understand what the High Priestess gained in keeping them attached to this planet for so long, but she was certain of one thing. It was more important than ever that she get to the tether.

Even if she had to break it again, and do it right this time. The City was meant to *move*.

She stood and wrapped herself in a big fluffy towel, then froze. Her purple mother had been at the *birthing houses*. Leela had said a birthing season had begun. Sera had not put it together at first, but . . . that meant her purple mother had been blessed to bear another daughter. She leaned against the wall, her blood rushing in her ears, her magic churning in her veins. Had she been forgotten so quickly? But she recalled the look on her purple mother's face and something strong and sure inside her said *No*. Her purple mother would never forget her.

But did her purple mother know she was alive, like Leela did? If they were friends now—strange as that thought was—wouldn't Leela have told her?

There was a light tap on the door. "Are you all done,

miss?" the serving girl asked timidly.

"Yes, I'm coming," Sera said, pulling herself together.

The girl led her to an opulent stateroom with a large bed, gilt-framed paintings on the walls, and a velvet-covered love seat beneath a sizable porthole. She brushed Sera's hair until it shone, pinning up one side with a comb decorated with tiny blue mussel shells and dressing her in soft lavender silk that draped across her chest and left one shoulder bare, clasped at her other shoulder with a heavy brooch fashioned in the shape of a dragonfly. She tried to put a pair of golden sandals on Sera's feet but she flat-out refused. Cerulean did not wear shoes.

The servant led her to an even more opulent dining room, ushering her inside and closing the door. A huge oak table with an exquisite candelabra in its center was set for four. Instead of a porthole, there was a long rectangular window covered with delicate latticework. The walls were painted in muted mauve and maroon stripes, the chairs upholstered in burgundy and gold. A large oil painting of a haughty woman with a black dog at her side dominated the wall opposite the window.

Leo was the only one in the room, dressed in clothes similar to those he'd worn on the journey from Arbaz, though the shirt was pale blue and not cut quite so revealingly; the sash that cinched at his waist was a rich indigo and decorated with tiny crystals like stars. His eyes were lined in kohl and his curls fell loose, a crown of soft white scallop shells nestled among them. When he saw her, his whole face lit up. Sera felt an odd lurch in her chest.

"Oh, thank god," he said, hurrying over to her. "This

whole day has been surreal, hasn't it? For a second, I worried my grandmother might have locked you up too."

"Do you think she would do that?"

"No," Leo said. "She's just . . . she's pretty intimidating. But she's agreed to help us get to Braxos."

Sera's heart leaped. "Oh, Leo!" she exclaimed. "That's wonderful."

"Yeah," he agreed. "And for now she's taking us to Culinnon."

"But—but what about Agnes?"

"Her people will find Agnes," Leo said. He seemed so sure, but Sera had seen him feign confidence before. "What about you? Rahel didn't hurt you, did she? She promised me she wouldn't. But when I saw what you saw in her mind, how brutally she treated that poor servant girl, I thought, I don't know, maybe she would. She's certainly capable."

"You *saw* that?" Sera's head swam. Though she supposed if Leo had been able to witness her meeting with Leela, it might make sense that he'd see the memories alongside her.

"I guess having your magic inside me comes with all sorts of unexpected side effects," he said.

Sera found herself relieved and not unsettled by this connection. She did not mind the thought of having Leo in her head. He could understand her without her needing to explain and there was comfort in that. "Don't tell your grandmother," she said suddenly.

"Of course not," Leo said, like it had never even occurred to him.

She took his hand and squeezed it. "Thank you."

His cheeks turned a delicate shade of pink as the door opened and Ambrosine entered the room. She wore a heather-gray gown with ropes of diamonds strung about the waist, and long sheer sleeves. At her throat, a massive diamond pendant gleamed. Her hair was swept up in a net of lacquered jingle shells. A woman in a simple dress of pink satin with a pretty junonia headband followed meekly behind her.

"Well," Ambrosine said, her face alight as she took them in. "Don't you two make a handsome couple." She turned to the woman. "Don't they make a handsome couple, Bellamy?"

Bellamy had features like a mouse, small and furtive. She bobbed her head, a mass of frizzy brown curls. "Very handsome."

Sera thought Ambrosine might introduce them all properly but she only clapped her hands and servants spilled into the room, carrying trays and decanters. Ambrosine took her place at the head of the table, Bellamy far away at the opposite end. Leo and Sera took their seats on either side of Ambrosine. Sera could not help wondering why Bellamy was here, and who she was, and why she was sitting so far away from them.

"Leo told me you are vegetarian," Ambrosine said.

Sera flashed Leo a smile and he looked almost bashful.

"I didn't want you to be deprived of a meal," he said.

"Of course, it is no problem at all," Ambrosine said with a wave of her hand. "My chef is one of the most skilled in Pelago. If you said you only eat rocks, I'm sure she would have whipped up a delicacy of pebbles."

The servants laid a plate in front of Sera—it was filled

with a colorful salad of radish and heirloom tomato with a drizzle of lemon oil and a smattering of fresh herbs. It smelled delicious. Sera took a bite and had to suppress a moan of pleasure. She hadn't realized how hungry she was.

"It's good, isn't it?" Ambrosine said.

"Very," Sera said as another servant poured her a flute of pale gold sparkling wine.

"Now this is called scintillant," Ambrosine said as her own glass was filled. "It is made from a very special grape that only grows on Culinnon. It is the most coveted wine in all of Pelago." She raised her glass. "To family and new friends. May you both find everlasting happiness and peace here."

The wine was delicious, Sera had to admit—like peaches dipped in nectar, and it fizzed on her tongue.

"You will love Culinnon when you see it," Ambrosine continued. "Won't they love Culinnon, Bellamy?"

The mousy woman nearly dropped her fork at being addressed. "Yes. Very much. It is truly a magical place."

Leo and Sera exchanged a glance.

"But it is Braxos you need to get to," Ambrosine said to Sera. "How remarkable that it appeared just as you . . . arrived." Sera had never thought of it like that—that her presence on the planet had something to do with the reveal of Braxos.

"Yes, I suppose it is," she said, taking another sip of wine.

"As I was telling Bellamy earlier, it is simply marvelous that we have a chance to help my grandson's friend. His return to Pelago is a gift to the family, a gift that will only grow once dear Agnes is found and can join us."

"A gift," Bellamy agreed. Ambrosine's eyes flashed and the woman looked down at her plate, quickly shoving a tomato in her mouth.

"Are there more of your kind on Braxos?" Ambrosine asked, turning back to Sera.

She shook her head. "My City is tethered there. I am the only Cerulean on this planet."

"Fascinating." Ambrosine tapped her jaw with a bony finger. "Well, I have plenty of ships that can take us. I've lost some, of course, trying to find Braxos myself." She said it dismissively, but Sera got the sense that she was more upset by the loss than she let on. "But now you are here and can show us the way. I assume you know the way?"

Sera blinked but Leo said, "Of course she does." Sera was grateful that she didn't have to lie, but she didn't know how to get to Braxos any more than Ambrosine. She hoped Agnes would not abandon Errol. He was their only hope.

Sera also did not like the thought of taking Ambrosine to Braxos—but she was not in a position to do much about it. They needed to get past Culinnon and they needed a ship.

"You know, there are so many tales of the Lost Islands in this country," Ambrosine said as their salads were cleared and a second course of hazelnut profiteroles with blue cheese and grapes was set before them. "Many that involve the Byrnes directly, though we don't like to talk about that with outsiders. But since we are among family and . . ." She turned to Sera with a smile that felt vaguely poisonous. "Close friends, there's no harm in a little storytelling, is there? Perhaps you, Sera, can add your own tales as well."

"Are you family?" Leo asked, turning to Bellamy.

She started. "I'm—"

"Bellamy is my son Hektor's wife," Ambrosine said. "I take her with me whenever I travel. She brings me such comfort."

The words held the indistinct shadow of a threat. Bellamy's shoulders tensed and her lips twitched.

Ambrosine picked up the conversation as if there had not been any interruption. "There are stories of riches, of course, wealth beyond measure that await those who find a Lost Island, but those are dull. In the Byrne family, however, we know of an inexplicable power that resides there. Some say it is the power of time—past, present, and future accessible all at once. Or else the gift of immortality. Or perhaps the ability to compel those you wish to obey you. No one knows for sure." She looked to Sera, as if hoping she might affirm or contradict these tales.

"On Adereen they say the Lost Islands can allow you to speak to those who are dead," Bellamy piped up, then looked like she immediately regretted it.

"Why would you bring up such a sad topic over dinner?" Ambrosine snapped. "And in front of our honored guest? My sincerest apologies, Sera. Bellamy is not from a particularly noble family. Her manners can be atrocious at times."

"It's all right," Sera said. She wasn't offended in the slightest and tried to express that to Bellamy with her eyes, but the woman would not meet her gaze.

"My daughter-in-law is a little out of sorts, I'm afraid. She and my son have been trying to have a child for years.

She miscarried again recently, her sixth."

"Seventh." Bellamy barely whispered the word and yet Sera felt her own heart crack with the pain of it.

Ambrosine sighed and finished her wine as the main course of spinach and mushroom pie was set before them. "I admit we've all been a little worried, haven't we, Bellamy? But now, Leo, you are back, and Agnes too. All the Byrnes back where they ought to be. What a relief. I'm sure Alethea would have wanted you to see her home, to meet her family, to . . . to spend time connecting with your Byrne heritage." She paused. "Family is everything, isn't it?"

Bellamy looked close to tears. Ambrosine's remarks felt like needles, small but sharp.

"Now," Ambrosine said, cutting into her pie. "Sera, do tell me some about your City. Leo was frustratingly vague earlier."

Sera flashed him a grateful look and he gave a small shrug as if to say, of course. She told simple details, of the seresheep meadows and the stargem mines, the gold-tipped temple of Mother Sun and the great rush of the Estuary. She did not mention her magic or the sacrifice that caused her to come to the planet in the first place. By the time dessert was served, Sera felt exhausted.

"My goodness, look at the time," Ambrosine said, taking her last bite of raspberry sponge. "You both must be more than ready for bed."

As if on cue, Leo let out a wide yawn. "Sorry," he said. "We haven't slept well the past few days."

"Bellamy will escort you to your rooms," Ambrosine said. "I've lodged you on the same hall. I thought you would wish to be near each other. You seem such *close* friends."

Leo's cheeks turned pink, the way they did when he was embarrassed. They *were* close friends, though, weren't they? So why did it make Sera's tummy go all wriggly?

Bellamy led them to their rooms in silence. Sera was trying to think of something to say to her when she stopped abruptly.

"Here you are," she said. "I hope you had a pleasant dinner."

The words were mechanical, more obligation than warmth.

"It was very nice," Sera said. "I wish we could have spoken with you more."

Bellamy gazed at the red-carpeted floor. "She doesn't like it when I talk."

"We noticed," Leo said dryly.

"You must miss your husband very much," Sera said. "If Ambrosine always brings you with her when she travels."

Bellamy's eyes filled with tears. "She likes to take me away from him," she said. "A punishment."

"A punishment for what?" Sera asked.

"For marrying me." Bellamy ducked her head. "Good night." Then she turned and scurried down the hall.

Sera and Leo looked at each other.

"For being all about family, Ambrosine doesn't like her own daughter-in-law much," Leo mused.

"No," Sera agreed. "Poor thing."

"Ambrosine's going to be disappointed when she realizes you don't know how to get to Braxos."

"I know," she said wearily. "But we can face that hurdle another time."

Leo chuckled. "True. Let's get some sleep." As she moved to open her door, he said, "Sera?"

She turned and he was looking at her strangely, in a way that made her feel like her insides had turned to clouds, airy and weightless. "Yes?"

He cleared his throat. "You look beautiful tonight."

"Oh." Her heart picked up speed in her chest. "Thank you," she said. "So do you."

He laughed and she felt her magic stir inside her, embarrassed. Perhaps that had not been the right thing to say.

"See you in the morning," he said.

"In the morning," she repeated.

She barely noticed the grandeur of her room as she stripped off her dress and crawled into bed, and when she at last drifted off, she dreamt of an indigo sky covered with stars, and a crown of shells in a nest of curls.

18

AGNES

Matthias led Agnes and Vada to the very back of the library, to a solid copper door with an imposing lock.

He drew a ring of keys out of his pocket and used a large brass skeleton one to open it.

"These are the archives," he said. "They hold the largest collection of Pelago's most ancient texts."

The archives were dim and cool, with a domed ceiling and walls made of stone. Sconces held lamps with glass so thick it distorted the flame within. The air was dry and musty and smelled faintly of peppermint. The shelves contained all manner of written work, leather-bound books with peeling spines, scrolls with fraying edges piled on top of each other, sheaths of yellowing paper. They followed

Matthias to the back, where the oldest tomes were kept. Very carefully, he took a thick scroll out from where it sat in its own pigeonhole.

"These came from my family," he said. "Writings from one of the earliest matriarchs of the Byrnes, a woman named Agata. They were donated to the archives by my great-great-grandmother. I'm sure my mother wishes she could get them back, but they belong to the university now. She came today, though, to read them. Secretly too—if the Triumvirate knew she was in Ithilia, they'd call her to Banrissa. It was the first time I'd seen her in . . . oh, years now. Not since Hektor's wedding." He held out the scroll to Agnes. "You should read this. It's part of your history too, after all."

The paper was so thin, she worried it would disintegrate in her hands. Vada leaned over her shoulder as they read. Most of the words were illegible, smudged or faded with time. But there was enough left that Agnes could piece together.

> . . . *set out to explore the north and discovered . . .*
> *island with palace atop a cliff. Jewels filled the*
> *waters . . . wanted to turn back but we had come too*
> *far to return to Culinnon with nothing . . . my duty*
> *as a Byrne for the f . . . a power greater than anything*
> *I ever thought possible . . . past, present, and future,*
> *all contained in . . . spoke to me and gave gifts that*
> *will keep this family strong for generations to come.*
> *I did not think at the time to . . . fog descended and*
> *became . . . off course and for days . . . there is more*
> *I know there is more. And it rightfully belongs . . .*

power that this country could not even begin to
understand . . . will be tied to Culinnon for all time
and therefore must be protected at all . . . rested and
will journey again once the leg has healed. I must
return to the island. It calls to me. It belongs to . . .

"An island," Agnes murmured. "With a palace atop a cliff. This scroll is speaking of Braxos."

"I am not liking the sound of this power greater than anything possible," Vada said darkly.

"But we know Braxos holds power," she said. "It has the tether."

"How do we know that is what this scroll speaks of?" Vada said. "If humans cannot see the tether, as Sera says, then perhaps this Byrne is meaning something else."

Agnes bit her lip. "Past, present, and future together, it says . . . and the power she found is tied to Culinnon somehow." She looked up at her uncle. "Did she ever go back?"

"No," Matthias said, running a hand over his thinning hair. "And she disappeared trying to find the island again. In our family it has long been known that she was searching for a Lost Island. It was just never known which one." Then he frowned. "What is this tether you mentioned?"

"It's . . ." Agnes debated how much she should tell him. "I can't really explain it, except it's the thing my friend needs to get home. It's on Braxos—that's why we need to get her there."

Matthias sighed. "Agnes, it is valiant of you to want to help a friend, but I do not think anyone will ever reach Braxos. The waters are too dangerous, the fog too thick.

Even Agata could not find it again."

"We've got a navigator," Agnes said. "He's certain he can get us to the island."

"How much have you paid him?" Matthias asked warily.

Vada grinned. "Not a single aurum."

"He doesn't need paying," Agnes said. "Not that way. Besides, until we get Sera and Leo back, we aren't going anywhere." She paused. "What does Agata mean when she says gifts?"

Matthias opened his mouth but was interrupted by his own name.

"Matthias Byrne!" The voice that echoed through the library was rich and full of authority. Matthias started.

"Stay here," he hissed. "Stay out of sight."

Then he hurried out of the archives. Agnes and Vada crept forward at the same time, slipping through the doors and staying hidden behind the shelves. They peered over a row of books and saw an attractive, imposing woman standing in the central area, her sleek black hair unadorned, dressed all in maroon with a soft gray cape draped over one shoulder and pinned with a bronze brooch crafted in the shape of five stars.

"Nadia," he said, making a hasty bow. "What a pleasant surprise."

"Did you know?" Nadia demanded without preamble.

"Know what?" Matthias blinked at her.

"What your mother was planning to do."

"My mother does not share her confidences with me."

"Ambrosine was here, though." Matthias's face flushed

a blotchy red and Nadia pursed her lips. "Don't try to deny it, Matthias; you've always been a terrible liar."

"Yes, she was here. She wanted to see the archives. I let her. The archives are open to any who asks to visit them. You know that better than anyone."

Nadia gave him a wry smile and shook her head. "Let us sit," she said. "The news I carry has wearied me."

They took a seat at one of the tables. "What news?" Matthias asked. "How can I be of service to the Lekke?"

Agnes felt as if a spider had crawled down her throat and was scuttling around in her stomach. Matthias was working with the Lekke? But he'd told Agnes to stay hidden. If he wanted to sell her out to the Triumvirate, he certainly had the chance now and wasn't taking it.

"There will be a council soon. The Aerin is calling for war against Kaolin. You know how the Lekke feels about violence." Matthias nodded. "The decision to close the ports weighed heavily on her. As does the fighting that erupts there daily. She hates to see her country torn so. And now Ambrosine has made matters worse."

"What has my mother done?" Matthias asked.

"She has attacked Princess Rahel's pleasure ship," Nadia said. "And taken the Byrne and his companion away with her."

Agnes felt relief wash over her, heady as a dream. Her grandmother had Leo and Sera. They were safe.

Matthias did not seem to be having the same reaction Agnes was. He leaned forward and put his head in his hands. "Oh no."

"Yes," Nadia said. "It was the worst possible move at

the worst possible moment. Now the Renalt is more inclined to take action. She is even threatening to leave Banrissa and sail after Ambrosine herself."

Matthias took off his glasses and cleaned them on his sleeve. "Damn my mother," he muttered.

"The Lekke requires your advice before the council is convened and the vote for war is taken. I have been sent to bring you to her." She leaned forward and placed a hand on his knee. "Your queen needs you now, my friend. She needs the honest and unflinching guidance you have given her throughout your years of service."

Matthias took a deep, fortifying breath. "Yes," he said. "All right. Tell the Lekke I will arrive at Banrissa within the hour."

Nadia stood in one fluid movement. "I will never understand how you are related to that family."

He flashed her a watery smile. "Not all Byrnes are like my mother," he said. "You never met Alethea. She was . . ." He swallowed hard. "She was the very best of us."

Nadia turned and was gone in a swoop of her cape. Agnes didn't realize Vada had been clutching her arm until she released it and the blood flowed prickling into her fingers. Matthias yelped when he saw them hidden behind the shelf.

"I told you to stay in the archives," he said.

"You work for the Triumvirate?" Agnes demanded.

"I advise the Lekke when she requests it," Matthias said. "And, as you plainly saw, I have no interest in revealing your presence here in Ithilia. But you must leave the city at once."

"That's the plan," Vada said.

Matthias was shaking his head slowly. "I never thought she would go so far as to actually physically attack the Triumvirate. Whatever scheme she has been stewing on for years, it seems the time is finally ripe to act. I fear for what that means for my country. It is bad enough, this threat from Kaolin. It is worse if we tear ourselves apart from the inside." He placed a hand on Agnes's shoulder. "I am grateful I got the chance to meet you."

"Me too," Agnes said, her throat tight.

"She'll be taking your brother and your friend to Culinnon," Matthias said. "That is where you must go. Leave at dawn; that's usually when the docks are quietest. Misarros are patrolling the waters heavily."

"What are you going to advise the Lekke to do?" Agnes asked.

"That is a very good question. But one you need not concern yourself with. I wish I could offer you better advice—in truth, I would tell you to avoid my mother altogether. But I know you cannot do that. I see Alethea's stubbornness in you. She would not abandon a friend she had promised to help."

Her mother would have done what she was doing. Her mother would have approved. Agnes looked around at the shelves and balconies towering above her. There was no way she could sit her interview now. She would have to give up this dream, to help Sera and get back to her brother.

Matthias seemed to read her thoughts. "You are thinking about your acceptance to this university," he said.

Agnes shrugged and hoped she looked nonchalant. "It's all right. Maybe I can apply again next year."

"There is no interview, Agnes. It was all a formality. My mother used it in hopes of getting you to Pelago. You have already been accepted to the Academy of Sciences— she decreed it since the day you sent in your application. But she hopes that once she gets you to Culinnon, you won't want to leave."

Agnes's head spun and the ground seemed to tilt beneath her. "Are you saying . . . I didn't . . . qualify?"

Matthias gave her a sympathetic smile. "I read your essay—I promise you, Agnes, you are eminently qualified. My mother just doesn't think Byrnes need to follow the rules like everyone else."

Hot tears filled her eyes but she didn't want to cry, not yet, not here. They had a job to do, a purpose, a mission. Her grandmother buying her way into the university shouldn't matter right now. And yet somehow it did.

"We have to go," she said. "We have to get to Leo and Sera."

Vada put a gentle hand on her shoulder but Agnes shrugged it off. She didn't want comfort right now. She didn't know what she wanted.

"I do hope to see you again, Agnes," Matthias said. Then he grinned, quick and catlike. "The semester begins at the end of the month."

Agnes managed a nod and left the library in a daze, Vada following close behind. She walked down the steps back to their waiting *metapar* on wooden legs, climbing into the seat as Vada said, "Take us to the Street of Lies. Bas's Secret."

The cart lurched forward. Agnes was dimly aware of the streets they wound through, but all the colors and sounds blurred together.

"This isn't how I wanted it to be," she said after a while. Her voice was thick with emotion. "I was supposed to deserve a spot, not have it gifted to me because of my family name."

"Hey," Vada said. "Do not be so cruel to yourself. You are the smartest person I know, Agnes McLellan, and one of the bravest too. Your grandmother did what grandmothers do—she tried to take care of you. Adults are not always knowing what is best for us."

Agnes shook her head. A tear slid down her cheek and Vada brushed it away with her thumb, a simple gesture that held more meaning than Agnes could put into words. True, her acceptance was not what she thought it would be. But Vada was here, Vada was touching her, comforting her.

"I am thinking you will be making one of Pelago's premier scientists," Vada declared.

"You're just saying that to make me feel better."

"Perhaps. But why would that mean it is not also true?"

Agnes gave in to the smile that rose up inside her and allowed herself to melt a little into Vada's arms. She could feel Vada's heart beat against her shoulder and it was exciting and calming all at once.

There were other things to consider anyway, she thought as the cart bumped along the streets of Ithilia. Her grandmother had attacked that princess. Leo and Sera were safe for now. She hoped Vada knew how to get to Culinnon. Her stomach pinched at the thought of this mystical island she never knew existed that would one day be hers.

She wondered if Ambrosine knew her estranged son was working for a member of the Triumvirate. Probably—her grandmother seemed like the type who knew everything.

The *metapar* rolled to a halt and Agnes looked around. They were on a narrow street lit with colorful paper lanterns. Wild music spilled out of the crooked restaurants and bars that lined the cobbled road, and the people here were dressed in slinky clothes and seemed like the sort who would not be out of place in Old Port's East Village—artists and musicians and philosophers.

"Where are we?" Agnes asked as Vada jumped down to pay the driver.

"The Street of Lies," Vada said. "Bas's Secret is one of my favorite spots in all of Ithilia. They have the best plum wine in Pelago and I am thinking we could both use a drink."

Agnes allowed herself to be led into a bar with no sign, just a painting of Bas above it, the goddess reclining naked, her long black hair covering her more sensitive parts, her red skin shining dully.

Inside, everything was red and black. Red painted walls with black tables, lamps with red-and-black checkered shades perched on each one. Smoke swirled through the air and there was a small stage in one corner with a jazz quartet playing. The bar itself was fashioned out of a coffin, Agnes realized, which seemed awfully morbid yet also appropriate for a place named after the goddess of death.

"Vada," the bartender said with a smile as she approached. She was a wizened old woman with gnarled hands and a gold tooth. "It's been a while since I've seen your face around here." She eyed Agnes curiously. "Who's your friend?"

"We need a table and to use your washroom, Neve," Vada said.

The bartender laughed. "I could smell the sea on you when you walked in the door." She reached behind the bar and handed Vada a small silver key. "Lock up when you're done."

The washroom was tiny and cramped, with only a sink and some towels and a bar of patchouli-scented soap. Vada stripped out of her vest and unbuttoned her shirt before Agnes even had a second to think. She turned away quickly, her face hot, but not before she caught a glimpse of Vada's lean torso and small firm breasts. Agnes's heart was pummeling against her chest as she waited for Vada to finish washing. Desire and anxiety warred inside her, along with the abrupt inexplicable fear that Vada did not want Agnes the same way Agnes wanted her.

"It is nice to be feeling clean again," Vada said. "Even if only a little."

"Mm-hm," Agnes said. She began to unbutton her vest, but slowly, hoping Vada would be done by the time she stripped it off, and also sort of hoping she wouldn't.

But she peeled the vest off and turned to find Vada fully clothed.

"I will be getting us drinks and a table," she said. "Come find me when you are finished."

Agnes forced herself to nod, holding her breath until Vada left. She quickly washed her face and chest and under her arms, drying herself with a towel and feeling the buzzing of nerves in her stomach.

Vada was at a table with a carafe of plum wine and a plate of olives and feta cheese. "Wait until you try this," she said, pouring them each a drink. "You will never want to be drinking anything else."

Agnes took a sip of wine—it was strong and rich with a fruity aftertaste. She found she quite liked it.

"Ah! There is the smile I was hoping for," Vada said. "Tonight, we drink, we laugh, we enjoy ourselves. At dawn, we leave for Culinnon." She shook her head. "Never in my life did I think I would be setting my sails in the direction of that island."

By the time they finished the carafe, Agnes was feeling much better. Her shoulders were relaxed, her pulse not so rapid, a hazy calm settling over her.

"What is that look?" Vada asked slyly, and Agnes realized a dreamy expression had spread across her face.

"I'm going to be a scientist," she said.

Vada's smile was like a flash of sunlight on still water. "Yes," she said, leaning in close. "You are." She ran her fingers through a lock of Agnes's hair and Agnes shuddered with want, the muscles in her thighs tightening. "I am liking this mane. You are a lion on the outside as well as the inside now."

When Agnes spoke her voice was rough as sandpaper. "Thank you," she said, "for sticking with me."

Vada's feline eyes held Agnes's with an intensity they

never had before. They were so close, Agnes could count every freckle on the bridge of her nose, see each individual eyelash. She felt her breath stop in her chest. Very slowly, as if not wanting to frighten her, Vada took Agnes's face in her hands, her fingers calloused and sure. Agnes stayed as still as she could as Vada leaned in and kissed her softly on the lips.

Agnes had never dreamed she would be kissed by a sailor in a smoky bar in Ithilia. She never dreamed she would really be kissed at all. Vada leaned in again and this time their kiss deepened; she melted into the feel of Vada's mouth on hers, the taste of plum and salt on her tongue. Without stopping to think if she should, she wound one arm around Vada's waist, her other hand sinking into the girl's thick auburn hair. By the time they broke apart, she was breathless.

"We are needing more wine, I think," Vada said with a grin. Agnes barely managed a nod. Vada laughed and kissed her again, then got up to head to the bar. Agnes sat back, her head swimming. She had been *kissed*. She touched her lips gently, feeling dizzy, and bemused, and so very happy.

Vada returned and refilled their glasses. She laughed when she saw Agnes's expression. "You are looking at me like I am some kind of treat."

"You are to me," Agnes said. Vada's expression softened and she pulled Agnes toward her for another kiss.

There was a faint tinkling of bells as the door opened and two men walked in, one red-haired, one brown. The brown-haired man had a thick, bushy beard, and hair as wild as the sea, and Agnes felt there was something familiar about him, something she couldn't quite place . . .

"Oh my god," she gasped, and slid down in her seat, covering her face with her hands.

"What?" Vada looked around. "What is it?"

Agnes peered through her fingers, her suspicions confirmed. It couldn't be, though. It *couldn't*.

"Agnes?" Vada shook her.

"Those two men at the bar," Agnes said. "You see the one with the brown hair and beard?"

Agnes looked at Vada and her heart felt as though it was pounding through wet concrete.

"That's my father."

19

AGNES

WHAT WAS HE *DOING* HERE?

Agnes kept her face covered with her hands until Vada hissed, "Stop that, you are not looking normal," so she picked up her glass of plum wine and downed it in one gulp, nearly choking on the richness. Vada refilled both of their glasses and adjusted her seat so that she was partially screening Agnes.

"It is dark in here, remember, and you are not looking at all the Kaolin lady you were when you first boarded the *Maiden's Wail*," she said.

"Right," Agnes said breathlessly. "Right."

She peered over Vada's shoulder and saw her father deep in conversation with the bartender, who was treating him with a sort of surly familiarity. Her father's beard had all grown out; she recognized the other man as Kiernan, but his face was ruddy and wind chapped. Xavier had been looking for Braxos like everyone else, but Agnes never in a million years dreamed he'd actually come looking for it *himself.*

And what could possibly have compelled him to come to this bar of all places? It wasn't the sort of spot Agnes would ever have pictured her father patronizing, regardless of the country.

Whatever the bartender told him got a strong reaction from her father. His face grew stony, but at the same time his eyes seemed to burn. He shot another question at her and his reaction was, if anything, scarier—he began to laugh. He ordered a drink, took it in one long draft, then slammed the glass down on the bar. Kiernan said something to him and Xavier snapped back a response. Agnes nearly fainted with relief as they headed for the door. She held her breath until they were good and gone, then sat back and took a sip of wine, her blood pounding in her temples.

"Let's see what he was looking for," Vada said, standing and gesturing to Agnes to follow her to the bar. "Got a cigarette for me, Neve?" she asked the bartender sweetly.

The woman pursed her lips and reached into her pocket, pulling out a pretty silver case and opening it. Vada took a cigarette and lit it using one of the thick black candles decorating the bar. She exhaled a long stream of smoke and smiled. "Thanks. Hey, was that some Kaolin asshole I saw giving you attitude?"

"Aye, it was," Neve said, then spit on the floor. "You know him?"

"Nah, the beard gave it away." Vada flicked some ash off her cigarette. "What was he after?"

The bartender snorted. "You're too young to remember it all. That there was Xavier McLellan, the one who married Alethea Byrne and stole her away to Kaolin. He used to come in here all the time back when he was courting her. Courting her money more like, but that's none of my business. He's even staying at the inn on the Street o' Leaves, just like he used to. Old habits, I suppose."

Agnes's fingers clutched at her glass so tight she feared she might break it. Her father had met her mother in Pelago. *In Pelago.* She'd always assumed Alethea had come to Old Port.

Not to mention spending his nights *here.* It was almost too impossible for Agnes to believe, except she'd seen him with her own eyes and the bartender had no reason to lie.

"Lucky he was docking in Ithilia at all," Vada said. "Misarros and soldiers everywhere, locking up Kaolins left and right."

"Aye, but he knows the city plus he's got a Pelagan with him, red-haired fellow. Asking about Ambrosine, they were. Told 'em she'd cut off the passages to the Lost Islands. Didn't like that much. His attitude changed, though, when I told him about Princess Rahel's ship. You hear about that?"

Vada nodded.

Neve whistled. "She's gone and done it now, Ambrosine has. Xavier laughed like it was the funniest thing he'd heard in his life. Anyway, I told him if he wanted to escape the dungeons of Banrissa, he'd best be leaving and leaving soon."

"That was uncommonly nice of you," Vada said.

Neve shrugged. "He's a good tipper. Always was, still is. I remember one night, he took out Alethea and her whole entourage—she was always surrounded by actors and musicians and sculptors, the sort who are looking for a wealthy patron. Alethea didn't care a fig about money." She gave a derisive grunt. "Those who have it never do. They kept drinking and he kept buying. Were here until close. Left me a fat pile of aurums."

"Was that impressing Alethea?" Vada asked.

Neve chuckled. "Weren't you listening? Alethea didn't care about money. She liked him because he was different. Don't get more different than a Kaolin in Pelago. Besides," she said, pouring herself a shot and downing it, "it pissed her mother off and there's nothing a daughter enjoys more than that."

Vada finished her drink. "Thanks for the cig and the gossip, Neve," she said, tossing a couple aurums on the counter. "See you around."

Once they were outside, Agnes gulped the cool air.

"It is a lot to be processing," Vada agreed.

"My father met my mother *here*?" she cried. "In Pelago? In Ithilia? In *this* bar?" Agnes leaned against the wall of Bas's Secret and put her hands on her knees. "No one ever told me. Not even Eneas. Why would they keep this from me?"

"Your father is hating Pelago," Vada said. "Why would he wish to admit he met his wife here?"

That was a fair point.

"Where is this inn Neve mentioned?" Agnes asked.

"The one my father is staying at."

The one he had stayed at before, she said. It was bizarre to learn her father had regular spots in Ithilia.

"I am thinking she meant the Old Waves Inn," Vada said.

"Take me there," Agnes said.

The Street of Leaves was a narrow, winding road paved with a patchwork of smooth slate. The inn was perched at its top—Agnes had a clear view of Banrissa, illuminated against the night sky at the summit of the cliff.

Agnes and Vada approached the inn, which was made of white stucco with seashells inlaid along its door. The roof was simple and thatched, a curl of smoke winding its way out of the chimney. Light spilled from the large front window, open to let out the sound of voices. Agnes heard her father say, "We leave tomorrow." Then he chuckled. "Ambrosine is going to bring the whole Triumvirate down on her."

Her heart skipped and she looked at Vada and pressed her finger to her lips. Vada nodded and they crept forward, keeping out of the light.

Kiernan and Xavier sat together in the corner, right next to the open window. A map was laid out on the table before them, stretched between two mugs of dark beer and a plate of grilled sardines.

"We can't underestimate her," Kiernan said. "If she's confident enough to openly attack Princess Rahel's ship, she must have some plan in place."

"Why, Ezra. I didn't know you had so much admiration for her."

Kiernan's ruddy cheeks turned redder. "It's not admiration, it's the truth. I didn't want to come back here at all, if you recall. You promised me—"

Xavier's mouth twisted. "I promised to get you away from her and I did. I never promised I wouldn't bring you back. Don't worry, Ezra. I don't want her to get her hands on you any more than you do."

Kiernan wiped his forehead with a handkerchief. "I wish I believed that."

"So now you don't trust me?" Her father took a long drink of beer, then traced a line on the map with one finger. "She'll take them to Culinnon. Whichever one she's got, Leo or Agnes, that's where she'll go." He gave a snort. "How rich, if she only has Leo. She'll be so disappointed."

Agnes felt a surge of protectiveness for her brother.

"More bodies are washing up on the northern islands each day," Kiernan said. "And none of the ships that have left have returned. The last dispatch was from a schooner called the *Desperation*—such an unfortunate name—and all it said was, *Fog too dense. Must turn back*." He swallowed. "They found the captain's body on the shores of Adereen two days later. No sign of the ship or the rest of the crew."

"These stories don't scare me, Ezra."

Kiernan sighed and popped a sardine in his mouth. "I wish they would," he grumbled.

"She knows something," Xavier growled. "You're right, if she's confident enough to outright attack the Triumvirate, something's changed." He tapped the table with one finger. "Matthias might know."

Agnes felt she shouldn't be surprised that her father knew Matthias after all the revelations tonight, but somehow she still was.

"I highly doubt that," Kiernan said.

Xavier smirked. "Scared of a reunion? Matthias has no bite, Ezra, you don't have to be afraid of him."

Kiernan muttered something that made her father laugh, and it sent a chill down Agnes's spine. Then he drained the last of his mug and set it down. "It's late," he said. "And we must get an early start tomorrow." He scratched his chin. "I need to shave. I stand out far too much with this damned beard."

He stood and Agnes quickly pressed herself against the wall of the inn. She listened as their footsteps receded and the common room grew quiet. Next to her, Vada let out a low whistle.

"He's after Ambrosine," she said.

Agnes wasn't sure exactly what her father was after, but one thing was certain—he was headed to the same place she was. To Leo and Sera.

"We can't let him get his hands on Sera again," she said. She felt so small, stuck between these two imposing forces, her father and her grandmother. "Or on Leo. Or me. We've got to leave Ithilia. Tonight, *now*. We can't wait for dawn."

"It is too dark," Vada protested.

A slow grin spread across Agnes's face. "Not with Errol it isn't."

They hurried back to the docks and as soon as they boarded the *Palma*, Errol's head popped up out of the water.

Agnes smiled and took a piece of dried apple out of one of the satchels for him.

"Errol," she said, settling down at the sloop's edge. "We've got to leave now, tonight. Sera has gone to another island and we need to go there to find her. We need you to light our way. We have to sail to Culinnon."

At the sound of that name, Errol straightened and his lights burned in a flash of brilliant purple. Agnes and Vada exchanged a glance.

"Errol, do you know Culinnon?" Agnes said.

Again the lights blinked purple. Agnes leaned forward. "We need to get there quickly. Sera is going to Culinnon. Do you understand? Sera. Culinnon."

Errol snapped his teeth at them and flashed orange-magenta-white. Agnes got the distinct impression he was exasperated by her, as if he was saying yes, of course I understand.

Once Vada had readied the ship, Errol's scales began to glow greenish gold. He snapped his teeth again, then gestured with one scaly claw. As he slid beneath the waves, a beacon of light guiding their way, Vada let out the sail and Agnes felt a burst of hope in the dark night.

They were on their way. To Culinnon.

20

LEO

THEY HAD BEEN AT SEA A WEEK ON THE MORNING LEO'S grandmother burst into his cabin with news.

"A dove has come," Ambrosine said imperiously as Leo yanked the covers up over his bare chest, squinting around in the sunlight.

"Huh?" was all he could muster, his brain foggy with sleep.

She took a seat at the armchair by his porthole as Mckenna, the young servant girl, rushed in with a tray of coffee and breakfast pastries.

"From Ithilia," Ambrosine said, waving a small scroll at him as Mckenna poured her coffee. The smell of it filled his cabin, mixing with the buttery scent of the pastries, and Leo's stomach growled. He grabbed the robe that hung beside his bed and slipped it on as the serving girl handed him his own cup. He smiled at her gratefully and she blushed. Mckenna was always blushing around him.

"That will be all, Mckenna," Ambrosine said, and she scuttled from the room.

Pelago didn't have a telegraph system like Kaolin, Leo had learned, but instead used trained doves to deliver messages. Ambrosine had been waiting for a message since the day they left Ithilia and it seemed at last, news had finally arrived. Leo took a bracing sip of his coffee.

Ambrosine unfurled the scroll and Leo caught a glimpse of triumph in her expression. "Your sister made it to Ithilia," she said.

Leo's shoulders relaxed. "Agnes is okay?"

"She met my son Matthias—he is the university librarian." She said it as if it were something to be ashamed of. "There was another girl her age traveling with her."

"Vada," Leo said with relief.

"It appears they have a ship. They would certainly have heard of my attack on Rahel and my rescuing of you and Sera. Matthias would know I am headed to Culinnon. Let us hope he has instructed them to sail here at once."

She didn't sound certain, Leo was surprised to hear. From what he'd gathered from his time on the galleon, Ambrosine commanded ironclad obedience from everyone around her, her family most especially.

"That's great news," he said.

"There was a war council as well," she continued. "The Triumvirate has voted. Three to zero. War has been declared on Kaolin." She grinned wickedly. "Even the Lekke, after all this time, has finally found her backbone." She slapped her thigh. "But that's not all, Leo. The Renalt has *left Banrissa*!"

"And that's . . . good?"

Ambrosine's displeasure showed in the faintest pursing of her lips. "Of course you wouldn't know, your hateful father and his hateful ways. The queens rarely leave Banrissa, usually only for ceremonies or the occasional holiday. But she has taken her warships. She is coming after *me*."

Leo felt that the news of being hunted down personally by a queen should not have been said with such eager anticipation.

"The Triumvirate is fracturing even as we sit here sipping our coffee," Ambrosine said. "Oh, it is better than I could have ever hoped. I should have sunk Rahel's ridiculous pleasure ship years ago." Then she frowned. "No, I was right to wait. Agnes is coming." She looked up at Leo like she'd forgotten him. "And you are here too! And Sera. No, my patience has paid off."

"Great," Leo said, though inside he felt queasy. Ambrosine had not been entirely able to hide her disappointment that Leo was not Agnes—he knew she'd rather have his sister here than him. For all her talk of the importance of family, it was the women who really mattered, not the men. Every night at dinner they had been treated to a new story about some Byrne matriarch or other, of brutal punishments meted out to enemies or heroic deeds of exploration and advancement. "I'll leave you to dress. We are nearly at Culinnon."

"We are?" For the past two days there had been nothing except sky and sea stretching out around them. In the beginning of the journey they had seen the coastlines of other islands, the waters dotted with ships. But the farther north they went, the colder it got and the emptier the ocean became.

Ambrosine gazed out his porthole. "I can always feel when it's close," she murmured. "It calls to me."

Leo shuddered. Without another word, Ambrosine strode out of his cabin. Meetings with his grandmother left him with the feeling of being doused in cold water. He munched on a cinnamon roll as he picked out clothes for the day. No more billowing silk shirts and sashes. In the north, they wore thick cable-knit sweaters and heavy woolen pants.

He found Sera standing at the rail, gazing out over the whitecapped waves. Gray clouds blanketed the sky, heavy with impending rain. Leo shivered despite his sweater. Sera wore a fur-lined cloak with the hood down, her blue hair flowing in a river down her back.

"Agnes and Vada made it to Ithilia," he said as he approached her. "My grandmother just got a message."

"They did?" she exclaimed. "Oh, Leo, how wonderful."

"Ambrosine says they have a boat, so they should be heading to Culinnon." He told her about the declaration of war and the Renalt's decision to pursue Ambrosine herself. Sera's excited expression faded.

"War," she muttered. "Why must humans fight against each other? *Kill* each other. For what?" She looked out across the sea again.

"I guess it's just in our nature," Leo said.

She shook her head. "I don't think so. I think sometimes you forget who you are, or what is truly important in this world. . . ."

He felt like she was talking about something else, as if he'd interrupted her during a moment of deep contemplation.

"The moonstone?" he asked. He knew she'd been consumed with it, hoping to see more of her City. She'd had visions here and there—one of the gardens that surrounded the temple at night, one of the houses where all the purple mothers were waiting to get pregnant, and one in that spooky underground place but with no Leela this time. The visions felt scrambled, she'd told him, blurry. Leo thought the moonstone was acting like a radio with a busted antenna. It was trying to connect Sera and her City to the same frequency but static kept getting in the way.

"No," she said, her hand moving to caress the pendant. "The moonstone is the same. I do wish I could speak to Leela again, though." She turned her eyes toward the clouds. "I hope she's all right."

Leo did too, but Leela's dangers were far away and theirs were very much real and, apparently, chasing after them. He didn't want to imagine what would happen if the Renalt and her warships caught up with Ambrosine's galleon. Even if they made it to Culinnon, was the island's magic strong enough to protect them? Leo still wasn't even entirely sure what magic Culinnon possessed. It just sounded like a very pretty place so far, and that wouldn't help withstand cannons or gunfire.

"I was thinking about Rahel," Sera said.

"Really?"

"Well, not about *her* but about her memory. I think the memories can serve a purpose. This power of my people may have been lost for a time, but I am on the planet now and my magic is stronger than I have ever felt it before. In the City Above the Sky, we blood bond with each other to read hearts. It is sacred because we share ourselves, open our minds to each other the way you and I did when we bonded."

Even now, when Leo recalled that night in the theater, he could still see the memories they'd shared as clearly as if it had happened yesterday.

"But with this self blood bond, it is not the same," she continued. "Rahel did not see into my mind. And I was able to make her *feel* something."

"Yeah, she was pretty freaked out," he agreed.

Sera was shaking her head. "No, Leo," she said. "I made her feel *shame*."

"Oh." Leo hadn't thought about it like that.

"I've been wondering," Sera said, and she turned her back on the ocean and looked out across the deck. "If perhaps I can use it to instigate other emotions. Good ones. Or . . . I don't know, meaningful ones. Perhaps this was a way the Cerulean were able to spend time on planets. Sensing emotions, calming the occupants or making connections with them using their own memories."

"I can feel a plan being formed," Leo said, and Sera flashed him a mischievous grin that sent his heart tripping over itself.

"I am not trying to take this power lightly," she said.

"But I was just hoping I could test out this theory, this ability, and at the same time, give a gift to someone I think deserves one very much."

Leo followed her gaze to where Bellamy was standing at the prow of the ship, still as stone, her frizzy hair caught up in the wind. His chest grew tight.

"You're a very good person, Sera Lighthaven," he said.

"I haven't done anything yet."

"No," he said, offering her his arm. "But you will."

They walked over to Bellamy, who started when she heard them coming.

"Good morning," she said politely.

"Good morning, Bellamy," Sera said. "We were . . ." She looked to Leo, uncertain, and he gave her an encouraging nod. Sera cleared her throat. "I was hoping I might . . . I was wondering . . ."

Leo had never seen her so flustered. But then Bellamy looked away, back out over the prow.

"We are almost to Culinnon," she said. "Ambrosine always knows when we are close." Her fingers tightened on the rail. That small movement seemed to loosen something within Sera.

"You miss your husband very much, don't you," she said.

Bellamy tensed, then nodded.

"I can help you see him," Sera said. "Right here, right now."

Bellamy whirled around, eyes wide. "You can?"

"But it would have to be our secret," Leo said quickly, foreseeing the danger. "My grandmother can't know."

"A secret?" Bellamy said, tempted but uncertain.

"Ambrosine has plenty of secrets of her own," Leo said. "It only seems fair that we have some ourselves."

A slow smile crept across Bellamy's face. "A secret," she said. "All right."

Sera squeezed Leo's arm, then released him. "This might be a little startling," she said. "But I promise I won't hurt you."

Bellamy was only allowed a moment of shock before Sera's eyes began to glow, brighter and brighter until they burned, and Leo once again felt a gentle wind ripple over his body, freezing him in place as she drew up their veils of memory, of life. He couldn't see them—Sera had told him that they were colorful and that his was a patchwork of grays and greens. He wondered what colors Bellamy's veil was, and what thread Sera was plucking from it now. And then he saw, as clearly as he'd seen Sera's memories in the theater and Rahel's on the ship.

Bellamy was much younger, lounging in a rowboat with a man with dark blue eyes and handsome, hawkish features. One of her hands dangled in the water amid lily pads and lotus blossoms while the man rummaged through a picnic basket.

"Will you read me another poem, Hektor?" she asked.

"In a moment, my love," Hektor replied. "I'm just looking for . . . ah! Found it."

Bellamy giggled. "What on earth has kept your nose in that basket for so long?"

Hektor's cheeks flushed. "I seem to have misplaced my heart," he said, holding out his hand. "It appears to be yours now." In his palm was a small silver ring with a tiny snail shell in its setting in place of a jewel. "Would you do me the privilege of spending the rest of your life with me?"

Bellamy clapped her hands over her mouth, tears filling her eyes. For a long moment, she did not speak. "Hektor," she finally choked out.

"Is that a yes?"

Her eyes shone, then turned wary. "But what about your mother?"

"I'm not frightened of her."

Bellamy gave Hektor a look that plainly said, Liar.

"Fine, maybe I am a little, but it's my life, isn't it? Alethea got to marry who she wanted; why shouldn't I?"

"Oh, darling, you know it's not the same," Bellamy said, cupping his face in her palm.

"Is that a no?" Hektor asked, real fear in his voice.

Bellamy leaned forward so she could kiss him. "It is a yes. A thousand times yes."

He took her in his arms and she cried against his chest. "I have never loved anyone in my life but you," he murmured into her hair.

And then they were kissing again and the memory dissolved.

Leo could still feel the tingles in his stomach, the yearning for physical affection, a side effect of the memory share. He'd felt what Bellamy had felt, yet it was also mixing with his own feelings, the ones he fought against every night after he'd left Sera and closed the door to his room. Bellamy was frozen in shock but Sera was looking at him, and the expression on her face was . . . strange. Almost like she was seeing a different version of him.

Then she reached out very slowly and ran her fingers down the back of his hand. "Leo," she said, and his insides shivered.

"By the goddesses," Bellamy gasped, coming alive at precisely the worst moment. She gulped at the air. "What . . . what . . ."

Sera turned to her and the spell was broken. Leo felt himself shaking. He wanted her eyes back on him, wanted her fingers back on his skin.

"It was like I was there again," Bellamy was saying. "On that very day."

"Yes," Sera said. "I wanted to give you something to hold on to. A gift. Of love. You love him very much."

A tear fell on Bellamy's cheek. "I do. I . . ." She gazed out over the ocean again. "You know, she didn't let us marry for six years after that day. Six years and three other engagements, all made without his consent, all broken. You'd think after Alethea, Ambrosine might have figured out the sort of people her children are. But they aren't really people to her. They are pieces on a game board."

It was the most Leo had ever heard Bellamy say.

She turned to Sera, her face fearful. "You can never let her know about this. This power you possess. She will try and take it from you. She will never let you go."

Suddenly, a bell rang out from the mainmast and the water around the ship began to churn, waves frothing and raging against the hull.

"What's happening?" Leo asked. Bellamy seemed remarkably calm as a dark strip of land appeared in the distance.

"Leo, look!" Sera gasped. "There's so many of them."

"So many of what?" he asked.

And then he saw.

The ocean was filled with the colorful lights of hundreds and hundreds of mertags.

Bellamy turned to them. "Welcome to Culinnon."

PART FOUR

The City Above the Sky

21

SERA'S VOICE WAS STILL RINGING IN LEELA'S EARS AS SHE hurried to join the celebrations for Plenna's pregnancy in the Day Gardens.

"Where have you been?" Elorin hissed when she arrived. "Novice Loonir was looking for you. I told her you had just gone to the creamery for some cheese."

"Thank you," Leela said, glancing left and right. Cerulean were laughing and dancing, fiddles and drums and pipes filling the sweet-scented night air, and everyone seemed more relaxed than they had in days. Once again, the High Priestess had managed to distract the City.

Leela pulled Elorin behind a huge rhododendron bursting

with magenta flowers. "I found Sera," she said. "I *spoke* to her."

"What?" Elorin gasped. "Where?"

Leela quickly explained how the doors to the temple had told her to eat the golden fruit, and how Sera's form had appeared in the large pool beneath the cone of moonstone.

"Leela," Elorin said solemnly. "The doors to the temple can only be read by the High Priestess. If *you* are reading them . . ."

Leela waved the thought away. "Sera said the same thing. But she told me that *she* was able to read the symbols on the choosing bowl! And I am certain the High Priestess can no longer read the markings on the door—at least, not the ones that spoke to me. So it has been a lie that only the High Priestess can read the doors. I think they actually used to speak to all Cerulean, just in different ways and at different times." Elorin did not look convinced. "There's more," Leela continued. "She has discovered the location of the tether and is making her way to it now. And there are humans helping her. A male named Leo and a girl named Agnes. They are brother and sister."

She rubbed her temples, still not quite able to wrap her mind around Sera traveling the planet alongside humans, and befriending a male, no less.

"A male," Elorin echoed, her eyes wide. "Will the tether be able to bring Sera home?"

Leela bit her lip. "I do not know."

She had wondered that herself when Sera had first mentioned it. But what other choice was there? The tether was the one connection to the City from the planet.

"I wish we knew more about what the City was like before the Great Sadness," Elorin said. "It seems like that would give us the information we need. Remember when I told you what Acolyte Endaria had told me, about the fountain of moonstone that used to be in the Night Gardens?"

Leela nodded.

"Well, what happened to it?" Elorin said. "We know that moonstone is powerfully magical—it can show visions and allowed you and Sera to speak. But I do not believe Acolyte Endaria's story, that it was broken apart to protect from the sleeping sickness. Moonstone does not seem protective—it seems connective."

Leela had not thought of that.

"Your green mother said that moonstone had been used to communicate between Cerulean when they were on the planet, isn't that right?" she asked.

"Yes," Elorin said. "Perhaps that was a snippet of truth that survived the centuries."

It all felt like it was beginning to make sense. At least, part of it. "Elorin, I think you might be right," Leela said slowly. "The magic of moonstone is *connective*. It has connected this City to the planet—I can see visions of the planet, but only of what Sera sees or where she is, and that must be because of the moonstone. And it connects me and Sera to each other, like a blood bond. But instead of reading each other's hearts, we are able to actually speak!" Her mind was racing as her magic bubbled in her veins. "How did I not think of it before? Cerulean had to have had a way to communicate with those on the planet. And after we stopped going down on the planets, moonstone stopped appearing in the City."

Elorin clapped her hand over her mouth. "Yes."

Suddenly, the air was filled with cries of, "Plenna! Plenna is here!"

Leela and Elorin hurried to join the celebration. The Cerulean were gathering around a low plinth of stone, where the High Priestess stood with Plenna, looking radiant beside her.

"My children, let us raise our glasses in celebration of new life!" the High Priestess said. "Plenna may now join her wives in their dwelling, until her time comes to bear her daughter. Oh, what a joyous day for our City, so long plagued with doubts. But Mother Sun sees us and loves us all. Praise her!"

"Praise her!" the crowds shouted back, but Leela and Elorin said nothing. As Plenna fell into the arms of Heena and Jaycin, the moonlight caught the stone in the High Priestess's circlet. Leela felt her magic begin to burn within her blood, a startling heat that brought out the taste of the fruit in the back of her mouth. There was something special about that circlet, more than the obelisk or the statues or even Sera's pendant. Leela was certain of it, felt it deep in her bones. If she could just have the chance to hold it, to touch it in some way, maybe she could see . . .

Elorin let out a wistful sigh. "She looks so happy, doesn't she?"

Leela followed her gaze to where one of the acolytes was placing a wreath of flowers on Plenna's head. She felt a pinch of envy at the simple joy of Plenna's life.

"Do you think I am doing the wrong thing?" she asked.

"Should I just leave everything be? I do not wish to cause the people of this City more pain."

"You have not done anything wrong," Elorin said firmly. "It is the High Priestess who is causing pain, even if the rest of the City does not know or see it yet. Kandra believes you—well, about the High Priestess, if not about Sera. I believe you about it all. We will find a way to bring Sera home and prove it to them."

"If only I could bring the whole City down to the Sky Gardens," Leela said.

Elorin bit her lower lip. "But you could not get them all down there at once, and it would not surprise me if the High Priestess had some plan in place, some way to discredit or deceive. She erased Kandra's memory, did she not? And you would not be able to tell everyone at the same time, unless you called the City to the temple, and only the High Priestess can command to have the bells rung."

Elorin was right. There had to be another way. Leela's eyes were drawn back to the High Priestess. "I think there may be answers in her circlet, Elorin," she said.

"Answers that the other moonstone cannot give you?"

Leela nodded.

"But if moonstone is connective, then what do you think the circlet connects to?"

"I don't know," Leela said, her frustration returning. "It is just . . . a feeling."

"Well," Elorin said. "I am not one to doubt your instincts, Leela. They have not led you astray thus far."

"I am grateful to have you," Leela said, squeezing Elorin's arm. "You are a good friend."

Elorin beamed. "Come, let us try for one evening to forget our troubles. I think we may be able to sneak some sweetnectar from Novice Loonir if we are very cunning."

She wiggled her eyebrows, and Leela laughed and allowed herself to be led through the crowd to where Novice Loonir was filling glasses beneath the boughs of a poplar tree.

She had spoken to Sera tonight, after all. Surely that was worthy of celebration. The circlet could wait.

The next afternoon, Leela took a break from cleaning the doors. After the announcement of Plenna's pregnancy, no one was watching her closely, so she meandered around the Moon Gardens, seeing the statues in a new light after her conversation with Elorin. Perhaps, in days past, Cerulean would gather around them to see visions of their friends or family on the planet. Maybe it was a way for them to know they were safe, so far from home. She touched the statue of Aila, taking comfort in the moonstone's smoothness. For a moment, she had a glimpse of a room bedecked in pink and gold, and a table laid with all kinds of sweet foods. Then it was gone. Leela felt a surge of triumph.

I am with you, Sera, she thought as she returned to the temple. Perhaps she could try to speak with her again tonight. Would she have to eat the fruit again? She wasn't sure.

She was searching for a new jar of polish in the closet where the prayer cushions were kept when Elorin burst in.

"You scared me," Leela said. Then she took in Elorin's face. Her skin was pale and her eyes so wide Leela could see the whites all around clear blue irises. "What has happened?"

For a moment Elorin seemed too overwhelmed to speak. Her lips trembled and she took a deep, steadying breath.

"The doors," she whispered. "They spoke to me. I was tasked with washing the acolyte and High Priestess robes. I was carrying a load out to wash in the Estuary and as I passed the doors, the markings on them *moved*. And I understood them, Leela. I could read what they were saying."

Leela felt her heart soar. Whatever spell the High Priestess had cast on the City, it was slowly receding, like a veil being lifted. "What did they tell you?"

"*The circlet*," Elorin whispered. "Over and over, they spelled out *the circlet*. And then my feet were carrying me to the dormitory, though that was not where I had intended to go, and then . . . oh, Leela, you must come quickly!"

The two girls walked as fast as they could without attracting the attention of several orange mothers praying in the sanctum. Leela glanced at the doors, but the markings were inscrutable. She was certain her instincts had been right—the doors were meant for all to read, not just the High Priestess. It was a matter of showing the Cerulean not only the lies of the High Priestess but the powers they all should possess that had somehow, someway, been taken from them.

They made their way to the dormitory, down the stairs, and over to Elorin's bed, where a pile of robes sat. Elorin lifted the top one and Leela gasped.

The High Priestess's circlet gleamed up at her, the

moonstone a creamy confection in its center.

"How is this possible?" Leela said.

"I do not know," Elorin said. "It was just . . . here. But you said you felt it had answers. Maybe Mother Sun thinks it does too. Though I do not think we have much time. I will keep guard over the door to ensure no novice disturbs you for the next few minutes."

Leela nodded, then threw her arms around Elorin. Elorin gave her a squeeze and scurried out of the dormitory.

For a moment, Leela simply stared at the circlet. She wasn't quite sure what to do—the stone seemed so small, so innocuous. Her magic tingled in her veins as if waking up from a deep sleep. Every strand of her hair felt alight with anticipation. Cautiously, she reached out and picked it up.

It was heavier than she had expected, and old, the sungold tarnished in certain places. There were tiny white stargems dotted along the winding strands of gold—she had never noticed them, had never been this close before. The moonstone was a perfect circle, and reminded her of the one in Sera's necklace except maybe a bit smaller in circumference. She brushed her thumb across its surface, and suddenly, she knew what she must do.

With careful, deliberate movements, Leela lifted the circlet and placed it on her head.

The rush of images, of memory, overwhelmed her and made her neck snap back and her breath come out in one giant huff. She couldn't make sense of them at first, colors and faces and voices that were all foreign to her. A low whisper that felt vaguely sexual. A high-pitched laugh. Eyes the color of fire. A young Cerulean hanging sheets on a branch to dry. The warmth of a green mother's arms. And then pain, a pain unlike anything Leela had ever known. But it wasn't physical pain—it was guilt. Sharp, twisting, jagged guilt that made her double over and clutch her chest.

Stop, she thought. *This is not what I want.*

But what *did* she want? She tried to think through the pain. The first thing that came to mind was Estelle, trapped in a stalactite.

And the moonstone *reacted*. Leela felt a hard jerk in her stomach and then she was flying backward, but her feet stayed planted on the ground. Colors blurred her vision and it felt like traveling very fast through a narrow tunnel. For a moment she wondered if this was how Sera had felt when she had fallen.

Then everything stopped abruptly and Leela found herself in a dim room, kneeling over a bed. Estelle was lying on it, her eyes closed, her face slack.

"We must be careful not to take too many at once." The voice came from beside her and Leela turned to see a slightly younger Acolyte Klymthe.

"We will not need another," Leela replied, but her voice was not her own—it was the voice of the High Priestess. Some part of her went rigid with shock, but the High Priestess continued smoothly. "Her magic is very strong. I sensed it the day she was born. She will be an excellent addition."

Acolyte Klymthe frowned. "The City must move at some point, Elysse. We cannot stay here forever."

Elysse, Leela thought. *I never knew her name.*

"I know," she snapped at the acolyte. "But I have told you before—the time has not come yet. This plan was put in place centuries before you were born, Klymthe. Do not presume to tell me when it will end."

Acolyte Klymthe looked down, ashamed. "Of course. I did not mean to doubt you."

Leela sighed and reached out a hand with long, slender fingers so unlike her own. Gently, she lifted the acolyte's face. "I did not mean to snap," she said. "Please forgive me. You know how this takes a toll on me. And you know how much I appreciate your boundless aid and support. I would never have been able to accomplish all I have done without you."

Acolyte Klymthe looked relieved. "That means so much to me."

Leela felt a warm smile spread across her face at the same time there was a pinch of irritation in her stomach. She wished she did not need Klymthe's help, that she could do this all on her own. "I will find a place for her this evening," she said, gazing down at the unconscious Cerulean. "Her magic will feed the tether and keep the City strong. Like all the rest of them. They are saving this City and I know they would agree with me if they were to know the truth."

"But you fear they would not understand?"

"I *know* they would not. They were not there, Klymthe, nor were you. If you had seen it, the violence, the carnage . . ." Leela shuddered. "You would do as I have done, I am certain of it. All I have ever wanted is to protect this City. It is my one mission, my only purpose. It requires great sacrifice. But it must be done."

Acolyte Klymthe bowed.

"Now," Leela said, straightening. "Let us go and announce to the City that she has died."

The vision spun and swirled and Leela felt her stomach lurch and for a moment she thought she might be sick. Then everything righted itself and she was beneath the City, among the Sky Gardens. It seemed to Leela that they were not quite as withered as they were now—and the frosted vines were much heavier with fruit.

She was kneeling on the cold ground, pushing at Estelle's shoulders as her legs slid into an open stalactite. The young Cerulean's eyes fluttered and for a second, Leela's heart froze in her chest. But then she stilled and Leela exhaled and pushed the rest of her into the long cone of sunglass. It was filled with a viscous liquid that would help sustain her, suspending her in the sunglass. A fruit fell from the vines and she dropped it into the thick water. Then she passed one hand in a clockwise circle over the opening.

"For devotion," she said. She passed her other hand counterclockwise. "For wisdom." Finally, she passed both hands in a long line down the center of the circle. "For love. May your blood protect this City and keep it safe and whole for all time."

Icy fingers spread across the circle like spiderwebs until the surface was completely covered and Estelle was a mere blur beneath it. Then Leela pressed a palm against it and markings appeared, writing Estelle's name.

"So I shall never forget," she murmured. She gazed out over all the circles, each one etched with a name, each Cerulean donating the power of her blood to keeping the tether healthy, to keeping the City alive. She knew every one of them, their vibrancy, their magic. She was doing the right thing, she knew it deep in her bones. Her faith was being tested, but it had been tested before.

Acolyte Klymthe's words rang in her ears. *The City must move at some point.*

Yes, Leela thought wearily as she got to her feet. But not for at least another generation. She had time enough yet.

There was a sudden sucking feeling, as if Leela was being pulled up through a drain, and then she was standing in the novices' dormitory in the friendly light of the afternoon and it was all so completely bewildering that she wasn't entirely sure who or where she was.

She snatched the circlet off her head and tossed it onto the bed. Her magic thrummed with knowledge, and though it scared her, it comforted her as well. She felt *strong.*

She threw open the door and Elorin jumped at the sight of her.

"What happened?" she asked. "You look as if you have seen a ghost."

"I . . ." Leela felt a shiver run through her chest. "I know what the High Priestess is doing with the Cerulean in the stalactites."

22

LEELA GRABBED ELORIN'S HAND AND PULLED HER INSIDE the dormitory, shutting the door.

"She is using their magic to keep the tether strong and healthy," Leela said. "She is powering this City with the blood of its own people." She rubbed at the spot on her head where the moonstone had sat. "The stalactites feed the tether, which feeds the cone of moonstone, which creates the fruit—it's all connected, a cycle of stolen magic. And the more Cerulean she imprisons, the more magic there is to be stolen."

Elorin was shaking her head back and forth slowly, as if she could not believe it, but Leela could see in her eyes that she did. Elorin had been to the Sky Gardens, had seen the stalactites, and now the doors had spoken to her. Leela felt a sharp rush of gratitude that she did not have to bear this burden alone.

"And the circlet told you this?" Elorin asked.

"I don't . . ." Leela was not sure where to begin or how to explain. So instead she held up a finger, glowing brighter blue than it ever had in her life. Elorin's breath caught in her throat. They had never blood bonded before—indeed, Leela had only ever blood bonded with her mothers and Sera. But Elorin had earned this trust.

Elorin's face grew solemn as she held out her own finger. They touched and Leela felt the heat of Elorin's magic fill her as she poured her own into the girl. Elorin's magic was very much like Elorin, sweet and timid and kind—Leela's own magic usually felt similar, especially when she had blood bonded with Sera. She had always felt Sera's blood held the power of command. But now it was Leela's magic that poured into Elorin with an unfamiliar, writhing strength. Both of them gasped as the memories began to appear.

Instead of reading Elorin's heart, Leela was *showing* her the memories from the circlet. As if they were contained inside her and she could hold them up for Elorin to look into, like a mirror that showed the past. It was so much easier than explaining, and also slightly terrifying. How was she able to do this? Was some part of the High Priestess trapped inside Leela as well? She did not much like that thought.

The images—of Acolyte Klymthe, of Estelle, of the Sky Gardens and the stalactites and all the words the High

Priestess uttered—replayed in Leela's mind and projected themselves into Elorin's. By the time the memory faded and the girls broke their connection, Elorin was breathing heavily, as if she'd just run the length of the City.

"How did you do that?" she asked.

"I don't know," Leela said.

Elorin stepped back and leaned against the dormitory wall. "I didn't even know it was possible," she said. "To keep the tether strong with the blood of Cerulean."

"I think there are many things she is doing we never thought possible," Leela said.

"Yes," Elorin agreed. "The sleeping sickness is a lie, a way for her to steal Cerulean magic. So many have mourned for loved ones who never died. That is an unthinkable cruelty. And yet, the High Priestess seemed to believe all she did was for the good of the City. If she truly wished to help the City, she should have allowed it to move!" Her hands were balled into fists. "But the time *has* come for the City to move, hasn't it? She chose Sera to be sacrificed."

"I know," Leela said. "But she was not expecting it to go wrong. No wonder she has called for a wedding and a birthing season. The City must be distracted while she figures out what to do next."

"Why not just choose another Cerulean?"

"And if that ceremony fails like Sera's did?" Leela shook her head. "I do not think she can risk that. But I have a very bad feeling that something terrible is going to happen. And soon."

Elorin shuddered. "So do I," she said. "Oh, Leela, what do we do?"

Leela's resolve hardened. "I saw how she put Estelle inside the stalactite. Maybe I can get her out."

Unfortunately, Leela was not able to get beneath the City for several days.

Almost as if she knew something had shifted, that some danger to her schemes was lurking and drawing closer, the High Priestess announced there would be groups of novices saying devotionals at each of the three statues in the Moon Gardens at all times, day and night, for one week. They were to pray for the purple mothers still waiting to become pregnant in the birthing houses.

Leela was dismayed when her first shift was assigned and it was with Novices Cresha, Baalin, Reeda, and Flesse. They were all older and none of them had ever been very friendly with her. So it did not surprise her that while they held candles and prayed around the statue of Aila, they spoke almost as if she was not there.

"Never in all my years have I seen anything like this," Novice Cresha muttered to Novice Reeda.

"At least one other Cerulean should be pregnant by now," Reeda said. "I've never heard of holding devotionals to encourage fertility. Mother Sun has blessed them. There should be no need for anything else."

"The High Priestess is only trying to help," Novice Flesse said piously.

"Yes, of course," Cresha replied, but Leela could sense that there was no real conviction in her words. Her spirits lifted. It seemed the High Priestess could not erase the doubt spreading through the City for long.

"It feels as if nothing has been the same since Sera Lighthaven failed to break the tether," Baalin said. Leela's fingernails pressed into the soft wax of her candle. She hated the way Baalin phrased it, as if it was Sera's fault.

"I wonder why there has not been another choosing ceremony," Reeda said.

"Well, there wouldn't be until after the birthing season, would there?" Cresha said. "We cannot risk the City's journey to find a new planet until the next generation of Cerulean is born."

"But that could be years," Reeda said. "Surely if Mother Sun wished the City to move, she would not want it to be delayed for so long. Can the tether survive an entire birthing season?"

"The tether has survived for nine hundred years," Flesse reminded her. "What is a handful more?"

"You are awfully quiet, Leela," Novice Baalin said, turning to her.

Leela started and tried to look meek. "I am not as old or as wise as you novices," she said. "My only wish is for this City to be healthy and well."

That, at least, was not a lie. The other novices seemed placated and silence slipped around them, until their vigil was over and another group of novices came to relieve them.

The days passed and still no other purple mother became pregnant, and the devotionals continued. It seemed to Leela as if she would never make it beneath the City again, and her worry became a constant gnawing in her stomach.

"Be patient," Elorin whispered to her one morning as they returned to the temple from the orchards, carrying baskets of pears and apples for the novices' breakfasts. "A purple mother will become pregnant soon and this will all end. Then we can return and try to free Estelle."

Of course, that presented its own problem. If Leela *could* free Estelle, what should she do then? The High Priestess would certainly notice if one of her hostages was missing. And Leela would hate to think of forcing the woman to go *back* into the stalactite.

But she supposed she was getting ahead of herself. She didn't actually know if she could accomplish anything yet.

They came upon Plenna as they were crossing Aila's Bridge.

"Good afternoon, Plenna," Elorin said.

Plenna had her hands folded across her stomach, though she was so newly pregnant there was nothing to show yet. She looked quite like the Plenna Leela had always known.

"Good afternoon, Elorin. Leela." Plenna smiled at them. "I was just speaking with the High Priestess. She is so gracious to take the time to reassure me."

"Reassure you?" Leela asked.

"I have been hoping for another purple mother to become pregnant by now," Plenna said. "It would be nice to have someone I can speak to, who is in my same situation. Especially since this is my first time. Jaycin told me not to be a bother but I could not help myself." Plenna's face took on a dreamy look. "It seems only yesterday that I was falling in love with them. First Jaycin, then Heena. The joy of finding one person who draws you in, who excites you and challenges you. Then you become complete when you find the third part of your heart." She rubbed her stomach. "And now we will become four. I cannot wait to meet my daughter."

"My green mother always told me she and my purple and orange mothers fell into each other all at once," Elorin said. "That one day they were at the Estuary together and something simply clicked into place and they knew."

Plenna smiled indulgently. "I suppose falling in love is different for everyone."

Leela felt a deep, sudden sadness wash over her, taking her by surprise. The sort of life Plenna described was the life she used to imagine for herself. A triad, perhaps a daughter—Leela had no interest in bearing a child but used to imagine herself as a green mother. But all that felt far away, a distant dream that faded with each passing day. She mourned it even as she knew with all her heart that the life she was living now was more right for her than any other purpose she could have found in the City.

"The High Priestess has assured me that a purple mother should become pregnant any day now," Plenna was saying. "I do hope it is Kandra."

Leela tensed. "Why do you say that?"

"She was so sad and withdrawn. She kept to her house, the very last one on the edge of the twelve, as if isolating herself. She did not take meals with the rest of us, or sing, or pray. She mostly sat in her doorway and sewed. I wish she would move into my house now that I am gone. She might be happier if she were in the center of things."

"Mm," Leela murmured as Elorin said, "It is so good of

you to think of her well-being."

"Well, we purple mothers must stick together. Just like you novices." Plenna gave them a wink.

"Indeed," Leela said with forced cheer. But she knew that if Kandra became pregnant, it would not bring the joy Plenna hoped it would, only deep sorrow. Kandra had not believed Leela about Sera being alive, but what if Leela could free Estelle? Would that bring Kandra comfort?

After a week, the devotions finally ended, and all the novices seemed quite happy. There was something that felt forced about these prayers for fertility, something that did not sit well.

But still, no purple mother had been blessed with a child except Plenna.

Leela and Elorin did not need to speak to one another to agree to return to the Sky Gardens that night. The two girls waited until nearly the hour of the dark before slipping out of the dormitory.

The Moon Gardens were blissfully silent. Fireflies dotted the rosebushes as Leela and Elorin made their way to Faesa's statue—Leela making sure to move the statue over the opening to cover their tracks—and down the cold stairs to the City's underbelly. When they arrived at Estelle's circle, they both stopped and gazed down at her—the memory of putting her inside this stalactite was crystal clear in Leela's mind, and she sensed Elorin was thinking of it too.

"Do you think she will be all right if you take her out?" Elorin asked in a hushed voice.

"Yes," Leela said, trying to sound more confident than

she felt. "The High Priestess does not want to kill them. Besides, Estelle escaped once, years ago, and Kandra saw her—the High Priestess simply erased her memory of the meeting." She looked at the cone of moonstone, and its pulsing red heart seemed dim to her. "The stalactites absorb Cerulean magic," she said. "Which feeds the pool, which strengthens the tether." She turned her eyes upward to the boughs of vines. "The moonstone uses the magic of the tether to make the fruit, which she feeds to the Cerulean, replenishing the magic the tether is taking from them. Until it can't anymore and then she needs to make new stalactites and imprison fresh Cerulean."

"I wonder how she even thought to do it in the first place," Elorin said. "What could have caused her to make such a drastic choice?"

Leela felt that if she'd kept the circlet on longer, she might have found out. All she could do now was try to help those imprisoned. She knelt at the edge of Estelle's stalactite and recalled the movements the High Priestess had made when she'd first trapped her here.

She ran one hand in a clockwise circle over the ice. "For devotion," she said, her voice trembling. She passed her other hand counterclockwise. "For wisdom." Then she passed both hands in a long line down the center of the circle. "For love," she whispered.

Leela waited, hardly daring to even breathe. Suddenly, Elorin gasped and Leela saw cracks appear in the surface of the ice. Liquid began to weep from them, spilling across the ground and soaking the knees of Leela's robe. And then the ice was gone. Leela reached out and touched the inside of the stalactite—the liquid was clear as water but much more viscous.

"Estelle?" she called, unsure of exactly what to do.

For one agonizingly long moment, nothing happened. Then Estelle's whole body lurched, limbs flailing through the thick fluid, until she burst from the stalactite, coughing and choking and heaving up water onto the cold ground.

We should have brought an extra robe, Leela thought as she and Elorin helped pull her out. She realized how much she had doubted that this would actually work.

"I'll get her a robe from the dormitories," Elorin said, as if reading Leela's mind.

Leela nodded and Elorin quickly left. It was only after she'd gone that Leela remembered she'd sealed up Faesa's statue and Elorin would not be able to get out.

But Estelle had stopped coughing and now turned her eyes to Leela. They were flat black, no trace of blue at all.

"Who are you?" she croaked.

"M-my name is Leela Starcatcher," Leela stammered. "I—"

Estelle grabbed her arm so tight it hurt. "Are you working with her?"

Leela didn't need to ask who she meant. "No," she said. "I'm trying to stop her. I only found this place a few weeks ago, no one in the City knows about it."

"She lies," Estelle said, her grip tightening. "You could be lying too."

"Please," Leela said. "You're hurting me."

"How long has it been?" Estelle demanded. "How long have I been . . ." She shuddered and released Leela, slumping over and holding her head in her hands. "Is this real? I have had the freedom dreams before." She looked up and her black eyes sent a shudder deep into Leela's heart. "Am I dead?"

Leela knelt before her. "You are not dead," she said gently. "And this is no dream."

Estelle looked around, wild and frantic. "What do you want with me? Where are the others?"

"I want to help you. I want to help them too but I don't know how. I don't . . ." Leela felt ashamed. She stared at her hands and said, "I don't know what I'm doing."

"There are so many of us," Estelle murmured. "Can you hear them? I hear them in my dreams, when I wake, voices that whisper, that beg, that cry . . . some of them are so very old." She gazed up at Leela. "Does the City know of her treachery? Is the nightmare over?"

"Not yet," Leela said, and Estelle crumpled. "But I know of her lies and so does my friend Elorin." She took a breath. "And so does Kandra Sunkeeper."

"Kandra?" Estelle became at once alert, scrambling to her knees. "Kandra is still alive?"

"Yes," Leela said, grateful to be able to impart some good news. "She has a daughter. Sera. She is eighteen, like me."

Tears filled Estelle's unnervingly black eyes. "A daughter."

"The High Priestess made her forget about you," Leela said. "But when Sera was sacrificed, it all came back to her."

"Sacrificed?" Estelle gripped her head with her hands.

"I'm sorry," Leela said. "There is so much to tell and I fear I do not know where to begin."

Suddenly Estelle was pulling at Leela's robe, her face desperate.

"You must take me to Kandra," she said. "I need to see her. Please. I don't have much time."

23

"KANDRA IS AT THE BIRTHING HOUSES," LEELA SAID. "IT is a long way from here and dangerous."

"Please," Estelle said again. "I can't—none of this seems real." She released her hold on Leela and slumped to the ground. "I wish to see my friend again. And the stars. I have not seen the stars in years. I wonder if they look the same as I remember . . ."

Leela's heart spasmed with pain, at the thought of so many long years in darkness.

Just then, Elorin returned with a robe in her hands. "The moonstone moved for me!" she cried. "I realized as I was climbing the stairs that you had sealed the entrance, but then Faesa's statue just . . . slid aside." She caught sight of Estelle's flat black eyes and fell silent.

"She wants me to take her to Kandra," Leela said.

Elorin gasped. "Surely you cannot. It is too far, and too dangerous. What if someone sees her?"

Leela grasped Elorin's shoulders. "She has been in darkness for so long," she said. "Without light, without hope. How can I deny her the opportunity to see her friend? What if we fail and this was her one chance?"

Elorin looked to Estelle, then back to Leela. "You are right."

Estelle suddenly fell to her knees, clutching her chest. "The fruit," she croaked. "Please . . . I need the fruit. . . ."

Without allowing herself a moment to think, Leela stretched out a hand and a fat golden fruit plopped into it, as if she had called it down from the vines. Elorin gave an impressed half gasp half squeak and Leela felt a stirring of pride, but Estelle was already grabbing it, devouring it swiftly and discarding the pit. Then she lurched forward, her palms slapping against the cold ground, her skin beginning to glow, until there was a sudden flash. She rose to her feet slowly, straight and strong.

She stretched her arms out and flexed her fingers. "I feel . . . almost myself again." Then she looked at Leela. "Oh, thank you. It has been so long since I've felt my legs beneath me. It's been so long since I've moved of my own accord, or spoken, or seen anyone besides the High Priestess."

Leela helped her into the robe. "We must go quickly," she said. "It will take us time to reach the birthing houses."

Estelle grabbed her wrist. "What is your name again?"

"Leela," Leela said. "And this is Elorin."

Elorin gave a little cough by way of greeting. They climbed up the stairs beneath Faesa's statue and as soon as they emerged into the Moon Gardens, Estelle collapsed onto the earth, sobbing and pulling up giant fistfuls of grass.

"Stop," Leela whispered. "Oh, please, Estelle, stop, we cannot be seen or heard."

Estelle took a deep, shuddering breath. "I am sorry," she said. "The feel of grass, the fragrance of roses, the whisper of the wind . . . how precious these things are, that I once took for granted. How painfully beautiful the world is." She turned her eyes upward to the stars. "They do look as I remember." Then she rose to her feet, her legs unsteady beneath her.

"How long will the fruit sustain you?" Leela asked.

"I'm not sure. It lasts longer when I am . . ." She swallowed, and Leela knew she could not bring herself to name her prison. "A few hours, perhaps."

Leela turned to Elorin. "Wait inside. No sense in both of us getting caught."

Elorin nodded, then turned and headed back to the dormitory. Leela beckoned for Estelle to follow her. They crossed Faesa's Bridge in silence and headed past the stargem mines, down the lesser used paths that Leela had become familiar with over the course of her late-night visits with Kandra. Only when they reached the forest and slipped in among the trees, where no Cerulean could hear, did she begin to tell her tale to Estelle. She listened with surprising calm, Leela thought, though perhaps she was just grateful to be listening to anyone at all again. Occasionally she would pause to touch the wrinkled bark of a tree trunk, or cock her head at the chirp of a cricket as if there were no more beautiful sound in the world.

They had nearly reached the birthing houses by the time Leela had gotten to the part about the High Priestess's circlet. Estelle placed a hand on her shoulder.

"Never have I met a Cerulean as brave as you," she said.

Leela's cheeks warmed. "Sera is braver. And I could not have done half of what I have without Elorin. But we must be quiet now. Kandra is in the last house, farthest from the path."

Leela paid no mind to the sacred circle of white and blue pebbles, crossing over them without a second thought. The birthing houses were deathly silent. The garlands of flowers strung among them were leeched of color in the moonlight and the obelisk was a mere ghost in the darkness. Leela and Estelle crept forward, quiet and alert. They reached the last house and Leela gripped the knob, gave Estelle a bracing look, and turned it.

This birthing house was much the same as the one Kandra had shown her the first time they had met here—a single room, round and domed, with a bed, a table with a pitcher and basin, and a bassinet to one side. Kandra was lying on the bed and Leela assumed she was sleeping until she sat up abruptly.

"Who's there?" she called. But her voice was small and sad and flat, as if she did not really care that strangers were coming into her room in the middle of the night.

Estelle let out a strangled sob and stumbled forward.

"Kandra," she said. "Kandra, it's me."

There was the sound of a match striking and then a flame glowed inside a glass lantern. For several long moments Kandra and Estelle stared at each other. Leela did not dare to move for fear she would break the moment.

Very slowly, Kandra stood. "Are you real?"

Tears were falling thick down Estelle's cheeks. "Yes," she said. "I'm real."

Then the two women fell into each other's arms, and Leela felt tears well in her own eyes.

"I'm so sorry," Kandra said over and over as Estelle murmured the same thing.

"I ran away," Kandra said, pulling back and wiping her nose on her sleeve. "I should never have left you. I didn't believe it was really you but it was. Oh, Estelle, I'm so sorry."

"Shhhh," Estelle said. "It is all right. You have nothing to be sorry for. You thought I was dead. I'm sorry that I did not tend to our friendship as I should have. You got married and I felt like I had no place in your life. I drifted away out of fear and in doing so, I lost my best friend."

But Kandra was shaking her head. "That was not your fault. I should have been more attentive to all my relationships, not just my wives. You never lost me, not for one moment."

And then they were embracing again.

"How is this possible?" Kandra asked as they broke apart. "How are you here? How did you escape?"

"Leela," Estelle said simply. Kandra gasped and turned to Leela as if only just noticing she was there.

"But how?" she asked.

"You may want to sit down," Leela said. "It is a rather long story."

Kandra sank down onto the bed, her eyes growing wider and wider as Leela explained everything.

"The High Priestess made up the sleeping sickness?" she gasped. "To steal Cerulean magic for the tether?"

Leela nodded. "But the tether is dying—the City needs to move. I'm not sure if she knows what to do now since the sacrifice failed. Sera didn't break the tether. We may see another bout of sleeping sickness run through the City."

"No." Estelle's voice carried the chill of her underground prison. "We cannot let her . . . no one should be subjected to what she has put us through." She took a seat beside Kandra. "We can hear her. Through the glass. Through the liquid that suspends and sustains us. Bits and pieces. Sometimes she talks to herself. Sometimes she talks to others." Estelle grimaced as if in pain. "At least I think she does. The other voices, the ones who are trapped alongside me, they are very old, they know more than I do. . . ."

She fixed her black eyes on Leela. "They told me a secret. The circlet, Leela. That moonstone is connected to every Cerulean in this City. It has been the moonstone of the High Priestess since the forming of the City itself. It was meant as a way to keep the High Priestess connected with her people, so that she would best know how to guide them. But it has been twisted to a dark purpose." Estelle clutched at her chest. "She has been using it to siphon magic from the City's population, for centuries. She has been weakening us, been *stealing* the magic from every single Cerulean. That is how she has been able to survive for so long, why she looks so youthful after nine hundred years. That moonstone can draw out Cerulean magic like a moth to a flame, without us knowing or feeling it. The circlet may seem small but it contains more power than anything in this City." She shook her head. "She was feasting on our magic, she still is, and we cannot feel a thing."

Leela felt her face go blank with shock. Kandra had one hand covering her mouth, her expression frozen in disbelief.

"Our prison is like one massive spiderweb," Estelle continued. "Where we are all interconnected and yet individual threads at once. I feel the sadness and longing and anger of the ancient ones, as if through a blood bond. The High Priestess knows us, knows each of our names. She speaks to us sometimes and asks for forgiveness. She tells us it is all for the greater good. I do not believe she knows we can hear her."

"How did you escape the first time?" Kandra asked. "When I saw you here, by the obelisk . . ."

Estelle closed her eyes, remembering. "I was still new then, still strong. She was feeding so many of us she forgot to seal my tomb. I remember the feel of air in my lungs again, the cold ground beneath my hands. And then I was walking and I didn't know where I was going until I found a staircase. I began to climb. I felt like I was in a dream."

"How did you move the obelisk?" Leela asked.

Estelle blinked. "I don't know. I didn't realize I had. I remember feeling desperate. I remember thinking, I have to warn them, I have to tell them. I had bright new fruit running through my veins. Though my muscles felt weak, my magic was strong."

Elorin had moved Faesa's statue as well, Leela thought. Perhaps the brightness of Estelle's magic had called on the obelisk to move. Perhaps all Cerulean were as capable of moving the moonstone as they were of reading the doors. They simply did not know it. Or the High Priestess had siphoned that power along with their magic.

Estelle turned to Kandra. "You told me I was dead."

A tear slid down Kandra's cheek. "And you said no, and then yes."

"I am sorry I did not tell you truly what was happening," Estelle said. "I spoke in riddles, but it felt like everything was one big riddle myself. I have had more time now, to see, to feel, to listen. When you ran away, I tried to follow you. But my legs were so clumsy, my mind muddled. And then I felt the fruit begin to fade from my veins and I could not walk any longer and my lungs began to shrink and my heart beat slower. And that's when she found me. She put me back and locked me away."

"That must have been when she sealed the stairs beneath the obelisk," Leela said.

"The obelisk," Kandra muttered, her eyes faraway. When she looked at Leela again, Leela saw a small spark of blue. "I think . . . I think I saw her name. Written on the obelisk."

Leela frowned. "Whose name?"

"Sera," Kandra whispered. "I was bringing water to one of the midwives and I walked past the obelisk and I—I *felt* her presence. I felt as if Sera was watching me. And then markings appeared on the moonstone and I swear on my love for Mother Sun, the symbols spelled *Sera*. Then they vanished so quickly I thought perhaps I made them up, that in my grief I was seeing things. But you told me she was alive. And for a moment I wondered if I should have believed you."

Leela bit her lip. She had spent so much time feeling confused and overwhelmed, but now she was seeing that there was some purpose to all these events, these changes, and that she was a part of it, and if she could just embrace that, maybe she'd discover a side of herself she never knew existed.

"Kandra," she said, and her voice was infused with the steady thrum of her magic. "I'm going to show you something."

She held up a glowing finger. Even though they had spent so much time together, and grown so close, they had never blood bonded. And this would be no ordinary blood bond, Leela knew. But Kandra would have to see that for herself. She would have to make the choice.

Kandra stared at her bright blue fingertip for so long, Leela thought she would balk and refuse. But she kept her hand and her gaze steady.

Please, she thought. *Trust me.*

At long last, Kandra raised her own finger, and as the two lights touched, Leela felt Kandra's magic enter her, and though it was older than hers, wise and compassionate and crippled with grief, Leela once again felt her own magic was stronger. It wound around Kandra's heart and she gasped as Leela held up the memory mirror inside her mind and showed her.

Sera.

Sera standing on the prow of a ship, gazing up at an unfamiliar night sky as the wind whipped her hair about her face. Sera's form emerging from the pool of water surrounding the tether, her cry of joy at seeing Leela, her explanation of where she had been, her tales of the planet, her struggle to find the tether and return home. Sera's smile, Sera's voice, Sera Sera Sera.

"She's alive," Kandra gasped as the connection broke. "She's *alive*."

She collapsed into sobs, her hands clutching her face. "Leela, I am sorry," she said, through jagged breaths. "I did not . . . I could not . . ."

"I know," Leela said.

"What is this power you possess?" Kandra said.

"I ate the fruit," Leela said, and Estelle let out a shocked cry. "I did not know what it was," Leela explained. "Only that the doors told me to."

"What doors?"

"The doors to the temple. Sometimes they form symbols that I can read." Leela felt embarrassed all of a sudden, like she was bragging when she did not mean to.

Kandra and Estelle were staring as if they had never seen anything like her.

"Mother Sun has chosen you," Kandra said. "Leela—"

"Elorin has read them too," Leela said quickly. "And you yourself just admitted to reading Sera's name on the obelisk. The symbols are not a declaration of a new High

Priestess. They are for everyone."

Kandra reached out and clasped her hands. "That may be true, but look at all *you* have done. You have freed Estelle. You have given me back my Sera."

"I don't have Sera yet," Leela said. "But I will find a way to bring her home. That I promise." Her stomach twisted with guilt. "As much for myself as for you and her other mothers. I miss her desperately."

Kandra laughed and tears sparkled in her eyes. "There is no shame in wanting something for yourself," she said. "And this is the second time you have brought me back from the brink of despair. If anything, I am indebted to you."

Leela was about to protest when Estelle gave a great shudder.

"It is starting," she choked. "I have stayed too long away. I can feel it . . . I have to go back."

"No," Kandra said. "No, you mustn't go back there."

Estelle touched her on the cheek. "I will die if I don't."

Her knees buckled and Kandra caught her before she hit the floor. "Help me, Leela."

Leela supported her on the opposite side and they hurried out of the dwelling, Estelle stumbling between them.

"You are not meant to leave the birthing houses," Leela whispered as they approached the sacred circle.

Kandra snorted. "I am not bearing another daughter until Sera has returned to this City. If Mother Sun truly did bless me, she would understand. As my orange wife once said, she is a mother, first and foremost." She glanced at Estelle, whose breathing was becoming more and more ragged. "And you could not have gotten her back alone."

They reached the Moon Gardens faster than Leela thought possible, and had to walk in an awkward fashion to get Estelle down the curving stairs. Kandra's reaction to the Sky Gardens was much the same as Elorin's had been.

"I thought I believed you," Kandra said. "I saw this in your memory, but still . . . what *is* this place?"

"I don't know, but the High Priestess is killing it," Leela said. "Those gardens did not used to be so withered."

They found Estelle's stalactite—Leela helped her out of the robe, not wanting to leave any evidence behind. They gently slid Estelle back into the viscous liquid that contained her magic. As she slipped beneath the surface, Leela whispered, "We will come back for you. Tell the others if you can. We will free them all."

Then she sealed up the opening. As she stood, she found Kandra staring at her, and a blue light was burning in the depths of her eyes.

"Leela Starcatcher," she said. "What a marvel you are."

24

WHEN SHE AT LAST CRAWLED BENEATH HER COVERS IN the dormitory that night, Leela had a dream.

She was walking in the Night Gardens, past bushes of solemn gray roses and beneath the boughs of nebula trees, their black leaves heavy with clouds. A will-o-the-wisp floated in front of her and hung there, its eerie blue light pulsing like a heartbeat.

"Hello, Leela," it said, though it had no mouth and the words seemed to come from inside her, from the very depths of her heart. And though she knew it was strange, that will-o-the-wisps did not speak, she was not afraid.

"Hello," she replied. "What am I doing here?"

"*Remembering,*" the will-o-the-wisp replied. "*This is where it all began.*"

Leela saw the dais then, and the ghost of the crowds that had gathered on the day that Sera was sacrificed. Sera herself was in full color, almost more vivid than she had been in reality, her hair starkly blue, the bracelets at her wrist vibrant purple and green and orange. Leela could sense the moonstone pulsing beneath her robe.

"*I was lost for so long in the night, searching, searching,*" the will-o-the-wisp said. "*I could not find my children and I mourned for them. Oh, how I mourned.*"

Though none of this actually made sense to Leela, her dream mind seemed to understand it.

"I am sorry," she said. "That must have been so hard for you."

"*But a bond of love and an act of pure courage lit up my sky like a meteorite,*" the will-o-the-wisp said. "*Where once there was only blackness, I again saw stars. The sun rose at last and the moon waxed and waned and I heard the bubbling of the Estuary and the singing of laurel doves and I knew I could find my way home again.*"

"Home." Leela nodded in agreement. "How sad for you to have lost yours for so long." Then she frowned. "Where did you come from?"

She had never known a will-o-the-wisp to have a home or a family, much less children.

"*From nowhere and from everywhere,*" the will-o-the-wisp replied. "*But from love most of all. I come from within you, and within Sera, and each and every Cerulean heart in this City. My love is made tangible in a form you know so very well."*

The star pendant rose up in Leela's mind, and suddenly she was wearing the necklace she had given Sera, as she never had in true life. She gripped the dream stone in her hand and felt an overwhelming connection to her best friend, as if Sera's heart was contained within it.

"Do you know where Sera is?" she asked.

"Yes," the wisp replied. *"And she is in grave danger. There are forces at work on the planet that wish to clutch her in their claws and never let her go. You must help her, Leela. You must help her show them."*

"Show who what?" Leela asked. "I am only trying to bring Sera home."

"Home is not always what we think it is when our journey begins," the will-o'-the-wisp said. *"And it can change along the way. Home is ever shifting, because it is not truly a place. It is a feeling."*

Leela wasn't sure what she meant by that. "But I miss her," she said.

The will-o'-the-wisp glowed brighter. *"You will see her again,"* it said. *"But my children have forgotten who they are and it is time they remembered. It is my fault—I was broken with grief and I let this City drift out of my sight. By the time I recovered, I could not find it."*

"Why not?" Leela asked. She felt as if the will-o'-the-wisp should be capable of anything.

"It stopped moving," the wisp said sadly. *"If the City does not move, I cannot see it. And it has been still for so*

very, very long. There was a dark time when I worried I might never find it again. Little lights winked out one by one and my love was too far away to be made tangible anymore."

"The moonstone," Leela whispered, and the dream stone grew hot in her hand. "That's why it stopped appearing. Because you could not find the City."

The will-o-the-wisp shuddered in a way that Leela took as a nod. *"But it lives in the City still,"* the wisp said. *"It cannot be destroyed, only hidden."*

Another image came to Leela, an unfamiliar one, of a fountain being torn apart out of fear.

"Why?" Leela asked. "Why would she hide it?"

The wisp did not need to ask who Leela spoke of. *"She is consumed with guilt. She thinks she is doing what is right. But it has been too long. She thought she could withstand all those years, thought she could be strong enough to protect the City. But it is not protection. It is desperation. Her time has come to live in my light and love, to let go and allow the change she so desperately fears to happen."*

"How can she live in your light and love after all she has done?" Leela asked.

"She is my child," the wisp said. *"Just as you are. All children make mistakes. It is not for me to reject but to forgive. And her story is not over yet. There is still time for redemption."*

Leela did not quite agree with that, but felt it best not to say anything. The wisp was far older and wiser than her.

"But if she destroyed the fountain, then why not the statues or the obelisk?"

"*Even she would not destroy the images of my daughters,*" the wisp said. "*And the obelisk, too, is sacred. But all other pieces of my love have been locked away. They are yearning to be touched once more, to be owned, to be connected.*"

"But I don't know where they are," Leela said miserably.

"*Ah. That I can help you with.*"

The will-o-the-wisp floated toward her, so close Leela felt its heat, and before she could cry out or back away, it floated *inside* her. And suddenly, she was at the top of the temple spire, at the place where Sera always loved to perch and watch the stars.

"*Look inside,*" the will-o-the-wisp whispered from within her heart. "*See beneath the glitter and the gold. And then make a leap of faith.*"

Leela saw a flash of gold-silver-blue that she knew was the tether, then she felt the terrifying sensation of falling, and space was all around her, and the underbelly of the City swam in her vision and she woke up drenched in sweat.

Heal them, the will-o-the-wisp's voice echoed in her ears. The dormitory was quiet around her, the gentle breathing and light snores of the novices the only sounds.

Leela stayed there, stock-still, replaying the dream in her head. She could not have been asleep for very long— it was still dark outside. She wondered if she should wake Elorin, but some instinct said this moment was for Leela alone. For the second time that night, Leela crept from her bed and out into the Moon Gardens.

She gazed up at the temple spire, silver in the moonlight.

Sera did this all the time, she reminded herself. But the

sensation of falling in her dream was still thrilling through her limbs, and she found she could not move, her body locked in panic.

See beneath the glitter and the gold. And then make a leap of faith.

That's what the will-o-the-wisp had said. Though Leela knew in her heart it was Mother Sun who had spoken to her, she could not bring herself to form the thought. It felt too large, too scary, too significant. So she focused on the task instead.

The glitter and gold must be the spire. And in order to see beneath it, she would have to climb.

She used the eave above the dormitory door to heave herself up, the way Sera had always done. The outer wall of the temple was shingled in sunglass, and she gripped its ridged surface with her fingers and toes. The first few moments were sheer terror, but soon Leela found herself developing a rhythm, moving her feet first, left then right, and letting her hands follow. And slowly, she inched her way up the cone of the temple until she had reached the top. She was breathless, sweat dewing in her hair and trickling down her back, but she felt a rush of triumph as well. If only Sera could see her now.

She stared at the spire, wondering exactly what she was meant to do. She ran her fingers over its smooth surface, feeling the sharp point of it, then searching at its base.

She gasped as her fingers ran over a thin piece of metal that wrapped halfway around the edge where the spire met the sunglass.

It was a hinge.

Leela grasped the narrow point of the cone in one hand and pushed. The spire fell open, and though Leela had been told what to expect, she still stared in shock at its depths.

The space beneath the spire was filled with moonstone.

She could not see how deep it went—some pieces looked to be parts of the fountain, broken and shattered, but others were carved into shapes, doves and snails and beetles, while some were set in jewelry like Sera's necklace. There was a thin decorative cuff of moonstone within her reach, its ends gilded with sungold. Leela picked it up—it felt warm in her hand, and a tingle of magic glimmered up her wrist and into her arm as she slipped it on. It shone against her skin like it was happy, as if it had always meant to live there and had finally returned home. It was hers, Leela was sure of it, though she sensed a different owner, a faint whisper of some long-dead Cerulean who had once worn this bangle on her wrist. And she suddenly understood what the wisp had meant when it said moonstone was yearning to be touched, to be owned, to connect. It was a piece of Mother Sun's love and every Cerulean left her own imprint on it.

Leela wondered where the moonstone in Sera's pendant had come from, and what life it had lived before she had found it on the Estuary's shore. And how *had* she found it, come to think of it? If moonstone stopped appearing, where had that particular stone come from?

She would not find the answers all the way up here, though. Leela carefully replaced the spire and began the long descent back to the ground. Her arms and legs were aching by the time she reached the bottom, and she quickly slipped the cuff into the pocket of her robe. She could not wear it, but she would keep it on her person at all times.

Only after she snuck back into the dormitory did she think she should have gotten a piece for Elorin as well. But, she reassured herself, the cache was not going anywhere, and she could always go back up to the spire another night.

The sad tolling of a bell from within the temple woke Leela almost as soon as she had laid her head on her pillow.

Novices were rousing themselves and looking around the dormitory in confusion. Leela met Elorin's eyes across the room and Leela could tell they were both wondering what had happened.

Leela managed to slip her moonstone cuff into the pocket of a fresh robe as she changed. She and Elorin gathered cushions to lay out for the incoming Cerulean, but the temple was too crowded to talk. She could tell Elorin was bursting to know what had transpired with Kandra and Estelle during the night—and probably wondering where Estelle was now. Leela was dying to tell her everything, about the dream and the will-o-the-wisp and the cache she'd found.

Once the City had gathered, the High Priestess emerged onto the chancel and crossed to stand at the pulpit. Leela saw the moonstone in her circlet with new eyes, a fresh appreciation for its power.

"My children," she said, spreading her arms wide. "I fear I have grievous news. The sleeping sickness has returned to our City. And it has afflicted our most vulnerable member. Plenna Skychaser has fallen ill."

The shocked gasps and cries of despair felt muted in

Leela's ears. Plenna. Of all the Cerulean the High Priestess could have chosen, she had to pick the only one who had become pregnant. It felt impossibly cruel, and yet Leela sensed there was some reason behind it. The High Priestess did not choose who she trapped in stalactites by chance.

"We have survived the sickness before and will survive it again," the High Priestess said. "But for now, I feel a time of fervent prayer and meditation is needed." The moonstone in her circlet seemed to stare right at Leela and her heart swooped, her stomach churning. "Mother Sun," the High Priestess prayed, bowing her head. "Help us in our time of need. Keep this sickness at bay, and release Plenna from its fatal grasp. All we do, we do in service to your light and love. Do not abandon us now. Show us the way. This we pray."

"This we pray," the congregation echoed.

Leela tried to sense if she could actually *feel* her magic being siphoned away, but if she had not noticed it for eighteen years of her life, why would she now? She slipped her hand into the pocket of her robe and squeezed the cuff.

I have my own moonstone, she thought. *And I know what I need to do with it.*

Perhaps she had always known, ever since she realized it may have been her pendant that had saved Sera's life.

The City prayed, until the sun began to set and the moons and stars painted on the vaulted ceiling became limned with gold. Leela found herself gazing at the Altar of the Lost, the great sun dotted with teardrop-shaped stargems. She remembered the day, so long ago, when she had prayed to Mother Sun and the gems had turned to tears.

That was the day she became friends with Elorin.

It all must stem from the Great Sadness, she thought. That's when everything changed. She should have been more judicious in her use of the circlet. She should have tried to see if she could go back all those centuries and read the High Priestess's memory from that dark time. She recalled the story of Wyllin and the forming of this tether. Elorin had wondered about its truth just as Leela did. Who knew if the High Priestess had chosen Wyllin for some dark purpose the way she had chosen Sera?

When at last the High Priestess declared the day of prayer and meditation over, the congregation rose and whispers filled the room alongside utterings of fear. Leela saw Koreen being comforted by Daina and Atana—she wanted to say something reassuring to her old friends, but the words stuck in her throat. This City had reached a breaking point—Leela could not allow another Cerulean to be imprisoned beneath it.

A leap of faith, the will-o-the-wisp had said. There was only one leap Leela could make and the thought sent waves of terror rippling down her spine.

Sera survived, she reminded herself. But the thought did not comfort her.

"What happened last night?" Elorin appeared at Leela's elbow, her voice barely a whisper. Leela glanced around and beckoned for her to follow. They went deep into the Moon Gardens where no one would hear them and Leela told her everything.

"But . . . are you saying . . . did she just *siphon* our magic?" She looked down at her hands as if expecting to see magic leaking out of them.

"I believe so," Leela said gravely. "But she must not take enough to be noticed. We still have healing power. We can still blood bond."

"But we should be able to do more than that," Elorin said. "I can read the doors now, and Kandra saw Sera's name on the obelisk." She frowned. "But neither of us have eaten the fruit. So how were we able to?"

"Perhaps it is because you two know about the lies," Leela said. "There is a strength of will in our minds and hearts, not just in our magic. Your eyes are opened. So you are seeing things you never imagined possible."

Elorin nodded solemnly, but Leela was not finished. She took a deep breath and told Elorin about the dream.

By the end of the tale, Elorin's mouth was hanging open. "Leela," she whispered. "That was Moth—"

"Now we know where all the moonstone has gone," Leela said quickly, because admitting she'd spoken with Mother Sun still felt altogether too overwhelming. "The High Priestess may have bent her circlet to her will, but now *I* have moonstone too." She reached into her pocket and pulled out the cuff. Elorin marveled at it.

"I can feel the life inside it," Leela said. "The lives of the other Cerulean who have worn it. It will protect me when I—" She swallowed hard. "When I fall."

For a moment, Elorin just stared at her. Leela thought she would cry or beg or protest, but when she did at last respond, her voice was steady.

"You are going down onto the planet."

Leela nodded.

"Are you going to jump off the dais, like Sera did?"

Leela was so relieved she did not have to explain herself. "No," she said. "That way is not for me."

She remembered the flash of the tether from her dream. The Sky Gardens were where answers waited for her. It was through the pool that she must go.

"The High Priestess could not destroy the moonstone, so she hid it, in a secret cache," Leela said. "The fountain is there, and other moonstone as well, jewelry and figurines and all sorts of things. It is all beneath the spire of the temple—there is a hinge at its base. When you think it is safe, go and get a piece for yourself."

"All right," Elorin said, though she looked pale as she gazed up at the impressive height of the temple. "When are you going to the planet?"

Leela slipped the cuff on her wrist, the welcoming sensation rippling once again up her arm. "Now," she said.

Then she held Elorin tight, feeling the girl's weight and warmth, trying to memorize it in case she never came back. She was too frightened to say goodbye, so she released her and fled through the gardens, the statue of Faesa springing aside before she even reached it, as if it knew, as if it sensed this night was not like other nights.

Down the stairs she ran, and through the paths and past the pools until she came to the tether. It was singing for her tonight as it had once before, the cone of moonstone's beating red heart aflame with hope, and the song echoed in her veins and gave her courage. She stopped at the water's edge and stared down at the planet.

A leap of faith, she thought.

Then a voice said, "Good evening, Leela. I was wondering who I might find here."

From the other side of the pool, the High Priestess emerged. Her face was drawn and terrible. The circlet glowed a sickly green. Leela put her hands behind her back to hide her bracelet.

"I felt a change in my moonstone," the High Priestess said. "As if another had worn my circlet. But I could not sense who." She cocked her head. "Impressive, if I'm to be honest, that your magic was able to elude me."

But Leela had no use for the High Priestess's praise.

"What you are doing to this City is wrong," she said.

The High Priestess's smile was a sharp, jagged thing. "What do you know about right and wrong?" she said. "You have lived such a sheltered life. I have made it that way. It is because of *me* that this City survives. You could not begin to comprehend the sacrifices I have made to keep it strong and healthy, to keep it protected from the hungry darkness of space and the cruel dangers of the planets."

"This City is *meant* to move," Leela insisted. "And Cerulean are *meant* to go down onto the planets. It is just as Sera always thought. Is that why you chose her? To silence her?"

"I chose her because her magic was the strongest I have sensed in a century," the High Priestess said. Then she sniffed the air. "But yours is strong as well. In a different way, a way that I have not seen in even longer. You remind me of Wyllin."

"I'm not Wyllin," Leela said. "If she even was your friend, as you claim. You cannot keep stealing Cerulean magic." She glanced around at the icy circles beneath her and with a start realized a new circle had been added. One whose markings on its surface read *Plenna*. The High Priestess followed her gaze.

"It had to be done," she said, and for a moment she almost sounded sad. "Her magic is so much stronger because of the pregnancy. I needed it. The City needs it."

Leela glowered, her stomach twisting with disgust. "I won't let you imprison anyone else ever again. We deserve to be free."

"Freedom comes at a price, Leela, and a far higher one than I'm certain you are willing to pay." The High Priestess's voice grew silky. "If you come back to the temple with me, I can tell you all. Secrets of your magic that would open your mind and make you melt with joy. I can show you power that will stun you, power that will thrill and entice. It's wonderful, Leela. Like nothing you have ever felt or will ever feel again." Her eyes glowed with enticement. "I will let you return to your mothers and your dwelling if you wish. Or"—her voice turned as cold as the columns around them—"you may become another victim of the sleeping sickness. Tragic in one so young, but Plenna is young too. Young magic is always strongest." She swept a hand out at the circles dotting the ground. "So that is your choice, Leela. It is up for you to decide which path you will take."

Leela dared not look down lest she lose her nerve. "I know what path I will take," she said. "And it is not one you have offered me."

The High Priestess seemed amused. "And what other path is there?"

The moonstone began to pulse gently against her skin, as if it was saying, *go, go, go.* Leela steeled herself and looked the High Priestess right in the eye.

"I am going to bring Sera *home*," she said.

And then she jumped.

PART FIVE

The island of Culinnon, Pelago

and

The island of Braxos, Pelago

25

SERA

MERTAGS SWARMED THE WATERS AROUND THE GALLEON as the island of Culinnon drew near.

Sera watched as its coastline took form, trees painting its shore like jewels, shimmering in rich colors, richer than Sera had yet seen on this planet. Exquisite blue-green leaves and silvery-white bark that glowed like moonlight.

"They're *Arboreals*," she gasped.

There must have been hundreds of them. Sera felt tears well in her eyes. She had only ever known Boris, but now she found herself staring at a whole *forest* full of Arboreals.

"So many," Leo murmured, and his voice sent a sudden prickle up her spine. "This must have been where my father stole Boris from. Errol too."

"Ambrosine was livid when she found out," Bellamy said. "She blamed Hektor, for not protecting them better. She always blames Hektor when something goes wrong."

There was a flash of movement on the water and Sera saw a ship, painted in the shifting colors of the sea, sailing past them. Then she saw another just beyond it, and another.

"She calls them clandestines," Bellamy explained. "Ships that blend in with the ocean. Makes them harder to detect until they're right on top of you. They've been sinking any ship that dares to come north. That's why the waters have been so empty."

The memory sharing seemed to have stripped Bellamy of her fear, no longer scared to talk to them but eager. Sera felt a flutter in her chest and a clenching in her stomach, the scene of Hektor proposing to Bellamy still fresh in her mind, the embrace and the kisses that awoke a discovery in Sera herself, one that was swimming bright inside her.

She glanced at Leo, but he was staring at the Arboreals with razor-sharp focus, almost as if he was determined not to look at her. She bit her lip and tried to push the feelings down.

"We're here!" Ambrosine declared as she strode up to them. "Bellamy, go put on something decent. And get Mckenna to run a comb through your hair. Honestly," she said, rolling her eyes as Bellamy scurried away.

Sera had to grit her teeth to keep quiet.

"How marvelous are my treasures?" Ambrosine said, sweeping her arms out. "My family's most prized possessions."

Mertags and Arboreals were thoughtful, intelligent creatures, Sera thought, not possessions.

"They're remarkable," Leo said.

"My mertags will destroy any ship that comes within a mile of Culinnon's shore," Ambrosine bragged. "Unless it carries a familiar face or flies my banners. They're devilishly smart, you know. Very easy to train."

The galleon sailed around to a large inlet where an enormous mansion was perched at the crest of a hill, a long dock stretching out into the water like a silver tooth. The mansion was made mostly of glass and it sprawled across the grounds, disappearing into the forests surrounding it.

A man was standing on the dock, and as the galleon pulled up, Sera recognized him from Bellamy's memory— Hektor.

The gangplank was lowered and Ambrosine led the descent onto land. Sera was glad to have her feet on solid ground again. The air was cold and crisp, scented with heather and dogwood. The path up to the mansion was lit with lanterns, like golden will-o-the-wisps marking a trail to the door.

"Mother," Hektor said, bowing to her formally. He eyed Leo first, then Sera, but whatever thoughts he had about them remained hidden in his dark blue eyes.

"Hektor," Ambrosine replied. "May I introduce your nephew, Leo McLellan. And his friend Sera Lighthaven."

"Welcome to Culinnon," Hektor said. There was no warmth in his tone and Sera felt Bellamy squirm beside her, ready to embrace her husband as she had in the memory.

The thought made Sera's fingers itch and tugged her eyes in Leo's direction.

"I must see to a few matters," Ambrosine said.

"We received a dove from Ithilia," Hektor said. "I have sent out scouts to track the movements of the Renalt. She won't be hard to find with all those warships."

"Good," Ambrosine said. "Mckenna, show Leo and Sera to their rooms. The western sequoia should do." Without another word, she strode off down the dock, taking a different path than the one that led to the main entrance.

As soon as she was out of sight, Bellamy flew into Hektor's arms.

"I missed you," Sera heard him whisper in her ear.

"Come," Mckenna said.

Hektor briefly pulled away from his wife. "You look just like her," he said to Leo.

"I know," Leo replied, his shoulders hunched.

Hektor's mouth twisted. "So this is Mother's salvation for the family?"

Sera didn't know what he was talking about, but Bellamy shushed him. "Leo has been very kind to me," she said. "Sera too. Let them be."

Hektor turned back to her, and Sera and Leo followed Mckenna up the path to the mansion.

The foyer was huge, encased in glass with a thick growth of purple and blue hydrangeas climbing up the outside of one wall. There was a long, low firepit in the center, and the furniture was in strange shapes, armchairs that looked like eggs and couches with peaked backs. Everything was colored in browns and olive greens and watery blues. Without pausing, Mckenna marched straight across and through another door that led to a glass hall, then up a set of stairs, then down a hall that had a boulder for a wall, water flowing over its smooth gray surface in a thin sheet.

The farther they traveled, the less the layout made sense—it was as wild and unpredictable as nature, built around several towering sequoias. And there were no discernible floors except the ground one—staircases appeared as if from nowhere and sometimes when Sera looked up she saw four or five floors above her, where other times there was only one. Occasionally they would walk inside a tree, brightly lit corridors of cedar-colored wood.

Finally, they reached a sequoia with a spiral staircase winding straight up through the center of its trunk. Halfway up, Mckenna stopped.

"This is your room," she said to Leo, opening the door to reveal a glimpse of glass walls and cozy yet modern furnishings.

"I—" Leo looked at Sera as if reluctant to let her go. Her heart stuttered and she felt off balance.

"She will only be one room above you," Mckenna said. "You are safe on Culinnon. If you'd like, I can show you the Arboreal groves once you've changed."

She directed this only at Leo and Sera felt a flash of irritation, similar to how she'd felt when she'd spent time with Rahel. She hadn't understood it then but she did now—jealousy. She didn't much care for the emotion. It was prickly and mean and made her feel not at all herself.

"Sure," Leo said, and then Mckenna was leading Sera away from him, up one more spiral to her new room.

"Do let me know if there is anything you need," the servant girl said. Then she bowed her head and descended back down the stairs.

Sera's room was nestled in the crook of the great tree— the walls were glass that formed a little dome with branches crawling up around them. A fireplace was built into the trunk, a small fire burning in its hearth. Her bed was laid with a comforter as red-gold as a sunset and there was a table made of polished river stones with two chairs on either side of it. A pitcher of water and a basin for her to wash with sat beside an armoire, and she scrubbed her face and then wiped it off with a soft, scented towel.

At last, Sera sank onto the edge of her bed and allowed the feelings she had so ardently refused to acknowledge to swell up around her. When she'd felt the shudderings and shiverings of desire that fluttered inside Bellamy during the memory share, she'd recognized them in herself, in a way she had not expected but now could not unsee or unfeel.

All the wriggles in her tummy when Leo said certain things, all the lurches in her heart or the weightlessness that would grip her . . . it had all sharpened so clearly to one solid point. Desire. She *wanted* Leo.

She was so unfamiliar with the rules and signs. She had only ever been attracted to James Roth, the handsome performer from Old Port City. She'd assumed that was how attraction worked, an instant thing that was known straightaway. She had certainly not felt any desire toward Leo when they first met. But she knew him now, had seen him change, and grown closer to him. So it appeared attraction could develop over time. She'd never imagined wanting someone else on this planet. She had been so focused on getting home, on going back to her City.

In the span of one memory, Sera's whole world had shifted. Because this was no infatuation like with James; she knew it in her bones, in her soul, in everything that made her *her*. This was something much stronger and far scarier. Tentatively, she allowed her mind to imagine what it might be like, to touch Leo, to press her lips to his, to feel his arms around her, and not just in a friendly embrace. A knot of want clenched in her stomach so intensely it made her body jerk and her toes tingle, yet there was a distinct sense of panic there as well. She felt crushed beneath the weight of the silence in this room with nothing but the thought of Leo surrounding her.

She sat and let her mind replay so many memories, so many days that now meant something different from what they had before. How had she missed it? Now that she knew, it seemed so obvious.

Then a new thought seized her—what if Leo did not feel the same way? She wasn't human, after all. Why would he be attracted to someone like her? Perhaps he saw her only as a friend. The concept was a twisting ache in her chest.

"You should not be worrying about this," Sera said aloud to herself. "You are supposed to be focused on going *home*."

What did it matter if Leo liked her or not—her City was where she belonged. But she found she could not stop wanting him. Desire overrode logic, it would seem. How frustrating. But wonderful. Yet scary. She wished there were someone she could talk to about this. A Cerulean, not a human, someone who knew her world and could help her understand on her own terms. She wondered again, as she had done when she finally spoke to Leela in the Sky Gardens, if there were others in her City like her, if she was not so wholly alone in this. But even if there were other Cerulean who were attracted to males, they were far away and could not help her here.

What advice would her purple mother give, she wondered. Surely attraction followed the same principles, regardless of the object.

Sera closed her eyes and imagined her mother's voice in her head.

He would be a fool not to want you back, my darling, she could hear her say. She smiled and clutched the moonstone.

The knock on her door startled her. "Who is it?" she called.

"It's me," Leo said, and Sera's heart leaped like a sun trout jumping for a fly.

"Oh," she said, standing so quickly she felt dizzy. She opened the door and the sight of him, in a sweater the color of the sea and his curls tied back in a low ponytail, set her mouth watering. What an unexpected reaction. Desire made her all out of sorts.

"I thought maybe we could explore the Arboreal grove together," Leo said. "I can see it from my room; I don't think we need Mckenna's company."

Sera would be happy to never have Mckenna's company again—she nodded and said, "Let me put on a cloak."

She chose a plum-colored velvet from the armoire by

the fireplace, her hands shaking as she slipped it on. They walked down the staircase in silence—was Sera imagining it or did Leo keep glancing at her every so often? But perhaps because she was being unusually quiet.

"Your grandmother has a very nice house," she said.

Leo laughed and the sound sent little shivers over her skin. "I don't know if *house* is the word I'd use," he said. "But it's certainly impressive."

They stepped out into the cold air and followed a simple flagstone path that led them to the Arboreal grove. Seeing so many of them together made her heart seize up and tears fill her eyes. Their faces were just like Boris's, three eyes that formed a triangle and an odd slash for a mouth.

"Incredible," Leo said, marveling at the blue-green canopy overhead.

They walked deeper into the grove, Sera touching each trunk lightly as she passed, and she felt the Arboreals stir, their leaves rustling, and without consciously thinking it, she called on the seeds of light and love as she had done with Boris. It was so much easier this time, she thought as she held her palms up, her magic slipping through her skin as lightly as a thread through a needle. Leo gaped as tiny glowing seeds with feathery stems floated up and away, filling the grove with their light and melting into the Arboreals' leaves where they touched them. Sera heard creaking, tree-ish gasps of delight and cries of, *"Seeds! Seeds of light and love."*

"What are they saying?" Leo asked. Sera found she could not look at him. It was easier to focus on the Arboreals.

"They call my magic seeds of light and love," she explained. "And they are full of joy to see them."

The closest tree turned its ancient eyes toward her.

"Mother," it said. That was the same thing Boris had said to her, when she'd first heard the Arboreal speak. She didn't understand it any more now than she had then, and though she knew this tree was not Boris, she could not stop herself from wrapping her arms around its trunk.

"I have known one of you," she whispered to it, her voice coming out in the wind-like rush of the Arboreal language. "And she saved my life by sacrificing her own. She was the bravest soul I have ever met. I am so sorry."

Tears spilled down her cheeks and she felt a branch bend to gently brush her hair.

"Ahhh," the Arboreal whispered. *"The eldest of us, the one who was taken. Do not cry, sapling. She was blessed to have known you."*

"Mother," another Arboreal said, and then another, and another.

"Why do you call me that?" Sera asked.

"You bring us the seeds of light and love," one Arboreal murmured.

"Seeds of light and love as we once knew," a second said. *"So that we may grow throughout this earth as we were meant to. We have been on this island for so long."*

"You are not meant to be here?" Sera asked.

The first Arboreal's eyes turned sad. *"We are meant to be everywhere. We come from another island, far away in the north."*

"Braxos," Sera said eagerly. "I am trying to get there.

My home is attached to that island."

"*Home,*" the first said mournfully, and the others picked up the call.

"*Home.*"

Sera had forgotten how frustrating speaking with an Arboreal could be. She kept walking, telling Leo what they'd said to her as murmurs of "Home" and "Mother" followed them. Part of her wished she had come alone—she felt a deep connection with this grove, like a natural blood bond, almost as if she truly was their mother, reunited with her children at last. But that was only the fear talking, she thought. Her magic was zipping and prickling, focused on Leo even as she wandered among the trees.

She passed an Arboreal who seemed smaller and younger than the others, and it reached out a branch to touch her shoulder.

"*She wants the island too,*" the tree whispered, as if telling a secret. "*She claims she is our mother but she is not. She thinks to find more there.*"

"Who?" Sera asked, though she thought she knew. "Ambrosine?"

The tree just stared at her, and Sera knew she was right.

"What do you mean, more?" she asked. "What more does she hope to find on Braxos?"

"*More of us,*" the Arboreal said. "*More of the fish that talk with lights. More of everything. More more more. Humans have so much. If only they could see. But always they want more. She has so many of us and yet she will not share. She keeps us all together, all here, all hers.*" A leaf fluttered and Sera reached out to catch it. It was soft as her cloudspun dresses back home, and brighter than a jewel.

"*Not that one, though,*" the tree said, and its eyes were focused on a spot behind Sera and its mouth moved in what she thought was meant to be a smile. "*That young sapling has only one desire. You.*"

Sera turned. Leo was watching her from several feet away, and the look in his eyes made her head spin, her heart throwing itself against her chest as though trying to escape. For a long moment they both just stared at each other. Sera knew she should walk toward him—walking was not so difficult. Or she should speak to him, as she had spoken to him many times before. But everything that had once seemed so natural now felt insurmountable.

"What did that one say to you?" he asked, his voice rough.

Sera's throat went tight. "That humans have so much," she said, not sounding at all like herself, but breathless and shivery. "Yet they always want more. Not you, though. She says you only want one thing."

"What's that?"

Sera swallowed. "Me."

Leo's cheeks flushed pink and she understood it now, all those blushes, the delicate color she loved so much. She finally found her legs, taking one step forward and then another. Leo was frozen, watching her as wary as a wounded animal being stalked by a predator. Her body was moving of its own accord now and it didn't stop until she was standing right in front of him, so close she could feel the heat of his body, could see every detail of his face. His eyelashes were so long and so black. Had she ever noticed that before? It was like there were bees buzzing in her rib cage, making everything heightened and jittery and just a little blurry. Her eyes found their way to his mouth and she swallowed again, hard.

Leo's brow furrowed as if he could not quite understand what was happening. He smelled faintly of wool and leather and something musky that she felt was decidedly *Leo*. He looked ever so slightly helpless; Sera felt vulnerable too, as if just standing here in front of him was the equivalent of unzipping her skin and letting him see every part of who she was. But he knew who she was. And she knew him. All of him, the good parts and the bad.

With feather-light hesitation, she pressed her lips gently against his.

26

LEO

SERA WAS *KISSING* HIM.

Sera. Was. Kissing. *Him.*

His hands moved to cup her face, her skin so soft, her hair like strands of silk, her flower-starlight scent engulfing him. She tasted of sunshine and honey.

How many times had he imagined this moment? He'd been with lots of girls back in Old Port, but that was different. He hadn't truly cared about any of them. He wasn't sure he'd ever truly cared about anyone at all until Sera fell into the Knottle Plains and his whole life had shifted course.

Kissing Sera was something entirely new. This was a tingling upside-down, inside-out, disorienting joy that was so sharp it could almost be confused for fear. Her lips were timid, and he held her gently, as if afraid she might break. But then he felt something in her surge, and she was winding her arms around his neck and pulling him closer and his tongue slipped into her mouth and she gasped and sank her fingers into his curls. Leo's hand slid down her back, feeling the length of her spine beneath her dress and wishing there was nothing between them at all. He wanted to know her, to know every part of her. He wanted to taste her kindness and the backs of her knees and the generosity of her heart and the curve of her shoulder blades. He wanted to live in this spot under the turquoise canopy of the Arboreals and never leave.

Culinnon, Ambrosine, Braxos, the tether . . . it all ceased to exist. There was only Sera.

Even if this was all he got of her, even if he had to let her go at the end of this journey . . . it was enough. It was enough to have kissed her, to have held her close, to have felt her breathing against him. It was enough.

How long they stood and kissed, he didn't know. But at some point, the Arboreals around them began to speak in that strange tree language, and they broke apart.

"What are they saying?" Leo asked.

"They are happy we are happy," Sera said.

"Oh." Leo hadn't been thinking they'd had an audience. "Thanks," he said to the trees, and Sera laughed.

"They cannot understand you," she said.

"Right." He honestly didn't care if all the Arboreals and mertags and strange things in the world were watching them right now. He was acutely aware of every place Sera was touching him, of her chest pressed against his and her hands on his back.

She said something then in their own language and the trees rustled back at her. Before Leo could ask her what she'd said, she was smiling up at him with a look that was at once daring and shy, and he cradled her neck and pulled her in for another kiss. He felt he could spend the rest of his life kissing Sera and not feel the time wasted. She pressed her cheek to his, her breath tickling his ear.

"I never thought to be kissed," she murmured. "I quite like it."

One of the Arboreals began to hum—a rustling, whistling sound like dry leaves skittering down a sidewalk in the fall. But the tune was sweet and simple and one by one the other Arboreals picked it up until they were enveloped in song.

All of a sudden, hundreds of tiny sprites, golden and shimmering, emerged from beneath the roots of the trees, scampering and floating and twirling to surround Leo and Sera.

"Sprites!" she cried with delight, clapping her hands together.

One landed on Leo's palm and did a little jig while two more alighted on Sera's shoulder. One doffed its tiny crown as it bowed to her; the other did a dainty pirouette. Sera laughed and they set off spinning and whirling, emitting tiny sparks as they soared.

"They're dancing for you," Leo said.

"It's more than a dance," Sera said. "It's something else."

And Leo saw the sprites forming something; a shape began to appear, a trunk, branches, golden leaves . . .

"Oh," Sera gasped, her hands flying to her mouth as tears filled her eyes. "It's Boris."

Leo had not known the old tree the same way Sera had, but he'd spent a fair amount of time with Boris, and while the Arboreals all looked fairly similar, he was able to distinguish the difference in the tree the sprites were making. It was Boris, right down to her sad wise eyes. The sprite-Arboreal swayed in the wind, and it seemed to Leo that she was happy to see Sera.

The other trees around them began to sing again.

"What are they saying?" Leo asked.

A thick tear rolled down Sera's cheek. "They are honoring her spirit. They are comforting each other, and reminding each other not to mourn her loss. They did not know she had died until I came here, but they have been missing her. She has not gone, they say—she lives on in every tree and root and branch, in the whisper of the wind and patter of the rain and the rays of the sun. She will always be here."

The sprite-Boris craned its branches toward Sera and she reached out and touched a leaf with a gentle silver finger. The sprites exploded in a shower of golden sparks, the shade of Boris vanishing into a thousand dying embers.

Abruptly, the trees stopped singing. The silence was so sharp and immediate it almost hurt Leo's ears. He and Sera turned to find Hektor standing in the clearing, his expression somehow impressed and disdainful at the same time.

"You have a connection with the Arboreals," he said to Sera.

"I knew one in Old Port," she said.

"Of course. Xavier's show." He turned to Leo. "I was

wondering if I might speak with you a moment."

Leo did not want to leave Sera right now, especially not to spend time with this stern stranger-uncle, but Sera nudged him and said, "Go. I will be right here."

"All right," Leo said. Hektor nodded curtly and turned, leaving Leo to follow after him. He wound his way through the trees until they came to a small pond at the base of a hill. A waterfall splashed into it on one side, and pure white rocks scattered around its edge like misshapen pillows. The water was a rich midnight blue and tiny lights glimmered from within it like stars.

"Fascinating, isn't it," Hektor said. "Culinnon is filled with so many beautiful things, things you would never find anywhere else on this planet."

"It's certainly unique," Leo said.

"It's a prison," Hektor snapped. "A very pretty one, but a prison nonetheless. But at least it was meant to be mine. Now you are here."

"I'm not inheriting Culinnon," Leo said. "And Agnes and I didn't even know about this island till we arrived in Arbaz."

Hektor ran a hand over his sleek black hair. "Forgive me," he said. "I have no skill with words. That's Matthias's gift. It was Alethea's too—though she was gifted at just about everything. Used to drive me crazy." He took a breath. "Bellamy said you were very kind to her on the journey. I thank you for that."

"I didn't do it for you," Leo said. "She's a nice person."

Hektor's lips twitched. "I admit, I was expecting you to be more like your father."

"I used to try to be," Leo said. "Back in Old Port. It didn't really work out. As it happens, my father is quite a prick."

Hektor laughed, and for a moment his whole face changed. "He is," he agreed. Then he stared at Leo, his mouth pressing into a thin line. "I'm sorry," he said. "I can't help—you look so much like—"

"It's fine," Leo said, holding up a hand. "I'm kind of used to it by now."

"She was very special," Hektor said. "Full of light, full of life. Mother had so much expectation pinned on her—even after she married Xavier, even after she left Pelago, Mother still hoped. And then Alethea died and that hope shattered. It isn't easy, being the eldest son. Matthias ran away, he could do that, but not me. I had to stay and get married and continue the family line. Family is everything."

"Yes, Ambrosine seemed pretty clear about that on the way here."

Hektor's dark eyes flashed as they held Leo's. "Family is *everything*," he said again, slowly. "I do not know if Bellamy will ever be able to conceive. And I do not think Matthias will ever love anyone but his books. But the Byrne line must continue. My mother will insist upon it."

Leo blinked. "Sorry, what?"

"I didn't take you for an idiot," Hektor said. "The Byrne line must continue. That will start with you."

Leo felt as if the ground had just disappeared beneath his feet. "Are you saying . . . look, I'm only eighteen! And I just got here, for god's sake. I'm not some . . . some . . . stud to be let out for breeding. There's a girl back there who—"

"Exactly," his uncle said, cutting him off. "There's a girl back there, a very special girl, who would create a very special line."

"That's disgusting," Leo spat. "How can you even think that?"

"I'm not thinking it," he said. "My mother is."

"And you're, what, trying to help me out by giving me a heads-up?"

Hektor looked at him like he was utterly stupid. "Yes, Leo. That's exactly what I'm trying to do."

"Sera's going *home*," Leo said, feeling a bit like a petulant boy.

Hektor raised one eyebrow. "You really think my mother will let that girl leave? A girl who looks like a goddess? A girl with a connection to Braxos?"

It was just what Bellamy had said too. Leo's nostrils flared. "This planet doesn't deserve her," he muttered.

Hektor's face softened. "You care for her very much, that is clear. My mother delights in using the things we care about against us. Especially since she lost Alethea. And she is a very powerful woman."

"Sera has power too," Leo said, then wished that he hadn't.

"Yes," Hektor said with a sigh. "I'm certain she does."

He left Leo abruptly, as if he had said all he needed to and there was no reason for a goodbye. Sera found him there after a while, sitting on a smooth white rock and staring into the pond filled with stars.

"What did your uncle want?" she asked.

Leo could not bring himself to tell her the full truth. "Just to warn me that Ambrosine is powerful and won't want you to leave Culinnon."

"Well," Sera said, sitting beside him. "We knew that already."

He wrapped an arm around her waist and she melted against him. It made Hektor's warning all the worse.

"I like this island," she said. "But it seems sad. Beautiful, but sad."

"Hektor says it's like a prison."

"Hm. Yes, maybe it is. It reminds me of a caged bird, something pretty but trapped, struggling to be free."

Her description made Leo think back to Old Port, how he had been instrumental in locking Sera up in that crate, and for a moment he was overwhelmed with disgust at himself, at the person he used to be. But he wasn't that person anymore and he'd be damned if anyone tried to take away Sera's freedom again.

It didn't matter what Ambrosine wanted. Sera deserved to go home and Leo was going to make sure she got there. Even if it broke his heart to do it.

The storm started just as Leo and Sera were summoned to dinner.

The dining room was like a huge domed greenhouse. Glass panels climbed high above them, with all sorts of plants hanging from rafters or crawling along iron moldings. Heart-leafed philodendrons and peperomias dangled their rich greenery from ornate ceramic pots overhead; red ivy wound its way along the walls, while delicate peace lilies and soft, rose-tipped painted ladies dotted the ground. The table itself was made of a massive tree trunk, its rings preserved with enamel, carved out to fit the chairs. An elegant candelabra sat in its center, thick green candles perched in the mouths of copper roses.

A clap of thunder rang out and rain poured down the glass, distorting the world outside.

"Leo, come sit here," Ambrosine said, indicating the chair beside her. "I hear you and Sera visited one of my Arboreal groves today."

Leo glanced at his uncle, seated on Ambrosine's other side, but Hektor's face was a blank canvas, revealing nothing.

"We did," he said, taking his seat. "I didn't know there were more than one."

"Oh yes, we have seven groves on Culinnon," she said.

"Seven?" Sera gasped.

Ambrosine looked pleased. "Yes."

"But then why do you not share them?" Sera asked. "With so many, you could start groves on other islands."

Ambrosine frowned like Sera was being stupid on purpose. "They belong to the Byrnes," she said. "Not some ignorant Malley from Adereen."

Bellamy flinched, and Hektor changed the subject.

"A dove came from Ithilia," he said to Leo. "The Kaolin navy has arrived. The Misarros are keeping them at bay for now."

"For now?" Ambrosine's lip curled. "Misarro warships could trump a Kaolin frigate any day of the week and twice on Sundays. Ithilia can take care of itself. Though I'm sure they're missing the Renalt's forces at the moment." She smiled smugly as servants poured into the dining room, filling their glasses with sparkling scintillant and serving the first course. Bowls of a creamy pale green soup were set in front of them, a radish carved in the shape of a flower floating on top. Leo took a tentative bite—it tasted of basil and zucchini and was surprisingly delicious.

"You don't seem too concerned that your country's capital is under attack," Leo noted.

Ambrosine raised one elegant eyebrow. "I'm not."

Leo felt like he was missing something—shouldn't Ambrosine be upset that Kaolin was attacking Pelago? Yes, Culinnon was far away and well protected, but still. Though maybe she was happy this would mean fewer ships to sink in search of Braxos.

"I was thinking of taking Leo to the cove tomorrow," Hektor said. "He'd best start learning how to sail."

Leo had already learned some sailing on the *Maiden's Wail,* and it was really more Sera's thing than his. He didn't feel a need to learn more and didn't understand why they would want him to.

"An excellent idea, Hektor," Ambrosine said, and Hektor looked the happiest Leo had seen him since he'd embraced Bellamy on the dock that morning. "Perhaps start with—"

Just then another clap of thunder rang out as a servant rushed into the hall.

"Mistress, a ship has come," she said, panting.

Ambrosine was on her feet in a flash. "The Renalt?" she asked. But the servant was shaking her head.

"It's your granddaughter," she said, and Leo's heart flipped in his chest.

Agnes had made it to Culinnon.

27

AGNES

THE STORM HAD BEEN BREWING ALL DAY AND AGNES HAD been watching the clouds with increasing trepidation.

They'd made far better time than even Vada could have anticipated. Errol had led them from Ithilia to a hidden path, a network of rivers that ran *through* the island of Cairan, saving them days off their journey by not having to sail around it. He was exceptionally skilled at avoiding other ships as well, and so while they had seen them in the distance, they were never close enough to be noticed or bothered with. Then, just yesterday, the ocean had become empty for as far as Agnes could see. The weather had grown steadily colder the farther north they sailed, and the two girls would huddle together at night for warmth, which always led to kissing, which made Agnes very happy despite the chill.

But even kissing Vada would not keep her warm in a rainstorm.

"I wish Errol could tell us how close we are," Agnes said.

"I am thinking we must be nearing Culinnon," Vada said. "The passages around it have been closed, yes? And we have seen no ships."

"True," Agnes said. There was a faint rumble in the sky and Errol popped up, flashing purple, the colors of Culinnon.

"Will we make it there before the storm?" Agnes asked, but he only gave the clouds one sullen look and then vanished beneath the waves.

"It makes no matter to him," Vada pointed out. "He's always wet."

There was a flash of lightning and then a great clap of thunder and the heavens opened and rain poured down on them. There was nothing for Agnes to do but sit there and shiver. Rivulets ran down her back, her clothes soaked in minutes, her hair plastered to her face. Lightning streaked across the sky as the sea grew rougher. Agnes gripped the sides of the sloop tight, her knuckles white.

"Don't be falling in, little lion!" Vada called. Agnes glowered and Vada laughed. "It's only a bit of water," she shouted over the pounding of the rain.

Agnes wiped her eyes, which was pointless because the rain kept on falling. "A *bit*?" she shouted back. Vada grinned and shrugged.

The storm raged and the waves crashed against the hull,

sending sprays of water onto the sloop so that Agnes was being doused from above *and* below. She tried to think of warm things, of thick soft blankets and roaring fires and hot mugs of tea. Her teeth were clenched so hard her jaw ached, shudders ripping through her in violent bursts.

Just then Vada cried out, "Land!" and Agnes saw lights shining on the horizon. The water around them began to churn, and not just from the storm; Agnes leaned over the hull and gasped as she saw hundreds of colored lights.

"Mertags, Vada!" she yelled. "Look!"

The ocean was full of them, flashing and twisting, lighting up the water in colors more brilliant than a sunrise so that Agnes felt they were sailing through a living rainbow. Errol was wriggling his way among them, and the two girls watched as he flashed at this one and that, and the joy that radiated out from his scales was palpable.

It suddenly occurred to Agnes that he was *home*.

"Who goes there?"

The ship came upon them out of nowhere, the voice almost swept away on the howling wind. Agnes looked up to see a sleek schooner painted in muted colors with a Misarro with gold disks at her neck staring down at them.

"My name is Agnes McLellan," she shouted. "I am the daughter of Alethea Byrne. I've come to—"

But the Misarro cut her off. "Agnes!" she cried. "Your grandmother has been so worried about you. Come!"

The schooner turned and Vada adjusted the tiller to follow. Agnes felt a flurry of nerves in her chest.

Her grandmother was here, and Agnes was going to meet her at last.

* * *

The rain was so heavy, all she could really make out of Culinnon was lots of trees and a mansion of glass.

She and Vada stood dripping on the floor of an enormous front room, huddling close to the firepit that ran down the center of it. A servant had instructed them to wait while she fetched Ambrosine. Vada whistled as she gazed around at the glass walls and oddly shaped furniture.

"Nice place," she said as another clap of thunder rang out.

Several minutes later, Agnes heard the patter of feet, and then there was a flash of silver-blue as Sera darted into the room and threw her arms around her.

"I'm all wet," Agnes protested, but Sera held her tight. When she finally pulled away, Leo was there right behind her, a big grin on his face.

"You made it," he said. "We heard you were coming, but . . . you guys made good time."

"We had some help," Vada said.

"It's so good to see you both," Agnes said. "What happened? We heard about the princess's ship but then we had to flee Ithilia in the night and we've been out of contact with the world since."

"We have so much to t—" Leo began, but then there was a soft clearing of a throat and he fell silent and stepped aside.

Her grandmother was standing in the doorway, and she was more elegant than Agnes had ever imagined. She was struck by just how much she looked like Leo, except for the nose, and her black curls were done up and pinned with pointed venuses, her blue lace gown the height of sophistication. She exuded power and confidence and for a moment, Agnes's breath was taken away at the very idea that they were related.

"Agnes," Ambrosine said, and Agnes stumbled forward. Her grandmother held out her hands and took both of Agnes's. "By the goddesses, it is so very good to meet you."

"It's nice to meet you too," Agnes said thickly. Then she shivered. "Sorry. I'm getting your carpet all wet."

Ambrosine laughed. "No need to worry about carpets, my dear, I've hundreds of them. But you must be desperate for a bath and fresh clothes. You and your companion . . ."

"Vada Murchadha," Vada said, giving an awkward bow. "At your service."

Ambrosine's brows pinched together, but she inclined her head politely. "Vada," she said. Then she clapped her hands and two servant girls hurried into the room. "Take my granddaughter and her friend to bathe and find them rooms in the eastern glen."

"Yes, mistress," one said as the other bobbed a curtsy.

Agnes didn't want to leave Sera and Leo so soon, but a bath sounded like heaven.

"Don't worry," Leo said when he saw her hesitation. "We aren't going anywhere."

She smiled at him gratefully and noticed Sera slip her hand into his. That was a new development. Though they both had many stories to tell, Agnes was sure of it. For now she allowed herself to be led out of the foyer and through winding halls of glass until they came to a room carved into the trunk of an enormous sycamore tree. Inside was a bath-house, smooth rounded walls with a massive stone tub sunk in its center, steam rising gently from its surface. Agnes and Vada quickly stripped off their wet clothes and sank into the bath with identical moans of pleasure. Agnes could feel the hard knots in her muscles begin to thaw as the steam filled her lungs.

Once they were clean and wrapped in big fluffy towels, the servants led them to rooms on the ground floor of the estate, Vada's right across from Agnes's.

Clothes had been laid out on the bed for her, a woolen dress and velvet cape with a fur-lined hood. Agnes would have to see about some pants later—for now these garments were dry and warm, and that was all that mattered. One wall of her room was made entirely of grass, tiny red flowers scattered among the dark green blades. Another was paneled in glass that looked out onto a pretty garden with a jeweled birdbath, and a third was a quilt of smooth paving stones, a fireplace set in its center with a roaring blaze that coated the room in delicious warmth.

Agnes had just finished dressing when her door burst open and Vada strode in.

"This is the first time I am wearing a dress since . . . perhaps since ever," she grumbled. The dress was simple, gray linen with a scoop neck and a thin leather belt. "Not that I am complaining," she said, walking over and plop-ping down on Agnes's bed. "It is very fine material and kind of your grandmother to be giving me clothes to wear." She chuckled. "If only my mama could see me now. Dressed by a Byrne on the estates of Culinnon!"

"I think you look very nice," Agnes said, which wasn't a lie. The dress suited her; she just didn't look like Vada.

Vada reached out for her hand and when Agnes took it, Vada tugged her close, tucking Agnes between her legs and running her hands over her waist.

"What are you thinking about your grandmother?"

"I don't know," Agnes said, sinking her fingers into Vada's thick auburn hair, free from its usual braid. "She's much more elegant than I imagined, I guess. More . . . stately."

Vada laughed. "Stately, yes. This is true."

"I hope she can help us get Sera to Braxos."

"We are not needing her help," Vada reminded her. "We have a ship and we have Errol. That is all we need."

Agnes's heart swelled to hear it. "That's right," she said. She leaned forward to kiss her—their tongues twined and then Vada pulled her down so that Agnes fell on top of her on the bed, laughing as Vada left a trail of kisses down her neck.

There was a light tap on the door.

"Pardon the intrusion," Ambrosine said, and Agnes scrambled to her feet, her cheeks burning as she adjusted her dress and smoothed back her hair.

"Um, oh no, it's fine," she said, completely mortified and trying not to show it.

"I was wondering, Agnes, if I might speak to you in private," Ambrosine said.

Vada was on her feet in an instant. "I will go find Sera and Leo," she said. "We did not get to have a proper welcome."

She gave Ambrosine another awkward bow and left.

"How do you find your accommodations?" Ambrosine asked.

"It's a very nice room," Agnes said. "This whole estate is beautiful."

Her grandmother smiled. It wasn't the sort of smile Agnes had pictured, full of warmth and joy like her mother's smile in the photograph. There was something sly and almost aggressive about it.

"Why don't we sit," she suggested. There were two brocade armchairs nestled in a corner between the stone wall and the grass one, and Agnes took a seat opposite Ambrosine, her heart skipping erratically.

"Leo informed me your father told you nothing of me, or your mother, or this side of your family," Ambrosine said.

"No," Agnes said. "We weren't even allowed to mention the Byrne name. Eneas would sometimes slip and give me little details, but nothing concrete. Nothing that made her feel real."

There was a darkening in Ambrosine's eyes at the mention of Eneas, but then her expression smoothed out. "She was very real, I promise you that," she said. "And she loved you very much."

"She never even knew me," Agnes said.

"She held you in her arms," Ambrosine said softly. "And kissed your tiny little hands and whispered your name."

"But . . ." Agnes tried to swallow the lump in her throat. "But how could you know that? Leo and I were born in Kaolin, in some private facility outside Old Port."

Ambrosine traced the pattern on the arm of her chair

with a finger. "No," she said. "You were not. You were born right here, on this estate."

If her own chair were to suddenly swallow her up, Agnes could not have been more surprised. She . . . was born . . . in Pelago.

"Why would my father ever agree to that?" she said.

"We made an arrangement," Ambrosine said. "One that he did not honor, of course."

Agnes recalled the words from the letter Eneas had written Phebe. *A deal was made and a deal was broken.*

Before she could ask, Ambrosine continued, "But that is neither here nor there. We both know the sort of petty, conniving man your father is—I should not have entered into any agreement with him in the first place. And besides, there are more important matters to discuss."

Agnes's head was spinning and the best she could muster was a confused, "Huh?"

"The past can wait. It is the future that concerns us now."

Agnes blinked. "The future?"

Ambrosine rubbed her hands together. "Yes, my dear. The heir to Culinnon has come home at last. There is much you need to learn about this country, this island, our family's history, but there will be plenty of time for that. For many years now, the Byrnes have been subjected to the most brutal character attacks from the Triumvirate. They are jealous of our power, of the wealth of Culinnon and the mystery it is shrouded in. Many Byrne matriarchs have thought to separate themselves from Ithilia's control, but none have had the courage or the force of will to actually *do* something about it."

Agnes felt a sudden squirming of nerves in the pit of her stomach.

"The northern islands are loyal to us, loyal to Culinnon," Ambrosine continued. "Why should we submit to western rule? It would be far better to rule ourselves. I have spoken to the head families on all the major islands. They are with me, at last. The Malleys took some convincing—Ragna can be such a stubborn old witch—but everyone has agreed. Their ships are mine, their people mine, their loyalty mine. And now with Braxos in our sights and Kaolin ships attacking Ithilia, it is the perfect time to declare."

Agnes's palms went clammy. "Declare what?"

Ambrosine straightened her shoulders. "Why, declare our independence, my darling girl. To form our own state, with our own queen. And just one, not three who fight and bicker and scheme against each other and play favorites with the upper-class families. One queen to bring everyone together."

"Can you do that?" Agnes asked. "Just . . . break away from Pelago and form your own nation?"

"Why not?" her grandmother said. "Just because something has not been done before does not mean it *shouldn't* be done. Braxos has power, Agnes, and not just this tether that Sera is seeking to find."

"I know," Agnes said. "I read the scrolls. Or what was left of them."

One side of Ambrosine's mouth curved upward like a scythe. "Of course. I heard you met Matthias. What did you think of your uncle?"

"He was very kind," Agnes said.

The scythe twisted. "I suppose that is one way to describe him." Ambrosine roused herself. "So you know about Braxos and the power that rests there, greater than anything, a power tied to Culinnon . . . it *belongs* to our family. And together, you and I will create a new dynasty in a new country, all our own."

"A what?"

"The northern islands would not support me without an heir, you see," Ambrosine said. "But then I heard you had applied to the university and I knew . . . Alethea's daughter was returning to Pelago at last, to take her rightful place in the family. You were the linchpin I needed, Agnes. And once I am queen of the north, you will be a princess, won't that be grand?"

She was beaming at Agnes like she was offering her a large serving of chocolate and not domination over a territory. A princess? Agnes had no interest in being a princess. She was supposed to study at the Academy of Sciences. She hadn't come here to rule over anyone except herself.

Ambrosine reached out to take Agnes's hand in both her own. Her fingers were bony but surprisingly strong.

"Oh, Agnes," she said, triumph ringing in every word. "Don't you see? We will finally be who we were meant to be—a family, all together where we belong. I wouldn't want to start this journey with anyone else by my side. I had thought perhaps my son's wife could—" She stopped herself and shook her head. "But that was foolish of me and makes no matter now. Think of it—when you have daughters they will be princesses, and then their daughters and theirs after. We will make the Byrne family live in the minds and hearts of our people for generations to come. We will truly leave our mark on this world. And it all starts now, it starts with us together. It is everything I have ever wanted."

But Agnes didn't want to have daughters. Or sons. She didn't want to leave a mark on the world or start a new line of queens. Her grandmother pulled her to her feet and wrapped her arms around her, engulfing Agnes in the scent of lace and jasmine, and it was what Agnes had always dreamed of and yet not at all the way she'd pictured it.

Ambrosine released her and held Agnes by the shoulders, looking deep into her eyes. "I see her in you," she said. "Not the way she lives in Leo. But I see her."

"Really?" Agnes asked, her spirits soaring because this was truly all she had ever wanted to hear, her whole life.

"Really," Ambrosine said, and then kissed her lightly on the cheek. "We have so much catching up to do! I'm sorry to spring this all on you so suddenly, but there simply wasn't time to waste. Much has happened since your flight from Ithilia. Now, come. Let's get some hot food in you. And I'm sure you will be wanting to see your brother and Sera."

Agnes allowed herself to be led from the room, her thoughts in turmoil, her homecoming not going at all the way she had expected.

28

SERA

SEVERAL DAYS AFTER AGNES'S ARRIVAL, SERA WOKE EARLY
and crept down to the dock.

She was slowly learning her way around the estate, the
glass halls and winding stairs and huge sequoias becoming
familiar. She, Leo, Vada, and Agnes had explored much of
the island—Hektor took them to where the Misarros' ships
were docked on the eastern side, Ambrosine showed them
the vineyards on the western slopes, and once Bellamy even
led them to a place she said was her favorite, a cave with
walls that glittered with quartz in an array of colors, emerald and ruby and amethyst. It reminded Sera of the stargem
mines. And at the very back of the cave was a hot spring, the
water black and steaming.

Sera was growing impatient, though. Vada and Agnes had arrived with a ship but Ambrosine had sent it off for "maintenance," whatever that meant. They were so close to Braxos, she could feel it in her blood and in the way the moonstone shimmered against her skin, and yet she had no way of getting there without Ambrosine's help; and for all of her promises, that help did not seem forthcoming.

Agnes had told them about Matthias and the university and Xavier showing up in Ithilia—that had come as a great shock—and Leo had told her about their own journey and the war that was beginning and the queen who was pursuing Ambrosine. Sera had added her own stories, of the self blood bond and the memories and her ability to speak human languages—Vada had been so excited to understand her at last. And she had been thrilled to learn that Agnes and Vada were together—Leo had been surprised by his sister's newfound relationship, but admitted to Sera privately that it actually made sense to him now when he thought back on certain things from their days in Old Port. And he was happy to see Agnes happy. Culinnon felt like a little bubble, Sera thought, but its safety was a mirage. The outside world was in turmoil.

She reached the end of the dock and peered over its edge, her fingers lighting up as she called for Errol. The mertag's head popped out of the water as if he'd been waiting for her.

"Good morning, Sera Lighthaven," he said.

"Good morning," Sera replied cheerfully. She'd come every morning to speak to him, before anyone else was awake. She did not want Ambrosine to know she could talk to mertags or Arboreals. It was bad enough Hektor had seen her in the grove with the sprite-Boris.

"When are we making sail for Braxos?" Errol asked.

Sera sighed. "I don't know. I would leave today if I could. But we don't have a ship any longer."

Errol's colors flashed in sad gray-greens. *"No, the small boat is not in the water anymore. The humans must have brought it on land."* He cocked his head. *"My family thinks I am crazy to try and take you to Braxos."*

"Why?" Sera asked. "Because it is dangerous?"

Errol let out his croaking laugh. *"Dangerous? No, Braxos is not dangerous to mertags. There is nothing in these waters that can harm us. The human family who lives on Culinnon—they do not like us to leave. Keep to the waters around Culinnon, protect the island from unknown faces, unknown ships. It is all we have ever done. Not Errol, though. Errol likes to stretch his fins and explore the seas."* The corners of his mouth turned down. *"That is how Errol was caught. Too far out, too far away. A foolish mertag."*

"If you had not been caught I never would have met you," Sera said.

That made him brighten. *"Too true, Sera Lighthaven!"*

Sera wondered if perhaps the mertags were in a similar situation to the Arboreals—trapped on this one island when they were meant to swim the seas.

There was a creak of wood and Sera jumped. Agnes was walking down the dock, wrapped in a thick sweater with a big woolen scarf around her neck.

"I thought I might find you here," she said with a grin.

She took a piece of dried apricot out of her pocket and tossed it at Errol, who caught it in a flash.

"Agnes is always giving Errol food," Errol said happily.

Sera laughed. "You deserve it," she told him. "You got her and Vada here, safe and quick."

Errol puffed out his chest. *"I would do the same for any friend of Sera Lighthaven."*

Agnes curled up beside Sera on the dock. "It's nice here," she said. "Quiet."

Her brow furrowed and Sera knew what she was thinking.

"Has Ambrosine talked any more to you about her plans to rule the northern islands?"

Agnes shivered. "No. I think she realized she might have told me all that a bit too soon. I mean, I only just got here."

"She must have been thinking about it for a very long time," Sera said. "So it was hard for her to wait once she saw you."

"I didn't come here to be a princess," Agnes said. "We're supposed to be getting you to Braxos and here we are, touring Culinnon like we're on vacation. I get that she wants me to feel some connection with it, but that's not why I'm here."

"I'm not sure your grandmother is the type to much care what others wish to do," Sera said.

"No," Agnes agreed, scratching her ear. "She's sort of like my father that way." She chewed on her lower lip. "A princess," she muttered. "Why would she think that's something I would ever want?"

"She doesn't know you," Sera pointed out gently. "Only the idea of you. Perhaps in time, she'll learn. Your place is at the university. She'll have to accept that."

Agnes nodded, but there was no conviction in it, and even Sera herself did not believe her own words.

"*A ship!*" Errol cried out. "*A ship is coming, Sera Lighthaven.*"

Sera was on her knees in an instant. "Whose ship?" she asked. She saw a trail of lights in the water and listened to the other mertags, passing along the message in a chain of color.

"*Ship, ship, ship,*" they said. "*Friend not foe, friend not foe.*"

And then, "*Family, family, family.*"

"What are they saying?" Agnes asked.

"A ship is coming," Sera said. She stood and peered out across the water and sure enough, in the distance but growing closer, was the outline of a mast blossoming with three sails.

Agnes scrambled to her feet. "The Renalt?"

"Family," Sera told her. "That's what they said."

The mertags were swarming, their colors flashing wordlessly. The ship drew closer—she could see a flag flying the five stars of the Lekke and her heart seized up, but it was the Renalt who was after Ambrosine, and besides, the mertags were letting the ship pass. It was sailing very fast, its slender, narrow body cutting through the water.

There was someone standing on the prow, and as the ship came closer, Agnes clapped her hands to her chest.

"Matthias," she gasped.

Servants came rushing out of the estate at the sight of the ship, calling out orders to each other, and someone ran to fetch Ambrosine. Sailors jumped down from the rails and landed deftly on the dock, Agnes and Sera stumbling out of their way so they could tie up the ship.

Matthias wore a slate-colored cloak and heavy woolen pants, high boots laced up over them. He had thinning red hair and very pale eyes and there was something distinctly educated about him.

He strode down the gangplank, cloak flapping in the wind. "Agnes," he said, smiling broadly. "You made it." He turned to Sera and there was a brief flicker of shock before he gave her a deep bow. "You must be the friend she told me about."

"I am Sera Lighthaven," Sera said.

"Matthias Byrne, at your service." His gaze was keen as he took her in. "My mother must be ecstatic over you."

"Matthias." Ambrosine stood at the end of the dock, swathed in ermine, Hektor and a handful of Misarros behind her. The sailors parted to let her through.

"Mother," Matthias said.

She looked up at his ship and her lips curled. "How kind of the Lekke to lend you a clipper. Such a nice reward for all your years of work."

"The Lekke is very generous," Matthias replied.

"What are you doing here?" Hektor demanded.

"Lovely to see you too, brother," Matthias said.

"Hektor speaks the truth," Ambrosine said. "I seem to recall you vowing never to return to this island again, or some such dramatic nonsense."

Matthias flinched but stood his ground. "Desperate times, Mother," he said. "You've made it rather impossible to be a Byrne in Ithilia at the moment, what with your penchant for attacking the Triumvirate personally."

Ambrosine waved a hand. "It was they who did the attacking first," she said. "Absconding with my grandson like he was a piece of cargo. And dear Sera as well. Have you met Sera? She and Leo are absolutely devoted to each other. And Agnes, of course, you know Agnes. She told me you showed her the archives."

Matthias's nostrils flared. "The archives are open to everyone." He sounded faintly exasperated, as if he'd explained this more than once.

"Old rules for old times," Ambrosine said. "Things are changing."

"They are indeed," Matthias said, but just then Leo and Vada came running out to the docks.

"We saw the Triumvirate flag and thought—" Leo stopped short when he saw Matthias.

"Leo, this is our uncle," Agnes said.

Tears filled Matthias's eyes as he took in Leo's face. "By the goddesses," he murmured.

"The resemblance is striking, isn't it?" Ambrosine said, but Matthias was walking toward Leo like a man in a trance. He stopped in front of him and extended a hand.

"Matthias Byrne," he said as Leo shook it. "It is a great pleasure to meet you."

"Um, you too," Leo said.

"So you've run to the protection of Culinnon now?" Hektor said with a sneer. "After all these years of abandoning your family?"

"I'm not running away," Matthias said mildly. "I've brought a gift for you, Mother."

His eyes flickered to Agnes and then he turned to the ship.

"Bring them out!" he called.

Leo choked on his own breath and Agnes gave a half squeak, half whimper as Xavier McLellan appeared on the deck of the clipper.

"Oh my," Ambrosine said, folding her arms across her chest. "What an unexpected surprise."

A second later, Kiernan appeared beside him and Hektor let out a barking laugh.

"You found the bastard?" he said to Matthias. "*You* of all people?"

Kiernan was watching the two men with unabashed fear in his eyes.

"Now, Hektor," Ambrosine said. "Is that any way to talk about your older brother?"

"Brother?" Leo croaked as Ambrosine strode forward.

"Bring them down!" she called, and the sailors shoved at the two men and they stumbled down the gangplank. Xavier's face was cold as stone but Kiernan was pale and quivering.

"Well, Ezra," Ambrosine said. "I suppose I shouldn't be surprised that you attached yourself to . . . him." She shot Xavier a disdainful look. "You always did like serving the biggest bully in the play yard." She sighed. "What an embarrassment, to have to call you son."

"But . . ." Agnes was shaking her head, confused. "But his last name is Kiernan."

"His father's name," Ambrosine said. "One of the first mistakes I ever made, before I was married. Since Ezra is technically a Byrne, I raised him here, though being illegitimate, he was never allowed to take the Byrne name. And he has been a disappointment ever since."

Sera had never felt any great love for the man who had stuck needles in her arm, but he wilted before her now, a sad, pathetic creature.

"I see you've finally got what you wanted," Xavier said to Ambrosine, jerking his head in Agnes's direction. He had not even said hello to his children, no remark about their safety or comment on how well they looked. Sera knew she shouldn't be surprised, but it made her sad all the same.

"I always do," Ambrosine replied. "Even if I have to wait eighteen years."

"Please don't hurt us," Kiernan whimpered.

"Shut up, Ezra," Xavier snapped.

"Yes, Ezra, listen to your master," Ambrosine said.

"I didn't bring them here so you could hurt either of them," Matthias said.

"I'm not remotely interested in your intentions, Matthias," Ambrosine said dryly. "They are here and that's all that matters." She snapped her fingers and the Misarros sprang forward.

"Take them to the wailing caverns," she said. Kiernan let out a cry of despair as the Misarros dragged him off. Xavier yanked his arms free.

"I can walk myself," he growled. He strode forward, sparing Sera one curious, resentful glance before his eyes fell on his son. "I didn't think you could be a bigger disappointment than you already were, Leo. For once in my life, I was wrong."

Leo's face flushed blotchy red and Sera felt her vision blur with anger.

"I know this might be hard for you to believe, Father," Leo said. "But I don't live and die by your judgment anymore."

Xavier only smirked. "Don't you?" he said, then a Misarro shoved him in the back, leading him off the dock to follow Kiernan.

"Well," Ambrosine said, running a hand over her furs. "What a morning. Leo, Agnes, come with me. We are going to have a little family discussion with your uncles."

29

LEO

THEY LEFT SERA AND VADA STANDING ON THE DOCK AND entered the estate. Leo's head was spinning.

His father's words still echoed in his ears but their sting was quickly fading. For a moment, Leo had a flash of his old self, the shallow coward from Old Port who desperately needed Xavier's approval, but then he'd seen Sera glaring and felt a surge of heat in his chest. His father's opinion wasn't the only one that mattered anymore—in fact, his opinion didn't matter at all.

How Matthias had come to bring him here and why, Leo couldn't begin to guess. From the look on Agnes's face, she was just as confused as he was.

Ambrosine led Agnes and Leo and their uncles to a

small parlor—they passed Bellamy in one of the glass halls
and she stared at Matthias with shock. Hektor gave her a
look that plainly said, "I'll explain later."

The parlor walls were alternating strips of onyx and
glass, like zebra stripes, and the furniture was all varying
shades of green. Ambrosine folded herself into a high-
backed, winged armchair, Hektor skulking by one of the
glass panels as Matthias sank onto the sofa. There was a
low bench opposite him, across the coffee table, and Leo
and Agnes perched there in unison.

"So," Ambrosine said without preamble. "You have
brought the traitor and the thief. Murderer too, though he'll
answer for that in due time."

Agnes and Leo looked at each other, confused.

"Your father killed your mother," Ambrosine said, as
casually as if it were nothing. Leo felt the room begin to
spin. Hektor flinched but Matthias sighed.

"Please don't say it like that, Mother, they're his children," he said. He turned to Agnes and Leo. "He didn't
kill her."

"He should not have brought her here so late,"
Ambrosine snarled. "What was he thinking, waiting that
long. She was almost at her due date and in no condition for
a long sea voyage."

"She was fine when she arrived," Matthias said wearily,
as if they'd had this conversation before. "The doctor said
twins presented more danger than a typical pregnancy."

"The question is, what do we do with him now?" Hektor asked.

"He must be punished," Ambrosine said. "Both of them must be punished. A night in the wailing caverns should be a good start."

"Please," Agnes said. "He was never a good father to us, but we don't want him hurt." She glanced at Leo as if to confirm this.

"We don't," Leo said, and his sister looked relieved.

"He should not have said what he said to you," she whispered.

"Yeah. But was it really all that surprising?" Leo muttered back.

"He stays in the wailing caves tonight," Ambrosine said. "How did you find him?" she asked Matthias.

"I heard he was in Ithilia," he said. "I figured he was staying at the same inn he stayed at when he met Alethea. Didn't realize Ezra was with him."

"Now we know who stole the Arboreal and the mertag," Hektor growled.

Ambrosine rolled her eyes. "Please, Hektor, I suspected that ever since Ezra disappeared." She turned back to her youngest son. "Why bring Xavier here, if you have no taste for revenge?"

Matthias gestured to Agnes and Leo. "He's their father. I was unable to convince the Lekke to vote against war with Kaolin. The streets were getting dangerous. I didn't want Xavier to end up murdered or locked away in Banrissa. He's a Kaolin and was married to a Byrne to boot."

"How did you get him on the ship?" Hektor asked.

"The Lekke graced me with a small crew as well,"

Matthias said. "They aren't Misarros but they are still a force to be reckoned with. Besides, Ezra didn't put up much of a fight."

Hektor snorted. "No, I wouldn't expect him to."

"Mother, please," Matthias said. "I beg you, don't do this thing. Don't challenge the Triumvirate. I know the Renalt is after you. Her warships could be here any day now. Culinnon is well guarded, but can the mertags take on an entire fleet? Have they ever been tested that way?"

"You think it is only mertags I have protecting us?" Ambrosine said. "You're supposed to be the smart one, Matthias. The northern islands have joined our cause now that Agnes has arrived. We can finally break away from Triumvirate rule. With Agnes by my side, we will start a new nation, one that is loyal to *us*."

For a second, Matthias just stared at her. Then he gripped the couch cushions as if needing them to anchor him.

"She's only just come to Pelago," he said. "You can't expect her to acquiesce happily to your plans. She barely knows the country at all!"

"Agnes can make her own decisions," Ambrosine snapped.

"And what about Leo?" Matthias demanded. "What are your plans for him?"

"You saw the silver girl, didn't you?" Hektor said. "She and Leo are . . . very close."

Matthias was on his feet in an instant. "They're *children*," he hissed at his mother. "Goddesses be damned, you haven't changed one bit since she died, have you?"

Ambrosine sneered. "It is my duty to preserve this family for—"

"Yes, the family, the family, all my life I've heard about how important this family is," Matthias said, his jaw tight. "As if that's all we are, Byrnes and no more. Alethea couldn't stand it—you suffocated her with your talk of continuing the line, of changing the world. What's so wrong with the world the way it is, Mother?"

"For someone so well learned, Matthias, you can be blindingly stupid," Ambrosine said. "So obsessed with your individual life when there is history to consider."

"Do not speak to me of history," Matthias said, his pale eyes flashing. "The dead are dead and the past cannot be changed. Leo and Agnes deserve to live their own lives. I don't want to see them break under the weight of your expectations like Hektor."

"I haven't broken under anything," Hektor said.

"Oh, I'm sorry," Matthias said, turning on him. "Does Bellamy have a child I'm unaware of?" Pain spasmed across Hektor's face and Matthias looked contrite. "I apologize," he said. "That was cruel."

"It was the truth, Matthias," Ambrosine said. "Don't lose your spine now that you just seem to have grown one." She nodded to Agnes. "Your visit with him must have been inspiring. I've never seen him so . . ." She looked her son up and down. "Bold."

Leo and Agnes had been mostly bystanders throughout this conversation, but Leo felt now was the time to speak up.

"We came here to get Sera to Braxos," he said. "Not to

torture our father or turn Agnes into a princess or . . ." He swallowed. "Or anything else. She doesn't belong here."

"Oh, but doesn't she?" Ambrosine said. "I know she has been speaking with my mertags in the mornings. And my Arboreals. Did she think she can go anywhere on this estate without being watched?"

Leo's neck grew hot.

"She has a connection with Culinnon the same as you two," Ambrosine continued. "Why you both are so insistent to get her to this tether, I can't understand."

"So she can go home!" Agnes cried.

"Yes, I know, my dear," Ambrosine said. "And I said I would help get Sera to Braxos. I will not break my word."

Matthias opened his mouth but Ambrosine stood. "We will leave for Braxos in two days' time. I have called the Malleys and the Callases to Culinnon. If the Renalt arrives, we will be ready for her."

"And what about our father?" Leo asked.

"One night in the caves won't kill him," Ambrosine said. "Hektor, make sure Xavier and Ezra have water, and food if they want it, though I doubt they will. Matthias, come with me."

Hektor strode out of the room, Ambrosine on his heels. Matthias paused and bent down to whisper to Leo and Agnes, "There's a surprise for you on my ship. Wait until dark, when everyone's asleep."

Then he was gone.

Agnes wrung her hands. "What do we do, Leo?"

Leo felt as helpless as she looked. "I don't know," he said. He wasn't particularly surprised that Ambrosine was reluctant to let Sera go—but the fact that she had imprisoned his father in a horrible-sounding place left a queasy feeling in the pit of his stomach. "I think for now, all we can do is get on that ship and see what Matthias brought us."

The night was cloudy as Leo met Agnes in a little copse of trees near her room. Both of them dressed in black, and they took a roundabout route to the dock, avoiding the front door to the estate.

The clipper was like a skeleton in the night, its sails furled, its masts spindly. The ship itself was empty, the sailors all being housed in a separate part of the mansion. Leo and Agnes used the ropes tying it up to climb on board, Agnes pitching over the rail with a thud and causing them both to freeze. Leo's heart pounded in his ears as they waited to see if anyone would come running, but the only sound was the water lapping against the hull. The deck was so dark Leo had to hold his hands out in front of him to make sure he didn't walk into anything. Matthias hadn't said where exactly this gift would be found.

Agnes bumped into him with a muffled "Oof," and Leo shushed her just as a lantern appeared from the steps to the hold.

"Matthias?" a voice called softly. The lantern was raised and it took all of Leo's self-control not to shout.

It was Eneas.

He caught sight of them and his face broke into a wide smile. "Children!" he whispered joyfully. "Come, quick."

They hurried toward him and down into the hold, following the light of the lantern. Eneas led them to a small cabin with a hammock hanging in one corner and a low table with three stools around it. He placed the lantern on the table and Agnes flung her arms around him. Leo felt a pinch of shame. He'd never been particularly nice to Eneas, something he regretted now.

"What are you doing here?" Agnes asked as he released her.

"Once I arrived in Ithilia and heard what your grand-mother had done, I knew I had to come find you. Both of you," he said, nodding toward Leo. "I went straight to Matthias. Caught him just in time. He'd already locked up your father and Ezra. I believe we got out of Ithilia just before the Kaolin navy arrived." He shook his head. "What a foolish war. It would have been better if Braxos had never been found."

"Ambrosine locked Father away in something called the wailing caves," Agnes said. "Will they hurt him?"

Eneas touched her cheek. "He does not deserve you. No, the caves will not hurt him. Their walls shriek. He will have an unpleasant, sleepless night, that's all."

"We met Phebe in Arbaz," Agnes said. "She lent us her ship so we could follow Leo and Sera here."

Eneas smiled again. "I am glad she got to meet you. She has heard much about you over the years."

"She showed us that letter you wrote," Leo said. "About a deal made and broken."

"And Ambrosine told me she wants to found her own country, of just the northern islands," Agnes said. "And declare herself queen and me *princess*." Her nose wrinkled. Even after several days to get used to it, Leo still found the idea strange and ridiculous.

Eneas sighed and sank onto one of the stools. "I'm so sorry, Agnes," he said. "It is the exact fate your mother wished to avoid for you. Alethea felt trapped by her mother's expectations, the idea of becoming royalty, of being who Ambrosine wanted her to be instead of just herself. *Don't we have enough?* she used to say. Isn't Culinnon enough? But even Culinnon frustrated her. Why was all this power kept in one place?"

"We've seen the Arboreal groves," Leo said, sitting down at another stool.

"And all the mertags, of course," Agnes added, following his example.

"Culinnon is a special island," Eneas said. "But to your mother, it was a prison. Ambrosine never appreciated Alethea's thirst to be different, to explore, to create. She wanted to be an artist, she wanted to travel and experience new things and meet new people. And once she met Xavier, she thought she had figured out exactly how to slip from her mother's grasp. Who would follow a matriarch whose daughter married a man from Kaolin?"

"So *that's* why she married him?" Agnes asked.

"It was," Eneas said. "At first. But she underestimated Ambrosine's ambition. And her patience. Ambrosine is not one to scrap a plan because there are a few bumps along the way. I didn't know it at the time, but she had already approached Xavier herself, already made a deal with him. She very likely contacted him the minute she heard he was sniffing around her daughter."

"What was the deal?" Leo asked.

Eneas leaned forward, the light of the lantern casting shadows on his face. "He would be required to have all of his children born on Culinnon. That way she could make the claim they were truly Pelagan, truly Byrnes. If you had been born in Kaolin, no one in Pelago would have accepted you as her heir. And in exchange, she would give him something more powerful than money or jewels—she would give him an Arboreal and a mertag. One for each child born on the estate. It was a fantastic price that would keep him wealthy for generations. It would make him special. Different. The envy of Old Port City—and that was all your father ever wanted." He smiled sadly. "Well, until he fell in love with your mother."

Leo made a confused huffing sound and Agnes sucked in a breath.

"Until he *what*?" Leo asked. He couldn't imagine his father being in love with anyone, least of all his own wife. That had been the one thing about their relationship Leo had felt certain of.

"Yes," Eneas said. "He fell in love with her. And she with him. Not at first—oh no, they would have fights that you could hear from five streets away in the beginning. And she hated Old Port and all the smoke and smog and factories and uptight women and starched dresses." He shifted on his stool and his face softened. "But then it all changed. It was Alethea who introduced him to people who actually knew theater—she used to spend time in the East Village, meet the artists and dancers and actors, learn which producers were looking for what shows or what the next big thing was going to be. They came to respect each other, your mother and father, and out of that respect grew a fierce love." Eneas gazed up at the ceiling. "Oh, how I wish you could have known him in those days. He was so quick to smile, to laugh even. She brought out the best in him. She brought out the best in everyone." He rubbed his eyes. "I miss her so much."

"Were you . . . in love with her?" Agnes asked.

Eneas chuckled. "No, no, my dear, I am not attracted to women like that. Your mother was simply a beautiful soul. I was not the ideal choice of companion for her, a lowly merchant's son from Arbaz. But she would visit every summer and she did not care about my pedigree. We were so close, almost as close as she was to Matthias." He looked at Leo, his expression tender. "It must have been quite a moment for Matthias when he first laid eyes on you. Alethea reborn."

Leo didn't know what to say to that. He wished he could have known the woman whose face he bore.

"But I digress," Eneas said. "Xavier managed to convince Alethea to have her children born on Culinnon. I remember myself thinking it was strange at the time—Alethea had vowed never to return to the island lest her mother not let her leave. And Xavier did not tell her of the deal he had struck with Ambrosine. How he got her to go, I still do not know. But we went, very close to her due date, on a secret ship in the middle of the night. Swansea was tasked with telling anyone who asked that they had left Old Port to have you delivered in a specialized facility.

"The night before she went into labor, we were alone in her favorite room in the estate, a solarium high up in one of the sequoias that looked out over the Arboreal grove. And she said, 'Eneas, if anything happens to me, keep my children away from this place, away from my mother. Don't let her try to do to them what she did to me, or to Matthias, or to Hektor. I want them to live their own lives, the way they wish to. Make sure they know they are loved. Don't tell them about any of this.' Of course, at the time it was an easy promise to make. 'Nothing is going to happen to you,' I reassured her. 'You will raise your children and love them for who they are.' She patted my hand and said, 'Xavier will take care of them. He'll be a good father. That's where they belong. Not here.'"

Silence filled the cabin. Leo's heart felt like sludge in his chest, his throat painfully tight. Agnes's eyes glittered with tears.

"And then she died," Eneas said, staring at the flickering light of the lantern. "That night was one of the worst of my life. I found myself wandering the glass halls of the estate, not caring where I was going, not thinking about anything except loss. I came upon a study I was unfamiliar with—the door was ajar and there was a light shining from within. I pushed the door open, not really curious but more for something to do. The room was empty, the desk covered in papers—some were correspondence, others looked like property deeds, or legalese, or invoices. But one name caught my eye. *Agnes.* The name Alethea had chosen for you."

"*She* chose it?" Agnes asked.

Eneas nodded. "Xavier chose yours," he said to Leo. He felt as if he had become glued to his stool. The thought of his father picking out his name was too foreign a concept for his brain to fully comprehend.

Eneas turned back to Agnes. "Ambrosine was going to keep you," he said, the barest hint of a growl in his voice. "She was never going to let you return to Kaolin with Xavier and your brother. She was going to keep you here and use you as she had wanted to use Alethea. To make your life about power and Culinnon and a new nation to control. She wields this island as a weapon and you were the magic bullet. An heir, at last.

"And she was never going to hold up her end of the bargain. She had never intended to let Xavier have so much as an olive branch from Culinnon, never mind a mertag and Arboreal."

He pressed his hands against the table, fingers splayed.

"I took the papers and went to your father at once. He was still with Alethea, still cradling her on her deathbed as if she might yet wake." He swallowed, and it was loud in the utter silence. "I told him we have to leave, *now*. I told him what I'd seen, what Ambrosine was planning. 'She killed her,' he said. He kept saying it over and over again. He blamed Ambrosine for her death, for making him bring Alethea to Culinnon, though he had made that decision as much as Ambrosine had. As much as Alethea had. I shook him then, hard, and made him look at the papers. 'This is not what Alethea would have wanted,' I told him. 'Will you let her dying wish go unanswered? Will you leave her daughter with this woman?'

"That seemed to rouse him. We went to the nursery and got the two of you. I carried Agnes and he took you, Leo. He could barely look at either of you. But when we approached the dock where our ship was anchored, we discovered Misarros swarming it. We were trapped."

"How did you escape?" Agnes asked.

"Ezra," Eneas said, pursing his lips. "He wanted Xavier to take him to Kaolin, to get him as far from Culinnon as possible. She hates him, but he is technically a Byrne, so she couldn't let him go. He led us to a small ship that I was able to sail by myself. I told Xavier, we cannot take Ezra with us. It wasn't worth the risk. She would be furious enough when she discovered we had gone with the children; why add insult to injury. And personally, I had never liked Ezra, never trusted him. Xavier promised him, though—he promised him that once his children were safe, he would find a way to get Ezra out from under his mother's thumb. And he did. It only took eighteen years.

"The mertags knew me and let our ship pass. We made it to a port where we could purchase berths on a larger ship that took us to Ithilia and from there back to Old Port City. It was a long, dark journey, but your father grew even darker over the course of it. The change in him was startling. He never held either of you again after that first night. I never heard him laugh the way he used to. He threatened me never to tell the two of you about Alethea or what life was like before you were born. And I knew his threats were real—he could send me back to Pelago without a second thought, and then I would never be able to see either of you again. I would have broken my promise to your mother, to make sure you both knew you were loved."

Leo felt another twist of guilt remembering all the times Eneas had offered him a compliment or a sweet or even just a jovial good morning. And all the times Leo had scoffed or rolled his eyes or wished he hadn't.

"Your father became cold and hateful," Eneas continued, "and his hate was directed both at Ambrosine and at Pelago, at the country he felt had given him the only woman he had ever loved and then taken her away. Xavier was not going to look after you. It was left entirely to me."

He turned to Agnes. "But when you wanted to apply to the Academy of Sciences, I found I could not refuse you. I could not prevent you from living your life as you wanted it, the way your mother would have wanted you to. Even if it meant bringing you within your grandmother's reach. I thought, so much time has passed. Perhaps she is not the same anymore, does not have the schemes she once did. Eighteen years and not a whisper of rebellion in the northern islands. I thought she might have given up on that plan." He rubbed the back of his neck. "But once I left you at the Seaport, a growing fear took root inside me. I should have gone with them, I told myself. I should not have let them go alone. I purchased a berth on the first ship I could find." Eneas placed a hand on top of Agnes's. "I'm so sorry," he said. "You should have known all of this, from the very beginning. I tried to protect you and I fear I only made things worse."

Agnes squeezed his hand. "It's all right," she said. She looked at Leo. "We know so much now. It's better than never knowing at all."

Leo nodded. "But why risk coming here with Matthias?" he asked. "Won't Ambrosine be furious if she finds out you've returned to Culinnon?"

"Ah," Eneas said, a clever smile spreading across his face. "But this is not the end of my journey. Or should I say, *our* journey."

"What do you mean?" Agnes asked.

He gestured around at the cabin. "Matthias and I have brought you a ship." He leaned forward, candlelight shining in his eyes. "We are going to get you to Braxos."

30

AGNES

AGNES CREPT INTO VADA'S ROOM AFTER SHE AND LEO
returned from the ship.

"Mmph?" Vada mumbled, rubbing her eyes. But she
became alert once Agnes began whispering all that Eneas
had said on the clipper. When she told Vada about Braxos,
she sat straight up in bed.

"When are we leaving?" she asked.

"Soon," Agnes said. "Matthias will let us know."

"Sera will be much relieved."

"Yes," Agnes agreed, even as her heart sank at the
thought of losing her Cerulean friend. It would be harder
for Leo, though. She'd never seen her brother so content or
relaxed as he had been these past few days on Culinnon.

She wondered how Sera would feel, leaving him behind.

Agnes slept in Vada's bed that night—she'd grown accustomed to sleeping beside her on the *Palma* so it had felt strange to sleep alone. But it was a restless night. Braxos was so close now and Agnes didn't want to wait a second more than necessary to start the journey there. She felt a little guilty at the thought of deceiving her grandmother, but Ambrosine wasn't really the person Agnes had been dreaming of her whole life. And after the way she'd spoken to Matthias, and how she'd thrown her father into a terrifying cavern, and all that Eneas had told her . . . Agnes knew she would never be what Ambrosine wanted her to be. And Ambrosine wasn't the connection to her mother Agnes had hoped for.

But Matthias was. And Eneas was here. There was more to her mother's family than just Ambrosine.

The next afternoon, the four of them gathered in one of the sitting rooms. Vada was teaching Leo how to play dice while Sera sat listlessly braiding and unbraiding her hair, her eyes fixed on the glass walls that looked out over the ocean. Agnes was skimming a book on one of the past Byrne matriarchs, but her mind kept wandering to the fact that her father had actually *loved* her mother. She simply couldn't fathom it and now that she knew, she wasn't sure how she felt about it. It made her happy to know her mother had been happy, but it also made her resent her father even more for acting all these years as if he hated her.

There was a light tap on the door and Agnes sat up. Bellamy hovered in the doorway, her shoulders hunched as if expecting someone to strike her.

"Ambrosine wishes to see you," she said. "All of you."

Agnes hadn't spoken much to Hektor's shy, skittish wife, but Sera had told her how she'd seen into Bellamy's memories and that the woman had been devoted to her ever since. Agnes wished more people on this planet felt that way, instead of trying to control or trap or manipulate Sera for their own purposes.

They followed Bellamy down through the halls until they came to a large circular room Agnes hadn't seen before. The ceiling was glass but the walls were marble, pristine white with narrow, arched windows cut along them at intervals. There was an enormous chair that was more of a throne, upholstered in velvet with gilded wings, and two benches on either side. Matthias and Hektor were already there, seated on the right-hand bench. Bellamy scurried to sit beside her husband. Ambrosine, of course, was on the throne.

"Come," she said. "Sit."

The foursome dutifully took their seats on the left-hand bench, exchanging confused glances with each other. They heard footsteps down the hall and Agnes's pulse thrummed in her ears.

When her father and Kiernan were marched in, they looked awful: dark circles under their eyes, their hair wild, their faces gaunt. Kiernan's whole body was shaking.

"I trust you had an unpleasant evening," Ambrosine said to Xavier, who stared at her with a steely expression despite his unruly appearance.

"Mother, please—" Kiernan began, but Ambrosine held up a hand and he fell silent.

"Be quiet, Ezra, the adults are talking." She turned her focus back to Xavier. "Now. What judgment should be made on the man who stole my granddaughter and two of my prized possessions?"

Agnes kept waiting for her father to look at them, either her or Leo, but he kept his gaze fixed on her grandmother.

"I am a citizen of Kaolin," he said. "You have no authority to pass judgment on me."

Ambrosine's smile cut like a blade. "But you are far from home, Xavier. Your pitiful president and his silly navy have no power here. You should never have come back. Why did you? Was it to rescue your children?"

Agnes's heart twisted, sharp and painful, as her father, still not looking at them, said, "No."

"Yet you took Agnes away from me," Ambrosine said. "Why? If you care so little for her, why not leave her here?"

"I didn't say I didn't care," Xavier shot back. "She wasn't yours to keep. Alethea would never have wanted that."

"As if you knew what she wanted better than her own mother."

Xavier's nostrils flared. "You didn't know her at all. You only saw the Alethea you wanted to see."

"*You* only saw her money."

"I loved her!" Xavier snarled, suddenly turning as wild as his hair. His eyes bulged and a vein throbbed in his temple. "I loved her more than my own life and you killed her. *You* made her come here, *you* made her have them here. Why couldn't you just leave her alone?"

"You came too late!" Ambrosine shot back. "I told you. I *told* you, seven months at the very latest, but you had to wait to the last second, you arrogant bastard."

"It was your fault we had to come in the first place," Xavier said.

"Oh, please. You saw Culinnon and you wanted its treasures. Don't turn yourself into a victim, Xavier, it doesn't suit you. And you haven't looked once at your children since you've entered this room. How do you think Alethea would feel about that?"

Xavier's face darkened and his throat bobbed up and down. "I . . . can't," he said.

"Do you blame *them* for her death, as well as me?"

Xavier said nothing. Agnes heard Leo shift on the bench. She felt a dull ringing in her ears.

"So," Ambrosine said, steepling her fingers, "Alethea's death was everyone's fault but yours. How so very Kaolin of you. Men don't have to take responsibility for their actions where you come from, but here on Culinnon, you *will* be held accountable. So tell me again: Why are you here?"

Xavier's hands clenched into fists and for a moment, Agnes thought he might try to hit Ambrosine.

"Braxos," Kiernan cried, breaking the tension. "We came for Braxos."

Ambrosine's turquoise eyes glinted like chips of ice. "Braxos," she said. Then she sighed. "I admit, Xavier, I'm disappointed. I thought you would have some better motive than riches."

"It's not about riches," Xavier said. "You think she didn't tell me? About the stories, about the scrolls?" He pulled at his hair and for a moment, Agnes wondered if he'd gone completely mad. "She's supposed to *be there*!" he cried. "She said . . . the island where you could speak to the dead. She said so, she told me! Past, present, and future, all together, all at once. I just . . ." Suddenly he crumpled to his knees, and this frightened Agnes more than the shouting. "She can't be gone forever," he said. "She's supposed to be there. Everything else I had is gone. My work, my company, my children, all of it, gone." He glared up at Ambrosine. "Does that make you happy? You won. You've got everything now. But not *her*. I can still have her. If I can just get to Braxos."

For a moment there was nothing but a ringing silence. Xavier's chest heaved and even Ambrosine seemed at a loss for words.

"Your children are *here*, Xavier," Matthias said softly. "Look at them. You never lost her."

Xavier turned his head away and Agnes felt her chest collapse. But then, to her great surprise, Sera stood.

"I can show her to you," she said, and Xavier gaped at her, at his ability to understand her as much as at her words. "I can show you Alethea."

Her skin began to glow faintly and her eyes burned. Agnes felt a gentle wind wash over her body and her muscles seized up, just the way Leo had described the sensation, and she knew that Sera was calling up their veils of life, of memory. Part of her wanted to cry out and say no, don't let Ambrosine or my father know of this power, but she was frozen and could not speak.

And then the memory came.

Alethea was in the brownstone on Creekwater Row. She was trying to hang a mobile over a crib in the nursery, hugely pregnant, her red curls pulled up in a messy bun. She stood on a stool on her tiptoes, her legs wobbling.

"Alethea!" Xavier cried when he came in. "Let me do that."

She grinned and pecked him on the cheek as he took the mobile, stars and clouds and little golden ships. "I think our daughter will like this. It reminds me of sailing with Matthias in the summers." She spoke Kaolish with the faintest trace of a Pelagan accent.

"What about our son?" Xavier asked. "Is his mobile made of gloom and doom like Hektor?"

Alethea laughed and slapped him playfully on the arm. Then she bent down and picked up a different one, trees and fish and a yellow sun in its center.

"His will be his mother's home," she said.

"But you hate Culinnon."

Alethea sighed and let Xavier hang the mobile over the second crib. "I don't hate it," she said. "I wish it were different. Not so isolated or secret. I think that island has made my family crazy."

Xavier kissed her on the forehead. "Good thing I stole you away before you lost your marbles then." He made a wild, exaggerated face and she laughed again.

"It's good they will be born there," she said as he rubbed her stomach. "You were right. Our children are of two worlds and we should not shy away from that." She made a face. "Mother must be ecstatic."

"Eneas and I will be with you the whole time," Xavier promised. "I'll take any barbs she throws at you."

Alethea pretended to swoon. "My hero," she said.

Xavier caught her and dipped her back, and she shrieked with delight.

"Oh, my feet," she said. She looked down and sighed. "Someday I'll be able to see them again."

"I'll have Swansea heat some water," Xavier said. "A good soak is just what they need."

"Mmm, yes," she said, wrapping her arms around his waist. "That sounds perfect." She gazed up at him. "I love you, you know."

Xavier's smile was brighter than the sun. "I love you too."

The scene dissolved and the marble room returned, and Agnes had the impulse to reach out as if she could somehow grasp the memory in her hand and keep it with her. Her face was wet, and when she looked at her brother, she saw tears streaming down his cheeks.

"Bring her back," Xavier said as the whole room seemed to come to life.

"What just happened?" Matthias said, dazed, running a hand over his face and then down his arms. Agnes knew he had not seen Xavier's memory—only she and Leo had that power with Sera's magic inside them. But everyone had felt the strange breeze and the unpleasant sensation of being held in place, unable to even lift a finger. Ambrosine sucked in a huge breath, her whole body trembling.

"Bring her back," Xavier cried, scrambling to his feet. Leo was up in an instant and moving to protect Sera.

Sera, however, did not seem afraid. "I see you, Xavier McLellan," she said. "And I pity you. Matthias is right. She has been here all along. You do not need Braxos to see her.

She lives in Leo and in Agnes. And she lives inside you."

"Please," Xavier said, breathing heavily, still refusing to look at his son. "I can't . . . bring her back!"

"No," Sera said simply.

Suddenly, from outside, there came the long blast of a horn. Then another.

"The Renalt," Hektor gasped.

Ambrosine was on her feet in an instant. "Get the Misarros," she snapped at Hektor. "Ready the ships." She turned to Sera. "Once I have dealt with this queen," she said, hunger in her eyes, "you and I are going to have a chat."

She strode out of the room, Hektor at her heels. "Lock them back up," she said on her way out, waving in the direction of Xavier and Kiernan.

Agnes found her voice at last. "Father," she cried, and finally he looked at her. He seemed empty, lifeless. Agnes didn't know what to say. That she forgave him? She didn't. That she understood him now? She didn't think that was true either.

"We could have been a family," she said. "A real family. You could have told us about her. You didn't need to be so angry, so cruel."

Xavier's face clouded over. "You do not know what it is like to lose what I lost," he said.

"But I do," Matthias said, stepping forward. "And if you cannot see that you must change your ways, Xavier . . ." He gestured to Leo and Agnes. "You will lose what little you have left of her."

Then the Misarros were pulling them from the room, and the last Agnes saw of her father was a look of shame and grief etched across his face.

"We've got to leave," Matthias said. "Now."

They ran through the halls and out into the forested area toward the dock, but when they got there, they saw the clipper was being guarded by five Misarros.

"What do we do?" Agnes asked.

"I'll distract them," Bellamy said. Agnes hadn't even noticed she had come with them. Her thoughts were all tangled up in that memory.

Bellamy touched Sera lightly on the arm. "Good luck," she said. Then she ran out into the open. "The Renalt has come!" she cried. "Quickly, your mistress needs you!"

The Misarros jumped to attention, following Bellamy as she led them in the opposite direction and out of sight. Their group hurried to board the clipper, Eneas emerging from below.

"Can you sail this alone?" Leo asked Matthias.

"Not alone," Vada said.

"I can sail," Sera reminded him.

"Eneas can too," Matthias said. "Quick, there's no time to waste."

"Has the Renalt truly come?" Eneas asked as Vada and Sera scrambled up the masts to release the sails.

"She has," Matthias said. "And we'd best be getting out of here while my mother is distracted."

Agnes leaned over the rail and called out, "Errol!"

The mertag's head popped up as if he'd been waiting. His lights flashed anxious indigo and umber.

"It's time, Errol," she said. "Braxos. It's time to go to Braxos."

Errol snapped his teeth at her and a gust of wind caught the sails, pulling the ship out into the water and away from Culinnon. Agnes had one last fleeting thought of her father and her grandmother and everything she was leaving behind.

Then she turned around and set her sights on the horizon, on Braxos and all that waited there.

31

SERA

Once Culinnon was safely off in the distance, Sera climbed down from the mast.

Errol was swimming alongside the clipper, his lights flashing excitedly when he saw her.

"Braxos, Sera Lighthaven! Off to Braxos at last," he crowed.

Sera's stomach flip-flopped. She was eager to reach the tether and return home, and yet she would miss her friends on this planet. She wished she could help the Arboreals and the mertags too, free them from Culinnon and Ambrosine Byrne. And she wanted to help heal the wounds between Leo and Agnes and their father. What she had seen inside Xavier's memory only inspired pity—the sort of man he used to be, the sort of man he could be again.

Leo came up beside her, snaking one arm around her waist.

"Ready to go home?" he asked, and though his voice was steady, she felt his hand quiver.

She nuzzled into his shoulder. "We haven't reached the island yet," she reminded him. "It will not feel real until I see the tether with my own eyes."

Matthias walked up to them. "What happened back there?" he asked. Sera explained about the memory sharing, no longer afraid to declare her magic to humans. Matthias's pale eyes grew wide as she spoke. When she finished, he said, "It is a good thing we left when we did. My mother would never have let you go."

"How long until we reach Braxos?" Eneas asked, coming up to them, Agnes and Vada trailing behind.

Sera shrugged. "Errol does not understand distance like we do." She peered into the water again and gasped. "Leo, look!"

The waters around the ship were dotted with mertags. Errol was not their only escort, it seemed. Errol saw her and popped up out of the water again.

"*Some of my family has come along,*" he said. "*They wish to help the Cerulean who saved me. There is fighting back on Culinnon and they want no part of it. There will be death today, human and mertag both.*" He sniffed at the air and then looked back the way they had come. "*By snails and seaweed, let us hope it does not follow us.*"

"Yes," Sera murmured, her fingertips flashing. "Let us hope."

* * *

One day out from Culinnon, the mist appeared.

It was delicate at first, clinging to the water's surface like a cloud to a nebula leaf. The wind grew colder but Sera did not mind. It felt good to be sailing again.

She was standing at the rail with Agnes when Errol emerged from the water.

"Ships are coming," he said. *"Ships with golden suns along with ships of Culinnon."*

When Sera translated for Agnes, she pursed her lips, her face stony. "The Renalt *and* my grandmother," she said. "I suppose it was too much to think they would keep each other distracted. Ambrosine must have noticed that we left. She's coming after us. And the Renalt is coming after her."

"This ship is very fast," Sera said, gazing up at the billowing sails.

"Let's hope it's faster than those clandestines," Agnes said.

The mist grew heavier and heavier, slowing their pace, and then the fog took them and everything disappeared.

Errol led them carefully, even slower now. The fog left dewdrops in Sera's hair and sent little shivers down her spine. It grew denser by the minute, surrounding the sloop in thick clouds of pearly gray. When Sera looked down she could barely make out the water lapping at the hull—if not for Errol's light, they would have been lost in minutes.

The benefit of this was that there was surely no way Ambrosine or the Renalt could follow them in it.

The first destroyed ship took them completely by surprise. One second there was nothing but fog; the next, the prow of a half-sunken galleon was rearing up on their left.

Errol flashed and his family lit up the water, illuminating a safe path. The clipper veered, Matthias at the helm, narrowly missing the figurehead, a wooden dolphin with half its nose missing. Sera thought she saw a body floating in the water surrounding the wreck, but she couldn't bring herself to look too closely and then the fog swallowed it up.

They passed several more wreckages, ships with gaping holes in their hulls, tattered sails hanging from their splintered masts. They were ghost ships, shrouded in grayish white, silent forevermore. Some had shredded Kaolin flags draped over their prows, others the green-and-silver flag of Pelago. The fog did not care for country or allegiance.

"There is a presence here," Vada said. "It does not want us."

Sera had sensed it too, but not the same way Vada did.

"It's the tether," she said. "It is protecting itself from your kind. But it . . . it calls to me. It sings."

She could hear it faintly, could feel it resonating in her chest like a violin string. It kept her going, kept her hopeful as a silence so unnervingly complete fell around them. Even the water lapping at the ship had ceased to make any noise. Agnes had her hands pressed against her ears as if the silence was somehow too loud, and Leo was pale and drawn, gripping the rail so tight his knuckles looked about to split through his skin.

"It feels like this will be forever," Eneas said dully. "Silence and fog and nothing else and no one left to remember."

Sera clutched Leela's pendant tight, praying for the fog to end.

"Look!" Agnes cried suddenly, and though her voice was muted, there was a spark of life in it.

In the distance there was a crack in the mist—a thin strip of silver that was widening as they approached. Like the first breath after being underwater for too long, the fog parted and the ship sailed into a circle of bright blue sky, so stunningly clear it made tears well up in Sera's eyes.

Oh, thank you, Mother Sun, she prayed. The change in her companions was noticeable—Leo's shoulders relaxed, Agnes stood to get a better view, Eneas and Vada exchanged tentative smiles.

"*Braxos, Sera Lighthaven!*" Errol cried from the water.

"*Braxos,*" his family echoed around him.

The waters surrounding the island glittered with jewels, some as big as ostrich eggs, colorful spots shining beneath the waves like a garden of light. White-sand beaches stretched across the shoreline, the land covered with lush green trees. And high above them, perched at the top of an ivory cliff, were the ruins they had seen in the photograph, copper doors shining—and the many-pointed star set directly over them, the same as the star on Sera's necklace. The temple was made of rose-colored stone, with jutting, winding turrets and towers swirling up toward the sky like snakes. It was partially caved in on one side.

"By the goddesses," Matthias murmured.

"We did it," Leo said, breathless and a little befuddled. "We actually did it."

Then everyone on the ship was laughing and cheering, clapping each other on the back and kissing cheeks. Home was so close, Sera could taste it.

"Ships!" Errol cried, his lights flashing danger. *"Sera Lighthaven, the fog has gone. See, see, look, the ships are coming, the ships can see us now!"*

In front of her were two hulking warships flying the golden sun flag of the Renalt. Off to her right, Sera caught glimpses of clandestines, visible when the light hit their hulls in a certain way.

The ships were pointed in all different directions, lost amid the fog, but Sera saw them begin to turn now, as the island that was once such a mystery had suddenly become crystal clear.

"We need to land *now*," she said, but Matthias was already steering the clipper toward a smooth strip of beach. Once it hit sand, they all jumped out into water up to their knees. The ruins towered above and Sera had to shield her eyes from the sun. The tether was there, shining proudly up from its center, and she felt herself grow dizzy and eager and nervous all at once.

"Let's go before those other ships get here," Leo said.

There was a path from the beach, covered in leaves and smooth pebbles. They hurried along as quickly as they could—it was overgrown and sometimes they lost sight of it and had to double back. And always it climbed higher and higher. Agnes's breath began to come in sharp pants and Vada clutched her side. Leo's face was bright red and Eneas began to fall behind, Matthias even further back.

"Go on without me," Matthias said, but Agnes moved to walk beside him, letting him lean on her shoulder, while Leo helped Eneas.

Up and up . . . and all the while the moonstone grew warmer against Sera's chest, whispering to her in unknown words that spoke of home. When at last they reached the top, they were sweating and out of breath. Eneas collapsed onto his back, panting, Matthias slumped beside him. Leo leaned against a tree as Agnes sank to her knees. Only Vada and Sera remained standing.

"That," Vada gasped. "Was quite the climb."

A fat golden honeybee buzzed lazily by them and perched itself in the horn of an enormous purple flower. The sun shone like a golden aurum in the sky, and the grass was softer than seresheep fleece. The trees hung heavy with fruit, ripe plums and peaches, yellow pears and juicy red apples. And right in front of them, the temple soared upward, the doors open as if they had been waiting.

The many-pointed star pulsed out a welcome that Sera's moonstone returned.

"The tether is inside," Sera said. "I can feel it."

Agnes struggled to her feet. "We'll go with you."

Leo didn't say anything; he just straightened and looked at her with the blue-green eyes she had come to know so well, eyes that said to her now, "I will be with you to the end." She knew he would let her go no matter how much it hurt.

"We'll wait here," Vada said. "These men are needing rest."

"I am sorry, my friends," Eneas said.

"I can come," Matthias said, struggling to get to his feet. Sera stopped him with a gentle shake of her head.

"No, you have done enough. More than enough." Then she leaned down and whispered, "Take good care of them."

When she passed Eneas, he took her hand and kissed it. "Bless you," he said. "And all you have done for this family. I wish you could see it. It all began with you."

Sera's first thought when she stepped inside the ruins was that this temple was almost like the one in the City Above the Sky.

The ceiling was vaulted and painted with moons and a sun and stars. But the paintings were ancient and not well tended—they were chipped and crumbling in places. The room was huge, circular walls of rose stone with alcoves cut into them that held sconces of copper, though they bore no light now, no candle or wick to be seen.

"Wow," Leo said, and his voice echoed in the cavernous space.

When they reached the opposite side, they found a door so short they all had to duck to get through it. The next room was smaller and entirely overrun with plants. Ivy devoured the walls, saplings pushed their way up from the cracks in the stone floor, and dandelions and ferns and thistles carpeted the ground. The following room was so dark they had to feel their way along the walls to find the door to get out. It led them into an impossibly cold room with water trickling down the walls, lichen growing in the ancient stone.

At last they emerged into a huge courtyard that was

oddly shaped—it took Sera a moment to recognize the many-pointed star, various prongs of stone shooting out from the open center. The tether was stuck into a fountain of frozen water that curled and arched and glittered in the sunlight, as if it had once been bright and bubbling and was caught by a sudden frost. The fountain itself was made of pale pink stone, three tiers with carvings along their edges. The beauty of the tether would have struck her dumb if not for the other, more surprising feature of this courtyard.

Kneeling by the temple was a woman. Not just any woman—a *Cerulean*. Her blue hair was streaked with silver and when she looked up, Sera saw there were deep wrinkles around her mouth and eyes. Her irises were dim and milky, a blue as pale as the sky at dawn. She struggled to her feet, leaning heavily on the fountain for support, her gaze fixed on Sera.

"Elysse?" she whispered.

Sera's feet felt cemented to the stone floor. "I am Sera Lighthaven," she said in a quavering voice. "Who are you?"

"I am Wyllin Moonseer," the woman replied. Sera's rib cage seemed to collapse, her head spinning as Leo grabbed her arm to steady her.

"But . . . you are dead," she gasped. "You died when you created this tether."

The lines around Wyllin's mouth deepened. "I should have died many, many years ago, Sera Lighthaven. Have you come to break the tether and set me free to live in Mother Sun's eternal embrace at last?"

"I have come to go home," Sera said. "I was hoping the

tether could help me get back to the City Above the Sky."

"The tether cannot do that," Wyllin replied. "Only moonstone can." She frowned. "You must have some, if you are here at all."

Sera took the pendant from beneath her dress and held it out for Wyllin to see. "My best friend gave this to me before . . . before I fell. I was supposed to break the tether, but . . ." She trailed off.

"So," Wyllin murmured. "She decided it was finally time to leave." She stepped toward Sera and cupped the stone gently in her hands. "This was mine," she said. "I sent it to the City months ago, before the fountain froze. The tether can take things, as it nourishes the City, and I hoped . . ." She pressed her thumb to the pendant. "I do not know what I hoped. That someone would find it, and read my heart contained within it. That it would make a difference. I did not think to see it back on this planet again."

All this was a bit more information than Sera felt herself able to handle. "How are you alive?" she asked. "How is this possible?"

"Elysse is still the High Priestess, is she not?"

Sera had never known the High Priestess's name. "Yes."

Wyllin nodded and closed her eyes. "She had a plan," she said. "And I agreed to it. For the good of the City. For the health of our people. But it was not meant to last this long." When she opened them, they shone with tears. "I never thought I would see another Cerulean again."

"Can you help Sera get home?"

Sera had almost forgotten her friends. Agnes was

looking at Wyllin with a mix of awe and determination. "We have traveled so far. Please. We want to get her back to her city."

Wyllin seemed to only just notice them as well. "Humans," she said, confused. "Humans are helping you?"

Sera nodded. "They have risked much to bring me here."

Wyllin's smile was a private, gentle thing. "So she was wrong after all," she said. "I am glad to see it." She turned to Sera, but before she could say anything else, there was a flash of brilliant light and then something fell into the courtyard, sending up a cloud of dust that made Sera choke and her eyes water.

"What . . ." Leo gasped, coughing and swatting at the air.

When the dust cleared, a young woman was standing beside the fountain, looking utterly shocked as she stared around at the courtyard. And Sera felt all her fear and confusion turn to joy.

"Leela!" she cried.

PART SIX

The island of Braxos, Pelago

and

The City Above the Sky

32

LEELA

THE POOL HADN'T FELT LIKE WATER WHEN LEELA JUMPED through it.

She'd expected liquid to soak her the way the stalactite had when she'd freed Estelle, but instead she'd fallen through a thick gelatin-like substance and emerged completely dry. She caught a fleeting glimpse of shock on the High Priestess's face before she was tumbling through space, the stars bright around her, the stalactites swirling in her vision.

The descent took ages—at some point it felt like she was no longer even falling, as if she was simply suspended in the cold endless black of space. It *was* cold, colder than anything she'd felt before, colder than the glowing blue columns of the Sky Gardens or the frosty grass in the cloudspinners' grove. Her lungs expanded and contracted, but breathing wasn't comfortable here, not at all the same as she was used to. The planet never seemed to come any closer.

Until all at once, it did.

She hit the atmosphere and her skin sizzled for several painful moments, the tether turning from winking silver-gold-blue to a thin streak of fire. But before the terror was truly able to set in—that she might actually die and her theory of moonstone was wrong—a pearly mist engulfed her, cool and soothing like a balm against her skin. She hung suspended and sensed the mist was waiting for her to make a decision.

I need to find Sera, she thought, and then her whole body was wrenched back and flung forward and she was falling fast, too fast, everything blurred, the wind howling in her ears, and just when she thought she couldn't take it anymore, her feet hit solid ground and a cloud of dust engulfed her.

And there was Sera. Real, true, living, breathing Sera.

"Leela!" she cried. Then they were running, colliding into each other.

"You're here," Leela said breathlessly.

Sera pulled away, tears sparkling in her eyes. "*You* are here!" she cried. "How . . . *how*?"

Leela held up her wrist with the moonstone cuff. "I was right," she said. "It's the moonstone, Sera. It saved you. It brought me here. Moonstone allows us to travel between the planet and the City. It does so much that we never knew."

Sera was examining the bracelet with awe. "Where did you find this?"

"In the temple spire. There is a secret place beneath it. The High Priestess has been hiding all the moonstone inside it."

"Of course. She is so afraid."

Leela whirled at the sound of an unfamiliar voice and stared in shock at the ancient Cerulean woman standing before them. "Who are you?"

"This is Wyllin," Sera explained. "She did not die. She has been here on the planet all along."

"*Wyllin?*" Leela more mouthed the word than spoke it. "But . . . how can you be alive and also have formed the tether?"

"Because there is a way," Wyllin said. "A way to create the tether without death, though it leads to death in the end, anyway. Just a longer, slower one." Her words seemed to carry a weight that grew heavier as she spoke, and she leaned against the fountain. "The circlet Elysse wears is the first moonstone Mother Sun ever gifted the City, passed down from each High Priestess. It contains all the power and knowledge of every single High Priestess who has ever lived. That was how she learned about the fruit, about how to make Cerulean magic into another tangible form, one that could be consumed instead of one that was merely connective. It was done centuries before we were born, by a High Priestess named Elbeth, she told me. As a precaution against a long voyage through space. She wished to see if she could preserve Cerulean magic and use it to boost the magic within her people during the journey—it was she who first put a Cerulean in a stalactite. But it was done willingly and not for very long."

"It is not being done willingly anymore," Leela said sharply.

Wyllin's eyes turned sad. "No," she said. "I imagine not."

"But why has the High Priestess left you here all alone?" Sera asked. Wyllin gazed up at the tether with tenderness, almost the way a mother looks at a child.

"I am the tether and the tether is me," she said. "After the Great Sadness, Elysse changed. We all did. She wanted to protect the City. She was so afraid, so . . ." Her voice trailed off.

"Sorry, the Great *what*?"

Leela had hardly noticed the humans, she had been so focused on Sera.

"The Great Sadness was the biggest tragedy in Cerulean history," Sera explained. "When two hundred Cerulean were massacred on the last planet the City was tethered to."

"How horrible," the human girl said as Sera made hasty introductions.

"Leela, this is Leo and his sister, Agnes," she said. "They are the ones I told you about."

"Thank you for helping my friend," Leela said.

"You're—wait a second, we can understand you," Leo said, looking confused.

"Cerulean can always speak the language of the planets," Wyllin said.

"I could not, when I first fell," Sera said. "It was not until I arrived in Pelago that I was able to speak the human languages."

Wyllin frowned. "Perhaps such a long attachment with

no contact with the planet had crippled this ability."

"No," Leela said, her face darkening. "It is because the High Priestess has been siphoning magic from her people. To keep herself young and strong. She has somehow bent the circlet to her will, twisted its purpose to steal from us."

Wyllin slumped against the fountain. "Moonstone is connective. It links our City to the planets and the Cerulean to each other. In days past, the stone was used by Cerulean to communicate, whether between City and planet or while on the planet itself. Like an external blood bond. We can read each other's hearts, speak to each other by calling on our moonstone."

"Like how I called on it to let me speak to you in the Sky Gardens," Leela said to Sera.

"And how I could see my purple mother at the birthing houses," Sera said.

"But the moonstone in the circlet is even more powerful," Wyllin said. "It connects to *all* Cerulean. Imagine a blood bond so strong it can actually pull magic to it, absorb the power that lives within our blood. Instead of sharing, it only takes. That moonstone must be thrumming with Cerulean magic." She looked at Sera. "But you were out of her grasp. Your magic must have replenished, grown strong like it is supposed to be while you were here on the planet."

Sera looked down at her hands. "Errol was first because he was the easiest," she said to herself. "And then Boris. And the humans last. When I was at my strongest. When I arrived in Pelago."

"I beg your pardon, Ms. . . . Ms. Wyllin," Agnes said timidly. "But what exactly is this place? The, um, the humans all seem to think it contains wealth or powers."

Wyllin looked startled, but she spoke to Agnes with kindness.

"It is called the Alcazar," she said. "Wherever the tether plants itself, it creates an Alcazar to protect it, to enclose it. Each one looks different, depending on the planet. This one was very large and very beautiful at first. But it has crumbled into ruin." Wyllin's eyes grew sad and distant. "There is power here, yes, but not the way humans expect. The tether cannot be claimed by anyone, not even a Cerulean. But it has the power of connection and the wealth of life. Are there no more important things than that?" She looked again at the fine chain. "How I would love to return to the City Above the Sky. To walk the shores of the Great Estuary, to wander the moonflower fields and eat honeycombs fresh from the Apiary." Her expression turned so mournful Leela felt her own heart ache. "And yet I cannot go back. Everything I have to give I have given to this planet and to the tether. I am the tether and the tether is me."

"But—sorry," Agnes said, "if the moonstone is connective and it was the way Cerulean used to travel between the city and the planet, then why hasn't Sera just been able to go home already?"

"She was not strong enough," Wyllin said. "Not if her magic had been weakened." She half smiled. "It is easier to fall than to fly." She and Sera exchanged a look, then Wyllin turned back to Agnes. "It takes great intention to travel. And who is to say Sera was not *meant* to come here to learn this? That there was not some deeper meaning to your journey?"

Leela felt a tingle run up her spine as Wyllin addressed her and Sera. "I must show you the truth before you go, before I die. For I feel my death coming now, as certain as sunrise."

"The truth?" Sera asked.

"About the Great Sadness. About what really happened on that planet so many centuries ago."

Leela and Sera looked at each other and Leela felt a sinking dread creep all the way down to her toes. Perhaps the biggest of all the High Priestess's lies was about to be revealed.

Wyllin extended a hand to Sera. "I will need my moonstone. My magic is too weak. The moonstone contains my heart, my memories, faint remnants of my magic. As it will contain yours now."

Sera quickly removed the necklace and gave it to her.

"What's going on?" Leo asked.

"I am going to show these Cerulean a piece of their history," Wyllin said.

"Is that like the memory sharing?" Agnes asked.

"I have blood bonded with both of these humans," Sera explained. "They have my magic in their veins."

Wyllin's lips parted in surprise, but Leela already knew this. "Blood bonded with humans?" Wyllin gasped. Sera nodded, unashamed.

"They see what I see," she said.

Wyllin hesitated.

"You are very brave," she said. She looked first at Agnes, then at Leo, as if silently commanding them to respect what they were about to witness.

Leo gave a serious nod and Agnes straightened her shoulders.

Wyllin's mouth twitched, then she gripped the moonstone and bent over it with closed eyes. Leela thought she saw her lips move as if speaking to the stone, and when Wyllin looked up, her pale irises had turned brilliant blue like a light had been switched on inside her. Leela felt the same disorienting sensation she had experienced when she put the High Priestess's circlet on, as if she was being pulled very quickly through a narrow tunnel.

The courtyard they were in blurred and disappeared, and then Leela was in the Sky Gardens, but they were bright and cheery, with vibrant flowers and verdant trees growing overhead, not the dead, withered bramble she was used to. The vines that surrounded the moonstone were sea green and rose-gold and no fruit grew among them. The air was cool, but not cold, and the columns glowed pleasantly blue, the paths like ribbons of pure white. There was nothing eerie about the place at all.

"I want to go back," a young woman was saying. "Just one last time, before we leave. I want to see him again, to say goodbye."

Leela's shock at seeing the young High Priestess registered somewhere, but her mouth was moving, words unbidden coming out, and she knew she was Wyllin in this memory, as she had been the High Priestess in the circlet before.

"There are so many already down on the planet," Wyllin said. "To replenish it before we leave."

"Exactly," the High Priestess said, though in Wyllin's

mind she was Elysse, and only Elysse. She was not the High Priestess yet, though Leela knew (because Wyllin did) that she had already been chosen to succeed Luille, the current High Priestess. "No one will notice a few more additions."

The fragment of Leela's mind registered with shock that she was seeing a memory from over nine hundred years ago.

Elysse's face turned pleading, making sad eyes that Wyllin knew would win her the argument. They always did.

"You are certain it is just to say goodbye?" Wyllin asked. "You could stay with him, if you wished, as others have done before. Remember Ebereen, who stayed behind on the planet of roses and ice?"

"I am not a planet-keeper," Elysse insisted, though Wyllin felt skeptical.

"But you care for this male," she said.

"I do," Elysse admitted. She looked forlorn as she stared through the large, clear pool, down to the planet below. "But I care for my City more. And I have been chosen. I must accept the role Mother Sun has assigned for me."

Wyllin put her hand on Elysse's arm. "It is such a weight for one so young," she said. "Mother Sun must see greatness in you."

Elysse smiled at her, but there was doubt in her eyes. "I am glad I have you to keep my counsel," she said.

"Always," Wyllin promised. Then she sighed. "Very well. Go. Say your goodbye."

Their moonstones were almost identical, perfect circles of pure white, except Elysse's was larger than Wyllin's. They had both had them fashioned into rings—Elysse wore hers on the middle finger of her right hand, Wyllin on the ring finger of her left. They chose pools that were next to each other, and Wyllin gazed down at the planet, at the familiar sprawling brown-green continent. Then they both jumped.

The scene dissolved and suddenly Wyllin was watching from afar as Elysse embraced a male with alabaster skin and hair the color of moss. She was whispering something to him and he shook his head, and then she was crying, and he talked softly in her ear. She nodded. He asked her something else and she nodded again. When he held her close against his chest, Wyllin saw a gleam she did not like in his fire-red eyes. She had always found the eyes of the people who inhabited this planet to be unnerving, but this was different.

"The others are in the forest," Wyllin said, when Elysse left the male behind and joined her. "I spoke to Gailen through my moonstone while I was waiting for you. We have almost finished giving back what we took from this planet. It is time to go. Let's join them and return with the rest, and no one will ever know why you and I came."

She didn't like that Elysse kept this male a secret. But her friend had always been so reserved in her feelings. At first Wyllin had just been happy to see Elysse in love. But something had changed in her over the course of the City's time attached to this planet. Orial, it was called, and while some of its people were dangerous and fierce, there were others who were kind and curious. Not everyone on the planet was the same. Elysse had spent more and more time on its surface, and yet still insisted she did not want to stay behind when the City moved on. Wyllin sensed her friend was torn. She wanted both, her male *and* her City, and that was simply not possible.

The scene dissolved again, and Wyllin was in a grove of enormous trees with thorny trunks and dark purple leaves. Cerulean wandered through them, leaving behind wispy trails of magic that caused flowers to spring up in their wake, and the grass to grow thicker, and the air to become more fragrant. Wyllin loved this part, when they would come to the planet in large numbers to give back what they had taken using the gift of their magic. The City did not steal—it only borrowed from the planets. There were so many Cerulean this time, easily two hundred. Elysse was not the only one who had enjoyed being attached to Orial. Its weather was pleasant, its people fascinating, its waters and woods teeming with life. Wyllin's favorite were the fish that had appeared in the Estuary once they had tethered here, one of the planetary gifts from Orial. The fish had fine filaments that hung over their eyes and they would light up in spectacular colors.

She wondered where Luille was among the Cerulean gathered—it was tradition for the High Priestess to be present for the replenishing. Then she caught sight of her, several yards away, her magic like a cloak streaming out behind her.

Wyllin spread her palms and called on her magic and it flowed through her like a river, faint trails emanating out from her as she walked, blessing the ground with fertile richness. She passed an elderly Cerulean named Meranne, who called out a greeting, the orange ribbon around her neck shining against her skin.

"Last day on Orial, Wyllin," she said. "Are you sad to be leaving?"

"Yes and no," Wyllin replied. "It will be nice to see a new planet."

Meranne smiled and patted her moonstone, a brooch fashioned in the shape of a bumblebee. "I have just seen my green wife leaving offerings at Aila's statue for a safe journey. She is eager for a new planet as well."

"I will leave an offering myself when we return," Wyllin said. "Perhaps—"

The rest of her words died on her lips as there was a whizzing sound by her ear, and then the back of Meranne's head exploded in a burst of bright blue, her body crumpling to the ground.

Wyllin did not make the conscious decision to drop to her knees, but suddenly she was lying in the grass and there was whizzing all around her, and the Cerulean were running and screaming and falling.

Bullets, Wyllin thought, her mind clumsy as another whiz pierced the skull of a Cerulean running for shelter among the trees. *Bullets, they are called. From a gun.*

Cerulean magic had healing power, but there was no cure for a piece of metal that pierced the brain. Her vision grew black around the edges and Wyllin could feel her lungs shrinking inside her chest; there was not enough air, and she knew she should do something but she couldn't breathe, she couldn't remember, there were bodies everywhere.

And then she saw him. The male her friend loved so much. With a long, cruel piece of metal in his hand. A rifle, she remembered. That's what it was called.

"The head or else they'll heal!" he was shouting. "We need the blood, it's the blood that has the power!"

She told him, Wyllin thought in a daze. *And now he wants it for himself.*

"Wyllin!" Elysse was there then, shaking her. "We have to go!"

"It was him," Wyllin said, stumbling to her feet. "Elysse, it was *him*!"

Elysse turned and saw the male. Their eyes met, and the flames in his seemed to extinguish for a fraction of a second. Then he raised the gun and pointed it at her head.

"No!" Wyllin screamed, and her mind cleared, the thought of home vibrant within her; she gripped Elysse's hand, calling on her moonstone to return them to the City. The ring on her finger flared up and then they were spinning, their feet leaving the ground, everything a blur of color, and they burst through the atmosphere into space, but the stars held no comfort. When at last they emerged up through the pool and back into the Sky Gardens, Wyllin still could not find her lungs.

Elysse was shivering on the ground, sobs ripping out of her chest.

"He betrayed me," she gasped over and over. "I loved him and he betrayed me." She turned up to Wyllin, her face etched with agony. "He killed them, Wyllin. He killed them, he killed them . . ."

Wyllin held her but had no words to comfort. All she could see was Meranne's body falling to the ground. All she could hear were the screams of the dying Cerulean they had left behind.

The High Priestess, Wyllin thought with a sudden chill. Had she died on the planet as well?

A Cerulean shot up through one of the other pools, her long wail echoing through the lush gardens.

"Dead," she moaned, "all dead . . ."

Then a second appeared through a different pool, and then a third. They were crying and hugging each other the same as Wyllin and Elysse. Wyllin waited, holding her friend in her arms. And she waited. And waited.

No other Cerulean returned.

"Elysse," Wyllin said in a daze. "I think you may be the High Priestess now."

That was perhaps the only thing in the world that could quiet her friend's sobs. She sat up, rigid, and looked at the other three survivors, huddled together.

"Don't tell, Wyllin," she whispered. "Please. Promise me. I will make this right, I will protect this City with every fiber and spark of magic contained within me. I will never let anything like this happen again, I swear it on Mother Sun and all her Moon Daughters. But please. Do not tell the others of my shame."

And Wyllin believed her, because she knew Elysse loved the City Above the Sky—had she not forsaken her love on the planet, false as he was, for her devotion to it?

"I promise," she said.

The scene dissolved again. Time had passed. Elysse looked older, and no longer wore the moonstone ring, but instead bore the circlet, its stone gleaming against her sapphire hair.

"We will have to have a choosing ceremony soon," she was saying. They were in Wyllin's kitchen, a pretty room with brightly colored mugs hanging on the wall and a

window box of basil giving off a fragrant aroma. Wyllin sat
at the table while Elysse paced back and forth.

"But Mother Sun—" Wyllin began.

"She has abandoned us!" Elysse cried. "I told you. I
have had no hint, no whisper, no dreams . . . even the doors
have stopped speaking to me. We are on our own, Wyllin.
We must protect this City ourselves."

"Why not share your fears with the others?" Wyllin
said, as she had said so many times before.

"They would not understand; they are still too frightened, too traumatized . . . I will not hurt them further. They
are under *my* care now. I told you, Wyllin. I told you right
after . . ." She cringed, as if she could not bear to recall that
horrific day. "It is my duty to protect them. I failed once;
I will not fail again. I will do whatever it takes, and if it
means I must lie to give them hope, then I will. I will do
anything necessary to make this City feel safe. We can never
go down onto the planets again. Traveling through space is
dangerous, as this journey showed us. They were going to
die, the City was beginning to die and it was all my fault,
my fault I can't . . ."

She fell forward, gripping the table as her body trembled, and Wyllin knew she was holding back the tears.

"But the tether cannot survive forever," Wyllin pointed
out.

"It can," Elysse said, and when she looked up, her eyes
had an unnerving glow. "If one Cerulean is willing to make
a great sacrifice."

"Greater than giving up her life?"

"Yes," Elysse replied. "There is a way. I have seen it

in the circlet—it has never been tried before but the idea is there, just waiting to be tested. The chosen one must be brave. She must be braver than any Cerulean in the history of our City."

Wyllin swallowed. For a long moment, the two women held each other's gaze.

"What would you have me do?" Wyllin asked.

"I would imbue you with my own strength, my own power," Elysse said. "And you would keep your moonstone on you. You would survive the fall, though you would lose most of your blood along the way. But my magic can sustain you long enough for you to reach the ground, where your own magic will replenish. You can keep the tether strong. Keep the planet healthy. The planet is always at its strongest when a Cerulean is on it, remember? Keep us in one place, keep us safe. Could you do that, Wyllin? Are you brave enough, and willing? I know what I ask of you, my dearest friend. If I could do it myself, I would. But I cannot abandon my people, not now, not when hope is only just beginning to blossom in this City again. They need me, do you see?"

And Wyllin did see—this City was broken. To suffer the loss of its leader would be a devastating blow, one that it might not recover from.

"I see," she said, rising and trying to find her courage. "And I accept."

The scene dissolved and they were back below the City and Wyllin was dragging Elysse out of a stalactite, her prayer robe sticking to her skin, her breath coming out in shallow pants.

"Are you all right?" Wyllin cried. "Oh, Elysse, speak to me."

Elysse opened her eyes, but it was not Wyllin's face she gazed at.

"Look," she croaked.

Wyllin turned and saw a golden fruit had blossomed among the green and pink vines surrounding the cone of moonstone. She gasped and the fruit fell to the ground with a plop.

"You must . . . eat," Elysse said, her words faintly slurred.

"How much magic did you take from yourself?" Wyllin demanded.

Elysse's smile was blurry. "Enough. My strength will return. I know it. Give me time." She turned her head toward the fruit. "But you must eat."

With trembling hands, Wyllin picked up the fruit and took a bite. A wild gasp escaped her lips—it tasted like blackberries and honey, like the sound of her green mother's lute, like moonlight on the leaves of an apple tree. Wyllin felt herself fill with an exquisite power unlike any she had ever known and it thrilled her and terrified her in equal measure.

And then she was in the Night Gardens, standing on the glass dais, and Elysse was cutting the skin on the insides of her elbows with the ancient iron knife. Wyllin's heart stuttered but she steeled herself. Her people needed her, even if they did not know it. She had taken her moonstone out of its setting and hidden it in the pocket of her robe so the Cerulean would not know she kept it with her. She was grateful for it, for its warmth, for its connection to the City.

"Good luck," Elysse whispered, so that only Wyllin could hear. She turned, the blood flowing down her arms, and jumped from the dais.

33

LEO

THEY RETURNED TO THE PRESENT WITH A JOLT THAT SENT a shock through Leo, even though he hadn't moved at all.

The courtyard was too bright after the dimness of the Night Gardens. Leo felt mixed up, so many emotions coursing through him, most of them not even his. He could still feel Wyllin inside his mind, her thoughts, her fears, her terror as her feet left the dais.

He turned to the others; Agnes looked winded, Sera dazed, but Leela seemed to be one step ahead of them all, and Leo felt like she was satisfied in some way, as if she had finally found a missing piece that completed a puzzle.

"So that is why she has lied all this time," Leela said. Then she shook her head. "Her motives may once have been pure, but they have become twisted and rotten. She clutches her power now. She does not want to relinquish it."

"She has been through so much," Wyllin said, sinking to the ground as if her legs could no longer support her weight.

"So have you," Leela pointed out.

Sera found her voice at last. "What is a planet-keeper?" Leo had noticed that as well, when Wyllin had mentioned the Cerulean who'd stayed on the planet of ice and roses.

"A Cerulean who finds her purpose on a planet," Wyllin explained. She mopped at her brow, Sera's necklace still clutched in one hand. "There was usually one, sometimes two, who would find a deep connection to a planet—whether it was romantic love, or friendship, or simply a love of the planet itself. It was often a traveler, but not always. Those were some of the most bittersweet goodbyes, a Cerulean who chose to leave her City."

Leo tried very hard to ignore the way his blood was suddenly pumping through his veins, the tiniest ray of hope lighting up inside him. Sera was not a planet-keeper, no matter how much he might wish her to be.

"What's a traveler?" Agnes asked.

Wyllin seemed bemused by him and his sister, as if she could not understand why they cared so much.

"Travelers were the first to go down when we tethered to a new planet," Wyllin explained. "They would seek out life, assess the level of danger or intelligence, the richness of the earth and how long a tether might be able to hold. They would be the first to communicate, to make contact with the inhabitants if contact was deemed safe or necessary. Of course, there would be no more Cerulean travelers now. And there are no tether-tenders either, are there?" She dropped her head into her hands. "What have you done, Elysse?"

"So there *were* Cerulean who once looked after the tether," Sera said.

Leela grinned. "Koreen will have to eat her words." Then she frowned. "I am confused about something else, though. Elysse loved a *male*. That does not seem possible."

Wyllin gave her a curious look. "But of course it is possible. There are Cerulean who love men, though I admit they are rare. There are Cerulean who love men and women, and Cerulean who have no interest in romantic love at all. There are Cerulean who love planets more than people and Cerulean who enjoy the physical expression of love but not the emotional. Not every Cerulean is meant for a triad. Not every Cerulean is the same."

Sera seemed to be thinking very hard about something and Leo kept as still as he could. When she turned to Leela, there was a fierce sort of determination on her face.

"It is possible," she said. "I am proof. I am attracted to males, Leela. But I did not know it until I came to this planet. Finally, I understood every part of myself." She gazed up at the crystal-blue sky. "I had wondered if there were others in our City like me. Or not like me. Cerulean that are different in other ways."

Leela's eyes bulged. "Males?" She rubbed her forehead then and shot Leo a furtive glance. "Are you attracted to that male?" she whispered as if Leo wouldn't be able to hear her, standing where he was.

Sera laughed and Leo felt a sharp tug in his chest, knowing this might be the last time he heard that sound. "I was not at first," she said. "But yes. I am now."

Leela looked Leo up and down with a sort of hesitant mix of approval and curiosity, and he hoped he appeared more cool and collected than he felt. All this discovery, all this new information about the City Above the Sky, it was all leading to one thing: Sera leaving. Agnes had tears in her eyes and Leo wished she wouldn't—he wanted to be strong now. He didn't want Sera to see him falter, to see just how much it would hurt him to lose her.

"The tether must break." Wyllin had risen to her feet, breathing heavily. "The City *must* move. The tether cannot provide for much longer. And then the City will die, as it nearly did during the journey after the Great Sadness. The moonflower fields will wither, the seresheep and the bees and the birds will perish, the Estuary will dry up . . . and Elysse will cling to it anyway. Because her guilt has crippled her." She ran her fingers along the edge of the fountain. "We used to speak, from time to time. I could see her through my moonstone, hear stories of my home and news of my friends. And then my magic and my stone grew weaker until at last this fountain froze over and I saw my City no more." Her eyes gleamed for an instant. "I got the moonstone out, though, before it froze," she muttered. "I did that at least."

She held the pendant out to Sera, who took it and slipped it back around her neck. "This moonstone is yours now. Take it and return. But know that a sacrifice must be made. You fell before, and you—"

Then Wyllin gasped, staring over Sera's shoulder.

Leo turned and saw Ambrosine striding into the courtyard, Hektor and a group of Misarros at her heels. Hektor had a spear pointed at Matthias; one Misarro had a blade pressed to Eneas's throat, and another held Vada, sporting a freshly blackened eye, in a chokehold. Ambrosine herself looked slightly worse for wear after the climb, her hair lank and sticking to her face, her clothes torn and stained with sweat and dirt.

"What are you doing?" Agnes cried, as Leo instinctively moved to stand in front of Sera. "Let them go, don't hurt them!"

Ambrosine ignored her. She looked from Sera, to Leela, to Wyllin, her face gaunt and greedy. Then she turned to the fountain. Though neither she, nor Agnes, nor Leo himself could see the tether, he was certain she could feel the energy humming from it the way he could. It made the back of his teeth ache, it made his mouth water and his toes itch and his spine crackle. It spoke in a wordless whisper that made him think of green fields and warm summer days and the flapping of a butterfly's wings.

"The power here is tied to Culinnon," Ambrosine said, moving forward with a crazed gleam in her eyes. "I can feel it in my veins." She inhaled deeply through her nose. "It declares itself for *me*."

"Who are you?" Leela said, and Leo could not help but be impressed at her fearlessness as she stared down the most powerful woman in Pelago. But then, what was Pelago to Leela?

"Ambrosine Byrne," Sera growled. "She is related to Agnes and Leo."

"Byrne?" Wyllin asked. "Did you say Byrne?"

Ambrosine tore herself away from the tether she could not see, ignoring Leela and focusing her attention on Wyllin.

"I am Ambrosine Byrne, matriarch of—"

"But I met a Byrne," Wyllin said. "Soon after I fell. She found this island; she came to the Alcazar and I gave her gifts."

"Errol and Boris," Sera gasped, and Leo felt another ripple of shock run through him. It all made sense. The Arboreals called Sera "Mother." The mertags were devoted to her.

"I do not know those names," Wyllin said to Sera. "But I planted a strand of my hair and a tree grew out of it, a tree with silvery bark and turquoise leaves. A tree that could multiply and help replenish what the tether took from the earth. And then I cried a single tear into this fountain and a fishlike creature appeared, similar to the fish I had loved on Orial and yet different. And he was meant to keep the waters pure and healthy. The Byrne promised me she would spread this wealth throughout the planet."

"She lied," Leo said.

"I spoke to the Arboreals on the island of Culinnon," Sera told her. "They have been kept there, imprisoned, ever since that day. The Byrne family has coveted your gifts instead of sharing them."

Wyllin put a hand over her mouth. "But that is not how

it was meant to happen," she said. "This planet must be dying."

Leo thought about all the droughts in Kaolin, the wild-fires and the poisoned waters and the desiccated farms. The planet *was* dying. And it made sense now, why Pelago was always so fruitful when Kaolin was not—they had a concentration of Cerulean magic in this country, and regardless of whether it was being shared properly or not, it was certainly giving Pelago an environmental advantage over Kaolin.

"How do we fix it?" Agnes asked just as Ambrosine said, "*Share?* The people of this planet wouldn't know what to do with them if they ever got their hands on them. They need to be safe, they need to be tended by someone who knows, who respects them."

"No, they don't, Mother," Matthias said, speaking for the first time. "Alethea was right all along. Their power was meant for everyone, not just Byrnes."

"That is exactly the sort of traitorous comment I would expect from a man who abandoned his family," Ambrosine said, and Hektor jammed the butt of his spear into Matthi-as's back, forcing him to his knees. "Weak and a coward, just like your father."

"Are you really going to hurt me, Hektor?" Matthias asked. Hektor pointedly avoided his gaze.

Leo couldn't stand it any longer. He was sick of watch-ing people fight over something that wasn't even theirs to begin with. "There's nothing here for you," he said to his grandmother. "There's no power you can wield or control. It belongs to Sera and her city. It gives their city life. You can't *own* that. Don't you see? There are bigger things than some stupid plan to raise yourself up, to rule over a handful of islands. Wyllin just told you our planet is dying and all you can think of is Culinnon and your family legacy and keeping power for yourself."

"I see you inherited your father's arrogance," Ambrosine said to him, her voice dripping with disdain. "That does not surprise me. Agnes, however . . ." She looked at her granddaughter and shook her head. "I thought we had an agreement. I thought you and I were going to change the world."

"I never said I would join you in those plans." Agnes looked frightened, but stood her ground, her eyes flitting to Vada, still struggling against the Misarro. "I never wanted to change the world. I came here to be my own person, to study science. I thought I came here for you, too, for a connection to my mother, but you can't give me that, can you? No more than my father can. You both hoard her. You're both so wrapped up in yourselves." She jutted out her chin. "I am Alethea's daughter. She didn't want what you were offering and neither do I."

"I told you, Mother," Hektor said. "She is ungrateful. Let us go, let us leave them here. The shores are filled with gems; we can take the riches and return to Culinnon."

"I am not returning to Culinnon until I have the power the scrolls promised," Ambrosine said, turning on her eldest son with an expression of utter contempt. "And I am not leaving Agnes, no matter how many impassioned speeches she makes. Even if your wife were to somehow manage to produce a child, it would have nowhere near the claim

Agnes does. Besides," she said, her nose wrinkling, "Bellamy would probably just have a boy anyway, and then where would we be?"

Leo could not believe how cruel Ambrosine was to her own offspring. There was something perverse about it, like she enjoyed taunting him. He recalled the memory from his father, when Alethea had said, "I think that island has made my family crazy." Crazy, perhaps, and also cruel.

"There are no riches here," Wyllin said. "Those jewels you saw on the beaches were illusions. If you were to try to take them off of Braxos, they would turn to dust in your hands. Once the tether is broken, this whole island will crumble into the sea."

Hektor looked stunned, his spear trembling. Just then there was an enormous boom that made everyone in the courtyard jump.

"The Renalt," Ambrosine said. "That stubborn bitch. You'd think she'd have given up when we destroyed most of her warships."

There was another boom and the ground beneath them shook.

"Perhaps we should go, mistress," one of the Misarros suggested. Ambrosine silenced her with a look. Then she turned to Wyllin.

"This is your island," she said. "I see it now. What is your price? What do you want? I will give you anything you ask for. You met my ancestor. We have a connection, you and I. I swear to wield this power only for good."

The lie was so obvious it was almost sad. Wyllin looked

at Ambrosine for a long moment, her eyes clear as dawn, revealing nothing. At last, she said, "I will show you. But it will destroy you."

Ambrosine's lips curled. "I'd like to see it try."

Wyllin sighed and waved a hand over the fountain. Ambrosine gasped. She must be able to see the tether, Leo realized with a start. But he couldn't, and judging by the way Agnes was squinting, she couldn't either. Wyllin's words from before came back to him.

I am the tether and the tether is me.

Ambrosine's eyes grew round and bright—a dark hunger crept across her face and spread throughout her body, making her back hunch and her hands curl like claws.

"Yes," she hissed. "Yes, I see. I see it now. Oh, it's beautiful. Magnificent. It's . . ." She licked her lips. "It belongs to my family. It's mine. Mine . . ."

One claw reached out and Leo realized what she was going to do a moment too late.

"No!" he cried instinctively, having no love for his grandmother yet not wanting to see what would happen once she touched the chain of Cerulean magic. But Ambrosine had already reached up, wrapping her hand around the tether that Leo could not see. For one endless second, nothing happened.

Then she let out a choked cry, and her whole body was illuminated in a silvery-blue light—it shone out through her eyes, from the tips of her fingers, from each strand of her hair. She began to scream, and the light poured from her mouth in a torrent of brilliance. One long, high-pitched wail that pierced Leo's heart and rang over and over again in his ears. The light coming from inside Ambrosine grew brighter and brighter, until she was engulfed in it, until her body was a mere shadow, an outline, and then there was a flash like a solar flare and Leo had to shield his eyes against it.

When he looked again, all that was left of Ambrosine Byrne was bits of ash floating through the air.

"She would never have let it go," Wyllin said. "She would never have let it be until she saw it. It was consuming her thoughts and so it consumed her."

Agnes looked too shocked for words, which was exactly how Leo felt. Eneas was rubbing his eyes as if that would somehow help make sense of what had just happened, and Matthias wore an expression of horror. Hektor looked like he was going to be sick. The spear clattered to the ground as the other Misarros released their captives, staring numbly at the spot where Ambrosine vanished. Vada rushed to Agnes's side.

"She's . . . gone," Agnes said, her breath hitching in her throat as Vada held her. There was another loud boom and this time the wall shook, sending chips of rose stone down into the courtyard. Ambrosine may be gone but the Renalt was still very much here and very much a danger to Sera. She could not lose this chance to return home.

"You've got to go," Leo said, finding his voice at last and turning to her. The words tore at his throat on their way out but he swallowed down the pain. "You've got to get back to your city."

"I can't just . . . leave you," Sera said, looking helpless and torn.

"You can't stay here," Agnes said. "You can't let the

Renalt get her hands on you. You've got to go home, Sera."

Sera blinked and a tear fell on her cheek, glittering like a star. "But—"

Another blast from the cannon and this time it found its mark. A whole section of the wall crumbled, causing the Misarros to run for cover.

"Sera, go!" Leo cried. "Go home!"

Sera gripped the moonstone pendant in one hand. Her face was tender as she looked at him—he wanted to tell her how much he would miss her, how much she had changed his life, but the words wouldn't come. Sera pressed her lips together, another tear following the first.

There were two brilliant flashes of light.

And when Leo looked again, Sera and Leela were gone.

34

SERA

She'd wanted to say goodbye.

When Sera had gripped the moonstone, she'd felt her heart pulled apart, her mind in knots. Leo was right, there was danger on Braxos and she needed to go, but the thought of leaving him made her chest ache and her lungs shrivel. Besides, she didn't know *how* to get home—Wyllin had said it was about intention, but Sera didn't know what she was supposed to do.

But it seemed her moonstone remembered—it went cold in her hand and suddenly the thought of her City became bright and writhing inside her, and she could see it as clearly as if she'd called up a memory. She could see the banks of the Great Estuary and the glow of the moonflower fields, could hear the buzzing of the bees in the Apiary and smell the rich fruits of the orchards.

Home, Sera thought with purpose, and her magic stirred in a way it never had before. The word was more than just a wishful thought. It held the power of a command.

Then the world was spinning and her feet left the ground in a disorienting whirl of color at first, then fire, then she was in space and the stars were bigger and brighter than she remembered them. Leela was beside her, encased in a pearly mist, and Sera realized she was too. She hadn't noticed it forming, hadn't been able to make sense of anything. On her other side, the tether glinted and they were following its brilliant line, shooting upward at an incredible speed. It was the opposite of falling. It was like flying.

But she had left them. Leo. Agnes. She had left them behind.

Then she caught sight of the City, its cold stalactites reaching out for them, and they burst through the pool she had appeared in when she first spoke to Leela, landing on the icy floor and gasping for breath.

She was back. She was home.

But this was not the home she knew, this cold underground garden with Cerulean imprisoned beneath circles of ice.

Leela helped her to her feet and hugged her close. "We're back," she cried.

But Sera found she could not melt into the embrace. This was not the homecoming she had expected. This was not how it was meant to be. She was supposed to be happy, not torn. She was meant to feel as if her upside-down world had righted itself.

"Leela!" Elorin's voice cut through the silence. Sera turned and Elorin's mouth fell open. "Sera," she gasped. "You're here. You're here! Oh, but you both must come quick. The High Priestess has called for another choosing, and this time there was no ceremony. She has chosen *you*, Leela, to be sacrificed. She is saying you caused the sleeping sickness! She has called the congregation back to the temple, to announce it—even the purple mothers and midwives from the birthing houses. I only just snuck out. I was hoping I would find you here."

A piece of Sera's heart was still back on the planet, but her own City needed her too. "We have to show them I'm alive," she said. "Leela, we must show them the memories the way Wyllin showed us, all of them, hers and yours and mine . . . the memories that live inside us now. We can share them. Every Cerulean in this City must see the truth."

"Yes," Leela agreed. "But there is something else they must see as well." She turned to Elorin. "I need to bring Sera to the temple so that all can witness the High Priestess's lies. I need to confront her myself. But there is another, deeper lie." She gestured to the circles covering the floor. Sera saw markings on one that read *Plenna* and another that said *Estelle*. "You've got to release them, Elorin. You've got to feed them the fruit and bring them back to the surface. They deserve to be free. They deserve to face the woman who did this to them."

"Me?" Elorin squeaked. "Oh, Leela, I can't, I never—"

"You can." Leela spoke with a confidence that compelled, that made the hairs on the back of Sera's neck stand on end and Elorin's eyes pop. "And you will." She bent forward and gave Elorin a quick peck on the cheek. "You remember how it was done?"

Elorin nodded, her lips pressed together in a thin line.

"Good," Leela said. "Bring them up when you have released them all. Clothe them from robes in the dormitory." Her face softened. "They will be eager to see the trees again and smell the earth and feel the wind on their faces."

Sera felt a sharp pang of guilt at the thought of living so many years in her City unaware that Cerulean had been trapped beneath her. They left Elorin there, Sera following Leela down a green-lit path until they reached a staircase. When they emerged out into the Moon Gardens, Sera's throat seized up and her knees locked together, tears pricking her eyes. It was all just as she remembered it. She gazed up at the temple, its spire twinkling at her as if in greeting.

"Come on," Leela said, and they hurried around to the front of the temple. As Sera looked up at the doors, she cried out, her heart slamming against her ribs.

Home, the markings said to her.

"Can you read them?" Leela asked. Sera nodded. "What do they say?"

The word almost got stuck on its way out. "Home."

Leela gripped Sera's shoulder, a fortifying gesture.

"Are you ready?" she asked, and Sera felt like she was seeing an entirely new side of her friend, one she had never known existed. This Leela was still as sweet and caring as she had always been, but also brave and poised, with a fierceness that could not be denied.

She has become a leader, Sera realized with a start. *Though she does not see it yet.*

Leela pushed open the doors just in time for them to hear the High Priestess saying, ". . . ceremony will take place privately. Leela Starcatcher cannot be allowed to contaminate any other Cerulean. We must act with extreme caution. My acolytes will—"

"There will be no ceremony," Leela called out, and the entire congregation gasped in unison, hundreds of faces turning toward the two girls standing in the doorway. "The first one was a lie, and this one would be no better. See for yourself! Sera Lighthaven has returned to us."

Sera stepped forward, feeling the weight of all those eyes on her. The High Priestess looked utterly shocked, her acolytes confused except for Klymthe, who glanced to the High Priestess as if for instruction. Whispers of "Sera is alive" and "How can this be?" and "Sera, it's Sera!" filled the sanctum.

Then Sera heard a strangled wail and a voice called out her name and everything else faded to a blur as her purple mother came running up the aisle toward her, her green and orange mothers right on her heels.

"Sera!" her purple mother cried, and Sera fell into her arms.

"You're alive, you're alive . . ." Her green mother said the words over and over as her orange mother sobbed into Sera's hair.

Tears streamed down her cheeks as Sera inhaled their scents, honeysuckle and peppermint and thyme, never forgotten even after so long on the planet.

"I missed you," she whispered. And yet she also knew in her heart that she was not the same girl who had fallen.

Her purple mother cupped Sera's cheeks in her hands, her face fragile yet alight with joy. "Leela told me and I did not believe at first," she said. "I was so broken after you fell. Can you forgive me, my darling?"

"There is nothing to forgive," Sera said. "As long as the stars burn in the sky, remember? I kept your love with me throughout all my travels on the planet. You never left me."

"How is this possible?" Freeda from the orchards broke the moment as she stood with her hands on her hips, her broad shoulders casting a long shadow across the kneeling congregants. "High Priestess, you told us Sera Lighthaven was unworthy, and yet here she stands."

"You said more purple mothers would become pregnant," said Koreen, standing as well, much to Sera's surprise. "And none have, and now Plenna is ill."

"We have never had to sit devotionals for fertility before," Novice Cresha added.

"And the birthing season came so fast on the heels of the wedding season," said Baarha, the old cloudspinner.

"Nothing seems to have gone right in this City since Sera fell," Daina announced, clinging to Koreen's hand.

"My children, calm yourselves," the High Priestess said. The moonstone in her circlet caught Sera's eye, a sudden pinch of fear in her stomach.

"No," Leela growled, and then she was running up the aisle, Cerulean stumbling out of her way. She stopped at the foot of the chancel, glaring up at the tall woman who had once been their trusted leader.

"I know the truth, Elysse," she said, and Sera felt a thrill run through her as Leela called the High Priestess by her given name. "I have met Wyllin Moonseer."

At that name, the High Priestess's eyes went wide. Several Cerulean close by gasped.

"But Wyllin is dead," one called out.

"She died to form this tether!" another said.

"This tether was not formed the way all other tethers have been," Leela said. "This City has forgotten its true purpose. The tether is weak. The sleeping sickness is a lie. Wyllin Moonseer lives, trapped on the planet. And this woman"—she pointed at the High Priestess—"is responsible for the Great Sadness."

Freeda was looking at Leela skeptically and Koreen's expression had changed too—Daina seemed ashamed she'd ever stood up and said anything at all, and Sera realized Leela sounded rather insane.

But it didn't matter. They could *show* the truth of her words.

Sera stepped forward out of her mothers' embrace.

"We can show you," she said, nodding to Leela. Sera felt her magic begin to sparkle as it connected with itself and with the power of the moonstone she wore around her neck, the power of memory, of connectivity. Her skin began to glow and her eyes burned. The Cerulean closest to her drew away, confused and frightened, but when Sera saw the self blood bond glowing within Leela, she found nothing frightening about her friend's shining skin or blazing irises. Leela looked *free*.

"I am not scared of you anymore," Leela said to the High Priestess, and her voice echoed throughout the room. "You cannot stop us from sharing our knowledge with this City."

Then Sera felt Leela's heart beating alongside hers and all the memories poured out in waves. Sera was dimly aware of each and every Cerulean in this temple, their magic like candle flames she could see and feel, bright spots of heat that grew brighter as the memories swarmed them.

At first it was just Wyllin's memories of the Great Sadness and all that had happened after. But then Sera's own memories filtered in, falling to the planet, being captured and imprisoned . . . it pained her to remember the hard slats of the crate and the needle sinking into her skin when Kiernan drew her blood. But then the memories shifted and became softer, tinged with friendship and love, for Agnes and Leo, for Errol and Boris. The planet was wonderfully strange and frightening and new and unexpected, and Sera's attachment to it was palpable, even through all the hardships it had caused her.

Then Leela's memories took over and the visions changed and she shared with their people everything she had seen and learned over the past weeks, since she had first overheard the High Priestess speaking to Acolyte Klymthe in the Moon Gardens. The doors, the fruit, the Sky Gardens . . . Finding the circlet. Releasing Estelle from the stalactite. The dream. The cache of moonstone. The High Priestess threatening her. And then Leela jumping through the pool, down to the planet as Cerulean had done in days of old.

As they were meant to do.

When at last the memories were spent, Sera and Leela came back to themselves. The temple was as silent and somber as the Night Gardens. Many Cerulean were rubbing their eyes or the backs of their necks, or blinking around as if unsure anything they were seeing was real. Some were crying or holding each other. Some were shaking their heads, dazed. Sera felt a faint crackle in her chest, as if her moonstone was saying, "Well done."

"Was that real?" Sera looked up at the sound of Acolyte Endaria's voice. She was gazing down at Leela. "I felt . . ." She pressed her fingertips to her temples. "I felt so much. It had to be real." She turned on Acolyte Klymthe. "How could you have been part of this?"

"Sh-she made me," Acolyte Klymthe stammered. "She said it was the only way. She showed me with her circlet, showed me what could happen if we didn't . . . I was afraid, I only wanted to help."

"Silence," the High Priestess snapped, then looked to Acolyte Endaria with a smile that might have once contained warmth but now was sharp and brittle. "Endaria, I can explain—"

Acolyte Endaria stepped backward. "You have lied to us," she said, tears filling her eyes. "You have lied all this time. How could you?"

"Why?" It was timid Daina who spoke up, to Sera's surprise. "Why would you do this?"

The High Priestess looked trapped. She glanced behind her, as if searching for a way to escape, but then Acolyte

Imima stepped up, blocking her way.

"Where do you think you could go, Elysse?" Imima said. "There is nowhere to hide in this City. You must answer for these . . . these memories, these images we have seen. You have told us Leela Starcatcher is false, that she is dangerous. You have said Sera Lighthaven was unworthy. But we have felt their feelings and have lived the truth of them, and the only danger here is you."

"All I have done I did for my people," the High Priestess protested. "Do you want another Great Sadness? You speak of the memories—you saw what Sera went through down there. They locked her up! They tried to steal her blood! Is that the future you want for this City, for our people? To be at the mercy of humans who do not understand us?"

"Do not use my life to justify your falseness," Sera said, and every head in the sanctum swiveled toward her. "If I had known . . . if you had not stolen our magic and our knowledge and our history, I could have communicated with the humans from the very beginning. Yes, there are those who are greedy and arrogant and cruel, but there are also humans who are kind and loving, who risked their own lives and futures to return me to this City. We are meant to explore, we are meant to learn, we are meant to give back what we take from the planet. We are meant to be so many things we have been denied. I always thought I was the only one in this whole City who was different. But I know now that is not true. You have made us think we are all supposed to be the same. But that is not what Mother Sun intended. You kept us in one place for so long, we forgot ourselves. But we remember now."

"What would you have done?" the High Priestess demanded. "If you were in my place. You think you know so much, Sera Lighthaven, because you have been to one planet. Well, I have been to many! I have seen things you could never dream of. You think you know so much about our purpose? We are safe here! How is that not better for our City? Why should we risk the journey through space, the dangers of planet after planet, when we can stay right where we are!"

"Because life is risk," Leela said as if she was hardly able to believe she had to explain this to a centuries-old woman. "Life is uncertainty and danger. You have dulled our minds and our hearts. You have kept us so still and sedentary that Mother Sun could not find us any longer. That is not the way to be a Cerulean."

Sera felt her throat swell as all eyes turned back to Leela. Their people were looking at her with unabashed admiration.

"I must admit," Freeda said. "I have always thought about visiting the planet. But I never wished to acknowledge this, not even to myself." She turned to Sera. "I am sorry that I called you a nuisance. Perhaps I was envious. It seemed so easy for you to express your wishes out loud."

"I always wondered about the tether, too," Daina said. "If there were ever people who tended to it. I am sorry, Sera, that I made it seem as if you were strange for thinking so. I simply did not want to be seen as strange myself."

Sera's eyes were brimming with tears once more and her mothers were gazing at her, their faces alight with pride. Her purple mother took her hand and squeezed it gently.

"You were happier that way!" the High Priestess shrieked. "I kept you safe here, I kept you healthy and whole, I—"

"You stole from us," Leela said. "You took our friends and our family and our purpose, but most of all you took our magic. So that you could stay young and strong."

"This City needs a leader," the High Priestess insisted. "Only I can protect it."

"Like you protected *them*?" Elorin's voice rang from the doorway.

She strode into the sanctum, and once again the air was filled with gasps and cries, as the hundred-odd Cerulean who had once been imprisoned beneath the City filed in after her.

35

LEELA

LEELA'S HEART WAS BURSTING AS ELORIN LED IN ALL THE
Cerulean who were now free.

"Plenna!" Heena shrieked as she saw her wife, and then
she and Jaycin were falling into Plenna's arms.

"Estelle?" Sera's green mother gasped as Estelle rushed
to embrace Kandra.

"Iona?"

"Beleen! But . . . but you died, you . . ."

"Kirtha, is that you? Can it be?"

The group of Cerulean from the stalactites were
swarmed, even the ones who were so ancient they no longer had family alive to welcome them. For a time, the High
Priestess was forgotten as the Cerulean hugged and cried

and rejoiced, gazing at each other with wonder and amazement. It was like they were all waking up from a very long sleep. Sera and Elorin joined Leela at the front of the temple.

"You did it," Leela said to Elorin.

She beamed. "I did." She turned to take in the room, the change that was happening, chains finally being broken. "We've shown them who they were meant to be, Leela. We've healed them."

"Not yet," Leela said, feeling crestfallen. "The City must move. There must be another sacrifice."

Elorin glanced at the chancel, where the High Priestess was boxed in by her acolytes. "Perhaps it should be the High Priestess," she whispered. "After all she has done. Perhaps it is for her to right this wrong."

Leela looked to Sera to see what she thought, but her friend did not appear to be listening. She was clutching the necklace, her eyes distant.

"Sera?" Leela asked.

"I have to go back," Sera said. "We have begun to heal our City, but the High Priestess's schemes affected the planet as well. And my friends are in danger. I don't know what the Renalt will do if she gets her hands on Leo and Agnes."

Leela swallowed. She did not know what a Renalt was and she did not wish for her friend to return to the planet, but she knew when Sera had made her mind up about something there was nothing else to be done. She cared deeply for those she had left behind, Leela had seen that. And then she remembered a snippet of Wyllin's memory—of how, before the City moved again, the Cerulean would go down onto the planet one last time.

"I will go with you," Leela said. "We must give back what we took from this planet."

"I will come too," Elorin piped up, and Leela smiled at her. She wasn't sure how much the three of them would be able to give, but it was better than nothing.

"Where are you going?" Leela had not noticed that Koreen, Daina, and Atana had approached them, but Koreen was looking at her with interest now.

"I have to return to the planet once more," Sera said. "To help my friends."

"And we must replenish the earth," Leela added. "As Cerulean did in times of old."

"To the planet?" Atana gasped. "But it's dangerous down there."

"Do not be a scaredy-cat, Atana," Koreen said. "It is our *purpose* to go onto the planet. Sera survived, and Leela too." She tossed her hair over her shoulder. "I will go with you as well."

"What?" Atana yelped, but then Daina said, "So will I."

"What's this about going to the planet?" Freeda was looming over them and other Cerulean were gathering around, curious and interested.

"I wish to join you," Acolyte Endaria said, after Leela had explained why they were going.

"We will go too," Kandra said as she joined them, holding Sera's green mother's hand, her orange mother close behind.

One by one, Cerulean volunteered, agreeing to something they had no concept of, something that had been kept from them for generations. Twenty were coming in total.

Leela had never felt so proud of her people.

"But we need moonstone," Leela said.

Sera grinned. "It's in the temple spire, you said, right?"

And Leela laughed, because there was nothing Sera loved more than climbing the temple, and this whole time she had been perching atop all the moonstone in the City.

Leela turned to the High Priestess. "You are coming with us," she said, and Acolytes Endaria and Imima flew to her sides and gripped her arms. But the High Priestess did not struggle. She merely looked at Leela with the eyes of a woman who saw her world shrinking, who saw everything she had built begin to crumble and fall apart. The fight had gone out of her.

As they left the temple, the news of what they were about to do spread and there were cheers of encouragement for the knot of . . . what had Wyllin called them? Travelers. The knot of travelers that Leela and Sera had gathered.

Leela's eyes filled with tears as she passed the doors and the symbols of Mother Sun shifted and became readable, a short cluster this time, not a waterfall like she had grown used to.

I am so proud of you, my child, the markings said. They shimmered, and for one moment, Leela saw the will-o-the-wisp from her dream reflected in their gilded image.

And then it was gone and the markings melted away.

Once outside, the travelers waited as Sera climbed up the temple spire as quick and lithe as a sunlizard. Leela saw the golden point shift and then moonstone was raining down on them, figurines and rings and bracelets, necklaces and circlets and brooches, along with shattered fragments of the old fountain from the Night Gardens.

Elorin chose a moonstone ring set with pink stargems and Kandra was fastening a brooch to her robes as Freeda tucked a long shard of moonstone into her belt. Leela could not believe so many had volunteered to come. She did not want to put her people in danger, but she knew in her heart that this was what they were *meant* to do. Sera might have another motive in helping her human friends, but Leela knew that if the City were to really, truly change and return to the way it was supposed to be, it had to begin now.

Besides, trying to keep the Cerulean away from all harm was what had led them to this stagnation in the first place. There were worse things than death, Leela thought as she looked at the High Priestess, still flanked by two acolytes.

Sera climbed back down the temple and Leela turned to address those who would be coming with them.

"We will have to go down beneath the City," she said. "If anyone wishes to change their mind, now is your chance. There is no shame in being afraid."

Daina trembled and Koreen twirled her hair nervously, but no one said a thing. The gathered Cerulean were watching her with faces set and backs straight. Leela felt a quiver in her stomach. She was in charge now. She must lead them.

She turned to Elorin and Sera. "Let's go," she said.

She led them to Faesa's statue, revealing the stairs that descended into the cold blue light. There were more cries of amazement as the Cerulean took in the Sky Gardens, the glowing columns and green paths and clear pools. Leela brought them to the central pool where the stalactites lay empty and the tether shot up into the cone of moonstone. Leela turned to the ice-white vines above—there was a flash of heat in her heart and suddenly all the fruit fell, plop plop plop, juicy orbs of gold littering the ground.

"You must take one," Leela said. "And eat it. It will enhance your magic and make you strong."

She was a bit shocked at how quickly her orders were followed. Without hesitation, everyone bent to grab a fruit. Koreen's eyes widened as she took the first bite, Kandra gasped, and Freeda shuddered. But when the High Priestess began to bend, Leela reached out a hand to stop her.

"No," she said. "Not you. You do not get to consume our magic anymore."

The High Priestess pursed her lips and straightened.

"Everyone take a pool," Leela commanded once the fruit was eaten. The Cerulean already seemed changed, their skin glowing bright silver, their eyes shining pure blue, as they spread throughout the space to stand beside the clear patches on the ground. "We will follow the line of the tether. Trust me. Trust Sera."

Elorin had a mix of fear and anticipation on her face as she gave Leela a tight smile. Sera's mothers were standing at pools right next to each other, their eyes flitting from the planet back to their daughter.

Leela and Sera stood together beside the largest pool with the tether shooting through it. "When I say jump, we jump!" Leela called out.

Sera grabbed her hand and squeezed it. Leela took a

deep, fortifying breath and cried, "Jump!"

She sank through the pool, Sera at her side. One by one the Cerulean followed them, filling the darkness like silver-blue stars.

36

AGNES

SERA WAS GONE SO QUICKLY, IT LEFT AGNES BEWILDERED, her mind unable to truly absorb the loss.

Then the cannons rang out again and Vada grabbed her hand. "We must be getting out of here!" she cried.

Agnes turned to Wyllin. "Come with us," she said.

The ancient Cerulean smiled. "My place is here," she said. "Go."

They fled back the way they had come, through the maze of rooms and out into the lush green trees. The warships had aimed their cannons at the Alcazar and ships carrying the Renalt's Misarros were being rowed to shore. The Byrne Misarros were racing from the clandestines to confront them. So much fighting, so much death, Agnes thought. Over nothing.

"We have to stop this," she said to Leo. But he was staring in the opposite direction. "What?" she asked, turning.

The Byrne Misarros who had come with Ambrosine were all kneeling, placing their weapons on the ground at Agnes's feet.

"We are at your service," said the leader, a woman with graying spikes and sinewy arms. "We will fight and die for you, Agnes Byrne."

"By the goddesses," Eneas gasped. "You are the matriarch now."

He looked proud, but Agnes didn't feel anything except light-headed and confused.

Matthias seemed to understand. "Ambrosine is dead," he said gently, placing his hands on her shoulders to steady her. "Culinnon is yours now. These Misarros serve the Byrnes. They serve *you*."

"I don't want to be served by anyone," Agnes protested.

"Let us not be making any hasty decisions," Vada said. "We are still having the Renalt to contend with."

That was a good point. Agnes could deal with the fact that she didn't want to be a matriarch later. "Please," she said to the Misarros, feeling horribly awkward. "You can stand, it's all right. We—we've got to get off this island."

"Our fleet is yours," the head Misarro said. "This way."

She led them down the winding path, an easier journey than the climb had been, though nearly as long. The sound of cannon fire chased their steps, along with the shouts from both Renalt and Byrne forces alike. They reached the beach and Agnes stopped short. Misarros were locked in combat, swords and knives flashing, whips cracking, spears flying through the air.

If Agnes was the head of these Misarros, they should have to listen to her. "This isn't what I want," she said to the leader. "I don't want them to fight. Ambrosine's dead. There's no power or wealth on this island. There's nothing to fight over anymore."

The Misarro gave her a curt nod. "Halt!" she cried out, running toward the fray. "Drop your weapons, by order of the matriarch!"

The other Misarros followed, but they were only pulled into the fighting instead of ending it, as the Renalt Misarros focused their attacks on the newcomers.

"No," Agnes moaned. She had lost her best friend and her grandmother, and the weight of her grief, of the unfairness of it all, ripped out of her in a wild, untamed cry. "Stop fighting!" She began sprinting toward the fray, sand flying up beneath her heels. "Stop!"

Someone behind her called, "Agnes!" but then her brother was running in time with her. Though his face was expressionless, Agnes could see the pain in his eyes, the agony of Sera's loss fresh within him. He didn't cry out to stop the fighting—he didn't speak at all, and Agnes had the sense that he was here simply to be by her side, to protect her in any way he could. A spear whizzed by her head and a dagger shot past Leo, grazing his shoulder, a fine line of bright red blood seeping through his shirt. Just as Agnes thought, *Maybe this wasn't such a good idea*, there was a flash of light on the beach in front of her. Then another. And another.

The cannons ceased and the fighting stopped as the beach was suddenly filled with Cerulean.

Half the Misarros stood stunned, eyes wide and mouths agape, the other half readying their weapons as if waiting for the knot of silver-skinned women to attack. The Cerulean seemed just as surprised as the humans, taking in Agnes's world with its blue sky and white sand and salty water as if spellbound.

"Sera!" Leo cried. And there she was, her head turning at the sound of his voice and they were running to each other, and Agnes was running too. Leo and Sera crashed into each other, and Agnes's brother was shaking with joy.

"You're here," he gasped as Agnes caught up with them, panting. She realized her family had followed her, Matthias and Hektor, along with Vada and Eneas.

"I couldn't leave you in danger," Sera said. "And we must give back what we took from the planet."

"So many of you came," Agnes said. Matthias took off his glasses and wiped them on his sleeve, as if the Cerulean might be a mirage.

"I am taking it things went well with your High Priestess?" Vada asked.

"She will not be High Priestess much longer," Sera said grimly as Leela hurried up to them.

"Sera, what should we do?" she asked. "Are the humans going to hurt us?"

Agnes felt resolve set in, strong and steady. "No," she said. Then she called out, "Byrne Misarros!" The warriors with golden disks at their necks all turned. "I command you to drop your weapons and cease this fight."

For a moment nobody moved and Agnes felt her confidence begin to crack. Then Matthias stepped forward.

"Ambrosine is dead," he shouted.

And to Agnes's utter shock, Hektor strode up next to him.

"Agnes is the Byrne matriarch now," he said. "You will do as she commands."

One by one the Byrne Misarros dropped their weapons and fell to their knees. The Renalt Misarros didn't seem to know what to do. Then Agnes saw them begin to kneel as well and wondered just how powerful a being the Byrne matriarch was, until she saw a woman stepping off a small boat and striding up the beach toward her.

"The Renalt," Vada gasped, and then she was kneeling too, and Matthias and Hektor and Eneas. Leo and Agnes looked at each other and knelt in the sand alongside them. Only the Cerulean remained standing.

"Rise," the Renalt said. Agnes stood and found herself looking at a woman in her late forties, with brown skin and liquid black eyes. She was clad in an elegant gown of glittering, champagne-colored beads, a crown of oyster shells nestled in her thick dark hair. A silver cape streamed out from her shoulders and she held a small scepter in one hand, topped with a smooth white dosinia.

The Renalt cocked her head. "So you are Alethea's daughter," she said. She looked at Leo. "And you are very clearly her son."

"I am," Agnes said as Leo gave a swift nod.

"Matthias," the Renalt said, acknowledging him with a flicker of her eyes.

"Your Grace," Matthias said.

The Renalt gazed down at them all imperiously. She turned to Sera and Leela with the same expression Agnes had seen on Ambrosine's face, a famished greed.

"It appears that my daughter and her guard did not exaggerate," she said. "You are all Saifa incarnate." Sera opened her mouth to protest, but the Renalt was snapping her fingers. "Arrest them," she said, and her Misarros leaped at her command. "The silver ones too. We will sort them out in Banrissa." She gave Agnes a hard, discerning look. "It seems as though the Byrne stranglehold over this country is finally at an end."

"No!" Agnes cried as the Cerulean stumbled away, confused, and the Misarros moved toward her, and then her own Misarros were picking up their weapons to defend her. "Ambrosine is dead and I'm not the woman she was at all. I don't want to fight you and I don't want to rule over anything. Please just . . . let us go. There's nothing on this island for any of us—no power, no riches. And we are no threat to you."

The Renalt's eyes were pitying. "I know you are not, my dear," she said. "But your grandmother attacked my daughter. Someone must pay for that."

"Take me, then," Matthias said.

The Renalt sighed. "Matthias, you know the Lekke would be at my throat if I did."

"Then me," Hektor said, standing.

The queen rolled her eyes. "That would be no punishment at all."

Hektor's cheeks flushed an ugly red and Agnes felt an

unexpected surge of love for her cold uncle.

Then Sera stepped forward, serene and unafraid.

"You will not be taking anyone anywhere," she said. The Renalt looked startled at being addressed so bluntly.

"My daughter told me about you," she said. "She says you are a witch."

"I am a Cerulean and my blood is magic," Sera replied. "And you will not take my people or my friends. There is another, better path open to you, if only you could remember it."

Her irises began to burn as Agnes felt once again the sensation of her body locked in a vise, a ripple of wind fluttering over her skin. She had a fleeting moment to wonder about what memory Sera would reveal before her joints all snapped together as she saw.

Alethea was kneeling in a triangular room, with high ceilings and three thrones in each corner, long steps leading up to them so that they were perched halfway up the walls.

One was carved into the trunk of a large olive tree, its scrubby branches spreading out above the head of the queen who sat in it, its leaves dense with green and purple fruit. The queen was young and dressed in scarlet, with pale skin and a crown of laurels in her honey-colored hair. The second throne was made of seashells: conches and scallops, mussels and lion's paws, blending together in a quilt of muted color. A younger version of the Renalt stared down at Alethea with an interested expression. The third throne was crafted out of bones, sharks and whales and dolphins, skulls and fins and vertebrae pieced together in a macabre fashion. The queen who sat in it had a shaved head on which perched a crown of fangs. Her face was skeptical.

Alethea's red curls fell freely down her back and she wore a dress of silver and green scales. She was young, perhaps no more than eighteen.

"Rise," the bone queen commanded. "Not that I don't love the sight of a Byrne on her knees."

Alethea got to her feet, her turquoise eyes flashing. "I thank you, Your Grace."

"So you have come to Ithilia," the Renalt said. "Is this another one of Ambrosine's chess moves? Is she trying to infiltrate our ranks now?"

"No one is trying to infiltrate anything," Alethea said. "My mother does not even know I am here and she would be furious if she did." She turned to the scarlet queen almost shyly. "My brother Matthias thinks the world of you, Your Grace, and greatly admires your wisdom. He is only fourteen, but he has a brilliant mind and a sharp wit. I have told him that perhaps one day he might come to Ithilia and meet the Lekke himself."

The bone queen snorted but the Lekke looked pleased. "I would be honored to receive him," she said.

"But why are you here?" the Renalt asked. "We were surprised to receive your letter and have, after much consideration, allowed you an audience."

"Yes, let's get to the point," the bone queen, who must be the Aerin, snapped.

Alethea took a deep breath. "I have come to ask—to beg—that you leave my mother alone. Not for her sake but for yours. The squabbling between all of our families has gone on for centuries. Isn't it time for it to end?"

"*And you believe we should just forget all the wrongs, all the insults?*" *the Renalt asked.*

"*If you do not, you are only giving her what she wants. Invite her to Banrissa. Form a truce. Show the northern islands that the Triumvirate is wise as well as powerful, and able to overlook the past.*"

The Aerin let out a sound of disgust. "*The northern islands do not frighten me,*" *she said.*

"*They should,*" *Alethea replied sharply.* "*And they are your subjects, as much as those who live on Cairan or Thaetus or any of the other islands of Pelago. It is the working women and men who suffer most from these petty feuds. The more you fight her, the more her position strengthens in the north.*"

"*And what is her position, exactly?*" *the Lekke asked.*

"*Domination,*" *Alethea said.* "*She wishes to rule.*"

There was silence and then the Aerin let out a barking laugh and the Renalt chuckled.

"*She will never rule Pelago,*" *the Renalt said.*

"*She may try to rule some of it,*" *Alethea said.*

"*You are a very brave child,*" *the Lekke said kindly.* "*But Ambrosine has no hope of ruling over anything but Culinnon. And we cannot reach out an olive branch to someone who has so steadfastly antagonized us. Unless she would be willing to make amends? Apologize for her past behaviors and pledge not to repeat her mistakes?*"

Alethea pursed her lips and she looked down at the floor.

"*Ah,*" *the Lekke said.* "*I thought not.*"

"*Go back to Culinnon,*" *the Aerin said.* "*Go back to where you belong.*"

"No," Alethea said.

"Then you may remain in Ithilia," the Renalt said as the Aerin muttered something to herself, annoyed. "On the condition that you leave your mother's beliefs and attitudes behind you."

"As you have so astutely pointed out, Your Grace," Alethea said, "they are my mother's beliefs. Not mine." She bowed low. "I thank you, Triumvirate, for your time. May the goddesses go with you."

"And with you," the three queens replied.

Once she had gone, the Lekke turned to the other two.

"She is not her mother's daughter, that's for certain," she said.

"No," the Renalt mused. "Perhaps when she inherits Culinnon, there can finally be peace between the Byrnes and the Triumvirate."

"Perhaps," the Aerin said doubtfully.

The memory dissolved and Agnes returned to the present, gasping for breath. The Renalt was staring at Sera, stunned. For several moments there was only the sound of the waves lapping against the shore and the murmurs of the Misarros who had been frozen and were now shaking their heads or flexing their fingers or running their hands over their chests.

"What . . . was that?" the Renalt said in a daze.

"I am a Cerulean," Sera said. "My blood is magic. And Agnes is more like her mother than her grandmother. The opportunity presented itself once before. Alethea's request was wiser than you realized. How much death and pain could have been avoided, if you had listened to her then and forged a truce with Ambrosine?"

"Ambrosine would have broken any pact that was made," the Renalt said, and Agnes knew that was true.

"Perhaps," said Sera. "But she is dead and Agnes is here. Isn't it time to put aside old grudges? Isn't it better for Pelago to be united rather than divided?"

"The Lekke would agree," Matthias said, rising to his feet. "And the Aerin would not be able to protest, not with two votes in favor. Let us move forward into a new future, Your Grace. One where our families can live in peace."

"And how can I be certain that Agnes is truly the woman you say she is?" the Renalt asked.

Agnes had a sudden flash of an idea. "I told you, Braxos holds no magic or fortune. The jewels you see beneath the water are illusions. The only power here belongs to these women, to these Cerulean, and it will fade when they leave. But there is something I can offer you, something you have long coveted." She steeled herself, wondering how her uncles would react. "I will share the riches of Culinnon with you."

Matthias gasped and Hektor made a choking sound. Leo was smiling at her grimly, nodding his head.

"The Byrnes have hoarded its wealth for generations," he said. "We'll give it back to Pelago." He jutted out his chin. "Kaolin too. The secrets of Culinnon were never meant for one country alone. They should be shared with this whole planet."

Sera was beaming at him. "Yes," she said.

Eneas dabbed at his eyes with the cuff of his shirt and Matthias looked moved to tears. The Renalt stared at Leo for a long moment.

"You really do look just like her," she said.

"I know," Leo replied, and for the first time Agnes heard a ring of pride in his voice as he said it.

Agnes turned to Matthias. "You should go with the Renalt, back to Banrissa," she said. "To ensure the Lekke's support."

Matthias gave Agnes a low bow. "As you command." Then he winked at her. "I'll see you at the university." Agnes felt a tingle run through her veins, but then she pushed the thought of the school aside. Now was not the moment to celebrate. Not yet. She turned to Hektor. "We'll take the clandestines back to Culinnon. There are plans to be made."

Hektor held her eyes for a moment, then bowed low like his brother had done. "As you command," he said, echoing Matthias.

Agnes looked at Sera. "What are all these Cerulean doing here?"

Sera smiled wide. "We are here to give back some of what we took. Come with me."

37

SERA

Sera led Leo and Agnes away from the Renalt, who was calling upon her Misarros to ready their ships to sail for Banrissa.

Leela came with them and the cluster of Cerulean stared in awe, at Leo especially, as they approached. She noticed her mothers exchange looks of curiosity mixed with delight.

"We have stopped the fighting between the humans," Sera announced. "Now we must do our duty and return some of our magic to this planet." She looked at Leo and Agnes, her heart thrumming with joy. "My friends will do the rest once we have gone."

She was so happy to think that the Arboreals and mertags would be freed from Culinnon, and that they would at last find their true purpose. Not to be sold, like Xavier wanted, or hoarded, like Ambrosine had done. Cerulean magic was meant to be shared. The planet would be replenished.

Sera felt a sharp twinge in her chest—she wished she could be here to see it, to help.

Leela was instructing the Cerulean on how to self blood bond. "Our minds are as powerful as our magic," she was saying. "Look within yourselves. The fruit has made you strong, the way you should have been all along. Look inside and release some of this power. A gift for what was taken."

One by one, Cerulean eyes lit up like fires. Daina gasped and Freeda sucked in a hard breath and Koreen made a sound like a giggle and a cough. Sera's mothers looked fierce, as Sera had never seen them before.

"Now walk the beaches," Leela said, and Sera knew she was thinking of Wyllin's memory, of the Cerulean wandering through the forests of Orial. "And give back."

Faint wisps of magic emanated out from Acolyte Endaria as she took the first steps. Acolyte Imima followed after, then Sera's mothers, then Koreen, then all the travelers were walking the white sand, leaving the faintest trace of silver trailing out from behind them.

Sera beamed, so proud of her people.

Until she realized someone was missing.

"The High Priestess," she gasped.

"Where could she have gone?" Leela asked.

Sera's eyes turned upward to the ruins of the Alcazar. "Wyllin," she said.

She and Leela left the others on the beach, Agnes, Leo, and Elorin coming with them. Leela was breathing heavily by the time they reached the top of the cliff.

"I never dreamed I'd see a planet," Elorin said, gazing out over the ocean. "It's not quite what I thought."

Sera grinned. "What did you think it would be like?"

Elorin paused. "Smaller," she said. "And not so green."

"The city we come from isn't as green as this," Agnes said.

"No," Sera agreed. "And there were dwellings as tall as the temple piled up next to each other, made of all sorts of materials, with hardly any trees."

Leela wore a curious expression, one that made Sera's stomach twinge with an inexplicable sense of foreboding. "You have seen so much," she said.

"I suppose there will be even more to see when we leave this planet," Sera said, trying to sound brave. She saw Leo flinch out of the corner of her eye but could not bring herself to look at him. She'd have to leave him. Again.

They passed through the doors to the Alcazar and made their way back to the courtyard. And there, by the fountain, was the High Priestess. She and Wyllin stood several feet apart.

"You abandoned me," Wyllin was saying, though there was no anger in her tone.

The High Priestess crumpled. "Forgive me, Wyllin. I didn't know how it would work, not really. I was frightened. I thought I was doing what was right."

"I know," Wyllin said. Her eyes caught Sera's and then she pointed. The High Priestess turned to find Leo and Agnes gaping at her.

"Do you see?" Wyllin said. "These humans are devoted to Sera. There is hope after all. Not every planet is Orial. Mistakes can be made and atoned for, but not like this. Not this way. We have lived for so long, you and I. Too long. It is time now. You have carried this burden for years more than you expected. You cling to life the way you cling to power. Aren't you tired, Elysse? All the fears you had no longer exist. Not all planets are safe, but they are not all as dangerous as you think. And we are killing this one. By staying here, we are draining it dry. It is time to let go."

"I don't know how," the High Priestess said, and she sounded small and pitiful.

"Together," Wyllin said. "We will let go together."

Tears filled the High Priestess's eyes. "I'm frightened."

Sera did not think she would ever be able to feel sympathy for the High Priestess, but as she looked at her now, she could not help thinking what a sad creature she was, and how lonely she must have been all those centuries. It did not excuse her actions, but it helped to smooth the rough edges of Sera's grief for her City.

"I know," Wyllin said, walking forward to clasp her hands. "But balance must be returned. By keeping the secret of the Great Sadness, you deprived the City of its very right to choose its fate for itself. How many travelers and tether-tenders and planet-keepers have been denied their true purpose because they did not know it was an option at all? How many different types of love have you prevented? I know you were only trying to keep them safe. But they *are* safe. And they deserve to be themselves, whatever that may mean. It is time for the City to move on. It is time for you and me to join Mother Sun in her endless embrace. It is time, Elysse. Can't you feel it?"

The High Priestess swallowed. "I don't know how," she said again. "I don't know how to let go."

Wyllin smiled at her. "I do." She bent and kissed their hands where they joined. "I forgive you," she said. At that, the High Priestess seemed to shatter, hunching over as tears fell, leaving tiny imprints on the floor of the courtyard. Wyllin rubbed her back and murmured soothing words.

"So will she be the sacrifice to break the tether?" Leela asked.

Wyllin turned and Sera felt a thrill run from the tips of her toes to the ends of her hair. Then, to her surprise, the High Priestess straightened and spoke.

"This tether is not like the others that have been created throughout our history," she said. "It was not forged by death, and so need not be broken by it. If one has the courage. To fall again." She looked up at the sky. "But she must live the rest of her days on this planet. She cannot return to the City."

"What?" Leela cried.

Sera felt a heady sense of relief at odds with a crippling sorrow inside her.

"You can't," Leo said, and the pain in his voice was palpable. Sera's heart swelled. How selfless of him, to insist that she go. She could hardly recall the selfish, shallow person he had once been.

"Sera, you don't need to do this," Agnes said. "You should go home."

But Sera remembered a fleeting bit of Leela's memory, of the dream she'd had when Mother Sun had visited her as a will-o-the-wisp.

Home is not always what we think it is when our journey begins. And it can change along the way.

The word she'd seen written on the temple doors when she'd returned to the City held new meaning now.

Home.

"Home can be many things." Sera touched the moonstone hanging around her neck. "I think . . . I think I have found a new one here."

"As long as you have a moonstone, you will be connected to the City Above the Sky," Wyllin said. "You will never truly lose your people, your friends, or your mothers."

Sera's heart was glad to hear it. Leela's eyes shone with tears.

"It will be all right," Sera said, though she wasn't sure those were the right words. It was all so bittersweet—no matter what choice she made, she would suffer loss.

But the City needed to move. And she had sworn to herself that she would set it right, that she would break the tether even if it meant falling again. And at least this time, falling did not mean dying.

The High Priestess seemed almost like the woman Sera had known all her life, confident and wise and strong. "If the City is to move," she said, "it will need a new leader."

She walked up to Leela and held her gaze for a long time. Sera had the sense that there was something akin to a blood bond taking place between them. Leela seemed so much older now, taller even. She stood proud and unafraid, facing down the City's oldest and most deceitful High Priestess where once she had been scared to sneak out of her house at night. Sera could not have been prouder of her friend.

Then the bond broke. The High Priestess removed her circlet and held it out with trembling hands.

"This belongs to you now," she said. "The City's new High Priestess."

Sera waited for Leela to protest, to insist that she was not meant for such an important role.

But Leela simply reached out and took the circlet, clutching it in her hands, her jaw set. Elorin pressed her palms to her chest.

The High Priestess turned to Sera. "There is something you will need," she said. She deftly plucked a strand of hair from her head and bent to bury it in the earth. She put her hand over the mound of dirt and a tiny sapling no more than a foot tall sprang up from the ground, winding through her fingers—a miniature Arboreal. And from its slender branches, a golden fruit appeared, growing larger and larger until the tree bent beneath its weight. The High Priestess plucked it and offered it to Sera.

"Eat this before you fall," she said. Sera took the fruit, its skin soft, its flesh warm in her hand.

Then the High Priestess walked back to Wyllin. "Together?" she said.

Tears leaked from Wyllin's eyes as the two ancient friends embraced. "Together," she whispered.

"It is time to go," Leela said, turning her gaze to the beach. "We have given all we can, I think."

Sera nodded. Leela touched the moonstone in the circlet

and Sera felt it beckoning, rippling through each moonstone on this planet, calling the Cerulean home. She turned to her human friends, looking scared and confused.

"Will you wait for me here?" she asked, and her voice broke.

Agnes was nodding and Leo said, "As long as it takes."

Sera looked up at the tether, the twinkling chain that had forever altered the course of her life. "I don't think it will be long."

Then she called on her moonstone to take her to the City Above the Sky, one last time.

The Night Gardens were quiet as Sera made her way to the dais.

The High Priestess's final fruit was running hot in her veins. Leela stood at the jutting glass balcony with Elorin beside her, an acolyte now that Klymthe had been stripped of her title. The circlet suited her best friend, Sera thought. It made her as powerful on the outside as she was on the inside. Cerulean bowed to Sera as she passed and the gesture of respect did not inspire insecurity and fear as it had before. This ceremony was so different from the last one.

Leela had returned the siphoned magic back to her people—she told Sera that the moment she had placed the circlet on her head and claimed the moonstone as her own that she could sense the Cerulean magic writhing inside it, begging to be released. She said it felt like turning on a faucet when she at last gave their magic back, a gratifying sense of release. The Cerulean held in the stalactites were healthy and well. Soon the City would move and the Sky Gardens would grow lush and green again and the Cerulean would explore new planets and learn the ways of the universe as they were meant to.

Sera touched the moonstone pendant, no longer hidden beneath her dress but shining proudly for all to see. As long as she had it, she would be connected to them, to Leela and her mothers and her beloved City. She would be able to see them and they her. She would not truly lose them.

Her mothers were standing by the dais, tears in their eyes.

"We love you so much, Sera," her orange mother said.

"We will miss you," her green mother echoed.

"I will miss you too," Sera said. "But you will always be with me."

"And you with us," her green mother said.

Her purple mother touched her cheek.

"As long as the stars burn in the sky," she said, "I will love you."

Sera's throat was too swollen to speak. She stepped onto the dais and stood in front of Leela.

"How far we have come," Sera said, "from climbing the temple spire at night."

Leela smiled. "That seems a lifetime ago."

Sera looked out over the sea of faces, staring at her with hope and admiration. "Take care of them," she said.

"I will," Leela promised. They held each other tight, their hearts beating in unison, and there was no need to blood bond for them to read each other. Leela pulled away and took out the ancient iron knife. When she cut into Sera's arms, Sera welcomed the pain. It sharpened her senses. She was not afraid. She was going to a different home, that was all. Home didn't have to be one thing or another—it didn't have to be the place where you were born. It could be wherever those you cared about were. Sera suddenly thought herself lucky, to have two homes.

She turned and gazed at the stars as Leela swept a hand to remove the barrier and Sera stepped out into space.

"Goodbye," she whispered, to the stars, to her mothers, to Leela, to her City. Then she fell.

She landed with a hard thud that sent her sprawling on the ground.

When the dust cleared, Agnes and Leo were standing over her.

"Are you all right?" Agnes asked.

Sera sat up. They were still on Braxos, in the ruins of the Alcazar. The fountain had cracked in two. The tether had vanished and Wyllin and Elysse were gone.

"They just . . . faded," Leo said. "And then the fountain broke."

Sera looked up at the sky.

"Is the city moving?" Agnes asked quietly.

"Yes," Sera said. "It is. At long last."

"Are you all right?" Leo asked.

"Yes," she replied. "I am sad to lose it. But I am also happy for them. I do not regret my choice. It was no choice at all, really. It was what I was meant to do."

He smiled and she laid her hand against his chest,

feeling his heart beat beneath her palm.

"So," Agnes said. "Should we go back to Culinnon? We've got a lot of plans to make. And we'll have to sort out what to do about Father."

"Maybe he won't be so angry anymore, now that Ambrosine and Braxos are gone," Leo said. "Maybe Sera's memory sharing can, I don't know, help him be more like who he used to be."

"Maybe," Agnes said. "Or maybe he'll just go back to Kaolin and stew."

Leo grinned. "Maybe that too. But at least Culinnon won't be so isolated anymore. We can do what our mother always wanted."

"Yes," Sera said. First Culinnon and then beyond. She would help heal the scars her people had unknowingly left on this planet. And besides, there was so much more to see and do and learn. She was still Sera Lighthaven, after all. Her curiosity had not been quenched by the fall.

They left the Alcazar and headed down to where Eneas and Vada were waiting for them, Hektor and the Byrne Misarros readying their fleet, the open ocean full of possibility.

Acknowledgments

I often say that every book is its own little monster, and this one was no exception. And no book is ever completed without the help of so many amazing people working diligently behind the scenes. First, to my editor, Karen Chaplin, thank you for the numerous phone calls and hand holding that went along with drafting this book, and for helping me keep all the storylines straight. Bria Ragin, thank you for your infectious enthusiasm for this story and for making sure I got everything in on time. Rosemary Brosnan, thank you for believing in me and this series. My wonderful copyeditor, Jessica White, and production editor, Alexandra Rakaczki, you were both so invaluable in keeping these varied worlds straight and making sure all the little details lined up. Jacquelynn Burke, my amazing publicist, thank you for all you did to help promote this series. To the fabulous illustrator and designer, Jeff Huang and David Curtis, I cannot thank you enough for such an incredible cover—people often think I somehow have any hand in them, which is absolutely laughable, and for which I am eternally grateful that I do not, otherwise my covers would all feature stick figures. And a thousand thanks to Tim Paul for the gorgeous map of Pelago, which made all my fantasy-writer dreams come true.

Charlie Olsen, slayer of self-doubt dragons and defender of insecure hearts, I am eternally grateful that I have you in my corner. And many many thanks to Lyndsey Blessing for handling all things foreign rights related.

Jess Verdi, there is literally no world in which I could write a book without your support and encouragement, your sharp eyes, or your shoulder to cry on. Thank you for always finding the time to have wine and snacks while I ask you a million plot questions. Jenna's thesis.

Alyson Gerber, you were there for so much of the initial drafting of this book, reading revised scene after scene with such care and always making me feel like I was improving even when I thought I'd gone off the rails. Caela Carter, thank you for the boundless support and for your ability to see the sense in my always weird and often tangled mind.

So many friends have been there for me during the birthing of this book and were instrumental in keeping me sane throughout the writing of it. Thanks to Corey Ann Haydu, Jill Santopolo, Linsday Ribar, Steven Salvatore Shaw, Heather Demetrios, Mike Hanna, Erica Henegen, Clark Solak, Melissa Kavonic, and Ali Imperato. Matthew Kelly, my oldest friend in the world, who could have guessed way back when we were in nursery school together that one day I would be dedicating a book to you. All I ask in return is that you make me the Chef pasta on demand.

To the steadfast crew at Mess Hall, thank you for cheering me on through this process, especially Derek, Max, Cherry, and Dana.

To my Aardvarks, every year I get to work with you I am reminded of why I do this in the first place and leave inspired by your dedication and talent. Thank you all for being so generous and amazing. Special thanks to the merch squad—Anika, Carissa, Daniel, Mary, and Alin.

My incredible family who has supported me from day one, I am so grateful for your love and encouragement and your belief in me as I struggle along this crazy path of being a writer. Thank you to Ben, Leah, Otto, and Bea. And to my parents, Dan and Carol—you guys have been my champions since way back when my dream was acting, and I couldn't have done any of this without you.

And for Faetra. I miss you every day.